FEB   2009

W9-BWG-268

THE CONTRACTOR

Also by Colin MacKinnon

Morning Spy, Evening Spy

Finding Hoseyn

THE CONTRACTOR

COLIN MacKINNON

ST. MARTIN'S PRESS
NEW YORK

This is a work of fiction. All of the characters, organizations, and events portrayed in this novel are either products of the author's imagination or are used fictitiously.

THE CONTRACTOR. Copyright © 2009 by Colin MacKinnon. All rights reserved. Printed in the United States of America. For information, address St. Martin's Press, 175 Fifth Avenue, New York, N.Y. 10010.

www.stmartins.com

Book design by Jonathan Bennett

Library of Congress Cataloging-in-Publication Data

MacKinnon, Colin.
    The contractor : a novel / by Colin MacKinnon. — 1st ed.
        p.   cm.
    ISBN-13: 978-0-312-35578-4 (alk. paper)
    ISBN-10: 0-312-35578-5 (alk. paper)
    1. Nuclear physicists—Fiction.   2. Nuclear weapons—Fiction.   3. Terrorists—Fiction.   I. Title.
    PS3563.A3176C66   2009
    813'.54—dc22

                                                                2008034060

First Edition: February 2009

10   9   8   7   6   5   4   3   2   1

For Diane

Contents

CONTENTS

ACKNOWLEDGMENTS

MY THANKS first to a wonderful agent, Phil Spitzer, who encouraged me greatly as I was writing this book, and to my editor at St. Martin's, Marc Resnick, whose suggestions for shaping the narrative were invaluable. I am grateful also to Bruce Schneier, Chief Security Technology Officer for BT (British Telecom), for helpful comments on cell-phone security, and to Steven Aftergood, Director of the Project on Government Secrecy of the Federation of American Scientists, for guidance on U.S. government classification procedures. If I've made errors writing on these subjects, they are my errors, not Bruce's or Steve's.

More than all, though, I am grateful to my wife Diane for the love and patience she showed while I worked on this book.

A point on sourcing: The fictional Project CIRCLE in the following pages was partly inspired by Sam Adams's memoir on American intelligence in the Vietnam War, *War of Numbers*. The character caught up in Project CIRCLE, Walter Behringer, is not, however, based on Adams or anyone mentioned in Adams's book.

But it wouldn't be make believe if you believed in me.

—From the song "Paper Moon,"
by Harold Arlen, Billy Rose, and E. Y. "Yip" Harburg

I cannot assert that no part of that network exists, but it's my understanding based on our conversations with the Pakistanis that the network has been fundamentally dismantled. But to say that there are no elements in Pakistan, I'm not sure I could say that.

—Undersecretary of State for Political Affairs, Nicholas Burns, speaking on July 25, 2007, to the Senate Foreign Relations Committee on the subject of the A. Q. Khan clandestine nuclear weapons network

PROLOGUE

The Interrogation of Sasha Geydarov

ISTANBUL, AN EVENING IN THE FALL

THEY GRABBED Aleksandr "Sasha" Geydarov—pimp, smuggler, liar, and longtime asset of the American Central Intelligence Agency—as he sauntered lazily down Yeniçeriler Avenue in the old city.

A brown Mercedes-Benz had come to a fast stop just beyond him, and when it did, two men—not friends—following him in the street pushed him into the car. They told him in Russian to shut up, and because the pistol in his ribs felt convincing, he did. The driver, maneuvering the car through the slow traffic on Yeniçeriler, turned south to the Coastal Road, then sped west.

Geydarov, forty-three years old, had been born in Baku, Azerbaijan, to an Azeri father and a Russian mother. He was a graduate of a technical school in Baku and had served as a combat engineer in the Soviet Army. He began his commercial life in the early nineties as a suitcase trader, ferrying merchandise between Russia and Turkey. In a short time his trade expanded to involve the trafficking of drugs from Central Asia to Europe and of young women from countries of the former Soviet Union to Turkey and elsewhere to serve as forced sex laborers. To the Americans who knew Geydarov, he described himself as a "beezneessmen," and in fact by the end of the nineties he had reached a kind of chancy prosperity.

Just past the resort town of Bakırköy, Geydarov's captors turned their Mercedes into the walled courtyard of a two-story beach house, and parked there. They jerked the terrified Geydarov from the car, frog-marched him

1

into the main hall, the reception room of the house where honored guests are received, and fastened him with gray duct tape to a heavy, straight-backed chair. When Geydarov noticed the plastic tarpaulin spread under the chair he fainted.

"Y OU FUCKED our deal," the man named Oparin was saying.
Conscious now, shaking and perspiring, his heart pounding, Geydarov said, "No!"

"Yes, you did, you shit, you trash, you pansy, you fucked our deal and you cheated us."

"My God, no, Vanya—Ivan Sergeyevich—my God no, God is my witness, no . . ."

"You queer, you traitor, you are the worst kind of criminal. You have no honor."

The first blow came from behind without warning, came as pure unexpected force, as if not through human agency, and struck Geydarov hard in the back of his neck.

The second and third blows came from behind as well, then more from the sides and front. Using truncheons, Oparin and the others struck Geydarov in his face, temples, and neck. They broke his cheekbones, nose, ribs, and fingers, and when a final blow fell on the top of Geydarov's head, his mouth opened reflexively in a kind of grin. He'd long been senseless.

They spooled duct tape around his head and left him slumped in the chair, sagging to the right.

O N THE beach, Oparin and friends roasted lamb kebabs and corn ears that they had soaked in salt water, then cavorted in the surf under a gray moon, yelling like schoolboys at a beach party. They were very drunk.

When they returned to the house—it was about midnight—and saw that Geydarov's breathing had stopped, they cut his body loose from the chair, dragged it in the bloody tarpaulin out to the courtyard, and heaved it, wound in the tarpaulin, into the trunk of the Mercedes.

Then, slewing drunkenly from lane to lane, they sped back toward Istanbul. They pulled off the Coastal Road just under the Sultan Ahmet Mosque and left Geydarov's body, still wound in the tarpaulin, on the beach near a fish seller's stall that was closed for the night.

I: SIGNAL

Gazelle Seven

"YA'LL DON'T watch the Sooners' games," Ray says, "but *Ah* see every one Ah *can*. Buddy Ambruster, you shoulda seen 'im last Saturday. Intercepted a pass—this was the Texas game, man—intercepted a pass on the thirty-yard line, ran seventy for a TD. *Man,* he's good."

Ray and I are having a late-afternoon drink in a café on a hilltop in Athens, a city he visits from time to time. Ray's real name is Raza Malik, but he likes to be called Ray. He's an electrical engineer with a degree from Oklahoma, where he picked up a half-Oklahoma accent and a love for American football. He is a civilian purchasing engineer with the Pakistan Military Communications Committee.

Ray's just slid a DVD in a white paper jacket across the table to me. The DVD contains the system designs for a fiber optics network PAMAC is installing. The project is called Ghazal Haft—Gazelle Seven. We think Gazelle Seven will link countrywide Pakistani military nuclear facilities with one another and with a command post near Islamabad.

We worry about Pakistan. The Pak military has at least seventy nuclear weapons. If the government falls and the military turns on itself, who will control those weapons? And the scientists who built them: What of them? Are any of them renegades? Islamists? Would any want to take what they know and build a bomb on their own? There's been talk of that.

Our ally Pakistan could be our worst nuclear nightmare.

I take the DVD and slip it into my pocket. With what we learn from this glittery little piece of plastic, we will be able to spook the Pakistani commo system. We will listen in on their conversations. We will, if the mood strikes us, take the system down, invade their country, and, if we can, seize those weapons.

The DVD is pure gold.

Ray and I share the fiction that I am an American telecoms consultant helping a small Danish company sell phone equipment internationally. Story is, my Danish client—a firm called Dansk Telefonik—manufactures fiber-optic cable and switching devices, and wants inside information on the Pakistani market, including the military, the better to write bids with. So, for a monetary consideration paid in cash, Ray supplies me with the skinny.

That's the fiction. In fact, Dansk Telefonik doesn't exist, though it has a street address in Copenhagen and a working telephone number in that city. The address is that of a friendly law firm. The phone number is back-stopped to the American embassy, where a young woman pretending to be a Dansk Telefonik receptionist will answer it. To Ray, I am known as Doug Lawson. My name is Rick Behringer.

In all this, only the DVD is real.

Ray and I have come up here separately and are sitting outside the restaurant on a terrace paved with white tiles. I see Ray every couple of months somewhere in Europe, usually at various places here in Athens. When he wants a meeting Ray signals with e-mails to me. They come in from Islamabad, from Dubai in the Persian Gulf, or sometimes from Frankfurt, a city Ray seems to pass through frequently. Ray likes to sign them "Grant." I have no idea why.

Ray's forty maybe. He's short and chunky and has thick black hair he combs straight up and back. He's got a short, well-trimmed beard. He's wearing an expensive-looking yellow shirt that has a silky buffed sheen. Around his neck he's sporting a gold chain and a gold religious medal. Ray's clothing makes you think he's well off, which is the point.

As the sun goes down, Ray and I talk a little football and watch the city change color from white to rose peach. It's a bright autumn afternoon and the sky is blue and cloudless. Look down, though, and you see a gritty, yellow smog hanging over the city. I tell Ray the Parthenon, off to our west, is burning away from the acids in the air. Too many cars in a closed place, I say.

"Yeah, like Karachi. Very bad, very ugly. When you fly into the city you can look down and see it. Ah go to the north in the winter to ski. In Swat. That's a province up there. The air is very good in Swat, very fresh. Fun place to be in the winter."

The mountains Ray talks about are blue-gray, and year-round they are capped with snow. When I was a child my father once took our family on a vacation in those mountains, but I don't tell Ray this. We don't get into much about me.

Ray's shown me a picture of his wife and children, a son and a daughter, the three of them sitting on a sofa, smiling. The children are very pretty. His wife, who is wearing no veil, not even a headscarf, has a darkly beautiful face, classic Pakistani. Ray says she works in a bank.

"Kids," he says. "You have kids?" Ray and I have met numerous times, ostensibly socializing, but he has never asked this before.

"No."

"Ah. They're the joy of life. Really. You live for yourself, but you really live for them. You start thinking that everything you do, you do for them. That isn't true, of course, but you start to think that. My son Ikram is such a clever boy. He's ten years old. He plays chess. He's very good. He is champion in his school. But I think Noosheen is smarter. She's eight years old. Very good in school."

Ray's conversing easily this afternoon, as he always does, but he's edgy. He fidgets with a pack of Winstons and keeps looking over to where the café opens onto the terrace. I don't blame him. Supplying us this information is hugely risky. If Pakistani security people learn what Ray's been up to, he's a dead man.

To get us this stuff I'm pretty sure Ray has hacked a password somehow and—I'm just guessing—has used a computer not his own, maybe one he's not authorized to use. He's told me before that PAMAC security people have been around, have been more active, maybe than usual in his section. He can't tell. He says they're smart. He's afraid they suspect something's amiss, that information's been accessed by someone not supposed to have it.

I'm pretty sure, one way or another, he's coming to the end of the road with us.

I slide a small package over to Ray. It contains $5,000 in cash, part payment for the DVD. He will get another $20,000 when our tech people confirm the value of the DVD's contents. Ray nods and smiles.

"You know, on this"—he eyes my pocket with the DVD in it—"there's more stuff. There's commercial information. Buyers, sellers. Things like that." He looks at me significantly.

I've thrown in a little extra, he's saying, more than you asked for. You owe me, he's saying.

"Okay, Ray, that's great. I'll let them know."

"And about the green cards?"

Ray's wife and children all have passports and exit permits. Ray wants American immigrant visas for all of them leading to American green cards, then citizenship. He says he wants to leave Pakistan and never go back.

"I'll tell them, Ray."

Ray nods a few times, then smiles and says, "Well, slowly, slowly . . ."— a phrase he uses with me when he's about to leave. "Ah'll see you, Doug," he says, "bye-bye," and departs nonchalantly with the package under his arm.

Later, on the network of paths that lead down from the café I deliver the DVD to a young man in a beige poplin suit. He is from the American embassy. He slips away into the dusk without saying a word.

On my slow and roundabout way back to my hotel I am followed. I think there are two of them, a shabbily-dressed young man carrying a blue daypack and a chic young woman, a brunette with long, straight crimson-streaked hair and lots of bracelets. As I pass through the turmoil of cars and buses at Omonia Square, through the shoppers, metro passengers, hookers, street peddlers, and out-of-work Albanians, Serbs, and North Africans, I notice the pair. They've been moving together, though they seem not to know each other. They stay with me.

I'm not sure I am being tailed, you just can't know with these things, and if these two are taking an interest in me, I can't know why. Ray, of course. But I've worked Athens a lot, done some black—very black— phone work here, and governmental interest in my doings in this city wouldn't surprise me. I doubt the people who set up the tail know a thing about Ray.

On St. Constantine I catch a cab west, then change to another on Achilles Boulevard, and head south. I've ditched them, I think.

If I haven't been imagining them.

M Y DAUGHTERS call me Telephone Man—good enough name, I suppose. I own a company, a real one, called Global Reach Technologies, which I started fifteen years back and which has done pretty well. Global Reach is based in the Virginia suburbs of Washington. We design and install communications systems for small businesses and government offices. And not just in the U.S. We've done a lot of work overseas, with firms in Athens, Amman, Dubai, Islamabad. We're also an Internet service provider. I've got a few full-time employees, but mostly I use a bunch of freelancers and outside experts. Depends on the job.

The name Global Reach I invented on a summer evening sitting in a lawn chair on the still warm concrete patio of the house I shared with my wife of the time. I was buzzed on scotch, which made the choice of name seem particularly apt, but even in the sober morning of the day after, the name—Global Reach Technologies—sounded good. I didn't want the name to say too much or get too specific; you couldn't tell how the company would grow, what undreamed directions it might take. And I didn't want it to say too little, either—my vision was all the wide world. Global Reach—just right. And as Duke Ellington said, "If it sounds good, it *is* good." He was talking about music, of course.

In time, and simply in the nature of things, Global Reach got into more secret work for our clients—detecting taps and other kinds of eavesdropping, setting up encryption for them, training them in security techniques, defending against hacks.

Then we got into the really secret work.

I am a contractor to the Central Intelligence Agency, one of their outside consultants. As I do with private businesses, I help design and secure their communications systems. I'm what's known as a "green badger," from the color of the ID badge the Agency has given me, a green and white plastic card, adorned with my name and Agency number, my photo, a washed-out looking identigram based on that same photo, and an impressive line of bar code that signifies I'm employed by the Agency as an outside hire. The regular Agency troops, the employees, carry blue and white badges.

I'm also—by mere chance—in what the Agency calls the "foreign matériel acquisition" trade. The phrase, like a lot of Agency terminology, doesn't quite say it. What I do is buy other countries' weapons—radar, rockets, commo systems, whatever—buy them from whoever will sell them to me and turn them over for inspection to CIA, DIA, and other U.S. intelligence agencies. I make use of funny banks and strange airlines. I work through middlemen in the arms trade—Russians, Brits, Israelis, most of them—and through officers on the take from various militaries around the world.

Over the years I have brought in a variety of toys for our spook engineers—a new Chinese shoulder-fired antiaircraft missile with its technical manuals; a Swedish mobile radio system used by the Iranian army and Pasdaran; a complete North Korean short-range surface-to-surface missile, also with technical manuals, this last a major coup.

Global Reach isn't the only company in the FMA trade. There must be six or seven others in town, most of them quiet little firms like us, with opaque company names and small staffs, situated, like us, in out-of-the-way little office parks in northern Virginia and the Maryland suburbs.

I got into the business a few years after starting up Global Reach. A man named Hawk Stedman called me about "doing some government work." Stedman—he wanted people to call him "Hawk" because he thought it sounded better than Hawthorne, his given name—pitched me over diet Cokes in a cluttered Agency suite (lots of filing cabinets and file boxes, too many chairs for the rooms) in a federally leased high-rise in Tysons Corners, Virginia, a few miles out Dolley Madison from CIA. The suite looked over the Tysons traffic mess and the distant green hills of northern Virginia.

"You're established," Hawk said. "Have been for three or four years now. You've got a track record. Global Reach does real jobs for real clients, has real employees. People can look you up in Dun & Bradstreet. You've got a legitimate Web site.

"We need some help. There's a company we want to deal with. It's a Lebanese firm, works out of Cyprus, in Larnaca. Town on the south coast. They buy and sell telecoms equipment. We want Global Reach to put in an order for a phone system through them. It's Russian-built. We'll give you the all the details on it, no problem. Just buy the system in your company's name and turn it over to us.

"You'll have to go to Larnaca in person—can't do this over the phone. We know the company CEO, he's trusted. Okay guy. You'll have to prove who you are and show bona fides. When that's all done, just shake hands and pay him. We'll reimburse for time, trouble, and expenses plus ten percent. That's all. Easy to do. I can't tell you much more than this. But I can tell you that if you do this, you'll be doing your country a great favor. I mean that."

I was no stranger to the Agency. My father, Walter Behringer, had been a high-level CIA officer before his death. A lot of Agency people knew me or knew who I was. (In fact, I did my first work for the Agency the summer between junior and senior year in high school. I was what they called a "records analyst"—that is, I helped decide where classified documents should be filed and carried them to the appropriate clerk.) That I was Walt Behringer's son is probably why Stedman called me. They'd checked me out beforehand. They always do.

Two days after Stedman made the offer, I signed a formal agreement and other papers—among them, my will—in that same cluttered suite in Tysons and became a player in our government's FMA trade. Stedman had an attorney from the Office of the General Counsel there to oversee the deal.

For its Non-Official Cover officers—its NOCs—the Agency makes up whole identities and furnishes them with props for their act, down to their pocket litter. Agency NOCs run bogus companies, like Dansk Telefonik, with arranged addresses and phony letterhead stationery. And like Dansk Telefonik, these phony companies often have working telephones that are backstopped somewhere, usually to Langley, sometimes to a foreign station.

But these days the Agency also has real companies out working for it— companies like mine, Global Reach. A kind of privatization, I suppose. The Agency likes energy companies, international law firms, banks with overseas branches—firms whose execs and employees travel around asking questions.

Business travel, when you think about it, is not just like spying, it *is* spying. On the road you meet your counterparts at conferences, or in clients' offices, or maybe the American embassy if you're visiting the commercial and econ officers or the mil attachés. And you trade gossip. If you're in sales to governments, you want to know who's who at your target ministry. You want to know the structure of the ministry, the ministry's budgeting, the personnel, who's at the ministries buying what. You also want to know about your competition: what they're offering, what they're charging. So you ask. And you become known as a person who goes around asking questions. Perfect cover for a spy.

The Lebanese company was called Cedar Telecoms, the Russian company, Golorg. The phone system—I found this out years later—was identical to a special network secretly ordered from Golorg by the government of Libya for its chief foreign intelligence organization. The network had an ingenious encryption-decryption capability the Russians had designed. CIA and NSA wanted to have a look at it.

Golorg had skirted international sanctions—you couldn't legitimately sell much of anything technical to the Libyans back then—by going through Cedar Telecoms in Cyprus, which happily supplied Golorg with a fake end-user certificate stating the system was going to a Lebanese government agency. Golorg wasn't averse to selling the identical system to— well, to whoever. Neither was Cedar Telecoms.

SHORTLY AFTER I sign that contract at Tysons, I fly into Larnaca. Tourist city: seafront, palm trees, Brits, Germans, noise. I meet the CEO of Cedar Telecoms, a chubby little man with sloping eyes named Fuad al-Khazen in an office owned by something called Eastern Trading Establishment. Cedar Telecoms, al-Khazen says, has no offices of its own in Cyprus, and the Eastern Trading premises are on loan. Eastern Trading occupies space on the second story of a dusty, paper-strewn commercial arcade south of the marina, near the bus station. We meet at night because al-Khazen wants it that way. Stores in the passage—Syrios Camera, an art-supply shop, a jewelers, a barbershop—are shut, steel gratings pulled down over their windows and secured to the pavement with huge locks. The arcade is deserted.

The goods, al-Khazen tells me, are ready to go. They will be air-freighted "tout de suite"—his words—from Russia to Larnaca and stored in a bonded warehouse for forwarding to Beirut. After they arrive in Larnaca, money will pass hands, and shipping documents and bonding records will be altered. The goods, labeled "telephonic equipment" and sourced to a Belgian manufacturer, will be flown to Dulles International, addressed to Global Reach Technologies of Fairfax, Virginia, Richard H. Behringer, CEO.

Tout de suite.

I present al-Khazen with a cashier's check for $100,000 written on a

Global Reach account at Riggs Bank, a now-defunct Washington institution once much used by the Agency. We shake hands. I leave.

At the foot of the stairs in the arcade, in dim light, I find three men loitering. When I try to pass them, one blocks my way and, putting his hand on my chest, says, "Back, back, back," prodding me gently with his fingers and showing me a small, steely semiautomatic pistol. I move backward, heart pounding, into the shadows of an archway. I think it's the entrance to the barbershop.

The man is thirty—something like that. The other two are kids. He's cool, they're nervous, but look happy. They are all dressed in casual suits and are tieless. They could be tourists, young guys out on a nighttime prowl.

The older one runs his hand up and down my chest in a kind of meditative, caressing motion. His eyes are bland, focused on mine, assessing. Still gazing at me, he says something softly to the others—Arabic—and the kids pull away, put some distance between the two of us.

"Who are you?" he asks.

I tell him my name.

"Why are you here?"

I say I'm a tourist.

He smiles. "You saw Mr. al-Khazen."

I say nothing.

He says, "Yes. Mr. al-Khazen." He smiles again. His hand stops on my chest, rests on my heart. He stares into my eyes, calculating.

After a time he asks, "Hotel?"

"Continental."

He calls out a name—it sounds like "Fawaz"—and one of the kids comes back. Fawaz has the beginnings of a mustache, and thick, long black hair that he parts on the side. Fawaz has an eery smile and he is armed too.

The two speak softly in Arabic.

The older man says to me, "You'll go with him. He'll take you to the Continental."

"I can walk there."

"No you can't."

He nods at Fawaz. Fawaz walks me halfway to the end of the passage, then stops me and holds his pistol to my left temple. He keeps the piece there for a time, then brings it down my neck, down my back, halts it at my rib cage. He's gripping my left arm. I can't see his face.

He pockets the piece and pulls me along to a street as desolate and trash-strewn as the passage, then out to a larger commercial street, where traffic and pedestrians begin. He turns in front of me, puts his fingers to his lips, motioning for me to be quiet, and nods authoritatively. He feels very good doing this. You can tell. Fawaz walks me for a time in the direction of the Continental, I'm not sure how long, and when we come to a girlie bar district, where crowds are milling and the scene is very boisterous, the kid suddenly peels off into the throng and disappears.

A T TYSONS, Stedman tells me that al-Khazen is alive and well. "The visitors? Who knows? He does a lot of business. Various kinds of clients. Some of them you wouldn't meet at Junior Cotillion."

"Drugs."

Stedman shrugs. "Larnaca's got a nice marina."

I cleared the shipment of "telephonic equipment," four small crates, through customs at Dulles—the Agency had done the paperwork—and turned them over to a young Agency officer Stedman had sent along. The officer, who was wearing a billed cap, wraparound sunglasses, and chinos, thanked me politely and drove off with the crates in an open black Ford pickup with Virginia plates.

If al-Khazen ever told us who his visitors were, I've never heard about it. And I never saw Stedman again, though I have continued to work for the Agency.

My ex, Liz, who liked to sum me up, once told me, "You need risk, you need to take chances. And basically, Rick, I think you're crazy." Maybe. All I know is I do like edge—I like facing fear, and facing it down. Doing that gives you a high like nothing else, keeps you realizing you are alive. When I think of that dimly lit arcade in Larnaca, of the older man's calculating eyes, the kid placing his gun at my temple, I think of facing risk that night—my first real brush with death—and coming out alive. I remember I liked that, liked that a lot.

I N THE evening at my hotel in Athens I turn on my cell (Internet SIM card in place, you save a bundle on the international calls), and check my voice mail. Among a dozen or so messages, this from my ex-wife: "Hi, Rick. Liz. Look, we got your message okay, so that wasn't a problem, but the girls were really upset. This is the second weekend in a row you've missed, Rick. Every time I call your office I ask, 'Where's Rick?' and they never know what to say." She pauses. "Uhh, give me a call and let's try to set something up with the girls, okay? Like something *definite*? It *was* Sam's soccer debut." Another pause. "Hope you're okay." Beep.

Liz and I have been divorced five years. She's a high-priced lawyer at a downtown law firm. She lives with our daughters Penelope and Samantha, at eleven and thirteen both charmers, in McLean Station, a wooded enclave of upscale though unflashy dwellings—earth-toned houses in among tall oak trees and cedars—just east of where the Beltway shoots over Old Dominion Drive.

The girls don't seem much worse for the divorce, which was rancorous, but we won't know that for a while. In any case, I am smothered in guilt for all that happened.

"I don't want the burden of bringing up these children alone," Liz said during the bust-up, "particularly the way this is ending. You have to contribute." I agreed. Child support payments will stop after each girl turns eighteen. Liz and I will split their college costs when the time comes. Since Liz has custody, she chooses their schooling—public, not private, a choice I back her up in.

I have visitation rights—I pick the girls up and bring them over to my place a weekend a month—and I try to do a week or two of vacation with them once a year. Sometimes, as now, things don't work out. Sam's soccer team had its first game Saturday, which game I was to attend and root for the good guys, but could not—Ray's appearance in Athens with his DVD was last minute, and I had to scramble to get here.

T o make sure nobody's getting away with one-upping anybody, I call Liz at her law firm, but it's 1:10 P.M. in Washington, and her secretary Patty coldly informs me Liz is out, then switches me without asking to Liz's phone mail. Ticked at Liz, and ticked now at Patty, I say, "Hey, Liz. Rick. Meant I was sorry when I said it the first time. I'll be back in a couple of days and we'll set something up. I know Sam was disappointed—so was I and I think she knows that. Talk to you."

I have a message from Ted Pappas, a guy I partner with occasionally and with whom I often trade information. "Hey, Rick. Ted. Gimme a buzz when you get back. We'll do lunch. Take care."

Ted and I never "do lunch." Ted has a need to talk, but he wants it face-to-face, not over the phone. Ted is ex-Agency. He's in his sixties, and has been out on the street for a decade, doing various kinds of security consulting. Like me, Ted works in the FMA trade, and in fact is regarded as a prodigy in the field—a little tricky, maybe, but then in FMA everybody's a little tricky.

Messages over, I scroll down to Frannie McClennan, my honey-blond and leggy significant other, and punch Call. Frannie counterpunches almost immediately, which doesn't always happen, and says, "Heya. Where are you?"

"Heya. Cradle of Civilization. Home of Plato and Socrates—that bunch."

"Being philosophical?"

"Oh, yeah. Where are *you*?"

"At my desk munching on a salad—*Greek* salad, believe it or not," she says, laughing her lovely high-pitched laugh. "And looking out my window. Clear day here—not that much civilization in sight, though. No philosophers at all."

Frannie, a real estate agent—and no slouch at the business, she's made the Three Million Dollar Club at Donnelly & Amstutz three years running—has a desk in a room of many desks, hers next to an immense window looking over Lee Highway, in Arlington, with a view of the road and the commercial strip opposite.

"What have you been up to?"

"Right now I'm sitting in my room and digesting dinner. Parthenon's lit up. I can see it from where I'm sitting. You'd like it."

"Umm. You sound tired. Can you sleep?"

"Yeah, but not at night."

"Trip turning out okay?"

"Just fine."

Frannie knows—we've "been together" six months now—that Global Reach does vague things for the government that have to stay vague. She's used to the concept. Her husband Jim—he's moved out and the divorce is under way, but they're still legally man and wife—has also done vague things for the government in his time that have to stay that way. (He was actually CIA for a while, a case officer overseas, and is now a senior aide on Senate Foreign Relations.) Vagueness is not as big a deal with Frannie as it might be for some women.

She asks, "Ready for some fooling around at the beach? Display your muscles?"

Day after tomorrow, a Monday, Frannie drives over to Henlopen Acres, a sandy beach town on the Delaware coast, where she has rented a cottage for the week and following weekend. I get back to town midweek, but will hang around attending to business, see Pappas maybe, then head over to Henlopen myself on Friday for what I hope will be plenty of "fooling around" with Frannie.

" 'Display your muscles'? Never heard it called that before."

"Heh heh."

I actually am muscular and bulky like the aging high-school football player I am—McLean Highlanders, 1979, 1980. I have a barrel chest and the accompanying biceps to envy (inherited from my mother's side of the family, the Conovers). I'm medium height, and now that I'm in my forties, I've also got the beginnings of a middle-aged gut, which I halfheartedly try to control by the usual diet and exercise, without that much success. Young chickies on the beach don't swoon when I walk past these days, and I've noticed they've started not liking even to make eye contact. Way it goes.

"My head'll still be spinning from the jet lag, but I will be there. And show my muscles."

Now's a good time of year for "fooling around" at Henlopen. It's post Labor Day and there'll be no people to speak of in Rehoboth, where Henlopen's summer visitors buy their six-packs and pizzas and dine out at overpriced and crowded restaurants. A fine time for walks on the beach (air chilly and the breeze high) and for romps under the covers.

Frannie and I talk a little more, then sign off with I-love-yous, well-meant and sincere enough, but which don't quite rise to the level of soul-to-soul. Between Frannie and me there's always been—call it a distance. Though since last spring we've been together steadily, enthusiastically, and as far as I go anyhow, faithfully, we both wonder where this thing is headed. We wonder, but we don't talk about it. If it ain't busted et cetera, seems to be our default approach.

Truth is, Frannie doesn't trust me. She knows my romantic history, if that's what you'd call it, which is nothing to be proud of. Third-time extramarital "fooling around" on my part is what caused Liz to pull the plug, and before, during, and after the divorce I saw a run of a dozen or so serial or overlapping "girlfriends" before settling into this grassy upland of a relationship with Frannie. Early on, in a mood of leveling, getting adult, taking responsibility—ever, by the way, an effective ploy with women—I let her know a lot of this, which of course has made her good and wary.

I'm wary myself. Frannie's an embittered woman. Her still-husband Jim moved out on her quite a while back, smitten with a Hill aide twenty years his junior. He bought a condo in the district in the Cleveland Park area, where he currently entertains his lady love, while Frannie, feeling sour and betrayed, but still glad to be shut of him, stayed in their big wood-frame house on Highland Street in Arlington.

Adding to her sense of betrayal is the particularly awful way she'd found out about Jimbo's roving. As she tells the story, she and Jim were among a large gathering of Hill people at some Hill event, when someone, unaware they were present, joked loudly and guffawed about Jim Mc-Clennan and his new girlfriend, and everyone present turned, frozen in silence, and stared Frannie's way.

"They all knew—*every*body—except me. Talk about last to find out. I didn't walk out of the reception," she told me. "I floated out in a trance, a fugue state. It was beyond horrible."

This was quite a while back. But Frannie, ordinarily a brisk, no-nonsense type, took a surprising while to get moving on Jimbo. After waiting for more than a year, and probably stimulated to the act by meeting me, she's finally gotten the divorce in gear.

Frannie is nonetheless, and for a while at least will remain, a woman scorned, and whatever issues she may have with my colorful past, I'm not sure how close I want to get to her, either. So, however much we profess love for each other and in some subsurface way probably mean it, we may ultimately pass in the night.

Thinking of other lovers and of those dozen or so girlfriends, I think also of bad timing, of wrong phases in coming out of divorces, of emotions too raw to allow people to find or accept the love in others that may actually be there.

I WRITE up my conversation with Ray for Mike Fiscarelli, my minder back at Langley. I tell him Ray's afraid that Pak security suspects something, that they may be closing in on him. I tell Mike—I'm guessing here again—that Ray may have downloaded too much, that big downloads can alert security people to a breach. If they detect a big dump, they'll be out looking for who did it. They may not know it's Ray, but they'll know it's somebody.

I e-mail the text, encrypted, to a Yahoo account Mike knows. We use these e-mail accounts—Yahoo, Hotmail, others—freely. Operational security on this modus operandi, if everybody encrypts, is much higher than you'd think. Ray's DVD, I'm sure, has already been copied at the embassy and also, encrypted, sent on to Langley. Sci Tech people in Virginia may be looking at its contents now.

The hotel is almost silent, though I hear elevator doors clunk faintly down the hall as they open and close. As I lie in bed trying to sleep, I think of Ray, of Pakistan, of nukes and jihadis.

On the plane home, as we pick up speed to take off, a thin, dark-haired girl next to me crosses herself repeatedly in the Greek way and says, "Jesus, Jesus."

THE CLOCK turns over.

It's very warm in the room.

They leave.

As they usually do in the midmorning, Miller's coworkers—Alexei, the lab technician, Fyodor, an older man and, like Miller, a graduate mechanical engineer, and Sonya, a chemical engineer—have left Laboratory G, a long, windowless, brightly lit room, perpetually overheated, summer and winter, for cigarettes and tea at the Institute canteen.

Engineer Vladimir "Vova" Alekseev Miller stays behind, as he sometimes does. Miller, a solid mechanics specialist, works in the Projects Development Laboratory—Laboratory G—at the L. D. Vygodsky Institute of Applied Physics, in Ryazhin, in hilly country east of Novosibirsk, Siberian Federal District, Russian Republic. The Institute, a large aluminum and glass cube, is sited in a bend of the Sakhra River called The Peninsula and is surrounded by chain-link fence, even where the building fronts the river. The Institute is named for a Russian physicist who had contributed crucial theoretical work to the early Soviet nuclear energy program. In the Soviet period Ryazhin was a secret city, closed to outsiders, not noted on maps.

Engineers at the Vygodsky Institute design and test space power reactors and nuclear-powered rocket engines. Miller and his coworkers are part of a team developing a fast neutron reactor type known as the Almaz IV, which will use small quantities of highly enriched uranium (HEU) to power a series of communications and surveillance satellites. They are currently working on problems of "packing"—attaining the most efficient long-term fuel configurations in small reactors that cannot be serviced regularly if ever. Laboratory G, on the second floor of the Institute, contains design computers, reactor mock-ups, and a variety of electronic measuring devices. Ten to fifteen engineers and technicians, all with high security clearances, staff the lab.

From the middle drawer of his black metal desk (along the far wall in a line with the desks of his coworkers), Miller, who is alone now, coolly takes a glasses case, an ordinary glasses case that he's lined with lead foil, and goes to the adjoining Storage Facility, also known as the "safe room," closed off from Laboratory G by a cipher-locked, lead-covered door. The door, typically, is left open during the workday.

The Storage Facility's walls and ceiling are painted light green; the room is illuminated by three bare fluorescent lamps. Filling the interior are five banks of floor-to-ceiling metal shelving. On the shelving, separated from each other by distances of at least one meter, rest seventeen steel pans, each fifteen centimeters wide by twenty centimeters long and five centimeters deep. Each has a fitted, though not locked, steel cover. The pans contain small, rectangular billets of HEU, a dark gray, heavy metal.

HEU, though toxic like lead, is not highly radioactive and can be held safely in the hands. With the lightest of shielding, small quantities of HEU can be carried past radiation monitors without setting them off.

From a pan on the fourth bank of shelving, Miller removes two of the billets of HEU and puts them in his glasses case. Then he returns to his desk and puts the glasses case back in the middle drawer. The entire operation has taken him less than one minute. This is the eleventh time in the past five weeks that Miller has removed HEU from the safe room.

This evening, Miller will carry the HEU out the Institute gate past radiation monitors and past guards who pay little attention to the comings and goings of the technical staff. He will return home today by bus as usual—he lives a forty-minute ride from the Institute—and add the material that he has just taken, a little less than one kilogram, to caches of HEU he maintains in his apartment. Today's theft will bring the total quantity of HEU that he is concealing in his apartment to 12.7 kilograms.

HEU is exceedingly dense, more than one and one-half times as dense as lead. Fifteen kilograms of the material can be held in a container the size of a coffee can.

The amounts Miller removes from time to time are too small to be detected by the Institute's perfunctory inspections—the last was nine months ago—and the loss of the HEU will not appear in the Institute's records.

The 12.7 kilograms of HEU have disappeared from the L. D. Vygodsky Institute of Physics without a trace. Miller is desperate to sell the material. And he has a customer.

I Laughed in Their Beards

I BEGAN my covert work for the Agency with FMA—that Libyan phone system—but the Libyan work led to other work (a Chinese GPS device, a Russian radar calibrator), which led to still other work. In time, I became a kind of private sector NOC, running agents like Ray, doing assessments, sometimes dreaming up operations that would never have occurred to them at Langley.

Here's one: I am in Tehran. It is December 2001. Nine-eleven occurred three months back. I have entered this country on an Irish passport as James Flaherty, businessman. I'm to assess the Ministry of Communications and Information Technology, and find out what I can about an organization we know little useful about. This stunt is breathtakingly daring. If the Iranians find out who I am, I cannot think what they'll do to me.

I'd lived in Iran as a child—Walt had been posted here—and I want to walk the old neighborhood, smell the smells, hear the sounds, catch if I can some of the feel of the street. But I want something else as well. Not glory—if this caper comes off without a hitch, no one beyond a few U.S. government bureaucrats will ever be the wiser. No. What I want is the *risk,* that feeling of edge. I want to walk in here under the eyes of the mullahs, perform a service for my country, and walk out again a free man. To laugh in their beards, as the Persians say.

Liz has filed for divorce, I have moved out, away from her and the girls. And I am in Tehran.

When I arrived in this country it was 3:00 A.M., and I slept until 10:00.

The first morning, staring down into this strange city from my sealed tenth-story hotel window, I realize that I am at the end of the earth and utterly alone. I have no diplomatic cover, and we—Rick Behringer and his employer, the Central Intelligence Agency—have no assets in the Iranian government who could rescue me if I am discovered. I am in mortal danger. As if to make the point, hanging on the wall behind the registration desk of my hotel is a large poster of Ayatollah Khomeini, a photo taken in three-quarter profile from the left, his face turned down under his black turban. He's looking up at the camera, his mouth and eyes slivers of cruelty.

IN 1969, my father spent a year with the Agency's large Tehran Station, working, I'm pretty sure, on the Soviet target, analyzing military and economic intercepts. On the Diplomatic Registry he was listed as Economic Officer, Department of State. My mother Marge, my sister Sue, and I were undercover with him as State Department dependents. I was seven years old.

Other embassy people favored living in the wealthy, far northern neighborhoods of the city, but in those innocent times, Walt and Marge chose to live closer to the center of town, within walking distance of the large compound on Takht-e Jamshid Avenue, where Walt worked. Urban guerrillas were known to be operating in Tehran even then, but had not yet targeted American citizens. Sue and I went to the International School, a more cosmopolitan institution than the American School, which served the embassy.

We lived just below a traffic circle in a new apartment built solidly of yellowish brick in a line of similar apartments fronting the *kucheh*. The landlord, a voluble man thickening with middle age, had been in the States and knew and liked Americans. We had a courtyard planted with cypress trees and roses, and at its center was a small blue pool, edged with purple and yellow annuals that an itinerant gardener came and planted. Beyond the pool, in the left rear corner of the courtyard stood an old persimmon tree. I remember a late snow—freak weather—leaving a dusting of white on the tree's orange fruit. I had a pet rabbit, which I kept in a cage and fed with grass and lettuce. I kicked a soccer ball around the *kucheh* with neighbor boys named Ali and Mehdi and learned some of the vernacular from them. I had a nanny named Zari Khanom, a sweet-faced peasant with a peasant's rough red hands, who taught me a child's Persian, and sang me Persian songs that I remember to this day.

Geryeh nakon, zar zar, she would sing,
"Don't cry, woe, woe,"
Mibaramet Lalehzar,
"I'll take you to Tulip Garden Street,"
Mifrushamet charezar.
"I'll sell you for four pennies."

M Y BUSINESS card announces that I am "James C. Flaherty, Vice President for Sales, Luxar Technologies." Luxar Technologies, its Web site proclaims, is a hi-tech firm, headquartered in Howth, north of Dublin, "offering superior mobility, optical, data, and voice networking technologies, which create new revenue-generating opportunities for its clients, while enabling them to quickly deploy . . ." and so on. Unlike Dansk Telefonik, Luxar really exists. The company CEO, a large man with a large manner, is friendly to the Agency, and has been kind enough to hire me on. Temporarily.

As Jim Flaherty I visit MCIT's old building on Revolution Avenue, where I, Jim Flaherty, jovial, smiling, gregarious—I'm from the new Ireland, you see, the hi-tech Ireland, grand place, forward-looking, great to see you, you should come visit us—meet top people at the Ministry, including the Deputy Minister, who is currently acting minister. I also meet the Ministry tech people, who are in less palatial quarters not that far from my hotel. We have cordial chats about IT while eating Persian melon and pastry off little plates using little knives and forks. We exchange business cards. I impress them with my song and dance—how Luxar might cooperate with MCIT, might for example invite MCIT training missions to Dublin, might if political conditions improve and let's hope they do, it's really time for it, undertake coproduction of telecoms components in Iran. I have PowerPoint charts, photos of Luxar telecoms equipment, and of course the company's glossy brochures.

Everything I say is moonshine.

My last afternoon in town—my flight leaves at 9:00 A.M. next morning—I am out strolling on a side street near my hotel, window shopping out of curiosity and boredom. After five days in town I still feel jet-lagged and light-headed in Tehran's thin, polluted air.

Then they come: four bearded young men, mean-looking and cocksure in sloppy, raggedy-ass uniforms, who pull by in an open jeep that coughs gray exhaust.

The men in the jeep and others like them patrol the city for women with too much face showing, for unmarried young couples out alone together, for people drinking alcohol—for anything strange or un-Islamic that may threaten the revolution's values. They call themselves *Sarollah,* God's Vengence, and maybe they are.

As they approach I make eye contact with one of them, just for an instant—a mistake—but then I edge away from the street toward the shops. They jounce past in their open jeep, one with a Kalashnikov between his legs, pointed at the sky. The jeep is Russian-made. It's spattered with mud, its tires bald.

The street runs one-way north to south, sloping down to a large boulevard, where it ends. Down there the driver, who, Iranian-style, is being very zippy with his vehicle, takes it around the corner fast to the right, not stopping, and God's Vengence disappears. Relief.

Across from where I'm standing is a large cleared space of dusty, brick-strewn, open ground. No buildings, there's been a demolition, who knows when. Over this space a flock of dirty-looking brown birds—I can't name the species, something like starlings—are flying in an enormous circle. The birds, screeching, hurl themselves in waves toward the street where I'm standing, then pivot, whirl back, and circle madly in the air over the empty, scuffed land.

Iran, I think. They don't know where they're going. They don't know what they're doing.

As I stroll back to my hotel, those four young men in the jeep, God's Vengence—return to confront me. They had noticed me—the eye contact—and, not liking what they saw, have come back around the block.

"Who are you?" one asks from the jeep. "Vot you are doink in Iran? Pahssport, please."

They take me in the jeep to central Tehran, to a grubby little office next door to a street-front mosque, where a heavy-set, unshaven man in a thick brown civilian suit, no necktie, goes through my papers very slowly, and looks closely at my Irish passport. He has copies made of the passport, though oddly he has to send a teenage flunky to a copying place down the street somewhere to have it done. His own copy machine is out of service.

Four or five other men in civilian clothing sit at three cluttered desks among a lot of comings and goings—people arriving to protest something or wheedle some kind of favor; others, like me, picked up in the street for questioning.

The room is chilly and underlit. They have a camp stove set up for heat, which gives off kerosene fumes.

Sitting silently at his own desk in a corner is a cleric, a little man with a round face and a bird's-nest beard, wearing a black turban and dark brown robes. He is scribbling awkwardly, holding a ballpoint pen in his left hand. His right is prosthetic, its original I suspect, blown off somehow. His black turban marks him as a descendent of the Prophet. He looks up from what he's writing and stares at me malevolently, though grinning and grinning.

The man who has been inspecting my passport turns out to be my inquisitor. He first glances at me cursorily with that look Islamic Republic officials have—it bespeaks a confined intelligence, clever in its way, but with small range—and tells me he is from the Interior Ministry. Then we go into it—reason for visit, length of visit, address in Iran, nationality, place of residence, contacts in Iran, travels. Business phone number in Ireland, cell-phone number, fax number, residential phone number. Business address, residential address.

After lengthy and repetitious questioning, they let me go. I walk out into the dark night, shaking, not just from the cold, and get a cab for my hotel. Next day I fly out on Swissair, never quite sure until the plane takes off that I will not die in an Iranian prison.

Thanks to my few days of doing the rounds at MCIT, I am able to put together a fair organization chart of the Ministry and its main players. I think, also, I have figured out who the principal grafters are, those who might be open to a polite offer from the Agency.

As to the mullahs, from the malevolent one-handed cleric in that chilly office to the pious ayatollahs who run the country, I laughed in their beards. I really did.

HQ: LURE, CASTLE, SLIDER

TOP SECRET

National Clandestine Service Operations Committee/Nonproliferation Task Group (OPCOM/NPTG) Session Audiotape, Session 11 (Excerpted).

Attending: J. Gutman (Chair), M. Fiscarelli, C. Lindquist, S. Kremer, R. Eisenberg.

Transcriber: D. Braithewaite.

Mr. Gutman: Okay, Operation LURE. What have we got? Mike?

Mr. Fiscarelli: Right. LURE. First off, Carl, you're new at OPCOM, I know you've had a lot on your platter, so you may not be familiar with . . .

Mr. Lindquist: No, no, I'm pretty much up to speed on the paper, but right, I don't know the recent stuff.

Mr. Fiscarelli: Right. Well, Operation LURE to recap, LURE is part of a, small part of a broad-range set of programs to electronically and in some other ways surveil the Pakistani nuclear program. LURE deals with their telecommunications. Right now it's small, though it shows growth possibilities. We have an individual, his crypt is CASTLE in the cable reporting on this, you'll run across it if you review the traffic, CASTLE, who is an individual, private sector friend of the firm. Reliable individual. He's in the telecommunications business himself. I won't go into more detail.

Ms. Eisenberg: And only this one person.

Mr. Fiscarelli: Correct. So far, anyhow. Yes.

Ms. Eisenberg: And this person's not an officer.

Mr. Fiscarelli: No. And we've got an asset, strategically placed asset, at the Pakistan Military Communications Committee—PAMAC—which is a highly classified office they've got, not that large but very sensitive, that oversees general commo in that country's military. So we've got a way in that has got major potential. PAMAC, as you all know, Carl, I think you are in the loop on this, you've served in Pakistan, they're the ones, PAMAC, that do the purchasing of communications gear for the Pak military. They handle of course clandestine purchasing and installation as well, which covers their military nuclear program. So of course we're very interested in them, as are DOD, NSA, others.

Mr. Gutman: Mike, this is not my bailiwick so forgive my aging memory, but we've got just the one internal asset at PAMAC and the one friend of the firm, as you say.

Mr. Fiscarelli: Correct.

Mr. Gutman: Not much.

Mr. Fiscarelli: No.

Mr. Gutman: And he's just a good friend? Where's the gravity on this?

Mr. Fiscarelli: He's under contract.

Mr. Gutman: Right, and that's a tenuous situation.

Mr. Fiscarelli: Granted, but for now he's what we've got. The asset, the Pakistani, SLIDER is his crypt, which you'll see in the cable reporting, has produced very useful material on PAMAC and what it's doing with PAEC [Pakistan Atomic Energy Commission]. Yes, we've been very, very happy with the product so far. We've just received some exceedingly detailed material on PAMAC and its dealings overseas, including work on the Pak nuclear force. The latest material is currently being analyzed. By the way, CASTLE has also produced useful intelligence on Russian matters.

Mr. Kremer: Russians? Commo stuff?

Mr. Fiscarelli: No. Actually, Russian military hardware, weapons systems, and whatnot. Not communications. The nature of CASTLE's business activities, which I will not go into, allowed CASTLE to produce some intelligence in this area, again, as I say, useful. But big picture on LURE: we know a major Pakistani fiber-optic project is underway. It will connect seven major Pak nuclear weapons sites. We now have the main outline of the project and what looks like a myriad of details, thanks to CASTLE.

Mr. Gutman: And SLIDER.

Mr. Fiscarelli: And SLIDER. The uses of this, of course, you can imagine.

"I'm a Spy"

I WAS born before dawn on a hot June morning in the far northwest of Washington, D.C.—Sibley Hospital, Loughboro Road. They named me Richard Henry after an uncle on my mother's side, who had died in the Korean War. They called me Ricky.

First memory: outdoors, a brilliant sunny day, probably hot, and a wooden table two feet high (eye level for me) and the table painted a dull grass green, with drop leaves that folded down on each side—they *were* folded down that day, I remember as surely as anything—and on that green table, a white frosted cake, and on that cake three candles. I am three years old—it's June 30, 1965—and I am standing before the table in an Arlington, Virginia, backyard.

My father Walt and mother Marge must have been there presiding over the event, probably with my sister Sue—who is older by two years—but I remember only the bright sun and the white cake on the dull green table.

Second memory: a wooden onion the size of a house looming over me. And in front of that onion, a wizened old man, bent over a cane. The old man has Asian features and is wearing a light brown cloak and a white turban. It is Jakarta, I learn later, and now I am four. I am with Walt standing before the wooden onion, which in fact is a mosque, though I did not know it at the time. Yet again, a hot day, probably in November.

Walt, holding my hand, smiles and waves from a distance as we approach the wizened imam of the mosque, who smiles back, and when we draw near, chucks me under my chin. The imam has a wispy white beard. End of memory.

The imam, I realized much later, was one of Walt's agents. Had to be.

And when I thought about it further, in my adulthood, I realized, too, that one of the props for Walt's drama, one of the ways Walt made connection with the wizened old imam of the mosque, was none other than pale-skinned, tow-headed, bumptious Ricky (they love kids, the Indonesians, love them crazy). I felt fine about that. Still do. My first foray into the Black World, I like to think, was at age four.

It was Walt, too, in a way at least and pushing my history back to very first things, who started me in my career as Telephone Man. One day he took me up to the attic—"Come on, Skeezix, let me show you something"—and from an old, battered military footlocker, hauled out two Japanese army field telephones that he'd brought home from the war. (In January 1942, Walt had quit grad school—Minnesota, Econ—after finishing one semester, and joined the Army Air Corps. They put him in intelligence, and he served on Saipan and Tinian and probably elsewhere in the Pacific, his first taste of the Black World that later became his life.)

"What do you think of these?" he asked as we sat on the bare planks in the attic, the phone sets open in front of us. "Pretty neat, huh?"

Walt installed one of the phones in his office, one in the basement, wired them with a six-volt battery, and there we had it, our own working commo system.

I'd never seen the phones before, he'd never mentioned them, and why he decided to go up and get them that day I can't say. I do remember it was a lazy summer afternoon—I'm guessing it was a Sunday since Walt often worked Saturdays.

Each of the phones was about the size and shape of an automobile battery. One was your standard field clunker in a beaten-up wooden case that was painted camouflage green. It had a scuffed black plastic handset and a cracked earpiece, and it looked as if it had truly been through a war.

The other was an altogether different affair. Its body was a polished blond-wood box and it came in a leather carrying case. Its handset was made of a satiny silver-gold metal and shaped like a horn. The handset had no visible mouthpiece; instead, the horn opened at its base and conducted the speaker's voice upward to a small receiver near the earpiece. The phone came with an extra, separate earpiece made of the same satiny silver-gold metal so that a third party could monitor the conversation. On top, the face plate, made of that same satiny silver-gold metal, was printed in mysterious paragraphs of black Japanese characters. An instrument fit for a general, and in perfect condition.

Walt put the clunker in his office for himself and the general's phone in the basement for me. To talk, you held down a long switch on the handset. You released it to listen.

When Walt and I spoke over those phones, we didn't say much. Our style. We were a little jokey as I remember: "Engine room to deck, engine room to deck, full speed ahead," and pseudo-military, "Do you read me? Zeroes at eleven o'clock. Roger, wilco, over and out"—that kind of thing.

My boy's imagination conceived the Japanese and Americans fighting a tremendous battle over those phones on some palmy South Pacific island. Walt told me that in the field the Japanese—he never used his generation's term, "the Japs," he was scrupulous about not using racial slurs—rigged only one wire between the phones and grounded each phone to complete the circuit. Our Marines, Walt said, would sneak close to the Japanese lines when they could, and using their bayonets, insert ground wires linked to American telephone equipment farther back, where interpreters could eavesdrop on the Japanese conversations.

You had to get really close, Walt said.

I had no idea what "grounding" meant, but I thought the Marines were way cool to take such risks. And I marveled at the idea that by planting a bayonet in the earth you could hear your enemies as they plotted against you. My first whiff of telephone security problems. Age ten, I think.

For most of his working life, my father had been an officer in the Central Intelligence Agency. He served overseas in Jakarta, Tehran, and Saigon, among other places, and for his work in Vietnam was awarded the Distinguished Officer Medal.

At the height of his career with the Agency, at the age of fifty-five, he shot himself at our home in McLean with his .44 caliber service pistol. He left no note of explanation, and his death has been an enigma that we—family, friends, coworkers—have never been able to interpret.

The brute facts are these: At about ten o'clock in the morning of July 3, 1975, a few days after my thirteenth birthday, my father took an embroidered pillowcase from the first floor linen closet of our home in McLean, got his semiautomatic pistol from the safe in his den, and, most likely concealing the weapon in the pillowcase, walked out to the raised garden at the far end of our backyard. There he lay down among the azaleas—which must have been green and woody, having dropped their spring blossoms—pulled the pillowcase over his head, and shot himself in the right temple. The heavy slug drove an inch into the garden soil.

I'd been playing basketball that morning in a nearby park. When I came home for lunch I saw two police cars and an ambulance parked on Davidson Street, and in the front yard grim-faced neighbors staring at the house. Some, when they saw me, backed away, actually backed away from a kid whose father had just died. One, though, Mr. Corliss—Eddie to his adult friends—a balding widower, silently put his arm around my shoulders. Kids from McLean High—summer school was in session—drifted past, staring, puzzling, not knowing, then learning what happened, stopped, and like the neighbors kept their distance, staring silently.

Marge, who'd been in the house talking with a police officer and watching for me, I know, came out of the house, walked over to me, calm and dry-eyed, and said, "Ricky, there's been an accident. Walt's gone."

The scene is as brief and indistinct in my mind as that first memory of birthday cake when I was three: I'm standing in the July heat, in a shaft of light that cuts through the oak trees, the sun glaring down onto me. I am dazed and voiceless. I do not cry. I cannot think, cannot react. I am taken to a neighbor's house.

For a time, days, I think, Sue cried uncontrollably; then like me, became taciturn. I thought of her then as a spirit waif, and in some ways she still is. No career, not a great marriage, problem kids.

P EOPLE WHO knew Walt think the fall of Saigon to the Communists earlier that year had something to do with his death. Walt had spent serious time in Vietnam both as analyst and intelligence operative, and had had much emotion invested in the war. The American defeat, the loss of the city, must have weighed on him and, perhaps with other factors, caused him to take his own life.

There was something else few knew. Walt had had a short affair with a nurse in Vietnam. I learned of her through a diary Walt kept of his Vietnam years. The diary, a small notebook, was among his papers in the den, in the back of a desk drawer. When he died Marge found it and didn't toss it out.

I'm not sure she'd seen it before, but I'm pretty sure she's read it. I've taken it and keep it in my own desk.

The diary is not a revealing document. Walt was a circumspect intelligence officer and never wrote anything an enemy—the Vietcong, the Chinese, the Soviets—could use if the diary somehow fell into their hands. He wrote in short phrases, often using abbreviations, some of which do not have obvious meanings. The entries detail his appointments, his times in the field, his meetings with CIA staff, the ambassador, military officers, including Generals Creighton Abrams and William Westmoreland—that kind of thing.

Still, you can leaf through it and get some sense of what it's like to lose a war. One example:

> *Wed. 17 May. 70. Explosion outside villa window, glass throughout room. 4:18 A.M. Mil. pol. in street say terrorist parked a bicycle full of plastique in front of American house. Timed fuse. Everybody jittery at this. Five of us.*

A little further in the diary there's this entry:

> *Thurs. June 1. 70. No electricity for half day. VC hit power plant. Embassy annex halls dark. Data collation dept. No reliable data VC force levels. Everybody unhappy. DB at hosp. Evening. Dinner.*

More of what it's like to lose a war, but also the first mention of "DB." There are others scattered through the notebook, "dinner with DB," "movies, DB," "DB on leave Tokyo." When I first came across the abbreviation I paid it little attention, but then began to wonder about it. Walt sometimes spelled out the names he abbreviated, but never DB. I wondered who DB was. I mentioned the diary and "DB" to Ted Pappas once, who was a young Agency officer assigned to Saigon when Walt was there. He looked at me evenly. "That'd be Donna Blalock," he said.

The affair was brief, and was probably the only time Walt ever stepped out on Marge. Donna I tracked down—this must have been ten years back—through a veteran nurses organization. She was living in western Massachussetts, south of Springfield. I called her cold, and after some surprise on her part we talked. "Yes, we were involved," she said. "It was a war and these things happen in war. He said he loved me, and I think he did, but we both knew it was going to end. He had a family. There was a huge age difference. Yes, I'd heard he died." Her accent was flat, out of the upper Midwest somewhere, like Marge and Walt's. The accent always sounds simple and honest to me. "He was a nice man . . . he was intelligent . . . his eyes were kind . . . and sad. He worried over right and wrong. We talked about the war, of course. He didn't say anything secret or about his work, just his general worries. He knew we shouldn't have been there at all—Vietnam, I mean.

"Walt would come to the hospital after his normal work to visit patients, the young men. He wanted to do that. He said it was to talk about field conditions, but that was BS. He was really more like a hospital volunteer, but he didn't want to say just that. We also had a small emergency children's burn ward. After he saw that he broke down and wept. I remember that. He was alone. I liked him. He liked me. Nothing special."

That was the conversation. We said good-bye and have never met, though she did send me a photo of herself—alone, Walt's not in it—from back then. The photo is black and white, wallet-sized. It shows her from the waist up. She is in military fatigues, arms crossed, head cocked to the left, stethescope around her neck. Her hair is short and boyish. Her gaze, directed at the camera, is friendly. All in all, a pretty woman. She's standing in front of an interior wall of some building. From an old-fashioned switch on the wall electrical wires run up and out of the picture. On the back of the photo she's written, "Saigon, 3rd Field Hospital, 1970."

Donna had done a one-year tour in Vietnam in 1969–70, three months of it in Long Binh, and nine in Saigon, which is where she and Walt had their affair. The affair ended in 1970; Walt shot himself in 1975. I doubt it was the romance with Donna that caused him to kill himself, though who knows—maybe it and the other heartbreaks of the war combined to push him over the edge.

Toward the end Walt had shown plentiful signs of depression that even I noticed—silences, withdrawal, long evenings spent in his den drinking beer. But he spoke to no one about his ordeal and as I say, left no note, his death as secretive as his life.

The Behringer family had known suicide before. Walt's own father John

Behringer, who owned a farm outside Long Prairie, Minnesota, died in what was called at the time a hunting accident. They said John Behringer had been out alone looking for rabbit—this was in the fall of 1933—and when he tried to climb over a fence carrying a shotgun that he hadn't broken open—not like him—he slipped and fell, discharging the piece and shooting himself through the chin upward. Such was the story the family told themselves and outsiders.

Down deep, though, most of the family, even John Behringer's wife Mary, thought his death was a suicide (it was the Great Depression, the farm was failing, the house was under threat of foreclosure).

After John Behringer died, Mary Loomis Behringer was able to hold on to the farm—barely, thanks to a small insurance policy on John's life and an unusually indulgent local bank. Despite the farm work, Walt managed to graduate from high school—Long Prairie Consolidated, Long Prairie, Minnesota, one hundred miles west of Minneapolis, almost to the South Dakota line—and in 1937 enrolled in the University of Minnesota to major in Economics.

Suicide isn't the only madness afflicting the Behringers. Walt's brother Harry in his early adulthood became psychotic. Voices spoke to Harry, telling him mysterious truths that Harry alone could hear and interpret. When he was thirty Harry disappeared and lived unbeknownst to family for years on the street in Denver, then San Francisco. He was eventually institutionalized, his identity discovered, and the family notified of his whereabouts. He died in 1994 in a mental institution in Bethesda, Maryland, at the age of seventy. Behringers seem given to mental illness. I'm a Behringer, of course. I think about that: Walt was thirteen when John Behringer shot himself, and I was thirteen when Walt, using a gun, killed himself out in the azalea bed. At some point—I can't say when—I saw the pattern: Behringers, guns.

IT WAS on an overnight canoe trip we took up the Potomac for my twelfth birthday that Walt told me what he did for a living. Because of that revelation the trip took on a kind of mythic resonance in family lore— Walt, an intensely private man, taking his son out to the forest primeval to say truly who he was, disclosing to his boy the secrets of his own adulthood.

"I'm a spy," Walt said, as we sat talking at our campfire. "I ought to tell you that. I work for the government, for the CIA. You know what that is. The Central Intelligence Agency. 'Fraid I can't tell you much about what I do 'cause my work is secret. Gotta be that way."

We had rented a canoe at White's Ferry, north of Washington, a crossing point where, then as now, cars are ferried across the river on a flat-bottomed boat, the *Gen. Jubal Early,* tethered to each bank by cables.

That first day we canoed six or seven miles, I in the prow, Walt steering. I wore a billed Baltimore Orioles ball cap and I carried a day pack on my back, pretending to be a frontiersman and thinking of Indians. The paddling was easy. Above White's Ferry there is almost no current, and we had a light, southerly summer breeze. Both days the weather was overcast, but it rained only once, just a fine light sprinkling that didn't last long.

The Potomac narrows considerably here, but at some points there are still islets, and we often paddled in the side channels, keeping the islets to our left as we paddled upstream. On our right, always, was the old C&O Canal.

"The Canal was built long back," Walt said, "to link people in the mountains of Virginia and Maryland with the sea coast and the ports down at Georgetown and Alexandria. They thought it would encourage people to go farther west. Supposed to go all the way to the Ohio River, but it made it only to Cumberland. Up in Maryland."

We pitched a pup tent on an islet that night. We broiled steaks and for breakfast in the morning, fried bacon and eggs. We pissed on trees.

At the campfire that night Walt told me what being a spy meant. "We find information," he said, "and we analyze it for our country, we try to give guidance to our government, to the president, to Congress, let them know what's going on in the world. Those years when we were in Jakarta and Tehran I was doing that kind of work, and it's the work I do now when I go off to the office. And also on my travel overseas, it's all for CIA."

The trip was utterly singular and, for Walt, out of character. He and I did little together as father and son. He was a sedentary intellectual, not an outdoorsman of any sort. He didn't fish or hunt, didn't even follow sports. For relaxation, he gardened. But for some reason—his idea, which he sprang on me one day in July—we took this one expedition together. A year later he was dead.

HQ: We've Got the Specs

OPCOM/NPTG Session Audiotape, Session 19 (Excerpted).

Attending: J. Gutman (Chair), M. Fiscarelli, C. Lindquist, S. Kremer, R. Eisenberg.

Transcription: D. Braithewaite.

Mr. Gutman: Okay, second issue on the agenda, the SLIDER DVD contents, the specs et cetera on the Pakistan weapons program and Gazelle Seven, and I want to congratulate Mike on this whole business. Quite wonderful.

Mr. Fiscarelli: Well, many thanks. We were very, very lucky to get this material. Rhoda, it's now with your people.

Ms. Eisenberg: Right, well, to summarize, these are just preliminary results, the first items we've gotten from what looks like a very rich trove, and because the customers, principally NSA, wanted work done on the specs, and they felt they needed it quickly, we're addressing that issue first. But as to the communications, the fiber optics, to summarize, it is quite a coup. We have the complete, what looks like the complete technical designs, but also the ongoing engineering plans, coordinated with the construction schedule, so you see . . .

Mr. Gutman: You love it.

Mr. Fiscarelli: You do.

Mr. Gutman: How sweet it is. So, Rhoda—upshot?

Ms. Eisenberg: Right, as I say, we've just gotten a complete picture of the program, their construction schedule, what looks like the whole nine yards on Gazelle Seven. Sci Tech people are still evaluating the designs and all that, the technical stuff, which will take quite a long time for a complete job. Plus the list of companies, the front companies, the clandestine suppliers and all to the Pakistani program—the DVD adds quite a bit to our knowledge and we'll be tracking these new leads down.

Mr. Kremer: This material, the specs, the designs, it gets handed on to DIA for possible action?

Mr. Fiscarelli: Well, actually, NSA and DIA. NSA will attempt to penetrate the system, perhaps need people on the ground. Who may well be DOD personnel, Special Forces of some type.

Mr. Lindquist: DOD obligation to us as I understand the new rules is to keep us fully informed on what they're doing.

Ms. Eisenberg: Dream on, Carl.

Mr. Lindquist: Hey, I'm just reading from the playbook. Like in the best of all possible worlds.

Ms. Eisenberg: It won't happen.

Mr. Lindquist: No.

Mr. Gutman: What those people are doing is called "preparation of the battle space." Nobody else's business, just Pentagon. As we all know, a lot of sins come under that rubric. Nobody here has input, nobody at ODNI, nobody on the Hill. And we may or may not know what happens. Just the SECDEF and his minions out there on the edge of the world.

Ms. Eisenberg: Well, I think we can be proud of ourselves on this one, specifically Mike and his work.

Mr. Fiscarelli: And CASTLE.

Mr. Gutman: Who is contract talent, which I emphasize is unreliable and you've heard me time and time again on these people. They have their own agendas.

"He Was Going to Get Me an Igla"

"HAPPENED A couple weeks ago," Ted Pappas is saying. "Heard it from a pal, a Russian—grapevine thing. You'd never see it in the papers."

A man named Sasha Geydarov has been beaten to death in Istanbul. Pappas has just given me the news. The murder is what he'd called me about in Athens.

Pappas and I are sitting on a bench in the park on Columbia Island. Across the river from us are the still-leafy oaks and sycamores of Potomac Park, and beyond them, the low skyline of Washington.

When we want private conversation, really private, Pappas and I will meet out of our offices. In good weather like today—blue sky, the early touch of an autumn chill, a little wind—we like meeting in open air. Makes it tough to put a mike on you. And wherever we meet—out in parks like Columbia Island or in bars and restaurants—we snap the batteries out of our cells.

You never know.

Pappas says, "My Russian pal was pretty sure his fellow Russians did it, but"—he shoots a look at me and snorts—"he wasn't sure *which* fellow Russians. Said it could have been a business thing or could have been the government—hard to tell. That's all he knew. Or, was gonna tell *me* anyhow."

Sasha Geydarov was a short, skinny little guy with pale skin and dark, alert eyes. He lived in the old part of Istanbul with a Turkish male lover, who ran a bed-and-breakfast just off the Hippodrome that catered to gays. Through his father, who had been a functionary in the Soviet Interior

41

Ministry, Sasha had connections to plenty of people, high and low, in the Russian and Ukrainian militaries. When the USSR fell to pieces, Sasha was in a position to cash in on black-market military equipment, which he did. Pappas and I were both customers.

I say, "I saw Sasha three months back."

"A deal?"

"Yeah."

On a thickly humid evening in Baku, on the harborside promenade, I paid Sasha $2,000 in cash for a Russian 1L21, a compact, handheld laser device used for guiding air-to-ground missiles. It was very hot. Sasha was in uniform—tight American jeans, tee, shiny Gucci-like shoes on his little feet—and I remember thinking his jeans looked heavy and wondering how the hell he could stand to wear them in the heat. I'd picked him up in a rented Mercedes as he walked along the boulevard. He jumped in and deposited the 1L21—wrapped in butcher paper—on the floor of the car. He was very jittery.

"This is it," he hissed, "give me the money." I drove him for about a quarter of a mile while he hurriedly counted his handful of bills, concealing them under the dashboard, wary, looking up now and then at the passers-by outside. When he'd finished he stuffed the bills into his jeans and under his breath said, "Okay, okay. Stop please here." He took a final glance at the strollers on the promenade, then jumped out of the car as quickly as he'd jumped in.

Fifteen minutes after dropping Sasha, I turned the device over to the usual furtive representative from the American embassy, this one a pale, plumpish man named Guthrie, whom I picked up in the downtown business section. Guthrie, as calm as Sasha was nervous, slipped the package into an expensive-looking woven leather lettercase, and when I stopped, got out, politely said good-bye, and ambled off into the night. I drove back to my hotel, job done. I never saw Sasha again.

PAPPAS TAPS my arm and says softly, "He was going to get me an Igla. Antiaircraft missile. Russian, shoulder-fired thing—like the Stinger? They got one now with a new design—longer-range, faster. Thing's got a whole new seeker nobody in America's ever seen. And a whole new guidance system, new logic—'proportional convergence,' whatever that is.

Harder to jam. Real good missile. They say kill probability is like fifty per-cent, even when you're using countermeasures. I mean, that's impressive."

Pappas notices a young man and woman ambling toward us on the bike path and goes quiet. The couple are in shorts and Georgetown Hoyas sweat-shirts, but they look older than college-age. I sense Pappas doesn't like that, the discrepancy. The young man has crazy-cut red hair that makes him look like Woody Woodpecker and he is wearing electric blue wraparound sun-glasses. He is spinning a red yo-yo. His girl has Afro features, but very light skin. They pay us no attention. They leave the bike path to wander down toward the water where they stop by a lone ailanthus tree, turn to face each other, and kiss, joining their hands. Beyond them on the river, a slim, low white power boat, its engine purring, cuts to the right and pulls into a nar-row passage running to Columbia Island Marina behind us. Pappas lets it disappear, then says, "Sasha was going to get one flown to Zagreb, I'd have taken it from there. Shit, we had it all worked out, no pretend third-party sale or anything, just Sasha and me." Pappas smiles mirthlessly. "Well, he sure fucked the deal this time."

"Didn't he."

Pappas works out of an old office building on Fifteenth Street, mostly shopping East Asia, where he spent his career with the Agency, though he works Russia, too. He looks like an aging gangster—dark, square face and heavy eyes, gray hair he slicks back in an old-fashioned cut. He's short and compact, thick in his build, and thick-wristed, and you can see how he must have been powerful once. His voice is hoarse and high-pitched, doesn't quite go with his thick body.

He glances over at me. "You wonder what happened."

"I got no insights. Ask me, we'll never know." Pappas rocks his head to the right, a Greek gesture of agreement, and we sit for a moment as waves from the now-vanished power boat slap the shore rhythmically, slowly dying out.

Pappas says, "You know, I often think of your dad. Still do."

In the sixties, when they were working in Saigon, Pappas and Walt had become close. Pappas spoke at Walt's funeral, a day that for me is like the day of his death—a hot, bright blur. I was sleepless and dazed, but I do remem-ber Pappas standing at a lectern, speaking—this would have been in an audi-torium in the funeral home, Loefflers, a two-storied brick place, looks like a savings-and-loan, still there on Old Dominion in McLean. When Pappas began his eulogy, he burst into tears, halted a few moments to grip the lectern in silence, then went on to speak eloquently of Walt, of Walt's decency, of his profound sense of honor, of his patriotism. I was told later that many of the upper-tier officers at the Agency, including Bill Colby, Director at the time, had attended the service. I remember only Pappas and the rows of folding chairs filled with solemn, older men in suits accompanied by a few women.

Later, Pappas would send me postcards from his overseas assignments, shots of exotic capital cities accompanied with short messages. "Hope you're doing okay, guy, you'd love Bangkok"—that kind of thing. After a while the postcards stopped.

A few years back Pappas got wind that I was in some kind of security business, and since by that time he'd left the Agency and was himself out in private business—"on the street"—he gave me a call. One thing led to another, and we now cooperate pretty frequently. Pappas brings along thirty years of Agency contacts and a large supply of smarts. And information. He stays in touch with his Agency buddies, both retired and active, and hears a lot—who's doing what, who got promoted, who resigned, who got fired and why.

P APPAS GESTURES with his head at a couple of teenage boys in knee-length, satiny shorts who jog past us on the bike path tossing a baseball to each other. At first they're side by side, then one moves out ahead, maybe ten feet, and glancing back over his left shoulder, gracefully snares a throw from the other kid.

"Makes me think of back when," he says, "playing ball at school. Beautiful game to watch, even better to be out there on the field." Pappas was once good at the sport. "I always wanted to be a ballplayer," he told me once. "Played ball in school—shortstop. I was good. Just not good enough to go pro. Could've made the minors, but that'd been it. So, hell, instead of playing ball, I joined the Agency. Had a good career. Never regretted it one minute. Been a great ride for a poor village kid from Greece, right? I love this country, I really do. Could only happen here."

Pappas's parents brought him and their four other children to the States in 1950. His father was a priest, and there was a church vacancy in Youngstown, Ohio. He learned his English in Youngstown and also—"it was a tough steel town, very raw place"—learned to use his fists. He went to

Kent State on an athletic scholarship because of his talent for baseball, did two years in the Army (drafted, Germany), then went straight into the Agency, where he had a long career and became known for adventurous, over-the-top operations. The older generation of senior officers, the ones from good New England and Virginia families who ran the Agency back then, liked Pappas, who was ethnic and by their lights maybe a little crude. They thought they were rubbing elbows with a tough guy and they liked that. It made them think they were tough themselves. Pappas ended up Chief of Station, Kuala Lumpur, Malaysia, then went private, using his contacts to make more money than he ever earned at the Agency.

Pappas stretches his right arm up and out toward the river, spreads his stubby fingers, then balls his hand into a fist, opens it, and repeats the action. "Arthritis," he says with a grimace. "Don't get old, Junior—it's the shits. I really feel it. Affects everything. Starting to hate the work. Flying all over, the security bullshit you have to go through these days, belt off, shoes off, that stuff, plus the time changes, living outta hotel rooms, eating hotel food, taking crap local taxis—taxis, Jesus, I been ripped off in at least twenty currencies. Goddamn, I'm too old for all this."

"You gonna hang it up? Live on Golden Pond?"

He makes a "tsk" sound that means "Who knows?" Then he glances over at me. "Hey, I'm still angling for an Igla. You game?"

"I'll look around." Like Frannie and her fellow realtors, Pappas and I split the fees down the middle when we collaborate. I'll work a couple of sources I know. I may hear something.

We sit for a time staring at the river and talking baseball. The series is coming up. We're both think Boston will murder the Rockies again. Doesn't matter much to either of us—Pappas is a Cleveland man and I follow the Orioles, neither team ever being much in the running.

Suddenly, Pappas gets up. "Hey, it's been good. Hear anything about, uh, an Igla for sale . . ."

"Will do."

He waves, then runs, hopping awkwardly, across the GW Parkway, dodging vehicles, over to the Marina, where he's parked.

WHEN I get back to Global Reach, my secretary Argaysha gives me a wave and a "Hiya." Her dreads are a gleaming coppery color this week, as are her nails, a new look she's testing. She's typing a contract for

Jimmy McKelvin, a fat, pink lawyer who subleases office space and buys secretarial time from us. McKelvin's a lone-ranger—he gets along with no fellow attorney on the face of this earth. We also have a deeply introverted CPA on the premises, Dick Smolen, under the same arrangement. I put the two of them around the corner and down the hall.

Our premises are in the WestTy Center, a small office park in Tysons Corners, Virginia, just off the hustle of Leesburg Pike, but secluded nicely from the Pike by landscaping. From the WestTy we have a fast shot to the Beltway and we're no more than fifteen minutes to CIA, even closer to a lot of the offices the Agency leases out here, including the building Hawk Stedman first pitched me in over a decade back, which is a five-minute drive from Global Reach (you don't walk anywhere in Tysons Corners, the place won't let you, you drive).

When you head into the WestTy from the Pike, you pass first under the Sheraton Premier, a cylindrical all-glass hotel tower the color of the sky, whatever that happens to be at the time, then you dip down into a small shopping strip (Easy Dry Cleaning, Elegance Nail Salon, Enterprise Rent-A-Car), then you find us.

We are in one among eight look-alike, two-story buildings of umber-colored brick, dark-paned windows, and phony mansard roofs. The buildings are unmarked except for their addresses. Their tenants are mostly small businesses like us—real estate franchises, little IT and other tech companies, security firms. Below our building an asphalted bike trail curls through a woody area; next to the trail, there's a "fitness cluster" with half a dozen exercise sites that no one uses. Beyond them are the garbage Dumpsters.

In the building across a parking area from us, DIA maintains a small satellite office. They have a retina reader and a card swipe for their spooky employees and visitors, and the place is monitored by videocams. Twenty yards or so down from their entrance an unmarked rent-a-cop car is permanently stationed. If you loiter at the entrance by the DIA's retina reader and card swipe, beefy rent-a-cops will emerge from that vehicle and tell you to move on.

The DIA presence just over there makes us uneasy. We sweep Global Reach regularly for bugs, we have a permanent monitor checking the phones, and of course have state-of-the-art burglar alarms. We think we're pretty safe from the more intrusive kinds of surveillance. But we're vulnerable to other kinds of hanky-panky. They—whoever "they" might be, DIA spooks, somebody else—could park a van out there in the lot, put a laser on our window, the one facing the lot, and catch the beam as it bounces back. The beam, a pencil-thin shaft of concentrated light, would be modulated by the faintest of vibrations—including the vibrations of human vocal chords—induced in our dark window. If "they" caught the ricochet when someone in here was talking, filtered it for voice frequencies, and recorded the result, they'd have the speech of a trusting, unguarded, thoughtless human being. The voice might sound like someone speaking through a long tube, but it would be a voice, and they'd know what that voice was saying. Which is why I sometimes meet people—Pappas, others—in the great outdoors.

In my office, as I troll through the afternoon's e-mails and Call/Please Answer messages—from the Israeli mil attaché, from a local United Way volunteer, from a DOD accountant—I think of Sasha thumbing through his twenty one-hundred-dollar bills and of his dark, alert eyes as he glanced warily at the strollers on that Baku promenade. And I wonder who killed him and why.

OPCOM/NPTG Session Audiotape, Session 23 (Excerpted).

Attending: J. Gutman (Chair), M. Fiscarelli, C. Lindquist, S. Kremer, R. Eisenberg.

Transcriber: D. Braithewaite.

Mr. Lindquist: On HIGHBEAM, report on his death and all, Analysis flagged it for us. They don't say why.

Mr. Fiscarelli: No. Right. Before your time. This Geydarov, he's HIGHBEAM in the cables, small-time con man basically. He's mostly shown up in reports on the Natasha trade. Girls, Russians or from other parts of the FSU [Former Soviet Union], want jobs overseas, end up, a lot of these girls, as slaves in Turkish brothels and elsewhere.

Ms. Eisenberg: Young women, Mike.

Mr. Fiscarelli: Yes. Right.

Mr. Lindquist: Okay, but again, why to us?

Mr. Fiscarelli: HIGHBEAM has also spoken to our people fairly frequently and he's been an asset, not high-level, on the Russian Mafia and sometimes nuclear security.

Ms. Eisenberg: Right. On the Mafia angle, Carl, it's the old worry that drug-smuggling outfits, Russian, whatever, Kazak and so forth, could be used to smuggle nuclear material too, which is our interest, OPCOM's interest in Geydarov. You read the reffed reports you'll get a better idea of the guy and his uses to us.

Mr. Fiscarelli: Geydarov's been helpful also in getting military items to us, pilferage from the Russian military, mostly smaller items though some larger pieces of equipment. Not in our portfolio, of course.

Mr. Gutman: I don't see it in the report, but the guy figured in an enriched uranium scam just last summer. As some of you will recall he acted as informant on that deal, among his many other talents. Passed on information to the Turkish police. Deal didn't amount to anything because the material as usual was junk, radioactive slag or something, not even low-grade enriched uranium.

Mr. Fiscarelli: There was this Georgian involved trying to scam it.

Mr. Gutman: Right, but the Turkish police decided to set up a sting, and the Georgian sold it to an undercover Turkish cop. He got three years or something like that, the Georgian. We still don't know where he got his slag.

Mr. Fiscarelli: Anyhow, Carl, to get back, that help on the nuclear issue is Geydarov's significance and why Analysis sent that over.

Mr. Gutman: Reminds me, back in the day, FSB officers used to run stings just to promote their own [expletive] careers. They'd talk some poor [expletive], a low-level guard or whatever at some nuclear facility, they'd talk him into stealing material of some kind. They'd make out like they had rich buyers—Arabs or something—on the other end. They'd offer the poor jerk a whole lot of money for HEU. They'd let him steal it, then bang, they arrest him, try him, put him away for a bunch of years. They did this a number of times we know of. Great for their careers, but it was all [expletive]. Higher-ups, Russian authorities, liked it. Showed they were being attentive and vigilant.

Ms. Eisenberg: Where in fact what arrests like this really meant was it was so easy to steal nuclear material.

Mr. Gutman: Exactly. As we know, Russia's a perfect [expletive] nightmare. Was and is. Okay, Turks say Geydarov was killed with a blunt instrument.

Ms. Eisenberg: Right. They found his body somewhere in Istanbul.

Mr. Gutman: Rhoda, I see here also Analysis says Turks don't have zip on the crime or motivation?

Ms. Eisenberg: Correct.

Mr. Gutman: Neither do we?

Ms. Eisenberg: Correct.

They Seem All Energy and Grace and Happiness

THE BEACH at Henlopen State Park, a little after noon—bright day, blue sky, few clouds.

Frannie's up on her elbows looking at the ocean. She's taller and leaner than Liz. Her skin is very fair. Her hair is a fine blond. Her eyebrows are thin and arched high, giving her a constant look of bemused surprise. The tip of her nose is sharp and as she talks mobile.

"You can see England over there if you try," she says, smiling. " 'Course, you have to try hard. When I was a little girl, Daddy'd take us to Cedar Point on the lake"—Lake Erie, Frannie's from Toledo—"and he'd say, 'If you try hard, try really hard, you can see Canada.' I knew he was kidding, but I looked anyway, and felt it—Canada—across the lake. You know it's just over *there*—and you think it's almost in sight, the water's so deceptive."

"We never came to the beach much," I say. "Overseas it mostly wasn't doable, not where we were. But Walt wasn't a beach guy, anyhow. He was like Richard Nixon—Nixon wore wingtips out on the sand. You ever hear that? Nixon'd walk out on the beach at San Clemente in a business suit and his wingtips. I think Walt would've done that, but he never went out."

We have stretched our beach towels in parallel on the sand up from where the waves are breaking gently, monotonously on the shore, and have plopped down with our paraphernalia—sunscreen, hats, sandals, sunglasses, newspaper (I've picked up a *Post* in Rehoboth). Frannie, who's fixed us ham sandwiches and packed them, along with bananas, apples, and little cups of yogurt, in a red-and-white plastic cooler, spreads them out between us. I break out the Miller's and potato chips that I've brought (we have our lifestyle differences). In the wind, always strong here, gulls circle, hanging over us, eyeing the food.

The beach is almost deserted. The nearest people are a couple of old folks in aluminum lawn chairs, high and dry like us, maybe thirty yards up the way. He—pale, bearded, wearing a billed cap the color of baby shit—sits there inertly, simply staring at the ocean. She—skinny, also pale, and wearing a floppy yellow hat, like Frannie's—is reading a book. They sit there un-moving.

Down the other way a lone surf fisher in green swimming trunks that reach past his knees has cast two lines out and has his poles anchored in white plastic tubes he's driven into the sand. He is sitting on the sand be-side his tube, no towel, leaning back on a huge cooler, also red and white, that he's brought. Way out, almost to the horizon, a white freighter steams slowly north, heading for Wilmington maybe, or Philly.

T HE AIR and water are still warm enough to take a dip. Frannie's suit is a demure one-piecer, dark blue, sleek over her body, tight on her thighs. When she heads for the water, she stands up, pulls the suit away from her lovely fanny, and lets it snap back on both cheeks—an attention-getter, though I don't think she particularly intends it. We both run yelling into the surf, holding hands at first, then we separate—she, sticking close to shore; I, ranging farther out, past where you can touch bottom, out where the surf gently bobs you up and down. Sometimes out here you will feel something brush against your foot and you wonder about it, this small hint of peril and of the mystery of the depths.

From way out I ride the waves in and get thrown onto shore, rolling in the coarse sand, stagger to my feet, reeling and a little dizzy, and head out again. Frannie joins the game, though never going as far out, and we do this a few times, then head for our parallel towels to lunch. Smiling, our swim-ming for the day done, she fishes out from her beach bag and puts on the sil-ver filigree Greek cross and silver necklace I presented to her last night just before some energetic fooling around. I had bought the cross and necklace at a gyp joint in the Plaka, an area of tourist razzamatazz just east of the Parthenon.

As we sit cross-legged munching our ham sandwiches and drinking beer, Frannie gives says, "Dick's sent the agreement over. He says it's a month, maybe two—that's it, then I'm free." She snuffles a kind of laugh.

Richard Hage, Frannie's divorce lawyer, has sent the last of her paperwork, the property settlement, to Arlington Family Court. According to Hage, it will take very little time now to sunder Frannie and Jimbo. The divorce, legally speaking, has been an easy deal for all concerned—nobody is contesting anything. Frannie doesn't want and wouldn't have gotten alimony; there are no kids, so there's no child support or visitation rights to haggle over; McClennan will pay Frannie half the value of the Highland Street property as assessed by a mutually agreed-on appraiser; and Frannie will stay in the house. Everybody happy, say amen.

My story was oh so different. When Liz let fly with a divorce suit, I dopily countersued to give her a run for her money. Huge mistake. Liz's lawyer, Abby, specializes in nasty breakups—she makes them nastier—and is a woman described by those who know her as a "pit bull." My guy, Bob, has no fear of combat either. The two of them strung the process out forever, billing us many happy hours as they went. In the end Liz and I split the property down the middle, which we would have done anyway, and agreed on the amount of child support we probably would have agreed on anyway, but were each about $20,000 poorer than if we had just "been reasonable" as my mother Marge said at the time—other people were forever failing to be reasonable by Marge's lights, among them, alas, for most of his life, her son.

I'm wondering, though, why Frannie didn't give me the news yesterday when I arrived out here. She'd had all evening, but never brought it up. No great rush—as far as I know nobody's particularly hankering to get hitched—but it's a kind of indicator of her wariness. And of course Frannie's news raises the question we've pretty much avoided up to now: When the divorce goes final, what then do we—Frannie and I—do?

We met in a Safeway (Lee Highway, just down the hill from Frannie's real-estate office), where on a freak snowy day in late March I noticed her—good bod it looked like under her long coat, pretty face, no ring—in the check-out line ahead of me, mugging at somebody's baby in the grocery cart just ahead of her. I joined in the mugging. She paid me not much attention.

Then, outside in the parking lot, I caught up with her in the slush as she was loading the last of her groceries into the trunk of a big maroon Chevrolet, a vehicle that suggested a large family—if no current hubby, then at least plenty of kids, the thought of which made me think of pulling back, but I didn't. I walked up to her and saying, "Excuse me, I've never done this before," gave her my business card, told her I thought she was attractive and that she might be unattached, that I was unattached, which wasn't much fun in Washington, and if she felt like it, would she give me a call?

She cracked the kind of smile you'd expect at the effrontery of the whole deal—which I'd actually pulled a couple of times before with up to then one success—and looking away from me, shaking her head, she got in her car, and still not looking back, drove off.

But did not throw away the card.

When she called, foiling my caller ID by pressing Star 67, we hit it off over the phone, met for a beer at the end of a day, and had a couple of dates—movie, free concert at a downtown church—chaste as a pair of sworn celibates.

The earnest, real thing began one spring evening as we sat side by side on Frannie's screened-in porch. The sun going down, well-thought-out and well-prepared dinner ingested, another Pinot Grigio uncorked, Frannie brushed my cheek with the backs of her fingers, and said, "This could work." Then came our quick ascent to her bedroom and the big king-sizer she once shared with Jimbo, time out to peel open a de rigueur condom from an extra large box of them (top drawer in the night table), a gift from her real-estate buddies when they learned Jimbo had moved out, and then scorching, exploratory first-time-for-us-as-a-twosome sex, followed by deep sleep, followed by breakfast in her "eat-in" kitchen, as she would put it in her sales pro way, then me heading home in the quiet, dove-gray Sunday morning.

A s WE sit watching the waves and the sandpipers—the white freighter has long since disappeared—I tell Frannie I've called Pennie and Sam and told them I would see them next weekend as scheduled, not of course this one.

Frannie says, "Your girls love you to pieces—total adoration, I can tell."

"I hope. They're sweet kids." They haven't quite gotten all the reasons for the divorce, don't seem particularly to blame me for it, and they like it when we're together because it's playtime as compared to Liz's earnest mothering and we concentrate on having fun.

"They do."

Unspoken: Down the line Frannie could be a good stepmom to them, and they wouldn't have some huge problem choosing between their real mom and her. Frannie and Jim, by the way, are childless. Jim, a true Washington-style workaholic (also, according to Frannie, a hyperfastidious control freak and lousy in bed), never wanted kids, and Frannie thought that would be all right. But it isn't all right. She's forty-two now and, except in the most theoretical way, the clock's pretty much run out on her. After a beer or two when she thinks about that her eyes mist over.

Frannie and the girls do get along. Sam, the outgoing one, was at first standoffish, while thoughtful, quiet Pennie, took to Frannie right off the bat. After a while Sam came around, and things these days seem fine for everybody. We have foursomes. We picnic (Belle Haven down the Potomac, Fletcher's Cove, up the canal from Georgetown in the District), we go biking (Washington and Old Dominion Trail, Mount Vernon). A couple of times when the girls were spending a weekend with me Frannie's come over and fixed dinner. Her rule, though, which I accept while not quite getting the point, is no mutual sleepovers. When the girls are at my place, Frannie heads for home.

THERE—HOW far from shore? a hundred yards maybe?—a dozen, two dozen dolphins, leaping and dancing in the sunlight, a large pod of them moving north to south past where we are standing in the sand. The dolphins shoot straight up out of the ocean, twist their dark, blue-gray bodies, and shimmy their tails as if walking on the water, cavorting balletically over the waves. They seem all energy and grace and happiness, so much so that I imagine them smiling in their dance. The show lasts a magic minute or two, then they're gone, leaving behind the dull, slow-rolling waves.

I've never seen this vision before. Frannie says they're a sign of good luck, and maybe they are.

HQ: Bunch of Phony Little Companies

OPCOM/NPTG Session Audiotape, Session 28 (Excerpted).

Attending: J. Gutman (Chair), M. Fiscarelli, C. Lindquist, S. Kremer, R. Eisenberg.

Transcription: D. Braithewaite.

Ms. Eisenberg: It's unbelievably good luck, the DVD. The CASTLE material on the Pakistanis is knock-your-socks-off stuff. Our Pakistan specialists assess the material to be high probability of genuineness. You've been supplied copies of the preliminary report on all this, NPTG 24/127. We finalize it in a couple of days, but it won't change much. Bottom line: We have almost the entire Pakistani military communications procurement program. We've got some companies we never heard of and they've been supplying, working for the Pakistanis. We all know in the '90s how the Pakistanis and Iranians, and Libyans, and North Koreans were cooperating closely in nuclear matters, thanks to Khan.

Mr. Fiscarelli: Just for some background here, Khan for the record, and for you, Stu—I know you're aware, but to make sure everybody's on the same page— Khan is A. Q. Khan, Pakistani scientist, so-called father of the Pakistani A-bomb, who sold nuclear know-how and even equipment to other countries, especially Iran, Libya, and North Korea.

Mr. Gutman: I was on that. Unbelievable. This Khan worked through a whole bunch of phony little companies and front men et cetera in Europe and the Far East. These front companies owned front companies that hired middlemen who opened more front companies. I mean, it was [expletive] endless. A lot of this seemed to shut down, go dormant, after the great man's arrest.

Ms. Eisenberg: Anyway, we know a lot of these Pakistani companies that Khan set up, and Pakistani individuals. We know their identities. And some still are functioning we know from this DVD.

Mr. Gutman: Big [expletive] surprise, right?

Ms. Eisenberg: We've got names of middlemen operating on behalf of the Pakistanis in Europe and Asia, including front men, front companies, service companies. Analysis is working very hard on this, high priority, what companies are still in existence, functioning companies, and what they're doing, and whatever else this DVD may tell us.

"The Jihad Is Ongoing, Thank God"

FRANNIE'S PLACE in Arlington, an evening in. We're in her "TiVo Room" at the back of the house with the wide-screen TV, a comfortable sofa, and a coffee table you can put your feet up on. Frannie's in the kitchen making popcorn for a movie we're going to see (*Kings Row*, the one where Ronald Reagan, back in his Hollywood days, asks, "Where's the rest of me?"). Surfing around, waiting for Frannie and the popcorn, I light by chance on BBC in America. They're doing something on terrorism—terror in the new millennium or some such. The anchorperson is a gorgeous young woman—nut-brown skin, long black hair, full lips, South Asian, she looks more than passingly like Ray's wife. She has a perfect British accent of the Tony Blair variety. She is speaking of al-Qaeda, its sanctuaries in northern Pakistan, its resurgence in Afghanistan.

Then there he is—his long, thin face, his untrimmed beard, his gentle, almost shy voice. He's standing before what looks like a rock escarpment. Behind him, leaning against the rock, is an AK-47. In the upper-right corner of the screen is the Al-Jazira logo, a little green-and-gold calligraphic arabesque, shaped like a candle flame.

"I have sworn to only live free," he is saying in Arabic, as English subtitles crawl across the bottom of the screen. "Even if I find bitter the taste of death, I don't want to die humiliated or deceived." He is looking directly into the camera, holding a microphone in his right hand. I notice he wears his watch on his right wrist. The shot is from the waist up and you can't see how tall he is. He's wearing a camouflage jacket and khaki-green shirt. His black-and-white checked *kaffiyeh* is wrapped around his head in a turban; the end drapes down the left side of his chest. He looks healthy, rested, and calm. The man is a living mockery of America.

"The war in Iraq," he says, "is burning without cessation, and operations in Afghanistan are in constant escalation in our favor, God be praised, and the Pentagon's numbers indicate an ongoing rise in the number of your killed and wounded, in addition to the huge material damage. The jihad is ongoing, thank God, despite all the oppressive measures adopted by the U.S. Army and its agents. In Iraq, there is a point now where there is no difference between this criminality and Saddam's criminality."

He speaks quietly of the September 11 attacks, and then says, "Any delay in similar operations in America does not stem from lack of ability to break through your security measures. The operations are in the stages of preparation, and you will yet see them, in the heart of your homes, immediately with the completion of the preparations, with God's help. They will match the enormity of your crimes in Iraq and Afghanistan and elsewhere in the world, God willing."

As the program goes to shots of the planes crashing into the buildings I click away from BBC in America. Enough.

"They call him 'Osama bin Forgotten,' " I say.

"Not by me," Frannie says, who's come into the room. "I watched the coverage the whole day. I called work and said I couldn't come in. I was catatonic. I saw the buildings come down in real time. They said the buildings could hold fifty thousand people, and I thought tens of thousands of people were dying. Miracle so many got out."

I say, "I'd been up there a few times—up in the Towers, I mean. Business stuff, conferences once in a while. The buildings were engineered to bend with the wind, and if you went way up, to the eightieth or ninetieth floors, where the planes hit, you could feel the motion, kind of a swaying. The windows were narrow. You could look down through them at an angle, at the harbor, maybe. You could get a good look uptown, too. You could see Central Park, which looked like a big green patch way in the distance. You could see all those cities over in New Jersey, all grown together. You couldn't look straight down."

You couldn't look straight down.

"I think of the leapers," I tell Frannie. Of their falling bodies. Of the people who crowded at the windows they'd somehow gotten open; of the secretaries, the ones who had come in by subway or bus and who'd packed their lunches and who wore walking shoes to work, which they'd changed on arrival to business shoes or heels; of businessmen, young sharpies, maybe, who'd come in in suits and ties ready to deal, or older guys, their bosses, overweight, thinning hair, not so much energy; of women execs who'd come in that day as on other days dressed for success—all of them at the windows looking down at the vast, helpless city. I think of the fearsome, necessary choice those people faced. At some point they started, individuals, or sometimes two together, hand in hand, perhaps staying linked all the way down. Those couples—were they strangers to each other? Office mates? Lovers? What did they feel at that moment of choice? And what did they feel in their descent? Terror, of course. But could there have been some kind of deeper connection between them, some kind of grace as well?

I once met a Special Forces parachutist who told me of a jumping technique call HALO—high altitude, low opening—used to clandestinely infiltrate enemy territory from the air. He told me that the human body falling from great height reaches a certain velocity, something like 125 miles an hour, which, because of air resistance, it does not exceed; and it makes a sound—an eerie, high-pitched scream, like the sound of a falling bomb, that trails it downward. I don't tell this to Frannie.

"They know the name of at least one," Frannie says. "Caught in a photo. They recognized him because he wore this orange undershirt. His regular business shirt, which was white, had blown up over his head, and you could see he was wearing this orange undershirt. That's how they knew. Plus the body type—tall and lanky. So they're pretty sure who it was."

After the attacks, all the civil air space around Washington was closed and Reagan National was shut down. No commercial flights for days and days. Usually on the Potomac it's a plane a minute coming in and flying out. But after the attacks there was just this eerie silence over the river.

Frannie says, "At night—you remember this?—you'd hear the military jets doing patrol. You never heard jets at night before. Not over Arlington. Not over the District. But you'd wake up in the night then, and you'd hear them, flying so low. Constantly patrolling.

"Couple of years back I was in New York. I visited Ground Zero. It was a dull day, gray, a little chilly. November. At the site where the sidewalk is wide and where most people gather to look, they'd put up a gray-steel wire fence. I guess it ran the whole length of the excavation. There wasn't any work going on when we were there. On the fence they'd mounted weather-proofed photographs from the day—pictures of fire-men, policemen, some who died, some who made it out, pictures of the people they'd rescued.

"There were a lot of people at the site, but almost everybody was silent. On the sidewalk there was this one, lone guy sitting with his back against the wire fence, his legs stretched out. He was maybe in his sixties, bearded, a long-hair, some aged hippy. He was playing 'Amazing Grace' on a flute. There was no other sound—just that flute and the passing traffic. The effect was unspeakably sad."

She pauses, then says, "So much innocent death. Nine-eleven was a tremendously cruel act. People who do that will do anything."

HEU: "Destroy and Burn the Land"

"THE INFIDELS might be in such a position that they cannot be resisted or repelled from Islamic territory and Muslims be spared their violence unless they are bombed with what are called weapons of mass destruction, as people with experience in jihad affirm. If people of authority engaged in jihad determine that the evil of the infidels can be repelled only by their means, they may be used. The weapons of mass destruction will kill any of the infidels on whom they fall, regardless of whether they are fighters, women, or children. They will destroy and burn the land. The arguments for the permissibility of this in this case are many. . . . If a bomb that killed ten million of them and burned as much of their land as they have burned Muslims' land were dropped on them, it would be permissible, with no need to mention any other argument. We might need other arguments if we wanted to annihilate any more than this number of them."

From a fatwa issued by Shaykh Nasir bin Hamad al-Fahd, dated May 1, 2003, shortly after the American invasion of Iraq, and entitled "A Treatise on the Legal Status of Using Weapons of Mass Destruction Against Infidels." Al-Fahd, a Saudi cleric, is said to have issued the fatwa at the request of Osama bin Laden. Under pressure from the Saudi government al-Fahd later rescinded the fatwa. It is unlikely, however, that those who accepted the fatwa in the first place take al-Fahd's recantation seriously.

HQ: Major, Major Red Flag

OPCOM/NPTG Session Audiotape, Session 31 (Excerpted).

Attending: J. Gutman (Chair), M. Fiscarelli, C. Lindquist, S. Kremer, R. Eisenberg.

Transcription: D. Braithewaite.

Mr. Gutman: Okay, first order of business, companies on the notorious CASTLE DVD. Analysis has done a preliminary report, which we have today. Rhoda?

Ms. Eisenberg: Right, Jack. Well, these firms, you can see in the report, a number of these firms raised concerns at Analysis. One in particular called Lahore Precision Engineering, LPE. It is a known Khan firm, and very mysterious. The DVD listing gives a list of sales to Iran and Libya made by this company, plus its coordinates, an e-mail address, which seems to be functional, and a PO box number, Central Post Office, Lahore. But we've got nothing else.

Mr. Kremer: Just address coordinates? That's all we got?

Ms. Eisenberg: Correct. We have almost nothing on them. Simply can't figure them out. The PO box, which still is there, was taken out in, we checked this a while back, in what we know is a phony name. How did that happen? Probably because it was some Pakistani government black operation—ISI, PAEC. More than that, in-house we've got no electronic take on Lahore Precision Engineering. We're waiting on NSA for e-traffic intercepts they might have or might be able to get, but they've got a long line of requests out there. We do know NSA's never flagged this company for anything. No nuclear keywords. Never came onto the screen. What we do know, though, and it's from this DVD, what we do know is that they made a number of major sales to the Iranians and Libyans totaling like $35 million. The DVD records these sales as "communications equipment," which is pretty broad and generic, so it covers, could cover a lot.

Mr. Gutman: But it's a Khan firm, so it's nuclear related, that's a no-brainer.

Ms. Eisenberg: Now about records, we've looked and gotten no records, for example international banking records, customs records, shipping records, for any of these Lahore Precision Engineering export deals. And we queried the Pakistanis and got nothing.

Mr. Gutman: The Pakistanis? Come on.

Ms. Eisenberg: Right, we queried the Pakistanis, and no, it's not believable that they would do an honest search or that they'd share what they found. So we've got no records. Nada.

Mr. Fiscarelli: The deals were disguised.

Mr. Gutman: Probably parts of bigger packages to throw off customs, the international bank reporting. Interesting the last sale was dated February 2004, which I think is significant. That's just after the Khan thing, I mean, when they folded, the whole Khan thing. So if this was a Khan firm, probably, it was run out of somebody's suitcase. Probably never a real company. My guess, dead and buried at this point.

Ms. Eisenberg: Jack, the LPE post office box is still there. The e-mail is functioning. This company is still around, that's the trouble. We just have no take on them after the Iranian sale and the bust-up of the Khan network, which as you noted was years back. Even without Khan, parts of the Khan network are out there and I bet operating, and we don't know anything about it. Major, major red flag.

Bethesda Medical Arts

"WE'RE GOING to put a hold on Malik's entry," Mike Fiscarelli tells me.

"Aw, *come* on!"

"No no no, it's not like that. They can start the paperwork—they can. I suggest that they do. Have them do it maybe outside the country, maybe Athens, and also let us know where and when so it gets processed here okay. The family can come in, not a problem. That means Malik will eventually. But he's going to have to stick around a little longer, stay on the job at PA-MAC. He just does. We may want more."

"Mike, the guy's scared to death. It's over. Strain on him's been major. They figure him out, they'll kill him."

"I know, I know, I know—I hear you. Ah . . . we *will* come through on the visas. And the cash. Assure the guy of that. But this is serious stuff and we may need some follow-up. It will not take too long to figure it out. Really."

"Mike, goddamn it, I can't keep stringing the guy along."

"You can't cut out, either, he'll be screwed. Look, the man will be paid and he will get his entry. Promise you."

"Mike, this is really crappy."

"We may have to ask for more."

"The Agency way."

Fiscarelli shrugs.

MICHAEL FISCARELLI is my minder from Langley. He tells me he's a Domestic Collections Officer, and he is if you push the definition a little, but I hear—"grapevine thing" from Ted Pappas in a bar around the corner from his office in the District—that Fiscarelli's main bailiwick is something called the Nonproliferation Task Group. The Task Group, which is secretive even by Agency standards, has a number of functions, mostly keeping track of who's trying to get the bomb. The Task Group worries about nuclear terrorism and tries to detect trade in nuclear materials. They run black operations.

"Fiscarelli's been around a while," Pappas told me. "Supposed to be a honcho in the Task Group. What the Task Group says goes up to DCIA, and from him to DNI, and from him to the president. Lotta layers, but that's the way it is these days. Jesus, whoever thought up ODNI ought to have his head examined. Unbelievable. Anyhow, the Task Group, they also send out foot soldiers, dickheads like you, to do the fieldwork. So they're both policy and actual operations. Obscure but significant. They glow in the dark way down in the mineshaft."

I don't know any of the other personnel on the Task Group, but whoever they are, I don't trust them. I never get the full story from Fiscarelli, and I wonder how competent any of them are, including Mike.

I usually meet him, as today, in the Bethesda Medical Arts Building, an aging, blocklong structure in what's left of the commercial strip on Wisconsin Avenue just above Old Georgetown Road. The neighborhood is the way they like it—banal, nondescript, none too prosperous. The building fronts on Wisconsin, which in this part of town runs along a ridge line, so its rear entrance is one story below its front. Behind it, across Woodmont Avenue, there is a municipal parking garage.

Fiscarelli's tiny office, on the third floor, has a plaque on the door reading, EGERTON ASSOCIATES, and next to the plaque a small American flag decal. The Agency uses the office mostly for debriefing and collection, as with me, though once in a while, Fiscarelli tells me, they will disguise an officer or agent in here—someone will walk in the Wisconsin Avenue entrance as Mr. A, pay a visit to Egerton Associates, and walk out the rear entrance, two flights down, as Mr. B. He'll be wearing different clothes, maybe have different hair. Maybe then walk over to the municipal garage and drive away into his—or her—new life. Fiscarelli's presided over some of these transfigurations.

Fiscarelli is usually available Mondays and Tuesdays at Egerton Associates, though you have to prearrange. To see him I use my Doug Lawson cell, and call an insecure line at a CIA facility in Suitland, Maryland, where a young person, usually male, will pick up and say, "Geodesics."

I'll say, "Hi, this is Doug. Can I talk to Ernie?" The other guy will say, "Ernie's away from his desk right now, can I take a message?" And I'll say something like, "Yeah, I just wanted to see if tomorrow at ten's okay."

"Tomorrow at ten?"

"Right."

"Okay, I'll give him the message."

Then I thank the person on the other end and hang up.

"Tomorrow," in this small drama, means "the coming Monday" ("day after tomorrow" would mean "the coming Tuesday"). "Ten" means "2 P.M." (you add four hours). If nobody calls back, the session's a go. Such are our—Fiscarelli and my—conventions. He uses other conventions for other people, I'm sure.

Fiscarelli is wearing his black suit today, a white shirt, a maroon tie. You look at him and you think, Who died? Pale skin, wide face, black hair, black-framed glasses. Paunch. He's forty, fifty years old, in there somewhere—you can't tell, the guy's so pasty. He has thin fingers and when he shakes your hand his hand is weak.

His eyes are stone cold gray.

I say, "I heard Sasha Geydarov got killed."

"We heard too. I was going to mention that. What do you think?"

"I don't know. How about you?"

"Nothing."

Meaning nothing to tell *me*. I wonder what he knows.

I tell Fiscarelli I think I was followed in Athens, and let that sink in. He absently picks up a paperweight, a clear blown-glass globe with a purple and white flower in it. The globe is about the size of a tennis ball and looks heavy in his hand.

"Well, all right," he says, "duly noted. We'll file that one away. For future reference."

I ask, "Happy with the DVD?"

Fiscarelli's eyelids lower, and he puts the paperweight back on his desk. "We're analyzing it . . . ah, looking at it very carefully. Malik could . . . could be helpful on some points. Which is why we want to encourage him to remain on the job a while. There's some information on the DVD . . . beyond the technical material . . . commercial information. We're wondering about a company, a Pakistani company called Lahore Precision Engineering. Seems to be nonexistant right now, or maybe, ah . . . dormant. They had a Web site once. Technical personnel have found some of it in caches around the world. We have their old phone and fax numbers, e-mail addresses—they seem to be alive, but just barely. Not used much. We know the company did significant business at one time with Iran and Libya, repeated sales. Supposedly communications equipment. We've looked at the company closely, but they're opaque. We can't get a fix on them, and we want to know more. We don't know the prinicipals, the investors if there are any. Last sale was in 2004. Big one, thirty-five million dollars. We don't know what it was. The Iranian sales are invisible. You look for records, there aren't any. Malik may . . . may be able to find out something about it. When he surfaces just put it to him, see what he says. We want to encourage him to get more info."

"He won't do it."

"Old spy's motto: 'You gotta ask.' "

"Mike, he'll sit on it. And after he's sat on it a while he'll tell us he's looked and can't find anything. End of story. Guy's scared shitless."

Fiscarelli sets his mouth, some kind of acknowledgment, and puffs air through his nose. "You're probably right. Still"—he shifts the little glass paperweight back and forth on his desk—"having to wait on his entry might encourage him." Fiscarelli's eyes light on mine. "You know." He hitches his shoulders in a small, tight shrug, meaning it's a sad world.

I agree to get in touch with Ray. I will post a query to a list-serve where we both check in regularly.

"As to the payment, it's a go. The usual way."

That means a transfer from my account with Bank Hügen, a small, discreet institution in Zurich. I have been to that city once in my life, to establish the account and get the modalities of transfer to and from Fiscarelli squared away. Every Agency financial transaction I've done since that day I've done through Bank Hügen via encrypted e-mail, as I move funds from the Zurich account to some receiver out in the great world, or receive payments from some well-laundered and bleached source the Agency has set up.

I will arrange to have the $20,000 we owe Ray sent from Bank Hügen to an account he has in Athens. Up to now Ray's gotten $56,000 for the information he's furnished us. He's probably given us plenty of value for our money.

And he's a worried man.

From a public library in Arlington, I send a signal to Ray on the list-serve we use. Our standard MO is a general query to all concerned:

"Wondering about Bush these days. Crazy man. Is he finally crazy? Cyclist5."

"Cyclist5" is one of my twenty or so screen names. Ray knows five and looks for them on the list-serve. When I mention Bush it means I want a meeting. Ray, who uses six screen names with me, usually picks up on my posts quickly, no more than a day or two after they go up, and puts up his own comment in coded and, we think, impenetrable language. Usually it's Ray who does the posting, telling me of travel possibilities, when and where we might meet. I've asked for a meeting only once before, and it took a while to set up—Ray travels at PAMAC's pleasure, not his own. I put up my post, and wait for a response from Ray.

R AY, MY agent. I found him a year and a half ago—or he found me—in Paris. He sidles up to me at EuroCom, an annual EU tele-coms trade show, held that year at the big Conference Center for New Technologies out in La Défense. The show is huge. Every major manu-facturer, every major customer in the world attends.

The Center is built on three three vast levels, and all were jammed with a mix of nerds and geek long-hairs, as well as barbered executives in suits, a thousand or so at any one time, milling around in a riot of company ban-ners, national flags, hands-on demos, new phones, new cells, flat-panel pre-sentations, braless and bare-legged models, music, performing animals, meeters and greeters, stand-up food courts, and general hullabaloo.

In all this, Ray, with his neat beard and his gray shark-skin suit strays from his group of Pakistani engineers and approaches me at my bogus home booth—"Engineering Associates, Fairfax, Virginia, USA"—and starts talking. As a kind of ice-breaker he tells me where and when he went to school—Norman, Oklahoma, 1990s. He says he works for PakTel—Pakistan's main private telecoms firm—that he's out looking at new equipment, seeing what to buy. He smiles as he talks, but under that smile he is nervous, intense, wired. I sense a walk-in.

I tell him I am Doug Lawson, telecoms engineer, that I actually work in Europe, that over here I represent some of the smaller European companies. We get friendly, relaxed, talk some tech stuff. He invites me to a nearby food court "for a bite to eat," where—why not?—I make my pitch. I tell Ray about this little company that I happen to know, Dansk Telefonik in Copenhagen. Small but dynamic, first-rate goods, first-rate follow-up support, but needing help, willing to do what was necessary, and so on. Ray takes no offense.

Walk-in.

We exchange business cards and say we'll stay in touch. I passed his on to Fiscarelli. A month or so later some heavy from Langley, a fairly high-up officer, I gather—it wasn't Fiscarelli—met with Ray at another one of these jamborees, this one in Qatar in the Persian Gulf. The officer assessed Ray, liked what he saw, and found that Ray indeed was open to a deal. He wanted money, of course. He also wanted a new life in the U.S.

But when it came to cooperating, Ray balked at working with anyone but me. I am the one person in the U.S. government he trusts enough to work with. Such behavior is not unknown. It's called "imprinting"—when a target refuses to be handed off from his first contact. As a result, I am Ray's sole handler. Imprinting drives them buggy at Langley, but there's not much they can do about it. Fine with me. Over the months, more than a year now, Ray and I have worked up a pretty good relationship.

B UT WHERE is Ray? I know the bank transfer, Zurich to Athens, went through. Ray's money should be sitting there in his account.

At home I check the pages from LPE's cached Web site that Agency techies found—Fiscarelli's given me the URLs. There are three screens. The screens aren't interactive, but you can get a sense of what the site must have been like when it was up and working.

The first screen I find is a shot of keyboards and flat-panel displays, all cool blues and grays and a text that reads, "Lahore Precision Engineering, Tools for the Future." The second screen is a shot of a darkly handsome young man wearing a white coat and clear plastic safety glasses. He is holding a fiber-optics cable that is glowing white. He is turned to us, smiling. Under him a text reads, "LPE Broadband Devices. . . . We are a pool of highly skilled and certified IT professionals answering the needs of our customers . . ."

A third screen, more cool blues and grays, gives the contact info: e-mail address, phone and fax numbers Fiscarelli was telling me about. There's a postal address, too. Fiscarelli tells me none of these function, they just sit there and do nothing, and you can't get past them.

I NOSE around my cell phone and call some people about LPE, Pappas first of all, who says he's never heard of the company. "Hey, this some kind of deal?"

"Nah, not yet anyhow."

"Found me an Igla?"

"Negative. Keep you posted."

Next day I call a banker in Bahrain I know who tells me he's heard the company name but that's about it, and that he'll get back to me. I call a couple of lawyers, one in Dubai, one in London, I call the Lloyd's insurance guy in Karachi, and a shipping agent in Kuwait, and get not much from anyone. "Sleepy little company . . . haven't heard much about them"; "Got started a while back . . ."; "Cell phones or something, I think, probably worth watching, might take off . . ." Nobody seems to have noticed that LPE's in a coma, a vegetative state.

I Wanted to Be Monk

LATE NIGHT. I'm at my piano, a black baby grand I keep in my den (along the outer wall of my end-unit town house—I've had no complaints from the neighbors, or even dirty looks, though sometimes I may be up searching for a tune at two or three A.M.).

As a kid, I entertained the notion of becoming a jazz pianist. Truly. The momentous year was 1979, when at age seventeen I first heard the recordings of Thelonious Monk. I was sampling disks in the old Tower Records store, Pennsylvania and Twentieth—why I was downtown I can't remember—when I came across some Blue Note reissues of Monk's quartet work and heard those unpretty chords, those strange rhythms that catch you the first time you hear them, catch you and give you a shake.

When other kids were doing grunge rock, their garages filled with banks of electronic devices, I repaired to our basement and pounded Marge's aged mahogany upright, playing solo, of course, nobody to be my Coltrane, my Blakey.

More: I wanted not just to play like Monk, I wanted to *be* Monk. For a time, some of senior year in high school, I affected what I thought was a Monk-like dark blue beret (Monk, in fact, didn't do berets), which I wore level across my forehead and pulled down in back—the way I thought Monk would have worn it—till Bobby Ringgenberg, my closest high school friend, and other buddies laughed me out of it.

After high school, to Marge's despair (*"Ricky, when are you going to grow up? You have to do something with your life . . . Oh, Ricky, I could just pull your ears!"*), I didn't go to college, but goofed around the campuses of friends who did, trying to pick up piano gigs, make some kind of sparse living that way. I traveled up and down the East Coast, the Ivies where a McLean student would normally go, and to little campuses out in the Midwest. As jazz pianist I failed, of course. Like Ted Pappas and his ball playing, I just wasn't good enough.

When I turned twenty, I gave up, and for no good reason other than to get the hell out, have some kind of adventure, I joined the U.S. Army. I did basic at Fort Bliss, and then I let them send me to Army Intelligence School at Fort Huachuca, south of Tombstone in Arizona. That decision, more than any other I've ever made, determined my life. At Fort Huachuca I learned the basics of electronic spying and shipped out to a forlorn army base on the west coast of Korea called Camp Humphreys. By that time I was serving in the 527th mil intel batallion—we styled ourselves the "Silent Warriors"— and helped listen in on North Korean and Chinese broadcasts. It was at those two barren places, Fort Huachuca, then Zoeckler Station, our corner of Camp Humphreys, that I learned real telecoms and computing and got a taste for the Black World.

And found my life. One year and three months later I was at Virginia Tech, with Marge footing the bill on condition I shape up, which I already had.

It was at Tech that I invented the Behringer Shell, a computing technique that earned me more than local reknown. The Shell was a method for linking data networks that speeded the encryption and decryption of data as it flowed between them. It was a kind of system of systems that you set up with its own encryption algorithm. I got the vision as to how such a baby would work as I was lying flat on my back staring at my dorm-room ceiling, thinking to quit school. I knew the idea, if I could work it out, would count as cool in the groves of Blacksburg; I didn't figure on its fame going beyond the campus.

But it did. When I sketched out my invention for my adviser Stan Meisel, an enthusiastic, voluble man with a springy way of pacing in front of a class, he was silent for a time, then told me, "You've got to patent this. Just have to." Approval came through senior year.

The Shell, a small contribution to the field, has long been superseded, but Meisel, who watched over and nurtured V Tech's crew of undergraduate electrical engineers from his underground office deep in Robeson Hall, put out the word to anyone who would listen that he had a comer in his class, a kid to watch for in due time. Among those receiving the news were some old friends of his at a Beltway company called M Systems, a defense contractor populated by mil intel types—the "M" stands for "military"—and spookier than a Halloween party. M Systems does such black work that all its employees down to the secretaries have to get clearances, and the corporate description it includes in its yearly prospectus has to be vetted by the lawyers at NSA.

I was hired on by a chubby, earnest little man who ran their Computing Security Division. He had mouse-brown hair, narrow-set eyes the color of his hair, and a twitchy smile. He wore boxy, bad-fitting sports jackets with pants that never quite went with them, and neckties a decade old, all of which said, *Look, here is a fellow engineer.* A fellow V Tech grad, too—what, ten years, fifteen years ahead of me at Tech? Before hiring me he lunched me at an Outback, his idea of a cool venue. He liked what he saw, and on graduation I began my work at M Systems, an engineer laboring in the shadowy labyrinth of computer security, doing secret work for secret clients.

B UT I still play piano, still find myself getting a high from the harmonies and the line and the beat, a feeling, when I'm really into it, I call "bo-plicity"—title of an old Miles Davis piece—cool, relaxed, true, right. Sometimes I'll take an old tune and jazz it up the way I think Monk would, well aware I'm not Monk. Other times, as now, I just rummage around the keyboard, looking for a tune of my own.

I hit some chords gently, then some more, keeping a four-four tempo, hearing in my mind the backup bass and drums, as I gently play two simple themes—ideas I concoct in the here and now—a couple of jagged lines, abstract, blues moody, each only a couple of bars long. I walk them by sixths into a higher key, listening to them, then play two new chords, banging down hard on the second, then lift my fingers, releasing all the keys but one—and that one the essence of the tonal idea, quavering out now, dying in its purity.

Then I break off.

SCI TOP SECRET GREEN SCI TOP SECRET GREEN SCI TOP SECRET GREEN SCI TOP SECRET GREEN SCI

OPCOM/NPTG Session Audiotape, Session 39 (Excerpted).

Attending: J. Gutman (Chair), M. Fiscarelli, C. Lindquist, S. Kremer, R. Eisenberg.

Transcription: D. Braithewaite.

Mr. Fiscarelli: One thing I do have to say at this juncture, we're very concerned about SLIDER. Contact at PAMAC. We haven't heard from him for some time. Usual commo procedure with SLIDER has been for him to check in with CASTLE by a certain method, very neutral, very secure. Hasn't happened since CASTLE met with him in Athens and got us that very useful DVD.

Ms. Eisenberg: SLIDER's been compromised?

Mr. Fiscarelli: No no no. We don't know that. Right now we just can't say. One other bad sign is his family was to apply for U.S. visas, precede him into the States, and they haven't done that. So that's another reason for worry. We're trying to check locally to ascertain SLIDER's status since he's on highest security level, which is taking a little time because we have to go at it on the quiet. If we make any sort of obvious inquiries, just by doing that we might in fact as Rhoda says compromise him. SLIDER is an absolute singleton. So right now we're blind here.

Mr. Gutman: [Expletive].

Mr. Fiscarelli: Second that. But again, bottom line is, we lose him, we lose sight of PAMAC, we've got nobody else in there.

Mr. Gutman: Right, and that puts us back to total blindness on the Iranian, Pakistani connection with Lahore, what is it, Lahore Precision Engineering. The nukes. I mean [expletive].

Mr. Fiscarelli: SLIDER's never been so out of touch with us. This, plus the fact that he himself reported that there's been CI [Counter Intelligence] activity in and around his shop. One positive: SLIDER worked solely through our contractor CAS-TLE, who is trustworthy and careful.

Ms. Eisenberg: Well, of course that brings up the issue, any risk to CASTLE?

Mr. Fiscarelli: If you mean personal safety, CASTLE used appropriate procedures to protect his own identity, so I'd assess his situation was low risk, low risk. And also, operationally I see no reason to think he's compromised.

Ms. Eisenberg: But we'll have to have an assessment of that.

Mr. Fiscarelli: Well, yes. Our CI people have been alerted to this. We will, they will produce an assessment.

Mr. Gutman: Kills me, really does. SLIDER's too good to lose. [Expletive] so's CAS-TLE, whoever he is, even if he is a [expletive] green badger.

"My Worst Nightmare, My Very Worst"

"WHEN I retired in '98, Jesus, was I bored," Jack Gutman is saying. "Out of my goddamn mind. I mean, Meg and I, hell, we'd travel, see relatives, old friends, tool around out West, whatever. And I worked on couple commissions with the Agency, internal stuff, mostly administrative, but hell, it really wasn't much, you do that stuff, you know the world's passed you by. But after 9/11 they went out looking for people who'd served, and I wanted to help out anyway, do something real again, so I talked it over with Meg, and she said, go ahead, do it. So I rejoined. Then Meg got sick. Her illness went on for a while, as you know, very rough—chemo, radiation, drugs, all of it. I got that leave of absence to take care of her, then, of course, she died"— Gutman doesn't go in for euphemisms, Meg Gutman died of a recurrence of breast cancer two years ago—"and I went back in. I'm going to stay a while, maybe stay till the fog rolls in, I don't know. It's something to do."

I'm with Jack in his rambler in Arlington, down in his basement den. I asked him why he was still working at his age, and that's his answer. I don't believe it's "something to do." Jack's passionate about his job.

Jack, a classical buff, has Mozart on the stereo, a collection of piano sonatas. The performer is just getting into the slow second movement of one, and Jack's gone silent, listening, waving his hand softly in the air to the beat. He says he avoids Schubert because it reminds him of Meg, her favorite composer, "although there's a piano sonata by Schubert," he said once, "the A minor, that Meg liked that I listen to sometimes." Alone, I think. He's never put it on for me.

He says matter-of-factly, "I think of Meg. A lot."

Jack's in his late sixties and he's built like a beer barrel. A fringe of short hair runs around his head, which is mirror shiny. He has a round, ruddy face, and flattened, pug nose, the result of a boxing injury long back. Tonight he's wearing a sweatshirt and gabardine pants.

I got to know Jack five or six years ago through a weekly poker session, which started I can't say when, long before I came on the scene anyway, as a bunch of friends, neighbors, guys from work playing once-in-a-while, pickup games, but which, when I joined, had turned into a serious, weekly poker group of fixed membership. Liz and I had just split, and the game was a good place to be. The group has since broken up—too many guys getting transferred, or having kids, or otherwise not having the time for it. Meg's death had something to do with it. After she died, even with no game going on, I took to dropping in on Jack, who doesn't live that far from me—north of Lee Highway on Quincy Street, not far from Frannie's office, and, as Jack puts it, "one block over from the Aldrich Ames place."

Jack's been noncovert at Langley since 9/11, meaning he can tell you he works there. He says he's in nonproliferation, so he probably knows Fiscarelli. He also knew Walt. He's told me that they'd met, but weren't close. I think he probably followed Walt at Tehran Station.

Jack knows, because I've told him, that in addition to being a telephone guy out in the private sector, I do security work for the Agency. He also knows I travel a lot. We don't go into the details.

The third movement of the sonata, a lacy, delicate rondo, ends softly in a major chord. Jack says, "You know, there's something ineffably sad in Mozart, even when he's being light. Meg liked him."

A picture of Meg rests alone on the end table. Before her illness, she was a strikingly good-looking woman. She had short salt-and-pepper hair, very thick and naturally curly, and beautiful dark eyes. When they stopped living overseas, she'd had become a lobbyist of some sort downtown for the beer industry. She'd been a smoker and had an assertive, gravelly voice—Jack called her Foghorn—that belied her prettiness. She was also a highly competent woman. She handled Gutman's investments for him, did their taxes and the bills, and thus freed Jack up to do nothing but work at Langley. They had no kids.

Jack says, "Meg was eighteen when I met her. College. I was Columbia, she was Barnard. Met her in this subterranean beer place—well, I call it a beer place, a snack place in the basement of a residence hall. You could get beer and pizza down there and meet girls, and that's why I'd go there. I went down one Friday night, and next table over there was a bunch of Barnard girls out looking for boys. And there she was. Beautiful face, you couldn't help notice. Smiled at me. I was a couple of years older. This was like '61. Well, I said hello and blah blah blah. We started dating. She was more or less local, Manhasset, out on Long Island, I was Queens. So we saw each other a lot, families got along. They were better off. Tennisy family—back then that was a class marker, maybe still is. Didn't matter to anybody, them or us. I graduated, Poli Sci, went into the army. I was going to get drafted anyway, so I joined up. Did Russian language school out in Monterey, then served on Rhodes. Greek island? We had a big listening station there, picked up radio chatter from Eastern Europe, Russia. Anyhow, Meg graduated a year after I joined up. Stayed in touch and after I got out of the army we got hitched, and I joined CIA. The rest is our life together. She liked it."

"The Agency life?"

"Yeah, yeah. Thought it was fun, thought Washington was fun, liked the foreign countries, the strange peoples, strange sights. She liked all that." Jack pauses, then says, "Toward the end, in the hospital, she was so weak. In her eyes she had this helpless look—same eyes she had as a girl, they don't change. 'Jack,' she'd say and try to smile at me, squeeze my hand. They had her on morphine, a line running into her with this little plastic thing you could push a button on, take care of the pain, keep it at a level you could deal with. She could choose to be clear-headed and in some pain or doped up and feeling better."

In the end the morphine brought on dementia.

"I've never gotten over her death. After forty years of marriage, how could I? And why would I want to? I mean, life goes on of course, as it must, but you don't 'get over' something like that. And you shouldn't."

Glancing up at his flat-screen Gutman suddenly says, "Yo, hold it, hold it, look who they got on." Rich Brody is holding forth on CNN. Brody was once an assistant secretary of defense for nuclear forces. He now runs a well-funded right-wing "policy research" group, the National Security Forum. He's been a fixture on the networks for two decades. He's in his fifties, balding, and has a neat little white beard. I've met Brody. He is a man without the capacity to doubt. Gutman puts the Mozart on hold and cuts the TV muting.

"Pakistan," Brody is saying, "I don't have to tell you is exceedingly fragile politically as we have seen."

"Are you saying the current government in Pakistan may fall?" Brody's interviewer is Karen Jeffries, a foxy blond with a light southern accent.

"It may, but even if the government doesn't fall, Pakistan is a very dangerous place. Its northwest is completely uncontrolled and it's the main center—the headquarters, you could say—of al-Qaeda and as such it's the center of Islamofascism."

"Which is?"

Brody leans into the camera. "Islamofascism is the violent, lawless, totalitarian ideology that we've been fighting since 9/11. Islamofascism seeks to destroy us, destroy Western civilization and institute a monolithic Islamic state over all the world. They are a mortal threat to America. We must be prepared to neutralize that threat."

"Neutralize? You mean military strikes?"

"Yes, of course."

"Invade Pakistan?"

"If necessary."

"Invade another Islamic country? While we're in Iraq and Afghanistan?"

"There would be consequences, of course, but we could handle them. America must act decisively when it is in her interests to do so."

Brody has piercing eyes and the manner of a believer. With Jeffries he is not conversing, he is proclaiming the Truth. He does not smile or frown or gesture much, and when he speaks, he speaks calmly and with an air of reason, but his eyes bore into the camera like twin gun barrels.

The Jeffries woman ends the interview. Gutman mutes his TV, but keeps the Mozart on hold.

"Brody," he says, pronouncing the name with disgust. "What an asshole. Islamofascism! Jesus. No such thing on this earth. Buncha shit, doesn't mean anything. It's a stupid term, an emotional term, makes people think they're fighting World War II or something. It's intended to make people stop thinking. And thinking hard and clearly is what we have to do.

"We got a new problem—people are calling it 'leaderless jihad,' which, of couse, is a buzzword, like Islamofascism, but I like it, at least it's real world and it means something. Me, I call it 'jihad of the Internet.' It's jihadis recruiting other jihadis in chat rooms, IMing and e-mailing each other, trading info. We got these virtual groups forming at random, disbanding, reforming.

You can't keep track of them. They're dispersed, free form, 'distributed'—another one of those buzzwords, but again it means something.

"Internet jihadis—they communicate like crazy. They shift Web sites, open new chat rooms, change names. They are very scary. So hard to tell what they're thinking, what they're planning. My worst nightmare, my very worst, is a smart *jihadi* getting nuclear material and setting it off in an American city."

"Think that's likely?"

"They're out there. They talk about it. They're trying. You get the HEU, it's not that hard to make a weapon. I could probably do it in my garage. And if they put something like that together here, they could take out half of Manhattan. Or Washington. Or Chicago. Tens of thousands could die. It would make 9/11 seem small. And mark my words, it would shake us, one detonation of one nuke would shake us to our foundations. For fear of the next one, people'd want total control, total surveillance. We'd have a police state. The constitution, civil liberties, all that would go down the tubes. The American experiment—that would be over. Our police state would be homegrown, not like the Soviets or the Nazis, but it'd be a police state nevertheless. And we'd set it up in the name of democracy. Scary."

He gives his glass a shake. "Want some more?"

"I'm good."

"Invade Pakistan," Jack says, shaking his head. "That asshole—that's how you *make* jihadis."

"Like Iraq."

"Like Iraq. And we don't need any more jihadis, not with nuclear materials all over this world, especially Russia. There is so much stuff there, highly enriched uranium, plutonium—it's very, very scary. This stuff is scattered among hundreds of sites, and the those sites are only partly secured. That's a problem, that's a big, big problem."

"WHEN WE were in school," Vova Miller is saying to Boris Mikhailovich Kolpakov, "you were such a swimmer, always the athlete."

"Yes, and you were the brain," Kolpakov says. "You were the son of an army officer. I always admired you."

Kolpakov and Miller are strolling on a cracked, weed-infested cement walk that runs along the top of a high levee overlooking the wet glint of the Sakhra River. Trailing them at a short distance is a bodyguard of Kolpakov's, a compact, taciturn man named Stegerov.

The levee, built for flood control, runs for a mile or so on the south side of the Sakhra through the part of town called Nizhniy Ryazhin. Across from them on a low bluff is Ryazhin proper, and upriver, barely in sight, is the L. D. Vygodsky Institute of Applied Physics, where Miller works. Though sunny, it's a chill Saturday afternoon, and a sharp wind is blowing down the river. Kayakers wearing wetsuits are out on the water piloting red and yellow fiberglass hulls.

Kolpakov is stocky, energetic, purposeful. His prematurely gray hair is elegantly styled. Always smiling with Miller, his face is the color of wheat, and his skin is pitted from a childhood disease. He has small, gray teeth. He is dressed casual-expensive: English sports jacket and trousers, English hiking boots.

"You joked at me a lot," Miller says.

"Out of envy. And we got along, didn't we? Well, didn't we?" That smile, those gray teeth. "We had good times, though you always had your nose in a book, and I—well, I didn't."

Kolpakov never forgets the people he's known. He's stayed in touch with Miller, followed Miller's career. One night, six months back, he called Miller at home. "Just passing through," he said, mentioning work in Novosibirsk. "Let's have a drink, talk about things."

After an evening's conversation in an out-of-the-way Ryazhin bar, before starting his rental car to take Miller home, Kolpakov mentions certain "business opportunities," possibilities that "material available at the Vygodsky Institute might be . . . might be valuable." That smile. "There might be quite a lot of commercial interest in it. Actually, I can guarantee it."

YOU WERE the smart one, Borya," Miller says. "When the collapse came you were ready for it. You took advantage of opportunities I didn't even know existed. It was all so chaotic back then. Now look—you live in London, you have a house in France. Success story."

"You do have to be fast on your feet in this life," Kolpakov says. "Well, this transaction will make you a rich man, should give you a leg up in the world, start your life again. I was sorry, shocked really, to hear about your situation with Marya." Miller's wife has left him for another man, a successful importer of luxury goods, taking with her their son and daughter.

The cement walk leads Miller and Kolpakov, with Stegerov continuing to trail them, into a small memorial park planted with fir and birch trees. A white marble tablet lists the names of the citizens of Ryazhin who fell in the Great Patriotic War.

Kolpakov says, "Vova, it is now a question of finding a proper buyer. I have . . . contacts who will prove useful for that purpose. Among other things, we'll have to demonstrate the quality of this material. Selling bogus material is not feasible these days. There have been too many scams over too many years, and the customers know all about them. They're quite sophisticated that way."

"They're animals."

"Sophisticated animals."

"If Chechens ever get this material . . ."

"Oh for God's sake, Vova—think! First of all, they won't—the purchasers will be Arab and the obvious target is the USA. And secondly, don't worry about the Americans, either. Making a successful device is much harder than it appears. Diagrams may be simple, but devices—truly working devices— are complex. Everything—you know this as well as I—everything has to work just right."

Kolpakov puts his hand gently on Miller's arm. "Listen, Vova, if these people ever get a device put together, and if they somehow elude the world's security services with their device, and if they actually detonate it somewhere—all of these are huge ifs—the result, believe me, will be a fizzle. They won't achieve anything like critical mass. At the very worst—worst— they'll get an ordinary explosion. Which will blow the contraband material here and there and everywhere. They'll see their expensive purchase scattered to the winds and they'll see that they've lost everything. Imagine their faces then! Vova, think about it: What's going to happen in the end is that we will take these shits, and take them big! I've looked on life that way—take the bastards for what they're worth and don't look back. It's why I am where I am."

Miller nods mechanically. His face has clouded over. He feels as if he is not ambling through a pleasant park among birch and fir trees talking to an old friend; he feels as if he is suspended in air, as if he is out of touch with the ground.

Marge Was Pretty Once

"HOW WAS Athens?"

"Oh, okay. Not much fun this time. Fast business meeting. I was in and out." I'm with Marge, sitting with her in her living room in the house on Davidson Street, here ostensibly to check on the house, but really to check on Marge, which I do weekly. It's a bright Saturday afternoon; sunlight is spilling into the room.

"We went through there once." She means she and Walt did on their Fulbright-paid sabbatical in India, in the mid-1950s. "Liked the place. Very sunny. Lots of white stones. Food's all olive oil, though. Gives you the tummy runs." I've heard all this before. Marge is sharp enough to know she's repeating herself, but she does it anyway, I think to relive, briefly and faintly, a happy time.

"Hasn't changed much."

"Well, no, they haven't moved the stones, I suppose. Beer?"

"Stay put, Marge, I'll get something."

She's eighty now. Hard to believe it, that she's been around all that time. Her skin looks translucent, and blue veins run across the backs of her spotted hands, along her arms. She moves stiffly, but doesn't use a walker or a cane—that's something, but her legs are stick thin and so fragile. You wonder how they can support anything, even wispy, aged Marge. Her voice, once gentle and caressing, is high pitched and withered now, its old sweetness, like the Conover prettiness, just a memory.

She still lives in the brick split-level on Davidson Street that she and Walt bought new in 1962, the year I was born. She won't think of a retirement home, so here she stays. Her taupe Camry's parked out in the driveway in front of the garage, reminding me that she still drives, though not at night anymore—she's stopped that at least. At some point I'm going to have to put an end to her daytime driving, too. There'll be a fight.

This house, where we—Walt, Marge, Sue, and I—lived as a family, is across from the back parking lot of McLean High. The neighborhood's not the fancy McLean, the Kennedy McLean, just middle of the middle. Skirting our modest front yard are pine trees and big, blue-green hostas. A pair of old boxwoods crouch under the picture window. The brick is a pale, liverish color, the vinyl siding beige, the shutters burgundy—'60s all the way. Yet, humdrum as this house seems to be, it will sometimes give me— fleetingly—an eerie feeling when I visit: Walt's mystery.

YOU CAN see—the carpets are all up, I'm having them cleaned. Buttons, stop that—*Buttons!*"

Buttons, Marge's yappy miniature poodle, has entered the room and is skittering around my shoes on the bare living-room floor, making short, inconclusive feints at my ankles. Buttons is the color of skimmed milk. He is small, nervous, and cowardly. He knows me well and knows I will do him no harm, but still, when he attacks my ankles, he does it in a fluttery, tentative way. He settles down finally and hops up onto a chair by the front window to keep an eye on the street and bark in utter safety at passers-by, the mailman, and the UPS guy.

On a bric-a-brac shelf this side of the front window, among other photos, there is a sepia-tinted portrait of Marge's brother Richard, my namesake. He is a smiling, bright-eyed young private first class in a crisp khaki shirt, dark brown tunic, and dark brown tie. He never grew old.

Richard Henry Conover joined the Army just after he graduated from high school in 1949. A year later, when the Korean War broke out, Rich got sent. In the rush of casualties of that autumn and winter, they made him a second lieutenant in the field, which was an honor but no great piece of luck—all the second louies, they used to say, died in action in the early days of that war. Not true, of course, but many did, and Rich was one of them, mortared in the snow somewhere on the western edge of the Chosin Reservoir. He was nineteen. They awarded him a posthumous Bronze Star.

Marge is a funny, jokey woman, never much given to melancholy, but Dick has always been in the house, a felt, unseen presence.

The decor at Davidson Street is what you see in a lot of Agency homes: artifacts from around the world, no one country or region dominating, a kind of historical museum of the family travels, though more like a junk store. From India, a round, white marble end table, inlaid in a floral pattern of red and green marble, blue lapis lazuli; from Turkey, a rusty-red woven wool salt bag; from Indonesia, paper cut-out puppets (grimacing demons, smiling heroes); from Cambodia, framed and hung on the wall, a silvery-maroon swatch of fabric, woven by some obscure ethnic minority. The earlier things they bought together, others are more from Walt's journeyings than Marge's, who stayed home in their later years while Walt traveled overseas a few months at a time. By then he was back on the analytic side, out of Operations, no longer a real spy.

Over on the lift-top card table by the door, next to the copper ewer they'd gotten in Iran, are Marge's boxy black glasses. Has them there for when she goes out.

"Susan called. Steve's quit his job. Again." Steve Ziolkowsky is Sue's strange husband. They live outside Cleveland, where Steve works—or did. They have two kids: Steve Jr.—Stevie—redheaded (he gets the hair from an aunt or uncle on the Ziolkowsky side), bad-tempered, and whiny; and Ann Marie, who looks like her father, has his face superimposed on Walt Behringer's head shape. Sue brings the kids *sans* Steve Sr. for visits every so often, why I don't know—Sue and Marge are forever on the outs, crabbing at each other whenever Sue's back.

"Steve's a software designer, Marge. They change jobs a lot."

"I know. But he doesn't *have* one now. It's not stable. The kids, the schools, all that moving around." She shakes her head.

Marge was pretty once. You can tell from old photos and slides, especially from shots taken in the forties and fifties. She had a lovely heart-shaped face, even behind those pointy glasses women wore back then, and for a time she sported a long red ponytail. She was athletic, too. There are shots of her at a tennis court, smiling, holding her racket jauntily, and one of her on a fifteen-foot-high dive board, legal back then. She has sexy hips and calves.

I noticed some of this athleticism as a little boy, though by then she was getting on. I remember once Walt telling her something out in the front yard, I don't know what, but whatever it was it made her giddy with joy, and—she was wearing a long, loose red-and-white striped dress and black pumps—she turned a cartwheel, actually turned a cartwheel in our front yard at the age of forty-five or so. The Conover exuberance.

"Liz called. Samantha—isn't she something! Soccer queen at thirteen."

"Yeah."

Marge goes silent, looking away from me. She's never gotten reconciled to the divorce, knows all the reasons for it.

"Well," she says, shaking her head.

"Don't say it." Marge has always hoped Liz and I would get back together. I don't want it. Liz won't hear of it. Case closed.

"Oh, Ricky."

I N 1947, Margery Reeve Conover graduated from Minneapolis West, the prestige high school in town, a big yellow brick building that has since been torn down. That fall she entered the University of Minnesota and majored in Economics, which is how she met Walt, a young instructor in the department. She graduated in 1951, but hung around the U, doing what young women did back then—working as department receptionist, and taking graduate courses in Econ, and thinking of getting an MA in the subject. She's never said, but I'm pretty sure that by that time she'd started up something with Walt. She told me more than once that she fell in love immediately with the tall, brooding intellectual.

Despite an age difference, nine years, they married in 1953, in North Presbyterian Church, St. Paul. As with a lot of couples, the age difference, not that great really, never seemed to matter. She got pregnant first in 1955, but had a traumatic, soul-searing miscarriage.

They spent the next academic year in India—Walt's Fulbright—in Kerala State, which was then governed by the Indian Communist Party. Communism in South Asia was Walt's research bag. They lived in a university town called Cochi.

Walt, though a Minnesota farm boy—maybe *because* he was a Minnesota farm boy—had a taste for the exotic, and Marge found she did, too. She liked the strange house they lived in in Cochi—a vast, open, two-story mansion, with lacy curtains floating in the warm breezes, "like dancers beckoning," she once said. She even liked the Kerala heat, though they were never there for the full midsummer experience. The less pleasant side of life in

India—the insects, the rats scuttling under the flooring, the small snakes and lizards lazing here and there around the house—these she took in stride. She liked the servants. She found the British presence and upper-crust Indian society amusing. In the Cochi academic community, the Behringers were considered suitable guests.

In 1957, they returned to the U, where Marge started taking Ed courses, but neither Walt nor Marge was satisfied with academic life in the Midwest. Walt published his work and drew some attention to himself. Halfway through the academic year 1958, he was approached by the Agency and asked if he wanted to do "consulting" on population and Communism in South Asia. He did. And the year after, he left the university for CIA and the life of a spy.

From Minneapolis my parents moved to a small house in Arlington, where Walt had an easy commute to Langley. Marge gave up any dreams of career, academic or otherwise, to raise babies, Walt being not much help on that score. Marge's next pregnancy was successful and resulted in my sister Susan, who was born in Arlington Hospital.

After Walt killed himself Marge never seriously thought of remarriage. She was a good-looking, witty redhead, even in her late forties, so she probably got offers. But she never married again, never dated. I doubt she even considered the idea.

I'LL SEE my father from time to time, see his long, white hair, his dark complexion, his stooped shoulders—in a crowd somewhere, or pushing a cart half full of groceries at the far end of a Safeway aisle, or—glimpsed from a cab—walking down a shaded street in the District, and for the merest, shortest instant, it really is Walt, the way he was in 1975.

In a more substantial way I have found my father in declassified CIA documents. The National Archives in College Park—in the close-in Maryland suburbs—has a bank of computers in its library linked to the Agency and to the Agency's vast collection of public documents. To find some one or some thing you punch in your search terms—"Walter"+"Behringer" in my case—and sometimes you turn up gold.

Walt gets a few scattered mentions in documents from Indonesia and Iran, but he shows up mostly in Saigon in minutes of meetings held in the embassy. (Cables he's written or signed off on don't seem to have been cleared for the public.) I try to picture him at these sessions, sober and serious, his hands folded on the conference table, discoursing quietly, his usual way, no sign of panic in his voice as the war slides away from us.

Walt was smart, and they knew it at CIA. One record of a meeting on March 22, 1972 reads:

> *Walt remarked agent networks shrinking as American presence is reduced.*
> *Battlefield deaths now down to an average of 10 a week, good, but*
> *serious problems on battlefield could ensue because of drawdown U.S.*
> *forces. Only 6,000 U.S. combat troops remain. Agents speaking of spring*
> *offensive.*

At the end of March, the Communists launched three waves of ferocious attacks all over the country, sending the South Vietnamese army reeling. Walt had been right on that one.

There are other entries from Saigon, mostly about running the agent networks. The last reference to Walt I've found is a conference note from May 3, 1973:

> *Walt wants to return home ASAP. Helms probably go along.*

I don't know why my father wanted to come home so quickly. I know that Richard Helms, Director at the time, okayed the departure because Walt did come home that summer, and stayed home, working at Langley, eventually of course going mad.

I have printouts of these documents, maybe thirty pages in all. They are simply random, scattered moments of his work life, and though they're helpful in a way, they really don't tell me much.

Walt also makes cameo appearances in a few books about the war written by journalists of the time, though he spoke little to the press and, therefore, took his licks from them. "A colorless bureaucrat," one *Times* reporter called him. "Cautious and standoffish, Behringer was referred to around the embassy as 'the dark ghost,' and lived up to his billing."

And once in a while Walt will appear in scholarly books about the Agency and its history, mostly because of his work in Vietnam. "Walter Behringer, the Station's top analyst at the time of the Tet offensive . . ." and so on. The authors of these books sometimes mention in passing

Walt's later breakdown and suicide, then move on to other, more important things.

And I am left pondering the enigma of my father.

BILLS OKAY, Marge? Need help with any of that stuff?" Marge pays all her own bills, manages her Medicare, does her own tax returns, which she lets me check, and which are always accurate and meticulously done. She uses a computer and a tax program to do them, a point of pride with her and which I, too, find impressive. I bet none of her old friends, those who are left, could manage the feat.

"Also, it's getting to be gutter time. I'll call Fernando, set up an appointment." The leaves will all be down by the first of December.

"Already done it."

"And the lawn needs a final cutting." Ordinarily a young German named Fritz does the job. Fritz has a huge lawn mower he stands on and rides around, like some Goth in his chariot, if Goths had chariots. The thing is built for parks and big open spaces, but Fritz hauls it around Fairfax and Arlington counties in his battered green pickup, mostly doing large jobs, but sometimes doing some neighborhood lawn business as well, small jobs like Marge's. He takes about ten minutes to rampage over her lawn and charges sixty bucks for his time and trouble. Fritz comes once a week till the middle of June, then every ten days or so. I've dismissed him for the season, and because it's what I do, I will drag Marge's old electric lawn mower out of the garage today and give the grass its last mowing of the year.

"Well, let me get some water, and I'll do the yard."

Marge's kitchen window looks out onto the backyard, where, square in the middle, stands a red maple, a Japanese cultivar that Walt himself put in forty years ago, and which has grown slowly with the seasons. It's probably a couple of feet taller than when he put it in. Its leaves are a rusty red now after their midsummer crimson, and are about to fall. On the south side of the yard runs a six-foot-high wooden fence, planted with hydrangea and rhododendron.

And at the very back, the raised azalea bed.

The bed is bordered by flat white limestones that Walt had collected from somewhere, and is filled always with dry leaves from two oak trees, one in each of the far corners of the yard.

I remember once seeing Walt standing out there on a twilit evening. This must have been toward the end. I am in the yard with him. The evening air is warm. He is facing the azaleas, his arms folded across his chest, inscrutable. He is wearing his pale straw hat, a green-gold shirt, white trousers, white shoes. Insects would be trilling, and fireflies glowing on and off in the deep blue light. Walt stands solitary, pensive, not moving, gazing at the azaleas. For how long?

After Walt died in it, the azalea bed was a no-go area for me. I couldn't even look at it. At some point in my adolescence, though—I can't say when—it went back to being, simply, the azalea bed.

Walt drank. On his travels he used an old, scuffed brown leather suitcase that was pigskin rough. Getting ready to leave on his Agency missions he would leave it split open, partly packed, on a cedar chest in their bedroom. It always contained a flat bottle of rye whisky. I tasted the whisky once, pressing my boy's tongue to the cork inside the cap and licking the strange flavor, which I found not bad, foreshadowing maybe my later career as drunk, though I never drank from the bottle.

Toward the end, when he'd given up traveling, he also gave up whisky and switched to beer. He would disappear into his den, put away a six-pack, and come out exhaling brewery fumes, distant, vacant-eyed, pretending to himself that he was steady on his feet. I don't know what Marge was feeling.

"You don't have to talk to Walt Behringer," Bill Colby, Director at the time, once told Pappas. Colby knew Walt had had some kind of breakdown, and had assigned him a small office on the fifth floor, where he did what amounted to make-work. Colby was planning to ease him out, but Walt killed himself first.

I FINISH mowing, and as I am reeling in the thick, orange electrical cord, twisted and knicked from years of usage, my cell rings. It's Ted Pappas. I punch him in. "Hey."

"Hey, howya doing?" he asks. "You okay?"

He wants to know if it's safe to talk.

Marge's backyard, what the hell. "Yeah, what's up?"

"Just had this funny thing happen, been bugging me, thought I'd call. I was talking with this guy I know, a buddy, lives in Boston. Where I am right now. Calling from the airport. Know that guy we were talking about the other day?"

Sasha Geydarov.

"Yeah."

"Well, my buddy is well connected, knows a lot. Had some stuff to say. Look, I'm gonna be back in town this afternoon. You want to get together later on? Might be a laugh."

"I got nothing on."

"Want to see Mr. McCabe?"

McCabe's, a raucous jock bar Pappas favors in Fairfax. "Doable. What time?"

"Sevenish?"

So THIS buddy, he's Russian," Pappas is saying, "he's been in the FSB, but now he's with a private security firm." The FSB is the Russian counterpart to CIA. "Swiss, believe it or not, Dempel Partners, got a branch in Boston. Founder was a dwarf. Knew him back in the day. Did breaking and entering for us. He's dead now. Well, anyhow, this Russian, I've helped him out now and then and he's helped me out, told me some stuff before that checked et cetera et cetera. So I decide, shit, why not ask him about Sasha, see if he knows anything, and I say, 'Hey, you ever hear of a guy named Sasha Geydarov? Know anything about what happened to him?' "

I've found Pappas at McCabe's. The decor here is dark wood, brass, and noise. Flat-screens are everywhere—there must be sixty in this cavernous hall, ten or fifteen behind the extra-long bar alone. All the screens are always on and all seem set to different channels—football games, basketball games, NASCAR races, tennis matches, and for the elderly clientele, golf games. When there's no sports you've got *ESPN News* and interactive trivia games. The owner, Steve McCabe, is a veteran center for the old Washington Bullets, renamed the Wizards. Blowups of *Washington Post* sports-page headlines from McCabe's long-gone era are on the walls. Hanging in freestanding glass enclosures are autographed jerseys of football heroes as forgotten as McCabe—Bruce Smith, Reggie "Miracle Man" Wims, others. Pappas loves the place.

"So I ask this guy about Sasha, and he immediately gets this look on his face, you'd think I'd punched him, real taken aback. I mean, it was so fucking *obvious*. Then he turns cool and says, 'I can tell you this. I have heard that Geydarov was involved in a deal, some kind of business, which resulted in his death.' Wouldn't say anything more on the subject. Then he wondered how the hell I knew anything about it, so I told him I heard it from another Russian and that's all I knew. He asked how I knew Sasha, and I gave him some bullshit, tried to pump him on Sasha but it didn't work, guy wouldn't say anything, and changed the subject. Definitely uncomfortable. Definitely. Anyhow, you hear anything more?"

"Negative."

"Well, keep what my Russian buddy said in mind. Funny thing about this guy, though, right? His reaction and all that?"

"Yeah."

And it is. It really is.

HQ: Worth the Risk

OPCOM/NPTG Session Audiotape, Session 42 (Excerpted).

Attending: J. Gutman (Chair), M. Fiscarelli, C. Lindquist, S. Kremer, R. Eisenberg.

Transcription: D. Braithewaite.

Mr. Gutman: Too much reliance on one asset—I don't like it. We will lose him. No no, I don't mean somebody'll off him, I mean he's a contractor, of a somewhat temporary relationship. He may just decide not to keep working.

Mr. Lindquist: Somebody might off him.

Mr. Gutman: Well, that too.

Mr. Fiscarelli: CASTLE's what we've got. He's the obvious asset on this LPE thing.

Mr. Gutman: Yes, okay. Madame Eisenberg?

Ms. Eisenberg: Only this, Jack. I'm concerned about the possibility they'll start peeling back the onion, notice CASTLE and get a line on the other work we've done via CASTLE and are doing. You know what I mean. It could compromise other programs. And of course there really is a question of personal safety.

Mr. Fiscarelli: We've managed pretty good backup on CASTLE and he's not been in, not in any gross, call it, physical danger that we know of.

Ms. Eisenberg: That we know of.

Mr. Fiscarelli: Well, that's right. Recently, he noticed a PST [Protective Security Team] though he was unaware of their function. Let me not say where.

Mr. Gutman: Well, physical danger, risk—something we all should think about on this thing. Carl?

Mr. Lindquist: I give it a go. Worth the risk.

Mr. Kremer: I'm negative.

Mr. Gutman: Well, this being one of the world's great deliberative bodies, it's a go. Carl, if you would, let's get an OPDESC [Operation Description] worked out for CASTLE and this Pakistani company, review it with us, and then Mike can address it with CASTLE and get things rolling. We can do it fast, like ASAP.

"Immature. Short Attention Span. Lies a Lot."

"LIZ, IT's stupid."

"Rick, they've all got them."

"A: no they don't. B: she's got to learn not to have things other kids have, to be able to deal with that."

I'm lunching with Liz at TenPenh, an Asian place at Pennsylvania and Tenth, a few blocks down the avenue from Liz's fancy law firm—Creighton, O'Connell, Lobel. Liz likes formal and public settings for our summit meetings. Keeps the yelling down.

The restaurant is packed and loud, and smells of garlic, soy, and ginger from the open kitchen at the back. Waiters in vaguely Asian apricot-colored jackets, with loop-and-peg buttoning, hustle around like coolies.

Liz is in her work clothes: dark gray pantsuit, pinstriped in light gray, white blouse buttoned up with a little burgundy bow tie just so. Makes me think of Fiscarelli. Her hair's the plain page boy she's had for years. Her skin is just beginning to crease now around the eyes, at the corners of her mouth. Not yet at the lips. That'll come.

Sam, Liz tells me, has become the proud owner of a cell phone.

"She had to be nice to Pennie for thirty days. Believe me, it was a long thirty days. Look, I know all the issues. The phone's fine. It's been zero trouble. *You're* Telephone Man—what's your *problem*? I'm telling you, the phone's been a really, really big help to me. I know who she's calling and who calls her. It's got a GPS function you can track them with—I mean you know where they are down to a couple of yards. You can use your own phone or your computer. *You*—if you wanted to—*you* could sit down in Paris or Caracas wherever the hell you are these days and track Sam at her slumber parties in McLean. I mean, it's amazing."

"I know all this."

"So okay, then—what . . . is . . . the . . . *problem*? Like *I'm* telling *you*— the world's wired, come . . . *on*! I want to have access to her. I mean, instantly. I want to be able to connect and I want her to be able to reach to me if there's some kind of emergency."

"She's got to learn *not* to be in constant contact with family. She's got to start learning responsibility. It's time for that."

Liz rolls her eyes. "Responsibility? Oh for God's sake, Rick. I work long hours. I'm lucky to have a free weekend. Juggling work and time with the girls is very hard, and the cell phone's a huge help." Liz looks away, puffs out a little laugh. "She *has* misused the thing. She called from her school cafeteria once, and then from Social Studies class."

"Great, from class."

"But—I told her to hang up immediately and not ever call from class again. And she hasn't. She's a responsible kid—responsible—you know that."

"You get her some cutesy little thing?"

"You wouldn't like it, but you wouldn't like anything. It flips open, you can text, it's got games the girls don't give a damn about."

"I'm just saying kids aren't kids anymore. They're all on leashes these days, virtual leashes maybe, but leashes all the same."

"They're not 'on leashes,' they're in touch. And they should be. There's a lot of danger out there."

"When I was her age, it was Song of the Open Road. I had the run of the neighborhood, so'd Sue. Shit, Bobby Ringgenberg and me, we'd be outside from when we got home from school—no homework—till dinnertime. What'd we do all that time? We messed around. Messed *around*! The creek by the high school? We told each other that Indians had camped there long back, and we'd crawl up and down the creek pretending they were there again. And we'd talk about George Washington riding through on his big white horse. No adults to horn in. I mean, we could . . ."

"That 'creek,' as you call it, is a filthy drainage ditch."

"Proves my point."

"Well, that was then, this is now. They're little girls, and it's an evil world. You never know, Sam might get talked into a car by some predator, or maybe the bus she's on'll have an accident."

"Kids can't tolerate being alone anymore. They don't have any time on their own, any imagination time. They have to be in constant contact with somebody. You ever listen to these kids' talk? It's dopey beyond belief. They call each other and ask 'Where are you?' What the hell is *that* about? You run around with a bunch of other kids in a park or somewhere—or up and down a creek—you're with somebody real, you interact, maybe you actually sit down and converse in the real world. Maybe you make things up, pretend, like me and Bobby Ringgenberg. These goddamn things . . ."

"Rick, it's a done deal, stop it."

L IZ, MAIDEN name Anne Elizabeth Yoder, is buxom and flaxen-haired and has emerald green eyes, as striking now as when I first saw them. She was born and raised in Mifflinburg, Pennsylvania, up in the mountains toward the center of the state, where her father, Hershal Yoder, was a local land and insurance magnate.

The Yoder forebears were Church of the Brethren Germans who came over here God knows when, before the Revolution, I think—Eastern Pennsylvania is full of them, Yoders, Prices, Wagners—pious, peasanty folk who settled around Lancaster and Reading, then headed out, some of them, for Ohio and beyond.

You can see their genes in Liz, who's always been thick at her ankles and a little clumsy and makes you think of a farm girl. With her hair pulled back she'd look at home in one of those Mennonite bonnets, the see-through, lacy kind.

But she is not a German milkmaid. She is a smart, by-the-numbers lawyer at Creighton, O'Connell, where she does mergers and acquisitions and is well paid even by Washington standards.

She went to Harvard Law after Penn State, graduated in the top 10 percent of her class, then went straight into Creighton, O'Connell, where she is on track to make partner. When she does—there's no if about it—she will be the first woman so honored by the other partners.

Creighton, O'Connell, your upper-tier Washington firm, is immensely prosperous. The firm's offices look as if they've been designed for a maharaja: oak paneling stained a dark rusty color, paintings that look expensive by artists you don't know, but who have probably been in the papers, fresh flowers here and there, carpet that puts a spring in your step.

Creighton, O'Connell is also an outhouse CIA firm. Their work for the Agency is so extensive they have a copy machine reserved solely for the purpose. They keep it in a cypherlocked secure area, a little room with a black and yellow McLeod tartan op-art piece, like a whisky ad, on the door, which you don't enter if you don't have the right security clearance. They do wills for CIA people as well, and get them out of trouble—or try to—when they get into it. (The Agency has a list of preferred lawyers as well as preferred doctors, dentists, realtors, psychiatrists, and at the end of the show, when the curtain rolls down, a list of preferred undertakers.)

Creighton, O'Connell oversees contracts the Agency makes with outside suppliers. Which is how, on a moist summer evening fifteen years back, I met Liz. I was working at M Systems at the time, a company wonder boy, and got dragged downtown to Creighton, O'Connell by an M Systems lawyer to explain the technical descriptions that had to go into a contract the company was negotiating with the Agency. Creighton, O'Connell's rep happened to be Stanley Bress, a senior partner, who listened politely to my little lecture. Stan, lounging back in his chair in one of the firm's well-appointed conference rooms—they have three—his fingers in a little tent, may not have understood what I was saying. Stan being Stan, though, we got to talking about other things, and discovered a common love for '40s bop and '50s cool jazz, which led to an invitation to a drinks-after-dinner thing at the Bress's Georgian Revival home in Kalorama.

As with most of these Washington soirees, people start showing up at 8:30 or so, chatter and work each other, then dash off to some other event. I showed up dateless. Stan with his wife Shirley were on the second-floor landing, Stan very dapper in a bluish Madras jacket, both of them smiling, greeting their guests. Stan introduced me to Shirley as "My young pal Rick Behringer, a bebop man"—an affectionate tap on my shoulder here—"a lover of Diz, Monk, Bird, that whole beautiful world." Shirley, a sweet, genuinely cordial woman, took me by the arm and led me in.

I knew no one there that night, and felt out of place, like a kid surrounded by adults who paid him no mind. After standing around for a time, nodding to people who nodded back and glanced away, I wandered into a large side room. It was paneled in dark wood. At the windows were green velvet curtains drawn slightly and held by golden cords—very elegant, Shirley Bress's taste—and on the floor a large Persian carpet. The room had lots of potted plants and lots of comfortable-looking furniture, and over in the far corner, its lid up, a polished mahogony baby grand. I had walked into the Bress's concert salon. Well now.

I went over to the piano and struck a key, a couple more, then a few simple chords in the mid range. The piano sounded in tune. What the hell, I sat down and started improvising some chords, no tune, no fixed key, then drifted into a tonality with an invented melodic line, a little too pretty, that went nowhere. So I started playing oldies—some Gershwin, I think, then, "As Time Goes By"—right index finger doing the melody—"You must remember this, a kiss is but a kiss"—left hand doing some tentative chords, and as I played—"a sigh is just a sigh"—a pretty woman floated into view. She leaned on the bent side of the piano by the lid prop, arms crossed, drink in her right hand, and said, "Play it again, Sam."

Flaxen hair with a touch of blond in it, skin like fresh cream, striking green eyes.

I said something like, "Greetings, music lovers."

She said, "Hi. You're not the entertainment. Stan and Shirley don't do entertainment."

"Not on purpose."

Get her name. Close the deal. "I'm Rick Behringer."

"I'm Liz Yoder." She nodded a few times as she said this, smiling.

I said, "You must know Stan."

"I get invited."

"The firm?"

She nodded.

"You play?"

"Nope. I'm just an admirer."

Next day, I called her at Creighton, O'Connell. A few days later we had lunch at a tapas place not far from where she worked. The weekend after that we went for a walk in Rock Creek Park, from Pierce Mill down to the zoo, and had a summery dinner Liz had prepared in her Connecticut Avenue apartment—chilled salmon mousse, crackling cold chablis.

And next morning I emerged into the light of day needing sleep, but happy as a billy goat.

I loved her for her green eyes.

"YOU DON'T drink so much anymore," Liz says neutrally. I'd shaken my head no when our apricot-clad waiter—his left eyebrow pierced with three or four tiny silver rings—asked if we wanted to start off with something.

"Hey, who's got the time?" I reply, a smart-dumb remark, tailor-made to avoid the issue, which is that Liz has picked up on some small something in me she genuinely finds okay—in the old days I'd have had a couple of scotches with lunch—and I am surprised, pleasantly, that she noticed and mentioned it. "I mean, I just cut back."

"See a therapist for it?"

"Hell, no." I didn't swear off, surrender to a Higher Power, or work my way through any twelve steps. I just cut back. You can do that.

Liz cocks an eyebrow. "That time you took the stanchion down."

Two brick stanchions painted white flank the entrance to the drive at Liz's place. With the divorce underway and Liz's bitch lawyer Abby hard at work, I drove crazy drunk and in fury one night to Dulany Drive. I remember stumbling from my car on the parking apron in front of the house, getting out, missing my footing on the first step of the porch, falling, bloodying my nose, then pounding with both fists on the front door—house's got a bell, of course—and yelling, "Goddamn your ass, goddamn your ass, goddamn your ass."

And Liz opening the door—glowering, enraged, but cold, controlled, steely—confronting me as I stood there, as she said, red-eyed and unshaven and smelling like a distillery.

"Liz, I hate your fucking guts."

"Oh, you idiot, go away."

"Fuck you, Liz."

Then, flooring the pedal, making the tires shriek, backing my silver Infiniti up the long curved drive, I ploughed the rear end of that sweet car into the leftmost stanchion at the beginning of the driveway, wrecking the rear end of the car, wrecking the stanchion, knocking it over—cost a fortune to get all this fixed—then getting out and stumbling, once again, stumbling, from my car, shoving the trash Dumpster down the driveway, turning it over, kicking at the cans, at the big plastic soft drink bottles, then—I don't remember this or anything else from that evening but Liz assures me it's true—picking up and hurling a glass jar at Liz's door, yelling at the top of my lungs, "Nightmare, nightmare, nightmare," by which I must have meant Liz. The girls—Jesus, what they thought, back in the den maybe, maybe cowering, I'll never know.

And inevitably, appearing at Fairfax County Courthouse after the harassment suit, sober as a judge, my lawyer Bob at my side. And attending the court-ordered "anger management" sessions. The County didn't go for jail time, and Liz didn't push it.

L IZ DROPS the subject. "Sam's navigating her new school just fine, and Pennie doesn't have any school issues, either, so there's that. Look, I don't want to harp on missing the soccer debut, I know things come up. But it happens all the goddamn time. It's the same old story—you are just not reliable, not even for your daughters. They notice, don't think they don't. You want to change the agreement?"

"Aw, shit, Liz, come on—I do what I can and you know it."

"You've got to be more serious."

Liz's voice easily shades off into the imperious these days, I think, more than before. As she's attained to a certain rank at Creighton, O'Connell, she's picked up more attitude, though she inherited plenty from her old man—Hersh always navigated as if the world was at his command. He used to hum around Mifflinburg in his white Cadillac, always white, passing the Amish as they clicked along in their black buggies on the one main street that goes east-west through town. He'd smile like the town seigneur, and they'd smile back.

Ten years ago Hersh had a massive stroke, which left him helpless. Couldn't walk, couldn't talk, couldn't focus his eyes. Incontinent, too. His hospital room smelled like shit. Hate to be a nurse. When I last saw Hersh he was lying on his side in a hospital bed, gaping, barely able to follow you with his eyes. When you moved into his line of sight he moaned something that might have been recognition, though you were never sure he really knew who the hell you were. A catheter ran under the sheets from his cock to a plastic urinal tethered to the side of the bed by its handle. When they'd stabilized him and made sure he wasn't dying on them, the docs castrated him for some medical reason of their own, after which he died anyway. What an end.

Mifflinburg is built under a hill to its south. On the softly rising lower slope is the town graveyard. Old Yoder's in there now, his Caddie gone to junk.

Liz asks, "Where were you, by the way?"

"Rome."

"Have fun?"

"Lots."

"I took the girls up and saw Mom. She asked about you. She remembers you, but forgets we're divorced. Ed"—Liz's brother—"and Judi"—Ed's wife—"are moving her to Harrisburg. Selinsgrove was fine, her old friends were in the area, but that was when she had her mind. Not much reason to stay now. I'll get up to her when I can. At some point she'll stop remembering you. Then me and the girls." Liz's eyes go liquid.

H E HAS many good qualities, Spence. He has courage, he has will. He is responsible toward the girls. He's also got personal charm, acres of that. He talks a really good line, very smooth. But down deep, he's a bullshitter, and a distant, icy, uncommunicative prick. He's lost in his goddamn Black World. That world is what he does, it is who he is. He has no more moral sense than a baseball. He has no tenderness. And he never forgets himself, never surrenders to affection or trust. Or to regret. I've never known him to regret."

Liz to marital counselor, Spencer Ott, before the smash-up. I was the one who suggested seeing someone, probably to pretend to Liz that I was willing to do whatever to hold the marriage together; Liz accepted, probably to demonstrate to me that nothing whatever would. She found Ott through a friend.

Ott was short and slight and had big staring eyes and an eerie manner. His fingernails were too wide for his fingers and wrapped around them. He looked like a lemur. He was always dressed casually: blue-and-white striped shirt open at the neck, no tie, white trousers, expensive-looking oxblood penny loafers.

Ott had his office in a one-story bisque-colored medical building out Leesburg Pike, just before Tysons, and not all that far from Global Reach. Typical therapist's quarters, I suppose: gray microblinds always half closed, pastel blue walls, and on the walls, framed pencil sketches of quiet harbors and boats becalmed. In the glass covering one of the sketches you could see the reflection of a clock on the rear wall and watch your fifty minutes run out—I am dead certain this placing was intentional. In the center of the room sat three wing chairs, two facing one (Ott's), and between the two a small table with a box of Kleenex on it.

"He's wired, hair trigger," Liz said. "When he's working a project he's all gotta go, gotta go. He's impossible to be with. He needs some kind of hit, and he needs it again and again, and he wants it so badly. He's up in the middle of the night, doesn't talk. When you're talking to him, he drifts off. Once he became a food compulsive. He put on fifty pounds and looked like a kangaroo—I thought he was going to explode. He's got this low threshold of outrage. He throws things, he screams, he's all on or off. He's a neurotic prick with no intermediate gears. I can't take that world he's chosen to live in."

In a vain attempt to establish civility, Ott had us "echoing" each other's feelings. One of us would say something personal, and the other had to interpret it, but Liz always drifted out of the game, claimed I didn't have any feelings to echo. Liz wanted to mangle me directly, anyway, with a bayonet charge, like the infantry: hey diddle-diddle, straight up the middle. Looking over at me, but talking to Ott, she said, "How to fill out Rick's résumé? I would say, 'Immature. Short attention span. Lies a lot.' "

Then: "Rick's like all the other guys in his business—you cannot trust him. Think of the affairs—I mean . . . I forgave him the first. I told myself, 'Well, it happens.' And I gritted my teeth for the second. I thought I should hold on to things for the girls' sake and all, try to get it worked out. Duh. Big mistake, happened again, of course. Third time I said, 'That's it.' There's no trust. I'll never trust the guy again. I can't believe in him."

I had no excuses and with Ott acting as judge I pled *nolo*. Attendant circumstances that justify nothing: my company had gotten into deep trouble, I'd borrowed too much, with the dot.com bust, we were losing contracts, I was working nights, weekends, drinking too much. I took too many foreign trips that ended up duds, nobody at home minding the store.

The first was Janine, Global Reach's slim, crazy-haired telemarketer. At our first steamy motel rendezvous Janine said she "liked it with older guys." I was thirty-seven. Then came a run of others—Anne, computer saleswoman I met at a conference at the Galleria in Houston, two nights.

Then Dottie, Sharon, Rosemary. There was a Marisa in there somewhere. All of this involved dispensing massive doses of untruth to Liz, much of which failed to fool her, though I am good at the art.

At a session in Ott's office she turned to me and said, "I loved you once. I loved you because you were crazy and I thought I was too sane. I loved you because you were funny, and distracting, and because you lived in a world that fascinated me. I loved you dearly, Rick, so help me. But there came a time when I just had to say, 'God, give me some sane.'"

One evening toward the very end I went down into the semidarkness of our basement and found Liz, tears in her eyes, sitting on an old daybed we have down there. She had our wedding album in her lap. The album was just your ordinary three-ring binder, but it had been sewn up in white-on-white brocade as a wedding present by the daughter of a friend. On the cover of the album, set out in a frame also wrapped in brocade, was a copy of our wedding invitation ("Anne Elizabeth Yoder and Richard Henry Behringer request the pleasure of your company at their marriage . . ."). Running around the frame was a border of red ribbon that was spaced every inch or so with knots tied in the shape of roses. Pathetic.

Liz looked up at me. "This was us. You happy?"

I sat down beside her on the daybed. "Liz . . ."

"Don't," she said. "Just don't." She got to her feet, and looking down at me, said, "A waste, Rick," and went up the stairs. I wasn't sure what she meant—the marriage? The album? Me?

The group pictures were shot in bright noontime sunshine in front of Mifflinburg's First Evangelical Lutheran Church. August. Hot and sticky. Liz's father, Hersh, with his round, gummy, larcenous face, looked like a dead man, not wanting his daughter to marry the likes of me. Ma Yoder—her name is Louise and she is known as "Weezie"—stood next to Hersh, appearing placid, her way of not dealing with stress. Then Liz's brother Edward, who was in "financial services" with some soon-to-die local bank in Harrisburg, and his wife Judi. Next to them were my family—Marge, Sue and her husband Steve, who had no kids at this point. And in the far right corner of at least one of the pictures, young Pastor Wagner in his strangely Catholic-looking raiment. Then assorted aunts, uncles, cousins, high school and college classmates.

This is 1993. Reception was at the Yoder house. No alcohol, by order of Ma Yoder. Okay with Hersh. Okay with everybody except me.

I closed the album. I heard Liz upstairs crying. I don't know where the girls were. I left that night for a motel, and never came back to stay. Liz pulled the plug on Ott—and me—after the third session.

AT TENPENH, as Liz pokes at her curried shrimp, a gesture she makes with her wrist, a quick turning movement, gives me a flash vision of her at our Dulany Drive place, planting impatiens at the shady bordered walk out in our backyard some early summer afternoon, using a narrow trowel to do the planting—making that same quick turning gesture. Her gardening gloves are soft, white feminine things. She's kneeling. There's a tracery of veins in her legs, and one pops out just above her left knee. Taut and assy when we first met and for those first few years, her body loosened later on, after the kids. She's lower slung now, but you'd still want in there.

"Stan Bress keeps showing up," Liz says. "Amazing, isn't it? Old lawyers never stop. Doesn't drive, of course. Takes taxis. He shuffles around now, and his back's bent over, but he reads a lot of the new cases, loves them. Stan must be eighty now if a day, hanging in there."

I hear Liz's voice and I make the appropriate facial gestures, but I'm not listening. I can't stop thinking of Sasha Geydarov, my Azerbaijani supplier, and the scuttlebutt about him from Pappas. I am thinking of a deal Sasha arranged.

About a year ago, Sasha introduced me to a beefy, puckery-eyed colonel in the Russian Missile Service. The three of us met at night in a small forested park in northeast Moscow, away from the city center, but inside the ring. The colonel, who was tall, came hulking out of the dark in a gray-green woolen overcoat and black karakul hat, Sasha in tow, shivering—the late March wind was up, it was not quite spring—in leather bomber jacket and his usual tight blue jeans. In English, Sasha told the colonel, "This is the person you want to meet." The colonel eyed me, nodded abruptly, then turned to Sasha and said something in Russian, some kind of insult, I think, because Sasha looked offended. He said nothing for a time. He just fixed his large, mournful eyes on the colonel, who stared back impassively. Then Sasha smiled and replied silkily, and it was the colonel's turn to look offended. Sasha then nodded to each of us, still smiling, and slipped off in that way he had. I have no idea what they said; I knew some small drama had just been played out.

The colonel turned to me. "You are Behringer?" he said.

"Yes."

"I can supply S-300 main internal radar. Upgraded. Full version. With new maintenance manuals. Extremely valuable. You cannot get these elsewhere."

The colonel was offering to sell me the latest version of the radar electronics of the S-300 antimissile system, their counterpart of our Patriot. I said I was interested. We exchanged cell numbers and parted company.

An FMA officer I knew at Langley (not Fiscarelli) got back to me quickly with a price: two million dollars, a figure that impressed me mightily. The next night I met the colonel in the same park and relayed the Agency's offering price. He accepted immediately. Then, saying he would "work on the modalities," he asked me to stay in the city and left.

Five days later, I got a call from the colonel asking to meet in the park that same night. This time the colonel brought a friend, a large man also in civilian clothing, but I think a military officer. The colonel and friend walked briskly up to me. "We can deliver Ostend Airport, Belgium," the colonel said. "Three weeks time. Definite. But, four million dollars."

"The understanding was two."

"It must now be four. Complications."

"I don't care about complications. The understanding was two. Two it has to be."

"Tell them it must be four," the friend said.

"No."

As we went back and forth on the price, the colonel and friend got a little menacing, raising their voices, leaning in, angry. They went silent for a time, then the colonel shrugged his shoulders. "We have made the arrangements," he said and the two of them disappeared quietly into the cold Moscow night.

This deal was not petty thievery, it was a major heist. The equipment was for sole use by Russia, Belarus, and Kazakhstan, their top stuff and not for export.

From Bank Hügen in Zurich I transferred two million dollars to an account in the Cayman Islands controlled by a Saudi go-between named Ismail Hamawi, a man the colonel and I knew and more or less trusted. Hamawi, an arms trader, is an Agency informant who also does favors of various kinds for the organization.

When the colonel received word from Hamawi that the money was in the bank, he had the radar system flown into Ostend on some bogus Kazak airline that ceased to exist soon after delivery. I was there for its arrival, waiting outside a long, low hangar at the edge of the commercial freight zone. The colonel turned the stuff over to me in person. I think he might have been leaving Russia for good.

The equipment came in ten aluminum boxes the size of large suitcases. A specialist from Sci Tech checked the engineering and gave it a preliminary okay. We scooted the boxes out the hangar on hand carts and over to a motorized baggage truck we'd gotten from the Ostend ground service. We drove the boxes—I was at the wheel—about half a mile to where an Agency cargo Gulfstream was parked and turned them over to a couple of crew members. An unmarked Citroën filled with Agency security, four young men in wraparound sunglasses, had followed me and parked a short distance away while the aircrew loaded the ten shiny aluminum boxes onto the Gulfstream.

The Agency flew the boxes from Ostend to Andrews AFB in Washington, then trucked them out to Langley. Sci Tech verified the goods, my FMA handler signaled me, and I had Hamawi, our Saudi go-between, transfer the two million dollars to the colonel's overseas account, in a Liechtenstein bank as it happened. Hamawi took 5 percent, his usual cut, to which the colonel had agreed.

Sasha was paid a $5,000 finder's fee. I don't think he knew the value of the goods.

Was this the deal—my guess it was the biggest sale Sasha ever arranged—that got him killed? The Russians had legal ways to get Sasha—arrest him, send him to Siberia, work him and starve him. But maybe they didn't want that, maybe the deal was too embarrassing for court proceedings, even proceedings conducted in secret. Maybe they just wanted to kill him.

HEY—HELLO hello hello? Anybody home?"
Liz is smiling that grim, disappointed smile she can get, the left side of her mouth turned down, eyes not taking part. Shades of Weezie Yoder. Liz is tapping my hand. "You're not here," she says.

LUNCH OVER, ultimatums and insults delivered, we walk out onto Pennsylvania. The day is cold, gray, and blustery. In the stiff October wind I catch a whiff, here now and gone, of perfume from Liz, a sharp, tangy fragrance that I don't recognize. I doubt she wears it for a guy. Still more that any guy gave it to her. "I'm not dating," she said once. "I could, but it's too much trouble to work boyfriends in when you have to do for the girls. Maybe I'm wrong, but I think guys basically don't like other guys' kids anyhow. Something Darwinian about that. And getting babysitters and all. So I just don't."

I believe her. Sam and Pennie report no action on the guy front at Dulany Drive and they probably would. When I bring it up now and then, delicately, I get honest-looking headshakes from the girls. Amazing how women can go without fucking—years, a lifetime even. Doesn't seem to faze them. You'd think they'd be ravenous for it. They explode on you, scary the way they abandon themselves, go crazy, thrash around, scream. But then next day it's as if nothing had happened, and you have to walk them through the whole drill all over again. Amazing.

"See you," Liz says, and turns up the avenue, heading back to Creighton, O'Connell in her sensible shoes. No high heels for Liz. Never wore them.

I walk down toward the plaza at the Navy Memorial. The ground of the memorial is a big map of the world, maybe fifteen yards in diameter, carved in gray-pink granite. There's a life-size bronze statue of a Navy swabby in a pea jacket standing face to the wind, duffel bag at his side, ready to ship out somewhere. I've always found the statue affecting. When the country's called them, the swabbies and the grunts and the jarheads have always shown up, however unworthy their leaders may be. In front of the swabby and the map of the world on the Pennsylvania side of the memorial stand two tall, white metal masts hoisting naval signal flags—pennants, swallowtails, burgees, of all colors—that snap in the wind, pulling at their metal halyards, the halyard links clanking against the masts. Those flags are saying something. I always wonder what.

"We Need a NOC. You're it."

"IT'S THAT company," Fiscarelli says, "LPE." Fiscarelli, his chair angled away from me, looks out his window over Woodmont Avenue toward the parking garage behind Egerton Associates. Rain is falling in sheets, beating against the glass. "We want to know what that company is doing. Who're the people who run it? What's the government connection? Military? ISI? We've tried to get a closer look, but without much luck. Embassy people attract too much attention. We need a NOC. You're it."

As the wind gusts, some metal contrivance on the building, the downspout maybe, moans.

"Business trip?" Fiscarelli says. "You've been there. You know the place."

I study Fiscarelli's blank, puffy face. They don't have the people. They can't do this on their own, they don't know how. They're paralyzed, and Ray isn't coming through.

That mysterious company, LPE. A little edge here, maybe.

"Sure," I say. "Sure."

II: TRANSMISSION

"EVERY DAY we get threat warnings," Don Rieger is saying. "I've seen five come in on one day. Every day you check your vehicle for bombs. Even here in the embassy compound. People are spooked."

Rieger is Deputy Chief of Station, Islamabad, and an old acquaintance— I won't say buddy. We are in Rieger's office in Annex One of the American embassy. Rieger is ex–Special Forces, tall and hefty, but his heft no longer means physical strength. It's become a burden. I'm seeing him because I am seeing everyone here—the Econ and Commercial Officers, the FBI. Tomorrow I get ten minutes or so of face time with the ambassador.

Rieger doesn't know why I'm here. The story Fiscarelli has cooked up is, I'm an IT contractor here to do work on the embassy communications systems. Plausible enough.

Fiscarelli does not tell people in the field that I am on Agency business unless there's an operational need—the DVD pickup in Athens, Sasha's laser in Baku—for station to get in on the act. Otherwise, they don't need to know.

In the Special Forces they called Rieger "Horse" because he is tall and long-faced. He went to a small, good college in the Midwest where he played basketball not particularly well and majored in Poli Sci. He thought he might be a lawyer.

On one of those life-changing whims, instead of going to law school, he joined the Army—in the late seventies—just when it was trying to find its way out of its post-Vietnam stress disorder.

In 1981, in the final months of his enlistment, a terrorist drove a truck full of explosives into the Marine barracks in Beirut and killed two hundred and forty-one men. Rieger was stateside at the time and had never been in Beirut, but the bombing made him rethink his life. Shortly after leaving the Army he joined CIA.

Rieger has the face of a tired man who doesn't realize he's tired. He's been here longer than anyone except the ambassador.

IT'S STRANGE out there," Rieger says, meaning the country he's supposed to circulate in and know. "In the street, I mean. You don't face overt hostility, people don't make nasty faces or obscene gestures or what have you. Most of them, when they see you just go about their business. But you are noticed wherever you go, and you think you're being followed. You may not be, probably aren't, but out there you have the feeling of eyes constantly on you."

"Sounds pretty paranoid."

"Maybe, but the truth is, there are people out there who want to murder you, really do, and no matter how benign a situation looks, you must watch your back. Didn't use to be this way. Now it is."

People like Rieger can't get out of the American bubble. They're well known to the government, to its police. They are photographed and registered. They can't travel incognito. Wherever they go, whoever they meet, it's all known to the security services. And they cannot penetrate the real targets of this place—the religious schools, the mosques, the Afghan communities, the indigenous opposition. They have no way in.

"One month back," he says, "police arrested a group of Arabs, a Yemeni and some others, Saudis, we think, who were al-Qaeda symps. They had three hundred pounds of various kinds of explosive in their apartment. Station is certain it was meant for the embassy."

"How so?"

"Some of them talked."

"Paks treat people rough. Think these guys told them the truth?"

Rieger shrugs. He doesn't believe in the results of torture any more than I do.

The Islamabad embassy is a fortress. You approach the place through S-curved roadblocks and three checkpoints. At each one you show ID. The embassy's thick brick walls are buttressed with steel pillars and topped with security cameras and silvery loops of razor wire. Outside, the embassy is guarded by Pakistani army units, inside by American Marines.

If you don't think of the thick walls and razor wire, you can imagine you're in a fancy country club in Palm Beach—pretty red brick buildings shaded by tall oak trees and planted with hibiscus and jacaranda. Beyond the embassy proper and its outlying annexes, you'll find a restaurant, a swimming pool, tennis courts, a softball field. Like home.

As Rieger and I are talking, a siren suddenly starts whoop-whooping, and over the intercom we hear, "Be advised, all personnel are to evacuate the buildings. All personnel must evacuate. Secure all classified materials. Close all windows."

Rieger screws up his face. "Aah, more of that bullshit. Come on, kids, fire drill."

Rieger and I, with everyone else, leave our building—we're in the one-story annex across from the swimming pool—and move with deliberate speed to a line of white vans, their engines running. A young marine in body armor and kevlar helmet is gesturing to us and saying, "Keep it moving, folks, keep it moving." A squad of marines, also in body armor and helmets and carrying M-16s, has taken position in front of the entrance to the main embassy building. The siren keeps whoop-whooping as Rieger and I board a van.

"Folks, squeeze tightly, please," a marine is saying, "make some room, more on the way." After a couple more embassy employees get in, the marine checks the inside, says, "Okay, van secure," and slides the side door shut, signaling to the driver to move out. Our van creeps toward the main gate, where more marines signal the driver to halt in place behind a line of other white vans poised to leave the compound. We sit for a few minutes in silence, until over the outside loudspeaker someone yells, "Okay, stand down. This has been an emergency drill. Stand down. Situation clear."

IN THE restaurant Rieger and I head for the buffet, a long table of large silver chafing dishes serving Pak food. A lot of the crowd is uniformed officers, mostly Army, with military bling on their tunics, as well as sleek, slim men in business suits from the upper reaches of the embassy, State maybe, or CIA. I see a couple of guys dressed like on-duty plain-clothes cops and think DEA or FBI. I see plenty of fellow contractors, too, men who have the look—some wearing mirrored sunglasses, some in cowboy boots, blazers and blue jeans, some in pinstripes. They're all selling something—services, weapons. I recognize a few faces.

The ambassador never shows. When he's around he's powerlunching in his residence. I know the man. He has a way of charming you, as if he's charming *down* at you, because he's got an important post and everybody knows it, and he didn't get here because he's a campaign contributor, he got here because he's a serious player in a serious place.

At our table Rieger orders scotch, and when it arrives he lifts it in a little salute. He sips at it, and in time his cheeks color and he relaxes. You can see his world getting better.

Rieger sweeps his arm around at the crowded restaurant. "There's almost one hundred percent annual turnover here. Nobody but nobody stays more than a year. Result, we got no institutional memory in place here. I don't mean CIA, I mean everybody—State, DEA, Commerce, everybody." Rieger gets out every couple of months for "family leave" in the States, to see his kids, not his wife. I can't imagine it.

"Hey, Rick!" someone behind me says. I feel a hand on my shoulder. It's a guy I know, Charley Phelps. Charley works out of the Defense Attaché's office. Charley knows Rieger, of course, and nods at him effusively, saying, "Hey, hey."

To me he says, "Rick, man, you don't call? What are you doing out here?"

"Heya, Charley, good to see you. Trying to make a buck, as ever. Always out there selling."

"Gonna be here long?"

" 'Bout a week."

Charley's DIA. I've been through here before trying to drum up local business—the phone companies, maybe, or the government, and like all American salespeople, I'd hit the rounds at the embassy for tips on who's buying what. In return, I'd give the embassy people, including Charley, commercial information I turned up. Charley more or less knows my status with the Agency. He's wondering what I'm really doing here.

I see he's been lunching with a large, florid-faced American wearing some kind of outdoorsy, semimilitary clothing who is staring over at us. The American has a white, handle-bar mustache and steel-rimmed glasses. Our eyes meet, then he looks away.

Charley says to me, "Well, give me a buzz, okay? We gotta talk. I really mean it!" He nods to Rieger again, smiling, then goes back to his table and the florid-faced American.

"You know Charley?" Rieger asks.

"In a way. Who's he sitting with?"

Rieger smiles. "The owner of an outfit called Talltree Security Services. His name's Gus Olstrom if you care. I don't. Believe it or not, DIA's out-sourcing HUMINT now, which is what Talltree does. Talltree's run by morons, Olstrom being *primum inter pares*. Olstrom has a DOD badge which he keeps rolled up in his rectum. You can laugh at these fuckheads, and we do, but the uniformed guys—Strategic Support Branch, so called—are about as bad. Strategic Support Branch—Stupid Sorry Bastards, we call them. A while back the dumb shits—SSB—were surveilling a big boy in the ISI, supposedly an Islamist. But you can't do that here, not if you're amateurs. They didn't even try to be subtle about it. Drove around with camcorders tailing him. General's people picked up on it immediately, of course, let it go for a while, but the general finally lost his patience and had them rolled up. Station had to get them out of jail. It's unbelievable they run whole operations. They are under nobody's supervision and they are out of control. Makes you puke."

R IEGER AND I finish lunch and head out. Off the entrance area to the restaurant is a kind of meeting room, currently empty except for— it caught my eye as I was coming in with Rieger—an ancient black baby grand piano and bench. As Rieger and I pass on our way out I give the pi-ano another glance. Why not? I say so long to Rieger at the restaurant en-trance and head back to the meeting room.

The piano is scuffed up, looks like it's been around the world. There's some old sheet music on the music desk, but I don't bother with it. I just sit down on the bench—also old, with a phony leather seat and a height ad-juster that doesn't work—and try out the keys. A couple of tones are off pitch and clangy, but the thing is basically playable. I improvise a tune, my own, in a minor key, soft and melancholy, old-fashioned, heavy on the chro-matics. Could have been written around 1910. The beat is ONE-two-three ONE-two, ONE-two-three ONE-pause, then the next phrase, no words—I don't have any—same tune, same beat, one tone lower, then a third phrase, this one starting low, rises, recapitulates the first phrase, and rounds things off.

I get into to some bouncy, jazzy stuff, kind of ragged, doing my Monk impersonation, then get into some Gershwin, some Ellington, Arlen. Out in the restaurant lobby the last of the lunchers are departing. It's maybe two o'clock. No lone looks in. I play on, lost in the music, and in time get into a groove, feel that high, when everything is right and true and beautiful: boplicity.

To GIVE Fiscarelli's cover story some traction—that I am here to check out embassy commo systems—I actually put in a couple hours of work on the Agency internal network. I know the system—I helped put it in—and, of course, I have the clearances. As if Red-teaming, I send test e-mails to Rieger and some of the other officers in Islamabad Station, nose around the networks, and look for vulnerabilities and signs of hacking. As expected, I find none. Then I communicate with other bases in-country—Karachi, Peshawar, Lahore, finally with Langley—pulling the same number.

I also emerge into the daylight to see people in the Defense Ministry and some Pak private phone and IT people in town. Rieger describes this activity solemnly to others in the station as my cover—sales trip, security software—for being here while working on the internal system. I duly visit a couple of local ISPs (BrainNET, FibreCOM) and shoot the shit with their managers and purchasing people. I see the local PakTel agent. I hang around a shopping mall in the Jinnah Market called the Hafeez Centre (Wrangler, EssJay Garments, Marshall Tiles, Mahmood Money Changer, PakMobile) and check out the computer stores and the pirated software and DVDs they sell. I even see a couple bank security people. Who knows, I might even get some business down the line from all this, but mostly it's smoke.

These covers can go as multilayered as you want. Walt and Marge once took me to an old movie playing at a Georgetown art house that had some long-legged babe in mesh tights—Cyd Charisse?—tap-dancing in a mirrored room. You saw an infinitude of Cyd Charisses, all in top hat and tails, dancing in synch, the reflected figures getting smaller and smaller till they vanished, and you couldn't tell which was the real babe, which the reflection.

So with my covers, which I spend three days spreading.

My real work in town starts this evening when I see a retired general I know. So, with time to kill in the afternoon, I head out of my hotel for a walk in the city to see the sights and stave off sleep till night. The day is bright and warm and clear, and I am the camera-bearing wanderer in my khakis and long-sleeved shirt out for a stroll, dodging the shrieking motor scooters and triwheeler cabs.

The few women you see here are covered, though some of the schoolgirls are wearing *shalwar kameez,* loose shirts and trousers. They have long black hair that trails down their backs plaited in pigtails with decorative inserts woven in at the ends. One young woman is carrying books, and despite stares wears blue jeans and sandals. Her whole attitude—body, face—shows defiance. She's the only one.

From a school down the avenue, teenage boys run past me laughing. One with a cricket bat, stops, turns my way, and says, smiling, "Please, sir, will you take a picture?" I agree, and they line up for a photograph, which I take on my cell. The kid with the bat also has a cell, and, obligingly, I send him the picture—through the regular phone channel. He tells me he's got Bluetooth on his cell, and so do I, but Bluetooth is way too interactive. Somebody, you never know, could hit a few keys and download all your stuff.

Even this kid.

In a few minutes of walking I come to a cement wall ten feet tall or so. The wall is covered with graffiti and plastered with advertisements and political posters. Behind the wall, through a small gate, I find another city different from the one I've been strolling through.

In here I find rows of cinder-block shanties no bigger than rooms. They have corrugated steel roofs. The street I'm on is paved, but the paving has cracked and has never been repaired. There's no drainage. In the mud a barefoot girl of about twelve, wearing an electric pink *shalwar kameez,* is carrying a large plastic bottle to fetch water from a communal pump.

Down the way, surrounded by noisy children, is a crude, wooden Ferris wheel. It is maybe fifteen feet high. It's got four gondolas, each full of children. A man in a lavender *shalwar kameez*—its owner-operator, I guess—is turning the wheel with a large crank. The yard around the Ferris wheel is full of debris—paper, plastic bags—all of it picked over. Across the way there's a smoking pottery kiln with a display in the street of orange and white pots. A crowded, wildly painted minibus splashes past me. Though shop owners pretend to ignore me, I get hostile glances from others—men in the street mostly, some of the kids. Two boys drive past in a donkey cart. The cart's wheels are automobile tires and it is loaded with an electrical generator. They yell something mocking at me.

Islamabad was built for the rich and powerful, but someone has to work it. Here's where they live. The city tries to hide these places behind walls and to a great extent succeeds. The people who run Islamabad don't have to notice.

I think Rieger has never visited this place. I walk back out the gate, go to my hotel, and get an early dinner in the Chinese restaurant next door.

Time to see the General.

"We Had a Damn Good Time with Those Koreans"

NIGHT IS falling and there's a chill in the air. I am in Ramna 5, on the eastern edge of Islamabad, downhill from the Melody Market—you locate yourself in this strange city, not by the municipal coordinates, but by what market you're near. On Ataturk Avenue, I pass a squad of blue-bereted police sitting in a truck, its canvas sides rolled down. Police have been stationed in conspicuous places in Pakistani cities since the anti-Musharraf demonstrations of the spring and Benazir Bhutto's assassination. I enter a clean, well-paved back lane and about halfway in find the villa I'm looking for. When I ring the buzzer at its tall, light-blue steel gate, a kid about fifteen years old lets me in—I'm expected—and leads me across a courtyard to the main house. We enter through large double doors with windows of stained glass—blue, red, yellow, white rhomboids—into a kind of front hall, then into a sparsely furnished sitting room—bristly red armchairs, white antimacassars—where I find the General. He rises stiffly from his chair, pads across the carpet in slippers to greet me politely, unsmiling, and gestures with his eyes to the servant to leave us alone.

General Shawkat Mir. The General has a circle of short white hair and a razor-thin white mustache. He is wearing a high-collared military tunic and loose *shalwar*.

Tugging at my arm the General says, "The night's lovely. Let's go out," and leads me back out into the courtyard. "Safar," he yells, on the way out, "whiskey."

The night's lovely. Let's go out. The General's house is bugged.

It's dark now. He takes me over to two wooden lawn chairs under a single, large eucalyptus tree growing at the far wall. Under the tree are two wooden lawn chairs and a small wooden table, where we sit in the moonlight. Safar appears with a bottle of Johnnie Walker Red, two glasses, and a small pitcher of water, and puts them on the table. Leaning toward me, the General taps the pitcher with his finger and says, "Produce of Scotland. Like the whiskey. I bought it in Edinburgh." The pitcher is cut glass and is etched with stylized thistles.

When Safar leaves the General says slyly, "We had a damn good time with those Koreans, didn't we?"

"We did."

It was, through the General, that I bought that North Korean missile, my proudest FMA moment. The General and I set up a daisy chain of intermediaries: a South Korean fixer whose contact in the north, a North Korean Ministry of Defense official, signed off on the sale to the General. The General attested that the end user would be the Pakistani Army. A Chinese army acquaintance of the North Korean vouched for the good faith of the General. All this took three months of arranging, but in the end the missile was carried from Karachi on a Greek-owned and Liberian-flagged freighter up the Delaware River to the Port of Philadelphia, from which it was spirited away to who-knows-where by a team from DOD.

T HE GENERAL has left the army. "I am a lonely old man," he says, "who is out of synch with his times. I was cashiered. They said it was peculation, but it was not peculation, it was politics. Nothing else. I am not PC as the concept is defined in this country, and they ousted me. I have many enemies. They said if I agreed to go quietly there would not be a trial. It has made me an insomniac. So, when I wake in the night, I get up and read. Never the television. It is for idiots. Except for the sports." The General is allowed to leave his house and to travel, though he may not leave the country.

"My son Haneef you know. He is in computer animation these days." The General bugs his eyes. "Cartoons! He works in Lahore. I have a daughter in Falls Church, Virginia. Her mother is in England. I was in England once, Sandhurst, special program, after the Military Academy here. Traveled.

Had a good time." He recites for me: "Oh, to be in England, now that April's here, Oh, to be in England drinking English beer.

"I am also one hundred percent out of the business, if that's what you want. But I think you know that. So—just what hat are you wearing these days? Telephone engineer, purchaser of missiles, something else? What do you want?"

"Do you know of a company called Lahore Precision Engineering?"

"Why are you interested?"

"It has traded with the Iranians and the Libyans and the North Koreans."

"Ah. What did they trade?"

"I don't know."

"Ah. Why are you coming to me about this?"

"I think they may be, may have been Islamist. And military. I was hoping you might know something."

"Well." He hesitates, his eyes fixed on me. "I am an old soldier. I am really quite retired and not plugged into the current situation. I have nothing to contribute off the bat. Sorry. Also, you have to be careful with these matters. These matters are very sensitive. Which raises the question—your personal safety. Are you going about asking questions? I think you are. You haven't come here just to talk with me. I can tell you that the security services here have many people in them who are Taliban sympathizers, al-Qaeda sympathizers, who know who you are and who would cut off your head if they got you in the right situation. Be very wary of these people. They are all around. They are scattered like germs throughout the military and particularly ISI, which they have infiltrated very successfully. They run whole sections. The government is most fearful of them.

"They are not democrats. They believe in something they call the 'umma,' which means the whole of the Muslim community round the world. They believe all these Muslims should be governed in an Islamic way by a caliphate. I do not. I like whiskey and I drink a tot every evening for my health. Sometimes several tots. It relaxes me. What is it to them? To hell with them. Also, they are buggers. They all are, these Taliban, Afghan shits, and their Pakistani followers. They learn the practice in the madrassas. Of course, wherever they are in power in Afghanistan or the Tribal Areas here, they make a great show of hanging their fellow buggers who have crossed them somehow. Hypocrites!

"I am a patriot. I was brought here from India as a small boy of ten in '47. We were from Ferozepur. They didn't want us there, and we had to get the hell out. We lost all our possessions. It was a bad business, and I remember our troubles very well, particularly those of my poor mother who was ill all the way on the train to Lahore. The Hindus, fuck them all, attacked our train on the way up. We—our guards—fended them off, but it was a close thing. They wanted to massacre us. It was then at the age of ten that I decided to be a soldier. I loathe the Hindus, India, all that. A dirty people—so backward, so superstitious. They worship elephants and snake goddesses. There's no reasoning with such people. You can't have discourse with them."

"The Islamists, General, can you discourse with them?"

His eyes widen. "Just as bad. All these people, silly people, oafs, all stirred up. Globalization, I tell you, is the great culprit. Think of the world one hundred years ago. If something happened in Karachi, no one in New York ever heard about it or gave a damn. And if something happened in New York, nobody in Karachi ever heard. Or gave a damn. Didn't matter if they did or didn't. But now, information moves instantly, and we are in effect cheek by jowl. So people in New York have acquired enemies in Karachi. It was never so before.

"Your enemies come out of places you do not begin to understand. Thanks to your information revolution, you impinge on these places, not even knowing that you do. You affect their lives in ways you cannot perceive or understand, and they resent your presence. And thanks also to the globalization that has produced them, they move easily from place to place, anywhere in the world. They move money and messages from anywhere to anywhere. Globalization has its hidden costs, Rick, costs I fear you Americans don't think about enough. Globalization is a great thing for investors, and a great thing for terrorists."

Suddenly he stands up and says, "Let's go in."

The General leads me into his "game room," where there is a large, dusty billiards table. "Snooker," he says. "Care to play?"

"Not my game."

"Too bad. It's good for the nerves. Steady eye, steady hand. There's my dartboard." The General points at a black cork dartboard on the wall with "BOAC Flies the World" printed on it. "Isn't it lovely? Historical artifact. I rescued it from a hotel in Peshawar, Dean's, before the hotel was torn down. They had it in a back room. When things became more . . . ardent in Pakistan it was considered slightly . . . not quite *haraam,* but not really licit, either, with its barroom associations, ideas of foreign frivolity and so on, so they moved it to an inconspicuous place, though they didn't throw it away."

At the far end of the room, the General has a huge wallscreen. He says he watches cricket matches, not much else.

"Will you be in Pakistan for a while?

I tell him a couple more days.

"Come back and see me." He nods significantly. "Really. Do."

Normal World, Real Life

I CALL Frannie in the morning, when it's early evening in northern Virginia, and I get her voice mail. She's probably showing a house. Half an hour later she calls back. She sounds muffled, and there's some voice delay, maybe half a second—that Internet SIM card—but it's Frannie. "Hey," she says.

"Hey." I've told her that I am in Pakistan and that beyond that I won't say much. So she does the talking. She didn't pick up my call immediately because she was out on a sale, but she's home now.

"The buyers—the Benners—are a young couple, no kids. He's a software guy, Bill, nice enough. Her name's Ronnie and she teaches Social Sciences, whatever that is, I think it's history, at Washington and Lee High School, and is a lot more outgoing. Very fun in fact. No kids yet. First-time house for them. I have to explain everything: loans, appraisals, money down, the whole nine yards."

And I think America, normal world, real life. "They like what they're seeing?"

"Well, their price range is okay, and we've got a lot on market just now, and with prices way down . . ."

Frannie proceeds to tell me about the Benners and her late afternoon sales tour with them, hauling them around in her Chevrolet, then says, "You okay?"

I know that's not just a routine question, though she makes it sound like one. She means physical danger, but doesn't want to say it.

"Yeah, I'm okay. Been running around." I give her the usual neutral facts.

Then I remember she told me once about showing a house to a single guy who was big and a little weird-acting just to start out with, and they're alone in this huge house on a huge lot, way back from the street, and the owners hadn't moved out yet and the furniture is still in the house, and as they're walking through, checking the rooms, she's more and more uncomfortable with the guy, the way the he's giving her looks, sizing her up, and finally they're in the master bedroom, and he comes on to her there, not strongly enough to call the police afterward—he doesn't lay a finger on her—but making suggestions, pushing into her space, getting between her and the bedroom door, and scary, definitely scary.

I'm glad it's a young couple. I don't tell her that, I tell her I love her and we sign off.

This evening I return to the General's. He's left a message at the hotel desk. He wants to talk.

"There's No Knowing Them"

"LAHORE PRECISION Engineering," the General says. We are seated once again under the big eucalyptus tree, talking softly, sipping Johnnie Walker. "I have made some inquiries. It is closed off. It is a black firm. It was once used by Dr. Khan for his scientific and engineering purchases." He means Khan's nuclear smuggling, deals with Iran and Libya, and general commercial shiftiness. "LPE still exists in some legal form today, I think under the Ministry of Defense, some office here in Islamabad. They are folded into ISI, however, and there's no knowing them—not who they are, not what they're doing. To contact them you must go through the ISI. You can't look them up in the phone book. Quite black."

"How do you know this?"

"I know it. Just listen."

The General is not telling me this for the money, though it is appropriate for him to be paid, and he will be. He is, of course, screwing someone, or trying to—the Islamists, I'm guessing, since they are the people who got him cashiered. The General will not tell me how he found any of this out. I will simply report it, sourced, to Fiscarelli.

The General says, "The company is under the direction of a man named Dr. Sajid. Ahmed Sajid. He is an engineer. He was a protégé of Dr. Khan. He was some kind of commercial representative for Khan back when Khan was riding high. Now he is working alone inside the Ministry of Defense.

"I would see Dr. Sajid from time to time in the '90s. We were 'friends'

so-called. Dr. Sajid, fuck him in the ass, is religious. Some time ago he became abstemious of alcohol and stopped his womanizing, which had become something of a scandal in various circles. They had parties in Lahore
back then with whiskey and prostitutes, and I think it was while working
with Khan that Sajid underwent a change of heart and became a devout
Muslim, very pure, with Islamist leanings. They, the Islamists, have a lar-
gish group in the Army and in the nuclear establishment. PAEC claims to
weed these people out, but don't believe it. They cannot be 'weeded out,'
they are too many and too clever, and have too many friends in the structure. Sajid also has a nephew, I can't recall the name, who is a great fellow
in Jund al-Haqq. You know the group? They are revolutionary Islamists.
They play the al-Qaeda game. They undergo military training in the
Tribal Areas and are thick with the Taliban in Afghanistan. They are illegal, though they have much support in ISI. The main thing is, Sajid's connected to them by blood. Remember that.

"Sajid was most contemptuous of the Iranians, by the way, odd in a man
who worked with Khan, but he had no use for them, didn't like them. I
suppose it was religious prejudice."

"Didn't stop him from dealing with them."

"Business is not theology."

L EAVING THE General's, I decide to walk back to my hotel. I turn into
a narrow side street of apartments and small businesses. The street is
dimly lit by one yellowish lamp. Far up ahead, one hundred yards or so, I
can see a well-lighted street with traffic passing back and forth.

Then I hear, "Sir, we don't want you here. Sir, you are up to no good.
You are from America. You are against us."

In the dim light of the street lamp I am being confronted.

Two men. I don't know where they've come from. They've caught up
with me from behind. They are wearing *chitrali* caps and gray *shalwar
kameez*. They have untrimmed beards. Islamists. One is wearing a beige
vest. He has thick wrists and hands, and looks like a manual laborer. He
looks away from me to the other man and starts talking in Urdu. His voice
is rough and hoarse. It sounds as if he has a cold. His companion is slightly
built, with a thin angular face and answers him, glancing my way, in a
high-pitched voice. They decide to walk along with me, one on each side.

Far down the way two military policemen armed with AKs stare at us. They know I'm getting hassled. They watch the scene, seems fine to them.

Now a third man in a green *shalwar kameez* comes from behind, swiftly moves in front of me blocking my way. They seem to know each other. "Why are you here?" he asks. "What do you want in Pakistan?"

I don't answer. I push past him, keep walking, heading for the cross street and traffic. It's a good fifty yards away.

As we walk along fourth man comes out of a shop, a small bookstore. He is young, fine-featured, dark, clean shaven. I can't tell if he knows the men who are hassling me. "Are you American?" he asks. "I like Americans. We like Americans." You can hear the hate, see the anger in his eyes. "Mrs. Bhutto, she was Made In America. Look at *her*. We liked *her* a lot."

The man in the green *shalwar kameez* is now on my right side. He says, "We like Musharref. We like him, too." He starts touching my arm, tentatively at first, then his touches turn to a grip. I jerk my arm away, he doesn't give up. He begins touching again, then tries to grip. I elbow him hard.

"Asshole," I say, teeth clenched.

On my other side the man with the rough hands says, "You come with us."

"No."

"Yes. Oh, yes."

I wrench my arm again from the grip of Green Man. The man with rough hands smiles and again says in his hoarse voice, "Yes, you will come." I feel hands on my arms. There are four of them. They are pushing me toward a parked pickup truck. They have no weapons I can see.

I punch at Green Man, catch him in the face. The slightly built boy springs back away from me, stands and smiles. The young man in front of me cocks his head, moves out of my way as I push back. He begins smiling too. As I leave the four of them, they take to laughing fake-uproariously, a kind of show.

The policemen with the AKs turn away and talk something over between themselves. Fun over.

I VISIT the General again the next evening, but he simply repeats his rant against the Indians and the Islamists. He has nothing more to say about

LPE or Ahmed Sajid. I raise the subject delicately with some people I know—an ISI officer, a journalist, a professor of political science, but learn nothing new. I've kept Fiscarelli informed of all this. We decide I've been hanging around too much. Time to leave.

HQ: Ahmed Sajid Rang Some Bells

OPCOM/NPTG Session Audiotape, Session 46 (Excerpted).

Attending: J. Gutman (Chair), M. Fiscarelli, C. Lindquist, S. Kremer, R. Eisenberg.

Transcriber: D. Braithewaite.

Mr. Fiscarelli: On Sajid, this stuff . . .

Ms. Eisenberg: Yes, right. On Sajid we have the biodata, at least what we know about him which is pretty slim, in NPTG 24/145, which is part of our discussion package today. It's on page twelve. Engineer, nuclear expertise. Trained in Germany. Somebody met him in 1992, wrote up a 201 on him, and we're basing almost everything on that. Disappeared, or so we thought, after the Khan network got rolled up, this was like 2003, 2004. We've looked and haven't been able to find him. NSA has gotten no electronic take. I mean, it's extraordinary how he's just jumped off the face of the earth. The Pakistanis have been no help. He's apparently a very sensitive issue with them.

Mr. Gutman: Meaning he's got influential pals.

Ms. Eisenberg: Yes, or perhaps simply his position in the Pakistani nuclear program keeps them from cooperating with us on this. In any case we've gotten nowhere with them, but here he is and our source in Islamabad connects him with the company on the CASTLE DVD, Lahore Precision. And this is scary, connects him with Jund al-Haqq, a major terrorist group about which frankly we know little.

Mr. Gutman: [Expletive]. Well, he's nukes and he's worked with the Iranians, and if Jund al-Haqq is in the picture [expletive]. It's all vague and hearsay, but obviously we need some follow-up on this, on this Sajid bird.

Mr. Lindquist: If I could put in here, we do have other fish to fry, you can't tell how allocating much in the way of resources to a company that's gone dormant, hasn't done anything since 2004 will pan out, including this guy, this Sajid, who may simply not have been doing anything that would attract attention. Just something to think about.

Mr. Gutman: That's so, but as Rhoda says . . .

Ms. Eisenberg: Carl, Sajid just leaps out at you. When I say nothing, I mean nothing. You can't locate the guy these days. That's just weird.

Mr. Gutman: Let's all agree we need to know here. I say a limited effort. Mike, your take?

Mr. Fiscarelli: One idea. CASTLE, of course, is no stranger to the Pak scene, and he got us the DVD, the recent information on Lahore Precision and Sajid. And that potential Jund al-Haqq connection. We could work up a thing with him. It would make sense.

HEU: "Significant Technical Weapons"

EVENING IN the desert, some twenty miles southeast of Dubai in the United Arab Emirates. A group of wealthy men have driven down to this informal campsite in their Range Rovers, Lexuses, and BMWs. They've left the tree-lined superhighway and driven a kilometer or so into the desert, and have parked their vehicles in a semicircle near a campfire attended by servants. The sky is deep blue and cloudless. A breeze is picking up from the southwest. On the western horizon the dying sun is glowing orange.

The men come here frequently for a *dowra,* an informal circle of friends who meet to discuss issues that interest them, primarily religious and political. They are merchants, bankers, attorneys, and currency changers—men named Khalid, Rasheed, Saleh, who know each other well. As they alight from their vehicles they greet one other with kisses, one occasionally lingering with another, softly intertwining their fingers, chatting. Some stroll and talk, others sit eating oranges and dates on wide Persian carpets spread on the sand. They are wearing white *thowbs* and red-and-white checked *kaf-fiyehs.*

This evening is special. They are awaiting a guest, a Pakistani named Amin Tajer.

As the sun is going down they see from the south, from the direction of the vast blank called The Empty Quarter, a faint light, which as they watch slowly dissociates into a number of distinct lights, weaving over the low dunes, becoming finally the bright blue-white headlights of a caravan of four Range Rovers.

The caravan stops opposite the circle of automobiles from Dubai. From the first vehicle a man alights carrying an AK-47, and looks around, fiercely scanning the silent audience. More men alight from the other vehicles, each carrying an AK-47, each scanning the group.

Finally, the guest, Tajer, a large and round-faced man in his forties, gets down from the rear seat of the third Range Rover and, accompanied by two bodyguards, approaches the group. He is greeted by the leader of the *dowra*, and is led toward the gathering, where in the flickering light of the campfire the two circulate among the other men, who greet Tajer with deference.

The leader of the *dowra*, a youngish man with a smooth manner, is a well-established member of the Dubai business community. He is a banker and though a Sunni Arab, his family has ancient ties to Iran. To the others, who are all seated now on the Persian carpets, he says, "You know who our honored guest is. He is, God be praised, a leader in the jihad. He is a man of courage and a man of steadfastness. He is also a man of education and knowledge. As you know he conducts the struggle in Afghanistan and Pakistan, but you may not know that he has lived in Spain and has traveled in France and Germany. He has studied in Germany and has gotten a university degree from there. His presence tonight honors us, and we welcome him."

Tajer begins to speak in English to his hushed audience, who know why he has come and something of what he will say. "I come to you from Pakistan, and from the valiant group Jund al-Haqq. I seek your help."

Tajer speaks first of Iraq and how the Americans are losing there to the forces of Islam. He talks of Israel and of the Zionists, of the Israeli wars in Lebanon, of the Israeli occupation of Arab lands, the Israeli seige of Gaza, and the Israeli oppression of Muslims there. He speaks of America's support for Israel and the Jews.

Then he says, "I'm sorry that there were no significant technical weapons in the planes that attacked New York and Washington." Tajer does not say "nuclear" or "chemical" weapons, preferring euphemism, but his listeners know what he means.

"By God, to defeat the Americans, to chase them from our lands is taking years and is requiring terrible work. Therefore, it is necessary to attack the United States with something more. To war on the Americans, we must form special brigades. We must make small groups. They should have a high technical knowledge. They should understand technological weapons, know to use such weapons on offensive operations. Just as the Americans are massacring Muslims using technological means we must be capable of conducting technological attacks on the Americans in their homes. We need above all a leader, one who knows science.

"We are fortunate for we have such a man in our struggle. They call him the Muhandis—the Engineer. He is educated. He is clever. He has been abroad and has studied there, and he knows the things the foreigners know. He knows their languages. He is a man not young, not old. He is working with Jund al-Haqq and is an honored member. He is with the government though he is opposed to the government. He is a great scholar and teacher. He is a pious Muslim. He is a great soldier, a hero of Pakistan and of the jihad. And he is an enemy of the the unbelievers. He uses his knowledge to the utmost to fight for the defense of of Islam, and to repel the Crusaders. He also fights for the honor of Islam.

"I know him. I've seen him recently, though because of the nature of the current regime in Pakistan, may God overturn and crush it, he must live and travel covertly. I can assure you he is at work.

"These days the Muhandis comes and goes. You can't follow him. He has friends, places to go, places to stay. You can't know where. Perhaps he is in Dubai in an apartment, perhaps in a village mosque in Pakistan. Perhaps he is gone to a foreign country, to England, to America."

Tajer ends his talk with an appeal for funds for the jihad.

The members of the *dowra* rise one by one, approach Tajer, and kiss his hand. Some make pledges of support, some deliver cash there on the spot, which subordinates collect in leather briefcases.

Then Tajer gets into one of his Range Rovers, and the convoy drives into the desert, the glowing taillights growing fainter until finally they disappear.

HQ: FLATTOP

OPCOM/NPTG Session Audiotape, Session 49 (Excerpted).

Attending: J. Gutman (Chair), M. Fiscarelli, C. Lindquist, S. Kremer, R. Eisenberg.

Transcriber: D. Braithewaite.

Mr Gutman: International Financial Crimes has sent over the report. On the desert meeting?

Ms. Eisenberg: Right. FLATTOP reports a large meeting of wealthy Islamists somewhere out in the desert in Dubai discussing WMD, which is why this got sent over to us. It's chilling if it's true.

Mr. Fiscarelli: FLATTOP, let me say, source FLATTOP is a plugged-in banker in Dubai. Very long relationship with us. Pretty reliable. We give him about eighty percent. FLATTOP was not on the scene, but heard some information, fairly specific, about what transpired there. Just hearsay, but FLATTOP has been accurate.

Ms. Eisenberg: And FLATTOP heard a Jund al-Haqq big-shot was there?

Mr. Fiscarelli: Correct. Major guy. Does not know, FLATTOP does not know who it was. Good speaker, the kind that goes around giving pep talks.

Ms. Eisenberg: Evidently there were pledges and actual cash contributions to Jund al-Haqq?

Mr. Fiscarelli: Correct. According to FLATTOP the money went to the Hassan Reza Trading Group—young Hassan Ali Reza himself was supposedly standing there and collecting the cash personally in a company briefcase.

Ms. Eisenberg: Disgusting.

Mr. Gutman: Where it goes nobody knows. Dubai ruling family won't do anything about this. Major political problem for them, which they will do their best to ignore. We will not get help on this from them.

"Shooting the Wounded"

LATE NIGHT, lights out. We're in front of the fireplace in Frannie's living room, lying side by side, half-embraced on her thin rug and listening to the burning logs snap and hiss. We are buck naked.

Frannie pulls at my hand, kisses it lightly, then puts it on her left breast, holding it there. "Missed you," she says. "I mean, you *can* pull a disappearing act! Funny to see you one day and get a call from you from who-knows-where the next." She moves her head in my direction, though still looking at the fire. "Not complaining, just remarking. I mean, you do call, after all. Any trips planned for the near future, or do I get to keep you for a while?"

"Nothing on the docket." But, of course, that's usually the case.

"Ummm. So nice to be alone. Just us in here and all that world out there. Great for recharging. I get burned out. I need regular down time. Especially," she says, "with my handsome and mysterious Rick."

Frannie says she's an introvert. Hard to believe, she's so outgoing and bubbly, and when you think about the trade she's in. But I know what she means.

"When Jim was headed overseas, our first foreign posting, Manila, we had to take classes in socializing, if you can believe that—how to be 'engaging,' 'courtesy in listening,' 'eye contact'—that kind of thing. They taught it at the Foreign Service Institute and it was really, really dumb.

"Did you know we naturally look people in the left eye when we're talking with them? That's what they say. And we should because it's the natural thing to do, but they told us if you want to freak people, concentrate on their right eyes when you're talking with them. Some kind of power thing. Don't do it too often, but if the need arises, do it. It makes them uncomfortable, but they don't quite know why. Increases your own confidence. Also, if you're nervous talking with some big high so-and-so, look at his nose—noses are funny, and the guy'll come across silly and vulnerable. I mean, they actually taught that. God, it was so phony.

"They called conversation 'returning the volley.' They told us not to be 'potted plants,' meaning don't just stand in the corner, get out there and work the room. You were supposed to choose a direction—clockwise or counterclockwise, didn't matter—and just keep moving until you hit everyone in the room. Well, I guess I'm just a potted plant by nature 'cause I sure got sick of 'working the room.'

"Jim liked all that. He's not an outgoing kind of guy, not really. He's very private, not at all friendly, but he likes talking to people the way normal people like to read the papers. He says he learns a lot that way, and I guess he does. That's how you become a good spy. You listen. Me, I'd rather just curl up somewhere with a book. Or with a someone." She is smiling up at me, her blond hair darkened and dense in the flickering firelight. At this moment she is as guileless as a child and as vulnerable.

Now she sits up, cross-legged, and in a down-to-business tone, says, "I'm going to get rid of a lot of the junk in this place. Lotta ghosts here. Memories I don't want."

I know what she means. Traces of the marriage. When I exited our Dulany Drive house, Liz repainted the front room a bright vermillion (it had been off-off-white, your standard sale color), filled it with Frenchified furniture, and put over the windows big magenta swags of Arabian Nights–looking cloth—all tulips, viny curleycues, and paisley cypress trees bending in the wind. The bedroom—I've seen it only when visiting the john—is all floradora now, poofy pink and white pillows, with lots of trimming, and pink sheets. ("I don't have to worry about your damn shoes or newspapers on the bed anymore.") White wicker chairs and dresser.

Liz to Rick: You're out.

Divorce is the loss of a kind of life. You say good-bye to the material objects—some of them anyway—that surrounded you, things you acquired over the years, things with a history, tangible memory, who you are in a way, and you have to start over.

I moved into a walled, though not gated, development of brick town houses—Hampton Court, it's called—just off Old Dominion Drive, where I still live. It's close to Marge's place, though that's not why I moved there, and not far from Global Reach. CIA is close by, just up Dolley Madison, and is well represented in Hampton Court. I know at least three Agency employees living in this enclosed little fortress.

Not far to the south is Pimmit Hill, tracts of modest little houses, where my boyhood buddy Bobby Ringgenberg lived. Bobby, at age thirteen, was the first of my friends to have actual sexual intercourse—the real thing, boy on top, pumping away—with overdeveloped, none too bright, Linda Quandt. Bobby was the first of us to smoke cigarettes, also at age thirteen. By the time he was fifteen Bobby was drinking beer and smoking pot, the same year he stole a car and wrecked it. Never got caught for that. He joined the Army right out of high school and made it a career. The Army straightened him out. He married a good wife he met in Texas and had three children. He drowned in Iraq south of Baghdad when his Hummer slid into a canal, turning over and trapping him under it.

In my Hampton Court bachelor pad I tried to make a new life. I started with a bed (no headboard, minimal linens), a La-Z-Boy chair, and a lamp. Instead of furniture, I bought gear—a humongous flat-panel TV, a stereo, a slim little silver laptop, a professional's camera I never use.

I made it a place for Pennie and Sam, too. I furnished and equipped a room for them, though they don't like sharing it, even putting in a stereo for them—mistake of course, they prefer their iPods—plus ethernet hookups. I keep a supply of Kotex in there for Sam, who's begun to need it. When they come over they bring their own makeup in little overnight bags—as with cell phones, I don't really approve; Pennie looks like a little whore when she's gotten herself painted. I follow up on schoolwork, on their projects, on homework that's due Monday—I do all of this, trying to make a life as a divorced father.

"Putting the end to a marriage is like shooting the wounded," Frannie says. She doesn't think of her sundering from Jimbo as any kind of victory or liberation. No kids, years that add up to nothing—she regards the divorce as basically a final defeat after a bad war, and I have no words of wisdom or comfort that would suggest otherwise. Same boat in a way, though I brought the divorce down on myself.

SCI TOP SECRET GREEN SCI TOP SECRET GREEN SCI TOP SECRET GREEN SCI TOP SECRET GREEN SCI

OPCOM/NPTG Session Audiotape, Session 50 (Excerpted).

Attending: J. Gutman (Chair), M. Fiscarelli, C. Lindquist, S. Kremer, R. Eisenberg.

Transcription: D. Braithewaite.

Mr. Gutman: Okay, word in on Pakistan, Afghanistan operations. DIA numbskulls have been through these countries trying to do HUMINT. They have successfully [expletive] a number of our operations. I'm not privy to the details, they don't come under our portfolio, but D/CIA is [expletive]. D/CIA hath protested to ODNI and has been told DIA and DOD activities are in accord with current guidelines. That's a direct quote. Now then, a bunch of these DIA yahoos are outside contractors.

Mr. Lindquist: Who used to work for us.

Mr. Gutman: Yes, many did, and you'd think they'd be smarter. But as I say, the nonofficial DIA personnel have compromised some CIA ops, maybe beyond recovery. We are having our own problems with outside contractors running amok. Some of you know some of the cases. Anyhow, it has been decided on high at ODNI that until things get straightened out, until we get a better handle on who does what, and what's rational here and what isn't, we are to curtail temporarily our outside and nonofficial work in Pakistan, Afghanistan . . .

Mr. Kremer: [Expletive].

Mr. Gutman: Pakistan, Afghanistan, Turkey, and the Persian Gulf area. I repeat, outside and nonofficial agents are to be curtailed since these are the people who are making problems. The personnel in question are agents involved in securing HUMINT. Other contractors—matériel suppliers, transport, most COMINT work—continue as before. As to DOD, their people get a pass because these countries, areas, are considered a war zone. DNI in his wisdom has so decreed and has sent said decree on to the D/CIA. Memo from D/CIA to OPCOM/NPTG 22/0009, me, just came through this morning. Want to read it? Take a look.

Mr. Fiscarelli: Jack, this is crazy. I'd simply point out that we have a number of outside nonofficial contractors currently falling under that definition and who are in fact doing good work, including one I'm personally handling and whom we've discussed here frequently, CASTLE. CASTLE is doing . . .

Mr. Gutman: CASTLE, no matter what his current work may be, has got to retract from the South Asian theater—Afghanistan, Pakistan, as well as work in the Gulf. Also Turkey. He cannot do that.

Mr. Fiscarelli: Well, that's just crazy.

Mr. Gutman: Yesterday when I got wind that something like this was coming down, which I am told is temporary, I tried to make the case with the Director that ongoing operations that show promise should be allowed to proceed. I got nixed. Look, people, I don't write the rules around here. We slog through no matter how deep the swamp or dark the night.

Ms. Eisenberg: Jack, this is really, really unfortunate and dispiriting. We are close to putting together a good study of Pakistani nuclear communications infrastructure plus purchasing operations. Nobody else is on top of this.

Mr. Gutman: Correct. And the greenbadger and other informal field work on it is now on hold. Regular operations can proceed and, of course, analysis here can proceed.

Ms. Eisenberg: We should protest.

Mr. Gutman: Been done, as I say, verbally yesterday and also in writing this morning soon after I got the memo. So a protest has been lodged. Formally. Don't bet on a fast or favorable response. Anyhow, upshot: Any contracted nonofficial operations in the Afghan-Pak realm are on hold till further notice. Same for the Gulf and Turkey. India's not a problem.

Ms. Eisenberg: But they're the people, DOD are the people who're causing all this, not us, and yet we have to pull back.

Mr. Gutman: Correct again. Right. I'm telling you, [expletive] you just think, I mean, when I joined, when, Mike, Rhoda, when we joined up . . .

Ms. Eisenberg: What?

Mr. Gutman: [Expletive], when we joined up this Agency used to be called Central.

"You Crazy, Mike?"

"RICK?"

"Yeah?"

"Ernie."

It is seven-thirty in the evening. Coltrane's on the stereo doing "Lush Life," and I am sitting in an after-dinner sated mood of well-being, thinking of not much. It takes me a sec to figure out who it is: Fiscarelli on my land-line home phone. Never done. Caller ID shows "UNAVAILABLE," which means I know not what, could be a cell, could be a pay phone in Kansas. Why is Fiscarelli such an asshole?

"Like to have a talk somewhere," he says. "ASAP. You got time?"

"Jesus. Kind of short notice. You mean right *now*?"

"Good time as any. How about that place we been? Know the one? I'll buy if it makes you feel better."

He's talking in code. We have met twice outside Egerton Associates, both times at a Gordon Biersch, a chain "brewery" in the Tysons Corner mall, where Fiscarelli shunned the beer and stuck to gin martinis. The place is ideal—very noisy and if we get crowded by other clientele we can easily go for a private walk and talk among the crowds.

Fiscarelli's serious. Something's going on. "Yeah," I say.

" 'Bout an hour?"

"Jesus. Yeah, sure."

THERE'S A problem with contractors," he says. "I can't go into it too much. But certain contractors supposedly have to be . . . ah, restrained from operating in certain countries. Pakistan, Gulf states among them. Also Turkey."

" 'Certain contractors'?"

"Meaning you."

I think of that large, florid-faced American lunching with Charley Phelps in the embassy in Pakistan. I think of his company, Talltree Security Services. "Turf war," I say.

"Well, I just can't go into it. I'm sure it's temporary. We will get things straightened out. But I want you to keep going. On the LPE stuff. Pakistan, anywhere else that looks good."

We're at a table for two in what they call "the patio" in the Gordon Biersch. Fiscarelli's not in his usual funeral outfit—he's doing casual this evening, a light blue parka, corduroys, gray wool-knit cap. The patio is a fenced-in area on the main mall promenade. Four wall TVs are showing a 'Skins game, and the sound is up.

Fiscarelli eyes an ordinary-looking young woman—brown hair, black top, brown slacks, black walking shoes—who is holding a silver iPhone in front of her face and is walking in circles past us, saying, "Hi . . . hi . . . hi . . . hi . . . No . . . no . . . no . . . no . . . Hiya . . . hiya . . . hiya . . ." She's speaking to no one, not even her iPhone. She's the mall equivalent of a street crazy. Fiscarelli watches her break out of her circle and wander off.

"We'll run your work just like any other op. Just the same, exactly, except we can't meet in Bethesda, not on this stuff anyhow, and we can't do the regular commo."

Egerton Associates has a taping system. That's why we're sitting in this shopping mall brewery. Fiscarelli doesn't want anything recorded.

"You crazy, Mike?"

"Maybe. But you're the honcho on this stuff, on this Sajid. We pull you, we're blind on the guy. I've bitched at headquarters about how this project is worth doing and about how these blanket edicts are screwing us. To no avail. Listen, I've thought it through. We can do it. You're a free agent. Nobody owns you. You are self-employed. You want to go somewhere on business you go. Nobody can stop you. Expenses? There's money in the Geneva account. Plenty. You can use it. Nobody's keeping track there. Just keep going. Want to?"

"What the hell do you mean nobody's keeping track?"

"It'll all come out in the wash. Trust me."

"They find anything funny, you got troubles."

"That's my problem, I'll deal with it."

"Might turn out to be my problem, too. And what do we do with the product? How do we handle collection?"

"Hey, we'll set up a new Yahoo account. Any info you get—reports, data, matériel, whatever—you turn it over to me and I'll deal with it. The meetings, we run them like now—you call Suitland and ask for Ernie. Same deal with the days and times and stuff, we'll just meet outside the Bethesda site."

"They log those calls?"

"They do, but they do it stupidly, and I'll handle it, never mind. Every time we meet we'll set the next venue."

"Other people at Langley? Somebody might . . ."

"Langley. There's . . . that's not something to worry about. Don't worry."

Fiscarelli's got other people in on this, you can tell. In his mind he's ginned up an op against ODNI. Proceeding like this—doing the forbidden—I would never have expected of a straight-out-of-the-mold, government-issue bureaucrat like Fiscarelli. Serious Agency operations have involved documentation. Everything they do, all the tricks of their trade—the phone taps, observation posts, surveillance teams, travel control, agent recruitment, use of access agents, COMINT operations, agreements with other services, and, of course, financial accounts—all are meticulously documented at HQ and included in the OPDESC. What we do, if we do it, will be . . . call it *ad hoc*.

And when an officer is in a dangerous situation—meeting a killer in the back room of a restaurant, breaking into a building in the dead of night— he's never alone, he's got backup, somebody out there watching over things. If I go it alone with Mike, I won't.

Edge.

"Look, you're a guy on a contract who does us favors," Fiscarelli says. "That's all. You know stuff, you learn about people—we debrief you. You buy stuff, we collect it. That's been the deal. We will just keep on doing it."

Fiscarelli will tell them he's got a special source . . . or he'll tell them it's word on the street . . . rumor in the souk. That's how he'll play it. They polygraph him, he'll pass. The issue won't even come up.

Fiscarelli says, "Now on this Sajid, he's a major thing. Your General may not know the half of it." Fiscarelli smiles tightly at the corners of his mouth. "By the way, I knew him." My jaw drops. "Oh, yeah. Met him long back—Helsinki, 1992—before all the Khan stuff came out. Nuke conference. I was a twerp, new hire, and they were sending me around to learn stuff. Well, he gave a talk on the peaceful uses of nuclear power in less developed countries. It was a huge joke though I didn't know it—at the very time he was talking peaceful nukes he was on a buying trip for Khan.

"The guy's very smart. And nationalistic. It's a big deal with him. When India set off its bomb in 1974, Sajid was one of the first guys in Pakistan to get up and demand that the Pak government make its own bomb. He was into it. Very committed. And got in on the ground floor. Worked in secret with Khan. He was a major player in the Khan network. He traveled all over—Germany, Netherlands, Canada—bought parts for the program. It was Sajid who put together this big network of companies, all the secret Pak purchasing firms and their foreign suppliers.

"We know for sure—we got it well documented—Sajid worked with North Koreans and Libyans. And particularly with the Iranians. The Iranian nuke program? You can thank Sajid for that. He sold them the P–1 centrifuges and helped install them."

Fiscarelli sips at his martini, glances at the wall TV over my shoulder—somewhere out in the American night a crowd is yelling like crazy—then looks back at me. "Anyhow, that's the idea. Want to or not? This Sajid business, I'm telling you, it's nukes. Sajid was a protegé of Khan, and he's gone under, disappeared, but he's still doing stuff. Something nonkosher's going on here and I want to know what the hell it is."

And so in fact do I. Like Walt, I suppose.

Mike tells me he'll give me some lists of questions, lists of people I ought to talk to. When I tell Mike I have my own list he doesn't ask about them.

"I Have a Stupid Fellow"

THE GENERAL'S young servant Safar has come to my hotel in Islamabad with a written note from the General. "I have a stupid fellow. You must come and listen to him. Urgent. I will drop by. Be in the traffic circle downstairs. Fifteen minutes."

He sent Safar because his phone's bugged. In this country you cannot tell which part of the government is bugging you, or where their sympathies lie. Makes it difficult.

THE GENERAL'S driver takes us down the main road toward Rawalpindi. The country here is dry and scrubby and is a pale buff color. Barbed wire fencing runs along the road to our left. Beyond the fencing you can see nothing—just gently hilly land and low-growing, woody brush, and far in the distance dun-colored hills.

We pass a caravan of military trucks, their lights on, also heading south. The trucks are full of soldiers and each truck is towing a howitzer. I count fifteen trucks, a major presence. The General tells me it's the usual thing these days. "Since Madame Bhutto's death."

After a time we turn into an opening in the fencing, a kind of gate, topped with a sign in Urdu and under it, in English, PAKISTAN HOME DEFENCE FORCES CAMP, and drive over a metaled two-lane road to a solitary checkpoint made of sandbags where two soldiers salute us and wave us past. The checkpoint simply straddles the road and has the look of the newly built and improvisatory. Anyone could simply drive around it.

THE GENERAL escorts me into a large hall, where, just inside, a guard stomps his right foot and brings his hand up to his forehead, palm out, in an old-fashioned, British-style salute. The General pushes a small button near the door and presently down the hall a junior officer appears, salutes, and nods silently to the General.

"These are tip-top officers here," the General says, "not Taliban sympathizers or Islamists. They continue to respect me. Now, this fellow was arrested and transferred to military authority under lawful order." Then he says quietly, "You'll like this. Come along."

He leads me into a long, dark room. At the very end of it a tiny red glow moves up, down, up again, pulsates. Down there at the end of the room someone is smoking. I smell opium. As my eyes get used to the darkness, I see a skinny, youngish man lying back in a large chair, one of four around a coffee table.

The General and I approach. The young man's long hair is down in his face. His eyes are lost somewhere. He is wearing Western clothing, a silky shirt, tight gray trousers.

"A friend of mine," the General says to the young man, poking at his shoulder. "This is Mr. Richard." Then to me: "Sit sit sit."

The young man looks at me, but says nothing.

On the table sits a small cassette recorder plugged into a wall socket.

THE GENERAL turns on the recorder. "Talk, you."

"*Mera nam . . .*"

"English, you idiot!" the General snaps, and slaps the young man's face lightly. He turns to me and says, "He is so far gone," then back to the young man, "Come, come, come, dear fellow, be a man. Let's have it. Start with your name."

The young man brushes his hair out of his face. "My name is Rizwan."

"Rizwan what?"

"Rizwan Aziz."

"What do you do?"

"I am an engineer."

"What sort?"

"Mechanical. Master of Science, Punjab Technical University."

"Employed?"

"No."

"Why not?"

"I was redundant."

"Liar!"

"My work was not what . . ."

"You are an addict, a heroin addict, and your work is shit. Admit it."

Rizwan ducks his head, not looking at the General. The General says, "For a time this fellow was sleeping in the corner of a vacant lot—*weren't you?*—between a bank and a tractor repair shop. His family disowned him for the dishonor. And I don't blame them. And who would come by, Mr. Aziz? Who?"

Rizwan stares away blankly.

The General says, "A sister. Sometimes. And she would drop off food. She was supposedly breaking some family rule, but I think they allowed her to bend it."

"Bad times. I'm ashamed," Rizwan says. His speech is slurred, as if his tongue is in the way. "I was a good engineer."

The General says, "We know that."

"I know the whole Windows XP. I was power user, goddamn. I did a lot."

"You did."

Rizwan blows air. "Opium—you smoke it, you go for days without food. I worked over there in Tararpur. That's why I started the opium. Tararpur is a goddamn city. Because of the opium, they put me in jail. It was very bad, the jail. My friend in the jail, Mr. Gailani, he was Taliban, from over the border, over there in Afghanistan. But he was a *heroinchi,* and he wanted someone to smoke with him. He got heroin in the jail, no problem, so we smoked it there. I became a *heroinchi* like my friend. We leave the jail, he was shot. There was a fight between the dope people. He was there. They shot him, I don't know, lot of dope people, somebody shot him. He didn't do anything. Just was there, just standing there. Mr. Gailani, where is he? He's dead." Rizwan begins to weep quietly.

The General says, "This fellow is the son of a cousin of mine. He was born in Lahore. Fifth of six children. Father, civil engineer. Works for the Water Authority, the father. Went to a private school for privileged little boys. Got a cheap local degree. He was very talented. Rising young fellow, attracted attention. Promised in marriage. Didn't want to marry the girl. Didn't want to marry any girl. Right? Doesn't like girls, right?"

Rizwan stares at the General.

The General smiles. "Are you hungry, Mr. Aziz?" The General looks at me. "He doesn't want food, he wants money." He looks back at Rizwan. "I can get you money, Mr. Aziz, have no concern. Now, tell me, where had you been working?"

"Tararpur Reactor Complex."

"Power generator," the General says to me, though keeping his eyes on Rizwan, "central Sindh province. Dreadful place, Tararpur, but enough water. Also well-located to feed our electrical grid. Doing what?"

"Working on water control problems."

"Who fired you? Who was the man? What was he like?"

"He's an educated man. In Germany. Not Pakistan. U.S. Yeah, sure. His name. Sajid. His name is Dr. Sajid."

"Sajid? Who's Sajid, Mr. Aziz?"

Rizwan's face goes clever. "Oh, Dr. Sajid," he says. "He's a big man. Engineer. Ahmed Sajid. They are a group. It is not one man."

"How many men?"

"Six, seven."

"Who are they?"

"Their names?"

"Yes, fool."

Rizwan recites Pakistani names and titles in his slurred, singsongy way.

"They meet for discussions. Islamic topics. They say they are Sufi mystics. But they are not."

"How do you know this?"

He looks at the General slyly. "I know."

"You spied."

Rizwan smiles. "They have a group. Funny group. They come around. You see them in Tararpur."

"You were with them."

Silence.

"Until they kicked your arse out of the group." To me the General says, "They thought he would be useful—his engineering, his computer work et cetera. But you weren't useful, were you, you little man? Oh oh oh, my poor cousin Hassan, the father of this idiot. You, these engineers, what did they discuss besides God?"

"Things, technical things. The need to create an *umma,* to arm and defend the *umma.*"

"You mean political things. What you are saying is *political.*"

"Yes, but also technical."

"Idiot."

As we are leaving the General says, "His family informed me of his condition, as to what he's been up to and where he's been et cetera, and I put two and two together. He claims this is all he knows, which may in fact be so, he is so stupid. It was easy to get it out of him. He has wants. I see that they are fulfilled. Temporary arrangement. He will go back to sleeping in his vacant lot. Here." The General snaps the tape cassette out of its player and gives it to me.

O N OUR way back to Islamabad the General says, "This Sajid is a dangerous man. We had many discussions. I remember he once spoke of what he called an 'Islamic Bomb.' He was speaking in a theoretical way, like a college boy discussing God and the universe with his mates, and he asked me what did I think of producing such a device? Something not under the control of a state, like Iran or Pakistan; something that would be under the control of a religiously pure organization with religiously pure motivations. The Iranians, our own government, he would say, would simply use nuclear weapons for typical statist reasons—for prestige and influence over others et cetera, perhaps as deterrence against attack, or as retaliation if attacked with nuclear weapons by some other state. But no state will ever truly act on behalf of Islam, he would say, not our Pakistani state, not the Iranians. No state will defend the Islamic *umma.* His eyes glowed when he talked this way of acquiring a nuclear weapon and defending the *umma.* Glowed! I think by that time he had lost his marbles. I told him it was rubbish. But of course he did not listen to me."

I N MY hotel I lie on the bed, TV on, sound down. Jay Leno is speaking to a sexy woman with long blond hair, both are laughing at something. I am thinking of the *umma,* of nukes and jihadis.

Once in Lahore an engineer friend of mine, a Pakistani telephone guy, said—I think jokingly at first, but then things got serious—"I know some jihadis. I wonder what you would make of one if you met and had a chat? Would you like to meet one? It would be safe, I think. These people are well known to the government, they operate quite openly and break no laws in any obvious way. They won't do anything to us. Actually I'm also curious as to what they would make of you. They come into contact with so few foreigners. Call me a matchmaker. Well, would you like to meet one?"

"Yes," I said.

Edge.

"Very well, I'll come round in the evening. We'll go for a walk, catch a cab, and then see."

M Y FRIEND comes by my hotel and we hail a triwheeler at a big inter-section they call Charing Cross, head up to the Delhi Gate, and enter the Old City. In here you catch the smell of rotting fruit and vegetables and dried dung and cooking odors. Strings of electric lights stretch across the fa-cades of the taller buildings, looping down from the second-story balconies. Music is blasting from a record store, and crowds of men shopping, carrying plastic webbed shopping bags, fill the streets. Green pennants with white crescents in their centers strung on ropes are draped across the street from a branch of Habib Bank to a glass-windowed police observation post, empty of police. We pass a blue-tiled mosque—"That is the Wazir Khan Mosque," my friend says. "And there also—see it on our left over there—do you see it?—the Sunehri Mosque." The Sunehri Mosque is smaller, and is set back farther from the street. It has three golden domes. The lights of the minarets are on in the falling dusk. "They are both well under the control of the gov-ernment. Not to worry, not to worry."

Past the Sunehri Mosque we turn south and my friend halts the cab and pays off the driver. From here we walk through the twisting alleys. We're to meet his friends—two jihadis, it seems—in a machine shop somewhere in here. We turn into an electrical supply bazaar, where open shops fronting the lanes display generators, light fixtures, electrical switches, cast-off arma-tures, piles of coiled wire, motors, drive belts, water pumps.

My friend says, "This fellow you are going to meet sells used automo-biles. In an off-hand, informal way. He has no store or showroom. To get customers, he relies on word-of-mouth among his friends and acquain-tances. He's embarrassed, though I don't see why. He makes a living of sorts.

But he says it's a temporary state of affairs, and that he will go on to do other things. Perhaps, but he's been doing this for the last year or so and as far as I can tell he has no other prospects. He and his group of fellows are in league with the Taliban. He is too old to fight, I don't think he's seen action, but does things, he organizes. In here," my friend says. We have arrived at a dimly lit shop with a small, dirty show window called the Haydari Electrical Emporium. Inside we find our contacts, our jihadis.

The older man is much older, in his sixties, I'd say, heavy-set, confident. The younger man isn't even twenty. He has a scraggly mustache and the thin, wispy beginnings of a beard along the lower part of his jaw, not yet up on his cheeks. He is short, thin, and intense, very much under the influence of his friend, like teacher and student.

As the four us sit on the floor and drink *sharbat,* the older man tells me through my friend that he has agreed to meet because he wants to tell me— tell "the Americans"—something. "We have ideology, you have greed," he says. "It is all the difference. We will defend ourselves from you. We have the power to do it. We want to be left alone. We will have the pleasure of driving you from Muslim lands—from Iraq, from Afghanistan, and you will suffer the way you have made us suffer. We are many, you are few." He smiles politely.

It's hard to take the measure of him or his young friend, who says, "We will establish an Islamic government here—here in Pakistan." Then, à propos of nothing, the young man says, "And we will have our atomic bomb. Our own. We will."

"For what purpose?"

"For defense of course."

"Would you use it? In defense?"

"Yes, of course."

The young man's eyes darken. He sits motionless, quietly furious. His older companion notices and nods approvingly. "You must go," the older man says. "You are not wanted here."

The message, as always: Leave us alone.

HQ: The Most Dangerous Man on Earth

OPCOM/NPTG Session Audiotape, Session 53 (Excerpted).

Attending: J. Gutman (Chair), M. Fiscarelli, C. Lindquist, S. Kremer, R. Eisenberg.

Transcriber: D. Braithewaite.

Mr. Kremer: MARLIN, I don't think MARLIN has contributed before.

Mr. Fiscarelli: No, that's right, we've had nothing on this problem from source MARLIN. I can say though this source, MARLIN, is highly reliable, has been operating in various fields for some time. And, beyond that I'd rather not comment.

Mr. Gutman: We're beginning to get take on Sajid, which is good, but I don't like what we're finding, particularly this group at where? Tararpur, that reactor.

Mr. Fiscarelli: If Sajid's involved it's nukes, it's that simple. And his connection to Jund al-Haqq makes him all the more worrisome. These people are not Pakistani nationalists. They may hate Indians, sure, but they're jihadi internationalists. They're rootless, stateless. They have no national loyalties. Their loyalty is to the *umma*. If Sajid's dealing with them, he's gone jihadi.

Ms. Eisenberg: Well, it's just this combination of nuclear expertise and what sounds like jihadism that is so worrying.

Mr. Gutman: Now think about him, this Sajid. Suppose as he experiences a conversion—maybe because of the American war in Iraq or the Americans in Afghanistan—suppose he begins thinking of ultimates. Why is he alive? To do what on this earth? What must be done? He has worked with A. Q. Khan, has been Khan's protégé. He knows the older structure that Khan put together to produce a Pakistani weapon. He has worked with the Iranians, the Libyans, the North Koreans, traded information with them, helped them buy their equipment.

Mr. Fiscarelli: He's beyond being a Pakistani. The nationalist paradigm doesn't describe him. He wants to assemble a weapon outside the control of any state. And he thinks this weapon can be used as threat on behalf of the *umma*. For whatever purpose. Maybe he thinks that with this weapon he can force the withdrawal of what he now calls the Crusaders from what he now calls the Abode of Islam. Maybe he thinks he can do something else, maybe construct a weapon and use it, actually use it.

Ms. Eisenberg: He wants to acquire HEU outside the Pakistani program.

Mr. Kremer: It's craziness.

Mr. Gutman: And we don't know where he is or what he's doing. He's the man who isn't there. Maybe some of the Paks—the Islamists in the military, the security services—are hiding him from the rest of the Paks. Maybe he's changed identities. Maybe he's slipped away into his own shadows. Whatever the case, he's competent. He's a jihadi and he's competent. He is the most dangerous man on earth.

HEU: The Baltistani

THERE.

The target appears—as arranged—on a broad avenue in Islamabad.

Fingering the trigger, keeping his pistol rolled his cloak, a man dressed like a Baltistani—a man from the northern mountains—follows the target, closes in. The target is a Shi'ite male. He is short, has thick black hair, a short beard. He has left his office in the Capital Development Building and is walking east on Suhrawardy Avenue, a secondary business road that parallels Islamabad's main southern avenue, Khiaban-e Kashmir.

The target passes clothing and electronics shops, banks, small hotels. He pauses at a florist's shop.

Saying, "There is no God but God," the man dressed as a Baltistani brings the pistol to Raza Malik's head and fires two shots from inches away, then leaps down from the high walkway onto Suhrawardy and springs into a waiting taxi, which first speeds east on Suhrawardy, then turns north onto Ataturk Avenue, and halts with a jerk.

Two men leap from the taxi to another vehicle, which has been waiting for them and which disappears north.

The driver of the taxi, freed now, but still terrified, falls from his vehicle, picks himself up, hesitates, trembling, not knowing what to do, turns in the street, one way, then another, then finds himself dashing south, waving his arms in terror, and finds a parked police patrol car.

Raza Malik—SLIDER—lies in a pool of his own blood. His heart has ceased pumping.

Direct, Open, Benign Face

WE'RE IN the General's Lexus, parked in front of the Jinnah Gardens. It's late afternoon. Couples with children and groups of young males are out walking in the park in the evening chill. The General hands me a photograph. "Sajid," he says.

The photograph is a three-by-five color shot. It is a portrait of a middle-aged man sitting in a chair. He is dressed in a dark brown suit, a white shirt, a light brown necktie. His complexion is dark. He has a direct, open, benign face. He has thick, gray-white hair that he combs straight up and back. He has a narrow mustache, a cleft in his chin. He is handsome. He's smiling. There's a twinkle in his eye. He looks like a sweet-tempered guy.

"How old is this? Where's it from?"

"It is recent." The General stops with that. He doesn't want to tell me the photo's provenance. I wonder who he's alerted that he has an interest in Sajid. And I wonder, therefore, if they know that I am looking for the man.

"And also," the General says, "I can tell you that this man, this Ahmed Sajid, this engineer, is the behind-the-scenes chief officer of a charitable fund called Islamic Relief. Islamic Relief is supposedly open and above board. It is headquartered in Karachi and registered with the authorities. It is very nice. They supposedly help Muslims in various war-ravaged countries—Afghanistan, Chechnya, Kashmir, wherever. They build schools and hospitals, and run food programs et cetera. I am quite sure they are crooks. Sajid controls it through a man named Amin Tajer. I don't know this Tajer. I believe Tajer and Islamic Relief are well known to the Americans, who could probably tell me a thing or two about them. Amin Tajer, Islamic Relief."

I TAKE Sajid's photo to the Futura Computer Centre in the Jinnah Market, rent a scanner from the one young clerk minding the store, and in among other documents—some newspaper clips, a magazine article—scan the photo of Ahmed Sajid, and save everything to CD. From my own laptop I WiFi the contents, encrypted, to Fiscarelli's Yahoo account. The whole process takes twenty minutes, no questions asked. I may have left a trail at the Futura Computer Centre, but if I did it's anonymous. I don't think I've attracted attention. The young clerk, when not harried by other customers, looks bored and oblivious.

In my room, studying the photo, I try to read the man's eyes. Who is he? What can he be thinking? What harm does he want to do? Why?

Jihadis don't do what they do just because of ideology. They get pulled into jihadism by friends, associates. Did Khan pull you in? If so, who pulled Khan in? Where does it start?

And where does it end?

I N THE evening I call the General's number from my hotel. Someone, not the General, picks up, and I am cut off. At the General's villa, I find a guard sitting on a plastic chair tipped back against the General's blue steel gate. He is wrapped in a long gray shawl in the night chill. Under the shawl, cradled in his lap, is the shape of an assault rifle.

He watches carefully as I approach from the end of the alley, and when I get close to the gate, he glares at me and raises his right hand, waving it negatively, his left holding the rifle's hand guard. The man's eyes are angry. When I move to ring the buzzer, he pulls away the shawl, aims the piece at me, and clicks down the safety. "No," he says. "No." I back away, putting up my hands in an appeasing gesture, back away, back away, then leave.

I learn the next day from Rieger at the embassy that the General has been put under 'restricted house arrest.' The General can see visitors only at the sufferance of the Military Court. That, in practice, means he sees no one except his court-approved attorneys. They're going to try him for embezzlement. The trial date hasn't been set.

Carrying a passport issued to one Frank Dudley—the name and person are Fiscarelli's invention—with my photo in it along with a nice-looking visa and convincing arrival stamp, I pass uneasily through Exit Control at Islamabad International and board my Emirates flight for Dubai, which takes off routinely. I am also carrying a Frank Dudley Maryland ID (Frank lives in Kensington).

At some point I'll have to stop using multiple passports and identities. At some point facial recognition technology at border control will start putting two and two together, and somewhere, perhaps somewhere un-pleasant, I will have a forced conversation with immigration and security officials.

The people who got the General knew about me. Had to. Nonetheless, I am on this Airbus drinking a vintage Burgundy and surveying from my window seat ships steaming into and out of the Persian Gulf below.

I am very, very lucky.

HQ: FLATTOP II

OPCOM/NPTG Session Audiotape, Session 56 (Excerpted).

Attending: J. Gutman (Chair), M. Fiscarelli, C. Lindquist, S. Kremer, R. Eisenberg.

Transcriber: D. Braithewaite.

Mr. Fiscarelli: We have the one lead on Sajid, which comes as you can see in the UAE and which is recent. FLATTOP reports with relative certainty, and this is something we do have to take seriously, that Ahmed Sajid has been in the UAE and was staying outside the city, outside Dubai, at some kind of desert hunting lodge. Owned by an old sheikh who's a sympathizer with Sajid and his goals, and a major contributor by the way to Islamist charities, fundamentalist charities, which we also know from a multitude of sources, some of them UAE, some of them Saudi. His name's there in the cable.

Ms. Eisenberg: Raising the issue, what is he doing there? And the obvious answer is, looking for money, for funding.

Mr. Gutman: Right. I would just say here that FLATTOP, our banking source . . .

Ms. Eisenberg: And source for that desert meeting, the Jund al-Haqq sympathizers . . .

Mr. Fiscarelli: Right, correct.

Mr. Gutman: FLATTOP has sometimes acted as access agent, and I understand that's how he's gotten this information—from a friend of the old [expletive] who owns the hunting lodge who's been talking to him, this friend, who in turn has been talking to FLATTOP.

Mr. Lindquist: It is secondhand again, more hearsay.

Mr. Fiscarelli: Yes, right.

Ms. Eisenberg: Did we ever get a precise location for that meeting?

Mr. Fiscarelli: Like GPS? No. We've just got a general sense and we will have to get better info. It may in fact have been at the sheikh's hunting lodge, we just don't know.

Mr. Gutman: Well, FLATTOP is an impeccable source, and I would put the probability of accuracy here very high, like seventy percent. We know who the individuals are, the sheikh and his friend, and FLATTOP is who he is, a good friend of the firm, so I will just leave it at that.

There Are No Friends in This Business

"I NEED it all, Omar. I have to have it."

Omar Lateef is clutching the steering wheel of his small gray BMW. We are parked in the shadow of the Burj al-Arab, an insane structure off the shore of Dubai in the Persian Gulf. The Burj is the tallest hotel in the world—taller, they say, than the Eiffel Tower—and is shaped like the sail of a dhow. Inside, the decor is hallucinatory Arabian Nights—riotous golds, crimsons, ivories, green silken banquettes, silver bolsters; curtains all flounces and ruffles; Babylonian columns lining the halls; vast stretches of Persian carpeting covering the polished marble floors. The Burj is excess beyond excess. We had met inside for a drink, but have fled here to Omar's Beamer because when Omar learned what I wanted to talk about, he panicked.

Hands on the wheel, Omar is breathing heavily, working his mouth. He stares ahead at nothing, not looking me in the eye.

I have just mentioned a bank in Beirut, an account password, and a sum of money. Omar isn't liking it.

Omar is a Pakistani national and CEO of a financial institution called Gulf Commercial Bank International. GCBI is headquartered in Dubai and has branches in Europe and Asia. GCBI has an investment arm and a merchant arm. The bank began life in the '60s, but in the '90s, made a series of bad loans. Then late in 2000, it collapsed. Omar collapsed with it and briefly did time in a Dubai jail. The Agency, Fiscarelli tells me, helped get him out. GCBI, in the manner of Gulf banks, was somehow resuscitated—

"reorganized" is what its owner-investors called the process—and is now back in operation. So is Omar. I think the Agency uses GCBI a lot.

Dubai has a magnificent port and is served by hundreds of trading companies and banks. Trading companies of some sort have been here since human habitation. The banks came later, attracted by easy-going regulations. Thus, Omar and GCBI.

Omar would not talk about what he calls "substantive matters" in his office, which he probably has bugged, though the Dubai security services may well be in there, too. So, we decided to take this drive over to the Burj al-Arab and have a chat.

Islamic Relief, Ahmed Sajid's charity, banks at GCBI, and Omar has access to their data. Omar has been on the Agency payroll and has done the Agency much service, but he has balked at one of our recent requests because, apparently, of the danger.

So, we have to encourage him.

Two weeks back, in a small French restaurant near my town house in McLean, Fiscarelli told me, "Omar's given the bank a haircut. Over the last eighteen months he's siphoned off close to two million dollars. We don't know how. We think he's paid off other officers in the bank. Can't tell. We'd like to know that, by the way, how he did it, so if he tells you, pass the secret on to us. He's sent the money to an account in Beirut. Just say, 'Bank of Beirut and the Levant, Greenwood, $1.9 million.' He'll crap his pants. After that, say, '$25,000 from us for the information on Islamic Relief.' Say it nicely, politely, maybe with a pleasant smile. The friendly approach is always best, at least at first. Ought to work."

R ICK, I just sent them some . . . some information, very sensitive." He looks at me plaintively. "Real stuff. You can't know how dangerous it was to send that. How can they . . ."

"We want all the Islamic Relief data, Omar. All their spreadsheets, all reported activity, all personnel using the account, all account passwords you may know or be using yourself."

Omar nods in understanding, biting his underlip. He says, "Look, I don't . . . Rick, it's not doable. I can't do this." He looks me straight in the eye and says, "It's not ethical."

"You'll download the data to this"—I tap my fingers on a slim, sterile computer the Agency has supplied—"then go somewhere neutral, a local cybercafé maybe . . . hey, maybe the lobby of the Burj . . . and from there WiFi the data to me at my Yahoo account. That's it."

Once I get the data, which this little laptop will encrypt automatically, I will forward it to Fiscarelli. Not a lot of fuss.

For Omar, though, there is risk, certainly legal risk, maybe physical. The Islamic Relief clientele are hard men and have hard men working for them.

Omar is petrified. We sit in silence. "This," he says finally, "this . . . Yes, all right, I will do this. But you must give me time. I will need a week. And after that I will need space. Please, Rick."

"I have to have this stuff, Omar. Serious business."

He nods grimly, acceptingly. He doesn't want this job. But he's got it, because, I think, we have another Omar in the Bank of Beirut and the Levant who tipped us off under who knows what pressure. Or no pressure at all.

O MAR KNOWS me as Rick Behringer, though he doesn't know who I am. Not really. He does know, because he financed the deal, that nine years back I bought a Russian antisubmarine torpedo from a Ukrainian Defense Ministry official, and air-freighted it—a large, very heavy package—from Odessa via Dubai to Savannah, Georgia. We've been friends ever since.

Omar is well aware that I operate somewhere in the American Black World, but he doesn't know quite where. That I'm asking about Islamic Relief shows pretty clearly that I am working on terrorist financing, though I haven't told him so in so many words.

M Y OLD friend drives me back to my hotel and lets me off in the hotel's small traffic circle. I've left the laptop next to him on the car seat. As I turn to wave good-bye he raises his right hand and flutters his fingers limply, then drives out onto Baniyas Road.

I watch Omar's gray Beamer disappear into the dusk and reflect: I played piano at his daughter's tenth birthday party. Her name is Zahra, and as I accompanied her, she sang shyly, "Twinkle, twinkle, little star, how I wonder what you are," in perfect American English. She was wearing a white satin party dress and little white gloves. Omar's face was alight with joy as she sang.

There are no friends in this business. No real ones.

THE SKY is a cloudless, brilliant blue, the air cool, and I decide to take a walk. From my hotel I wander down the Creek toward al-Ras. On Baniyas Road there's not much traffic. I'm over on the Creek side of the road, where I stop, lean for a time on the steel railing, and look down over the dhow wharfage. The boats are anchored, sails furled, and rest almost motionless in the easy water of the Creek. On the other side of the Creek is a small white mosque, its single minaret, built in the Saudi style, thrusting high over the buildings around it. As I lean lazily, the noon call to prayer begins over a loudspeaker. *Allahu akbar,* the voice proclaims, "God is most great." The voice will repeat the phrase three more times, then proclaim that there is no God but God, that Muhammad is His prophet, and will call the faithful to prayer and to salvation.

I move on.

I cross the road and head into a side street leading to the covered *souk,* and walk past its money changers and spice merchants, past the motorcycle shops, cheap textile stores, *tikka* restaurants, kitchenware emporiums. At a large intersection I see a KFC and, standing by the door, a cardboard cutout of the Colonel in his white suit.

Then over there, just past the KFC, I see Walt, walking away from me in the company of a European woman. He's wearing a long-sleeved light blue shirt with the cuffs rolled up, khaki Dockers, a Navy blue billed cap. He has the stoop, the long white hair, the dark complexion. He and his companion vanish in the crowd, in the direction of the gold *souk.* I let them go.

Why did my wandering father die? I have a need to know. And cannot.

A MAN calling himself Hussain picks me up at my hotel in a silvery green Range Rover. Hussain is slim and tense. He's in Western slacks and shirt. On his feet he's wearing blue Crocs. He's in his thirties. He has a bristly black mustache. He has a way of looking at you that seems to catch detail.

"He's the employee of a friend of the Firm," Fiscarelli said. "A flunky. He's going to take you someplace, a sheikh's hunting lodge way out at the end of nowhere. According to our friend who moves in all sorts of circles, Sajid spent time there recently. The sheikh is an elderly jihadi with bags of money. Big thing: We want the GPS coordinates. Take a look around, see whatever you can see. Anything else you can get would be fine—photos, whatever. But we do want those coordinates. Hussain doesn't know what this is all about. Total ignorance. All he knows is, he's gotten told to take you there." Our story is, we are engineers from the power company out inspecting lines. Hussain has the papers to prove it.

Leaving Dubai we are in thick traffic on the Khaleej Road, and it takes half an hour just to pass through the tunnel under Dubai Creek. Then we move faster and in a few minutes enter Sharjah, the next emirate over, where Hussain catches a palm-lined highway that heads south out of town past a racetrack and a cement factory. And into the desert, where traffic thins.

Forty or fifty miles out Hussain takes us off the highway, cutting down into a dry, flat creek bed, which he follows. "Shortcut," he says. "Rear approach. Faster." Desert scrub and a few low palm trees line the bed. "When there's rain there is a lot of water," Hussain says. "Otherwise, no."

We follow the bed a few hundred meters, then Hussain cuts left, up out of the creek bed, our vehicle tipping crazily, and we end up on a badly paved road that stretches over the low dunes. It looks traveled.

Far down the road I see a low, gray mass, buildings of some kind, and next to them a water tower.

"Hunting place. Once. To shoot gazelle. They use machine guns." Hussain thinks this is very funny. "Not used for hunting now." He rotates his right fingers at his temple, the universal sign for insanity. "No good place."

Our miserable road has been joined by a lone electrical line stretched on poles from a highway far across the rippling dunes. At the end of our road is a large compound with high, white-stuccoed walls. Some of the stucco is falling away revealing yellow brick. The walls are topped with red brick and on the brick broken bottles have been cemented in place.

Hussain parks our Range Rover at the front gate. We get out, and Hussain pushes the buzzer several times, then pounds with both fists on the door, yelling in Arabic.

Finally, someone inside replies and opening the gate part-way peers out at us. It's an old man.

Hussain and the old man exchange greetings, the old man nodding at Hussain, looking at back and forth between Hussain and me. He is wearing a black and white *kaffiyeh* wrapped like a turban around his head and a loose gray *thowb* and plastic sandals. He is blind in his left eye. Its iris is a cloudy dark blue-gray and it is immobile in its socket.

"Caretaker," Hussain says. "Muhammad."

Hussain flashes our power company papers in front of the old man's face, then flicks his hand, gesturing at the gate.

The old man unlatches the steel door, which creaks as he opens it, and lets us in. He's heavy-set and walks with a limp. He doesn't look either of us in the eye. His features are impassive.

The compound contains four houses—one large main building facing the entrance gate and behind it three smaller houses laid out symmetrically in line, all three alike.

"One house, one wife," Hussain says. The large house was for the preferred wife.

On each side of the walk leading to the main house there are the remains of a garden. Sand has blown over the tiled walk. Palm trees rustle in the wind. Hussain shakes his head, then opens his right hand palm up, index finger extended, and pumps his forearm up and down, an Arab gesture meaning, "What the hell is this?"

"Nothing," he says. "No one, no autos." I try to talk to the old man with Hussain as translator.

"Does anybody live here?"

"No no no. This place is for hunting, now nobody comes much. Some people. Sometimes."

The old man says he doesn't know who comes or goes, that he just keeps watch over the place. He's lying, but I don't push him. His function is to report to the old sheikh's family if visitors show up. Which he will do.

We ask the old man where the electrical box is—it's in the main house—and when we find it, we pretend to interest ourselves in it. It's 220 volts, not much amperage, enough for the lights maybe and an air conditioner or two, not much else. No phone line. Typical. They use sats. There is cell coverage down here too, though we're far into the desert. My cell gets a signal. I get Fiscarelli his GPS coordinates.

We walk from house to house to have a look, all the while I'm taking shots on my cell of not much. Each house has a main entrance hall and smaller adjoining rooms. In each, the interior doors are ajar, the cement-tiled floors dusted with fine yellow grit. Some of the windows are open. There is no furniture except for one gray metal desk in the entrance hall of one of the outlying buildings. It contains nothing. In one room of this building, we find an uncovered blue-and-white striped mattress on the floor and a pair of rumpled sheets, partly on the mattress, partly on the floor. This is the one house with equipment in its kitchen—a hot plate and propane tank, some cheap aluminum utensils. A refrigerator that's been unplugged. When I open it I see that it's dirty but empty and it gives out the smell of rotten meat.

Hussain says, "Someone was here. But only one man, I think."

Outside, footprints in the sand lead to treadmarks where a vehicle has been parked. The footprints, the treadmarks are recent.

Sajid. He's been here. And gone.

A T HOME. My place in McLean, bedroom, nighttime. Frannie, now just in panties, the briefest of briefs, body-tone of color and half-transparent, stands before me, as I sit naked on the edge of the bed, her hands on my shoulders, working her thighs in an excited, squirmy, back-and-forth, pumping motion, like a go-go dancer, though she's putting on no act. Her eyes are closed, she's off somewhere, panting, all on her own. Her skin is a snowy white, her thighs smooth. I pull her to me and kiss them.

In the morning, the two of us lie half asleep for a time, entangled in warm repose on this bright, lazy, Sunday morning.

She stirs first, yawns, eyelids heavy, pushes at me with the heels of her palms, smiling. "Hey."

"Hey."

"Missed you." She smiles that smile, laughs through her nose.

"I missed you, too."

"Poor me. You were off seeing the Sheik of Araby and doing big deals."

"You wouldn't like the Sheik. Dull guy."

"I bet."

Between her legs the hair is reddish, fine as silk, almost not there, like a pubescent girl's. Her eyes are inviting.

Best times are mornings, when you ease in and she gives a slight, tense shudder, and her face, as now, is a filmy, milky lapse into the faraway, like a child napping, and then back.

Do you love me? she asks at times.

I say, *Yes*, but I know she's not so sure, because I am not so sure myself. I'm her one and only, she says. More or less. There were "some boys" before Jim came along, she says, but nobody after Jim except me. I believe her, of course—why would she lie?—and I believe her frank, open, honest face.

Frannie calls me Frequent Flyer. For Frannie, as for a lot of women, these absences and the secrecy, especially that, are almost aphrodisiacal.

Once they believe you, that you're not just disappearing down the road to see some other Significant Other, that there is no other Other, they find the mystery seductive.

Liz never got used to it. Liz to Ott: "The life is just too much. The drinking, the hours, the running off in the night—Spence, I come home, end of the day, and there he is packing his bags, he hasn't even told me he's leaving on a trip. Last minute, he tells me while he's grabbing shirts and underwear that he's headed for somewhere, Belgium, Korea, India, and off he goes. Then I find out the guy was in Venezuela!"

F RANNIE AND I have breakfast and a late-morning coffee downstairs and read *The Post* for a time, sharing the sections, then she says, "Okay, lover, I'm off." Clients. She's heading into Arlington to Donnelly & Amstutz, weekends being her workdays. "The Millers's," she says, "he of the Department of Health, Education, and Welfare, she—I kid you not—of the Associated Tire Retreaders. They're trading up." She appraises herself in the mirror by the door ("baubles, bangles"), checks her purse ("thinggummies"), gives me a peck, and heads out into the bright day, leaving me to wonder, Do I love her? We've been together for almost a year. Where is this thing headed? And I have to say, I'm comfortable in this free-floating space. I don't think of marriage. The deal with Liz—all that makes me think, Never again. I just can't. Ten years married. Who thought it would end? And who needs it again?

HEU: "Considerable Risk"

BORIS MIKHAILOVICH Kolpakov, though he's being driven through a rolling landscape of farms and occasional bursts of urbanization, though his driver Stegerov is careful with Kolpakov's new Mercedes-Benz (fresh-smelling interior, cream leather upholstery, gleaming silvery accessories), though the road, the P459 south of Moscow, is a well-paved, four-lane, limited-access highway, Boris Kolpakov has this sudden sensation that he is being driven to his death. The feeling, something more than unease, something less than fear, lingers for a time around his heart.

Oparin does that to you.

Kolpakov is to meet with Ivan Oparin, a businessman who lives in a secret city of the wealthy hidden in forest not far from Moscow. Kolpakov knows that Oparin, in addition to operating his numerous legitimate enterprises, uses his airline to smuggle drugs from the East, from Afghanistan and Tajikistan, to Russia and to Europe, and to make illegal arms shipments to the darker parts of the world. Kolpakov has heard, and believes, that Oparin works for the Russian security services as a kind of contractor, carrying out clandestine work for them both at home and overseas, work, including assassination, they don't want to be connected to.

At their meeting, Kolpakov will propose to Oparin that they form a partnership to sell what Kolpakov has been calling "the commodity." Kolpakov approached Oparin through his own man Stegerov, who, after some trouble, finally found an appropriate intermediary of Oparin's, a tall man with red hair and a menacing manner. Stegerov was purposely vague in a number of meetings with Oparin's man, but hinted at enough to let Oparin know what Kolpakov would be proposing. Oparin, through his man, signaled interest.

S TEGEROV TURNS off P459 onto an unmarked secondary highway, this one two-laned but also well-paved, that leads through thick birch forest and arrives abruptly at a high concrete wall painted a dull green. Here, the road turns right, skirting the wall, and continues a few hundred meters until it ends at a gate of heavy steel pickets. To the left of the gate, built into the wall, is a guardhouse with a bullet-proof window looking onto the approach road.

When a guard inside has checked Kolpakov's license number against that day's guest list, he opens the gate electronically, and Stegerov eases Kolpakov's Mercedes into an inspection zone marked off by white lines on the pavement just inside the gate. Beyond the lines, the way is blocked by orange fluorescent traffic cones. Stegerov stops at the traffic cones and cuts the engine.

A young man in khaki uniform and khaki military-style cap emerges from the guardhouse and carefully checks Stegerov's driver's license and Kolpakov's Russian Republic identity card, giving as he does a seemingly casual look at Kolpakov's face. He inspects Kolpakov's car while a second young man in similar uniform emerges from the guardhouse and watches, restraining a large, brown, flat-faced, quietly threatening dog.

The first guard returns Kolpakov's documents and tells Stegerov, "Take the left and drive about a kilo. Mr. Oparin's house is number five on the right. You'll park on Mr. Oparin's circular drive. You'll remain in the car. Mr. Oparin's guest may walk the short distance to the house." The guard, saluting Kolpakov, says, "You may proceed," and pulls aside one of the traffic cones.

Stegerov drives Kolpakov through a community of newly built mansions of all styles and shapes—English Victorian, Old Russian, American Art Deco, Spanish, Japanese. One is a Bavarian *Schloss*. When they arrive at Oparin's circular drive, Stegerov, as ordered, stops the car and turns off the engine. In the grassy circle in front of Oparin's Mediterranean-looking mansion sits a bronze statue of a sphinx the size of a greyhound. The face of the sphinx is androgynous. It seems to stare into eternity.

———

A SERVANT sees Kolpakov into the mansion, where he meets Oparin, a bull-necked muscular man, in an elegant side room off the main reception hall. The room: bright red fabric on the walls, patterned in arabesques. Two blue and white Chinese vases, each a meter high, flanking the door. Hanging on the wall over Oparin's shoulder is a painting, a dark landscape, old-style Russian, nineteenth century—fields, small, pale figures walking on a country road, a rider on horseback. Bookshelves on the walls to the side containing neatly ordered volumes in leather binding, some in Russian, some in foreign languages, all with an untouched look.

K OLPAKOV REFUSED to discuss business inside Oparin's mansion and so the two are out walking alone in mist-laden air on a neatly tended footpath that parallels the service road leading around the colony.

"Ivan Sergeyevich," Kolpakov says, "I am a blunt man. Briefly, I have a quantity of highly enriched uranium. It is the genuine material, not radioactive waste. It would be worth a great deal to the right customer."

"You have this material in your possession?"

"I have access."

"Access. You're quite certain about its quality? Its genuineness?"

"The material is quite genuine, very pure. It could fetch an extremely high price."

"Highly enriched uranium is dangerous material, Boris Mikhailovich. With this material you're walking very close to the edge. You're perhaps over the edge."

"Ivan Sergeyevich, I think the time for selling radioactive waste is over. The market is aware that such sales have occurred. Buyers are much more cautious."

Oparin studies Kolpakov's face. "How much do you . . . 'have access' to?"

"A number of kilograms. A quantity for which they'll pay a great deal."

Oparin nods impassively. "Your proposal?"

"I suggest we partner in finding a suitable buyer and in shipping the goods. You, Ivan Sergeyevich, have many contacts. You have operated in regions where there are likely customers. You may know suitable candidates to approach. Also, you have a functioning aviation company—aircraft, pilots, ground crews. The quantities of material we are discussing could easily be hidden in . . . in anything—an automobile, a crate of ammunition, an air conditioner. No limit to the possibilities. I propose an agreement, Ivan Sergeyevich. I will pay you a flat ten percent of the purchase price on any . . ."

"Ten percent for *you,* you son of a bitch. I am to find the customer, which you have no chance whatsoever of doing on your own, I am to transport the commodity, at considerable risk, and which you cannot do. I would also have to handle the technical problems of passing national boundaries— all these matters are beyond your competence. For me dealing with them would be expensive and would involve further considerable risk, both personal and financial. You can lose people and aircraft on these missions. And the material you're discussing is extraordinarily sensitive. If something went wrong . . . Don't talk shit, Boris Mikhailovich."

I N THE end, Oparin agreed simply to pay Kolpakov some millions of euros for "the commodity," depending on how much Kolpakov was able to supply. There would be no talk of percentages. Kolpakov wanted to split the purchase expenses with Oparin as well, but Oparin refused.

"Statuesque Like a Goddess"

FISCARELLI SAYS, "The Islamic charity thing, Islamic Relief, that stuff came through okay. Thanks."

Omar. He sent to my Yahoo account—fowler_ken—the texts and spreadsheets and whatever else he got from Islamic Relief, which I then forwarded, already encrypted, to Fiscarelli.

It's a misty, chilly afternoon. We're in Zachary Taylor Park in north Arlington, following the steep bike trail up toward Marymount University and Glebe Road. Fiscarelli is making heavy weather of it, huffing as we walk—the guy gets no exercise—and we have to pause now and then. We sit finally on a bench about halfway up looking over Donaldson Run.

"I haven't heard from Ray," I say. "We've had long spells before, but he usually gets back to me. He hasn't this time. I haven't heard a thing from him. I'm worried. I mean, really worried."

"No . . . ted," Fiscarelli wheezes.

"Have *you* gotten any indication the guy might be in trouble?"

"No. Zero." Wheeze. "We've heard . . . nothing. I'll have it looked into."

Fiscarelli talks with not much emotion, which is his general pose. I've never seen him angry, or happy for that matter. When you're talking, he nods a lot. You never know what he's thinking.

We sit for a time as Fiscarelli recovers his breath. Then out of nowhere, astonishingly, he starts talking of romance. Flabbergasting. Nerdy, pasty

Mike Fiscarelli is in love with his secretary, an African-American woman named Dawn Braithewaite, fifteen or so years his junior (sounds like Jim McClennan) and a single parent with a daughter named Tameeka.

Fiscarelli's wife, Angie, was killed in a beach accident three years back. A freak wave carried her onto the shore, flipped her over, and snapped her neck. She died then and there. Angie's death, coming out of nowhere like an unseen fist, floored Fiscarelli. He's waking up now to his loneliness.

"Dawn," he says. "Beautiful, beautiful name. And so is she. She's tall, statuesque like a goddess. Gorgeous eyes. Dresses to kill, lot of Afro stuff. Drives a sexy little car."

I can't believe what I'm hearing. "Mike, you're in love."

"Sorta. She doesn't notice me. I mean, not like that."

"Mike, is this going to work?"

"Not a question of working. It just . . . is."

I marvel at this flabby, middle-aged bureaucrat in love with a young black chick from the District. What *will* the guy do?

"Ran into her last week at Tysons," Fiscarelli says, "just outside Bloomingdale's. I smiled and nodded—didn't know what else to do. She was friendly, smiled back, just beautiful. You melt." Fiscarelli makes a resigned face when he says this, knowing the whole business is crazy. The age difference, the race thing, office rules. Fiscarelli is top level at the Agency, and Dawn a typist. An office romance, even well intended, is off limits for him.

Dawn's a new hire, Fiscarelli tells me. She used to live on the Hill somewhere, but after a couple of months of commuting Hill-to-Langley she's moved over to Arlington. Like Jack Gutman, she is not covert. She can tell people she works as a word processor for CIA, though that's about all she can say. Working for Fiscarelli, she has to have a high-security clearance.

No way will this work. Fiscarelli's out of a nice white milieu some-where around Philadelphia. And yet, any way I sift his words about Dawn and watch him as he talks, this gooby bureaucrat is the dopey lover. The guy's hopeless.

Discussion of Dawn over, time to part. I hand Fiscarelli a cell phone, the one I have been using as Doug Lawson and which the Agency sup-plies. Fiscarelli hands me a new one. We exchange cells every couple of months. I keep the numbers of my contacts encrypted in a password safe on my home computer, and transfer them when I get the new phone and new SIM card. Before I turn over the old cell, I flush my contacts irretrievably from its memory. The Agency is aware of this and doesn't object.

"Are You Behringer?"

COLTRANE IS on the stereo doing "Lush Life," Billy Strayhorn's lovely piece, with Red Garland on the piano. Garland ordinarily has this wide chordal style, both hands playing the melody, which gives you a flood of sound, but on this rendition he holds back—it's Coltrane who's the master of this music, with his soft, meditative saxophone. In the work you can hear the Southern blues and Southern lyricism, but the music is urban, has a northern hipness, aware of where it came from, certainly, but no longer from Down There. You hear it, you think New York.

The phone by the window rings, and I go over and pick up.

"Are you Behringer?"

"Yeah."

"You must stop."

"What?"

"You must stop."

"Who . . . uh . . ."

"You know what. Remember you must stop."

And gone.

South Asian accent, Indian or Pakistani. Caller ID says it's a 703 area code number—northern Virginia. Could be from next door. But I don't believe it. It could also be from the other side of the world. With the right hardware you can use Internet phoning and make any number you want show up on somebody else's caller ID screen. It's called "spoofing." If you don't want to buy the hardware, there are Web sites you can go through

that do the trick. Or, you can buy a spoofing phone card for not much—
you dial a toll-free number, key in the destination number, then key in the
number you want to display on the destination's caller ID. No way for the
receiver to know the number's spoofed.

That accent. I doubt the call was from next door.

Across Old Dominion in the CITGO station an attendant is wiping the
windshield of a red Camaro. The driver's a Hispanic-looking kid in white
trousers and a pale blue jacket. He's hatless in the cold. His hair is cut high
and tight. The kid's probably military. Maybe on a big night off, heading
to Georgetown to meet a girl. Wish you all the best, kid.

Remember you must stop.

A little phone hassling never hurt anybody, but they know my real
name and number. Who are they? What do they want? And what'll they
do? That they never tell you. They worry you a little, let your paranoia
ramble, as mine is doing now. If they know who I am, they know a lot
more. Sam? Penelope? Liz? Maybe Frannie? Can't hide or protect everybody. They've always got a way.

I'll tell Fiscarelli, and he'll try to have the call traced. They won't find a
thing.

Target Range

POP . . . POP . . . POP . . .

I am at the Piedmont Firing Range, shooting. The range is south of Washington, way down I-95, almost to Quantico. It's run by buzz-cut ex-military types who walk around the place with holstered semiautomatics. They are far from unfriendly, but are nonetheless ready for what they would call a "situation"—attempted robbery, a shoot-out among customers—that never comes. They'll tell you the situation never comes because they're all packing pistols.

The gun I'm using is my own, a Glock 9 mm semiautomatic. The Glock's light, easy to carry, easy to maneuver, yet has an all-business feel. The bore is just slightly above the grip, so there's very little muzzle flip, and you get good accuracy. A very serious weapon. At home, I keep it locked in a desk drawer, its magazine empty. Next to it in the drawer is a box containing forty or so rounds.

I seldom think of using this weapon, using it in any serious way, that is. But that phone call—*Are you Behringer? Remember you must stop*—has me down here, practicing, though what I am doing here I know is mostly psychotherapy.

The ammo I use here are flat-ended, short cartridges, specially made for range practice, to cut well-defined round holes in the target. When I fire the gun—I've put on red plastic noise suppressers and am standing in a narrow booth facing down the target range—the shots sound like distant popping. I feel little recoil, though in time the fleshy mass under my right thumb will begin to ache.

My instructor Andy is young, short, and stocky with long hair that he parts in the middle. Andy has a Virginia good-old-boy manner and accent. Andy doesn't say much: He knows me.

Shooting is mental, Andy says: Stand. Grip. Aim. Fire. When you fire, you don't squeeze your hand—that brings the barrel down. You pull your trigger finger, and as you pull, you control your thoughts and your breathing. You get the single front vertical sight precisely in the center of the rear double sight. You get the tops of both sights precisely level, and you bring your sights, centered and level, on target. Then you pull as deliberately as you can.

The target here is a life-size black silhouette of a man printed on beige paper. It hangs on a retrieval line about fifteen yards downrange. Numbered concentric beige ovals emanate from its midsection.

When I come down here I shoot off three or four boxes of cartridges, regularly putting every slug in the 9 or the 10 oval, the innermost two, and then, triumphantly, I put one or two shots through a little man-shaped silhouette, just three inches high, in the upper left corner of the target.

I have good control over my breathing and my hands. No palsy yet. But I am forty-five and I feel age closing in on me, and the feeling scares me. Someday, if I live long enough, I'll have hands I can't keep from fluttering, I'll have all the rest of it that doesn't bear thinking about. To practice here at the target range, particularly to put a slug or two through the little three-inch-high man, I find life-affirming.

I bought this pistol ten years back against Liz's will, and so kept it in a locked cabinet in my office at Global Reach along with a good supply of ammo, out of Liz's sight and more or less out of her mind. Liz was afraid I'd use it on myself, maybe when Sam or Pennie turned thirteen—after all, John Behringer died of a self-inflicted gunshot when son Walter was thirteen, and son Walter Behringer died the same way when son Ricky was thirteen. Neither Liz nor I believe in luck, good or bad, so the number thirteen in itself is meaningless to us, but we do believe in patterns. We know family tragedies recur.

Your life can crap up in various ways, as mine surely has, but I have never had a suicidal thought. Walt, though—when did he begin to get serious about ending things? I saw his pistol, a large, black instrument, only when he took it out of his safe, supposedly to oil and clean it and check its workings. I remember also, my presence in the den at such times was discouraged. As far as I know he never took the gun to a firing range.

He acquired the piece in Saigon and brought it home, probably legally—he didn't transgress Agency rules or the law. When he died, the pistol was spirited away by the police, and I never saw it again. Marge, I'm sure, didn't want it back.

I won't use my Glock 9 on myself, I'm pretty sure. If I use it, it will be on someone else. I wonder who.

OPCOM/NPTG Session Audiotape, Session 59 (Excerpted).

Attending: J. Gutman (Chair), M. Fiscarelli, C. Lindquist, S. Kremer, R. Eisenberg.

Transcription: D. Braithewaite.

Mr. Gutman: Okay, on the Dubai bank thing. Stu?

Mr. Kremer: Right. IFC [International Financial Crimes] has been able to look at much of the material . . .

Mr. Gutman: Not to bust in, Stu, but for everybody's information, we've gotten a limited amount of material from our banking source in Dubai . . .

Ms. Eisenberg: This is FLATTOP?

Mr. Gutman: Right. And we have information developed from FLATTOP on the transactions of an Islamic charity, it's called Islamic Relief, which we've heard about from other sources, Pak sources, and it is run by a man named Amin Tajer, a Pakistani. It's been in existence a while and it was associated with the Khan network, and we believe it is associated with Ahmed Sajid, maybe backs his work. Like Khan's. Through this same information we've gotten a number of passwords to other bank accounts around the Middle East and Europe. Of course, it will take some time to exploit this material, but work on it has already proven really fruitful. Stu?

Mr. Kremer: Right. As Jack says, work is ongoing, but from the financials we've been able to look at we can conclude that the Islamic Relief account in GCBI—they have accounts in a number of banks, which we're seeing in this material and which it would be nice to know more about—Islamic Relief receives deposits from Saudi and Gulf charities, business firms, and individuals, mostly Saudi, but among them that Dubai company, the Hassan Reza Trading Group, which deposited a large amount right after the meeting in the desert . . .

Ms. Eisenberg: The WMD meeting. Money coming in to finance nuclear . . .

Mr. Gutman: You got it.

"OH, RICK, come on in. It is so scary. And thanks for coming."

There's been a break-in at Liz's place, and she called. "They didn't take anything," she said. "They broke in through the Florida room, got into the house, and rampaged around. Opened a lot of drawers, left stuff around, and probably got out in a hurry, maybe heard us coming. Oh God, look, Rick, could you come over? I think the girls would like it."

And so I took the familiar route from my place out Balls Hill Road, always a laugh that name, through the winding, two-laned streets of McLean Station, roads I know well, this dark, foggy night. I turned the familiar turn from Balls Hill onto Dulany Drive, made the big curve around to the right, and finally eased down into Liz's driveway on the left, just before the road bends again, the driveway and graveled parking apron where, once upon a time, I took down the white-painted brick stanchion at the driveway entrance and wrecked my beautiful Infiniti.

Liz has met me at the door, a drink on the rocks in hand, which looks and smells like bourbon. She notices I notice. "Not my drink usually," she says, "but God, it was scary. We've all looked again. They didn't take a thing, just left a mess. Police have come and gone." She gives me a rueful look. "I'm a wreck."

"Girls okay?"

"Blasé, believe it or not. Totally in stride."

I find Sam in the TV room. "Hey, Space Case."

"Heya, Daddy." Sam gets up, mutes the sound, and comes over and puts her arms around my neck. I give her a squeeze. God, she's tall. I've started marveling at her height. Only thirteen, tall as I am, and her front starting to push out. Behringer genes.

"So howya doin'?"

"Hangin' "

"You okay with all this?"

"Hey, no problem. Gone." Sam likes cool.

"Where's Pennie?"

"Around." More cool.

Pennie appears at the door, and runs over for a hug.

"Lot of excitement, huh?"

Her eyes widen behind her big glasses, and she nods, then grins. "They made a complete getaway."

"Well, maybe cops'll catch 'em, Boo Boo. No harm done, right?"

"They're not going to catch them," Sam says with finality.

"Maybe not."

Pennie says with not much seriousness, "So, maybe they'll come back."

"Nah, I doubt it. Not if they're smart. They'll go hit someplace else if they stay being robbers, which they might not. Might go into another line of work."

"As if," Sam says. She's signaling she's aware that Daddy is trying to soothe her naïve and dopey younger sister, signaling also that worldly-wise Sam is way above all this. So far, sibling rivalry has been minimal in these girls' lives, but we may be entering a new stage. Sam in puberty, Pennie on the cusp. It's due.

I rub Pennie's thin shoulders, so small still, so fragile and vulnerable. Memory: me sitting in "my" chair some evening, Pennie standing in socks on my thighs, not yet needing glasses, red hair in pigtails. She is smiling. I've said something. She says, "Silly Daddy."

Then I think about my phone call, that South Asian accent, no threat, just a single command:

You must stop. Remember you must stop.

Liz comes in. "There's homework, as I recall. Gotta get it done, young women, school tomorrow. This episode is no excuse to dork around. Sam, general science. Pennie, math. To your rooms. Chop chop."

Chop chop. A phrase old Yoder used when he wanted something done instantly. He'd clap his hands together when he said it, like a Chinese emperor. I wonder what the girls make of it. Probably heard it before.

"Hey, your mom's right," I say. "Run into trouble, either of you, I'll help out. Math, science, my kind of stuff, okay? When you're done we'll have some ice cream or something. Your mom and I need to talk about what happened here."

The girls exit reluctantly. They'll be listening.

"They broke in through the Florida room," Liz says.

Liz follows me as I go to the rear of the house to have a look. I see where they jimmied the flimsy, aluminum door, no great skill involved there, then, proceeding over the bright red tiles of the Florida room—Spanish, expensive, one of Liz's innovations after I moved out, another of her so-long-Rick gestures—got into the main house through a glassed, see-through wooden door that was left unlocked. (Dumb as hell, and Liz a lawyer.) Three lone women in a big, secluded house.

"Police dusted for fingerprints, but that's all CYA, they'll never get anybody. Except for wrecking the door lock, that's all the damage they did. Some drawers were yanked out, stuff scattered around. They didn't steal *any*-thing."

"How do you know it's a 'they'?"

"I don't. Cops said it's usually two guys. Takes two to work up the courage, talk each other into it. Probably kids, it was so slapdash and amateurish. I mean, they missed my jewelry, which was in a big box on the dresser, pretty obvious target, and I had some cash, couple hundred dollars, just sitting in the top drawer of the desk in my office. They never even went in there. As the police say, they probably left in a hurry."

She notices I'm drinkless, and she's half-sloshed on her bourbon. "I'm sorry, Rick, want something?"

"I'm fine." She notices this casual refusal. It makes her a little guilty, maybe. Which I like, truly.

I say, "Cops talk about recent robberies around here?"

"They did. Yeah, there've been some. Not on Dulany, but yeah, in the neighborhood." Her face unclouds a little. "We were out having pizza. We'd been gone maybe an hour and a half max. Then we came back and found this."

"The girls don't seem freaked."

"No, God, they thought it was funny." She swirls some bourbon around her mouth. "They see too much TV, too many cops and robbers. It's all fantasy for them." Her eyes go teary. The drink has loosened her.

I think again of that phone call: *Are you Behringer? Remember you must stop.* The people who came in here could have been truly evil. I do not like to think about what they—he, whoever—could have done.

"Probably really was a bunch of dumb kids" I say. "You'll be okay. So'll the girls. You look okay, considering," I say.

Her response to this is to sip some more bourbon, her face in neutral. She's pretty good at detecting lies, mine in particular.

HEU: "He Will Act as Merchant Banker"

ANTALYA, A resort town on the southwest coast of Turkey, where Ivan Oparin, through a Russian proxy, owns a large villa in a deluxe gated community: to the south, a view of the gleaming sea; to the east, a view of the blue-gray, denuded mountains of ancient Pamphylia that stretch down almost to the shore. Oparin is the first owner of this villa, a pretty place, two stories of beige stucco with white trim at the corners, a red tile roof, and, on the south side, a round tower.

Oparin is sitting in the second floor of the tower room—it's a cool, sunny day outside, the sea an achingly bright blue—with a Pakistani national named Amin Tajer, who has flown in from Karachi via Ankara. A tall young woman, Russian-looking, has served them tea, along with sugar in little cubes for the Pakistani, jam for Oparin, and has left them alone.

Each speaks fluent English. Oparin's manner, as ever when doing business, is brusque. He says, "All right, we will deliver to your client an agreed-on quantity of the commodity. It will be first-class quality. The quantity and price to be set."

"That has been discussed. The quantity is twenty kilograms."

"No. We will supply approximately thirteen kilograms of the commodity this time, no more. I don't know how you have set this quantity."

"Well, I'll have to discuss the issue with my client."

"A larger quantity I can tell you is not possible. We can supply more, but it will have to be in separate shipments, separate deliveries. Anything else is simply not possible."

"As I say, I must consult with my client."

"You've never said who your client is."

"No. Do you care?"

"No."

The Pakistani says, "Let's discuss the method of payment and delivery and also validation of the, ah, quality of the commodity."

"Good. Right. Method of payment. We will find a mutual friend who will be our intermediary. I suggest a man named Ismail Hamawi, a Saudi businessman. Mr. Hamawi, or someone else we agree on, will act as merchant banker. Like any international trading deal. Your client will deposit with this person the agreed sum. This person will not give the funds to us until your client signals that he is satisfied with the quality and quantity of the material. If you signal that you are unsatisfied, you may return the commodity, and your money will be returned to you. If you don't return the commodity, then our intermediary will deposit the money with us. There will be a transaction fee for our intermediary, some percentage of the total, probably no more than ten percent, probably less. You as purchaser will pay that."

"We'll split the fee."

"No. No, we won't."

"I'll have to discuss that, too, with my client."

"Will you accept the method of payment?"

"Another matter to discuss with my client."

"He may know Hamawi."

He Was Out on the Street
Just Walking Around

"SHOT IN the head from behind. We don't have much on it. Happened a week ago. We just found out. He was out on the street just walking around. Police say it wasn't robbery or anything, it was a planned assassination, a targeted murder, and they say they can't figure out why. Guy was a nothing—no big deal at the Defense Ministry, no political clout—why kill him like this? They say they got leads, but they always say that."

I'm with Fiscarelli in Pimmit Run Park, not far from where I live. He called. "Need to see you," he said, meaning emergency.

We're walking on an asphalted path. Now and then a jogger will pass, paying us no heed. I feel gut-punched. Ray died in Islamabad while I was in that city, wondering where he was.

"It was because of us," I say.

Fiscarelli shunts his head to the side, agreeing.

I say, "He was afraid. He thought security was closing in on him."

"Security? Maybe that's what this is all about. If they'd really found something, really figured out what he was up to, they might have done this. They have a pool of talent they can draw on. Easier than an arrest and a trial. This way they don't have to acknowledge the guy was important."

"Could have been somebody else. Inside, but not security."

"That, too. Don't expect to find anything out."

"I liked him."

Fiscarelli nods a couple of times, looking away. I guess he understands.

"Think about everything he said. Let me know. Some people are going to want to talk to you. Wrack your brain. Got any e-mails?"

"Yes."

"Give me copies."

I think of Ray's wife. The two kids: the little boy so good at chess; the little girl, who may be even smarter. I think of Ray's half-Oklahoma accent, how he followed the Sooners.

Fiscarelli says, "Family's distraught. Nobody can figure it out."

I say, "That threatening call I got. It wasn't long after they shot Ray."

"Right."

At Langley and the Fort, Fiscarelli tells me, they've tried to trace the call. No luck. It was nicely spoofed. The call most assuredly left tracks—they all always do—but it went through an anonymizing Web site, and we have no access to those tracks and probably never will.

When I get home I call Rieger in Islamabad—it's 2 A.M. there—who says, "I can't talk. Don't ever call me about this again. Check at home."

He means Fiscarelli.

"Gotta sign off."

Meaning, that's all.

Ray's gone. And there are people out there who will call me, probably from South Asia somewhere, and tell me, *Remember you must stop.* Would these people know enough, have a long-enough reach, to break into the house where my children live? Would they?

SCI TOP SECRET GREEN SCI TOP SECRET GREEN SCI TOP SECRET GREEN SCI TOP SECRET GREEN SCI

OPCOM/NPTG Session Audiotape, Session 60 (Excerpted).

Attending: J. Gutman (Chair), M. Fiscarelli, C. Lindquist, S. Kremer, Ms. Eisenberg.

Transcription: D. Braithewaite.

Mr. Fiscarelli: As you can read, word in from Turkish National Intelligence is that the guy got caught trying to sell nuclear slag, the Georgian, got three years, has told them that it was a Russian mafia guy who was the go-between, who he identified, that he named the Russian as Aleksandr Geydarov. Geydarov was an asset of ours.

Mr. Gutman: HIGHBEAM.

Mr. Fiscarelli: HIGHBEAM, who who got himself murdered in Istanbul, beaten to a pulp, and that the Turks find it is plausible that Geydarov was indeed in on the deal.

Mr. Gutman: That's his photo.

Mr. Fiscarelli: Yes.

Ms. Eisenberg: Jack, there's this issue with the flow of, the drug flow out of Afghanistan into Russia, and the issue of the Russian mafia and terrorism, including nuclear terrrorism. It gets very convoluted, but the drug mafia is also acting as smugglers of other commodities. And that includes trafficking in prostitutes, as we know. Very nasty people. My own area is this transnational crime, and I'm seeing that we don't know enough, that the nonproliferation people here at OPCOM don't know enough about simple, organized crime. All these criminals, they'll work with anybody, including terrorists.

Mr. Gutman: Right. Granted.

Ms. Eisenberg: I mean, the notion here on the fifth floor, Jack, seems to be that criminals won't risk their profits by dealing with terrorists, who are high-risk and supposedly in our gunsights. But they've got no national loyalty, the criminals, and they'll deal with anybody who promises to make them money. And there could be a lot of money, a lot of money, in nuclear smuggling.

Mr. Fiscarelli: We've had sixteen confirmed incidents of uranium and plutonium smuggling since the nineties.

Ms. Eisenberg: So frankly, I downplay this notion that you won't get common criminals and terrorists intersecting. They will intersect. And you'll get proliferation on a subnational level. I'm thinking of course of Ahmed Sajid and Jund al-Haqq.

Mr. Lindquist: We're not seeing it.

Mr. Fiscarelli: Well, maybe that's the problem, Carl, we're not seeing it. Rhoda's right.

Ms. Eisenberg: Frankly, NSA is not much of a help. All these groups are way too smart, way too good at avoiding electronic monitoring. It's a cloud of unknowing out there.

Mr. Gutman: In here, you mean.

Ms. Eisenberg: Well, yes, in here, too.

HEU: Kolpakov the Carp

KOLPAKOV IS driving the rented Audi, while Stegerov, alert eyes ever scanning for danger, has taken a seat in the back. Vova Miller is in front of Stegerov in the passenger seat. Kolpakov and Stegerov have picked him up on an almost deserted street corner in Ryazhin.

Miller is carrying 12.7 kilograms of HEU in a battered leather briefcase. Kolpakov is to pay Miller 300,000 euros in 50-euro bills. It is time for the exchange.

"Vova," Kolpakov says, "we'll all do well from this affair. Nothing will come of this except money." Kolpakov, smiling, showing his gray teeth, turns to Miller and nods his head vigorously.

Suddenly at his throat Miller feels excruciating, inexplicable pain. He has just exhaled and—this can't be!—cannot inhale.

Piano wire, a tight loop of it is contracting and slicing into Miller's larynx. His hands fly up to meet the pain, which he can't understand, his head pulled against the window. The street lamps have stopped flashing by, their lights are over the car, not moving. Kolpakov, unsmiling now, is peering into Miller's face, Kolpakov's eyes as emotionless as a carp's.

Struggling to turn, Miller feels himself pulled up, up, up, and back. The pain at his throat, his lungs burning, his eyes bursting, he kicks his feet, he thrashes his arms, swatting at his bleeding neck.

The pain, the pain, the pain, the pain, the pain.

Kolpakov watches, Kolpakov the carp.

K olpakov drives beyond Nizhniy Ryazhin on P 397 into flatlands, a plain covered with low, conical barrows, the funeral mounds of ancient Siberian peoples, long-forgotten nomads who once ranged through here on their shaggy ponies. Kolpakov pulls off P 397 onto an unmarked, unpaved secondary road, and stops by a tall barrow, ghostly in the light of a half moon. The fields around them are dusted with snow. In the distance lights shine from a cluster of buildings, probably a former collective farm, now privatized.

Kolpakov and Stegerov pull Miller's body from the car and drag it to the side of the barrow away from the road, to the shallow grave Stegerov has dug. They leave it there, covered in earth.

I WAKE. And I realize where I am.

Right. And it's after midnight. I give her a gentle shove, then another, but she's awake already, has been awake, maybe, for all this time.

Liz doesn't raise her head, doesn't look at me. She is staring at the ceiling, her face blank, her whole person unreadable.

She says, "Welcome back, guy. Land of the living."

I don't respond for a moment, then I say, "It happens." Then, "I'll clear out."

When I get up to collect my clothes she says, "Just . . . ," and breaks off.

Three hours back, Liz and I had been sitting on the sofa, she with her legs folded under in that too comfortable way she has. She was wearing a loose, coarse-woven flax-colored skirt, peasanty-looking, bought from one of those do-gooder, Third-World, we-are-the-world shops—she knows one in Baltimore—and a thick brown sweater, probably from the same place, looked like it, they went well together. TV off, Liz's house deathly silent without the girls, who had been conveyed to a slumber party at Stacey's, a plump, kindly redhead of thirteen I've met and like. Liz approves of her parents—I don't know them—whose house is one mile away, in Langley.

I dropped in—I'd called before—to check on things after the break-in.

On the sofa Liz said, "Thanks again for coming over that night. It was good of you."

"Cops have anything more to say?"

"Hey, come on. Break-ins like that, they never get the perps."

"Right."

We talk of the girls, get onto the subject of when they were born. The talk goes to our wedding, that hot day in Mifflinburg, after which we went whitewater rafting—New River Gorge, West Virginia, a six-hour drive down from old Yoder's place in Pennsylvania.

"Whose idea?" I asked.

"Yours."

"No no—yours. Not very ladylike or lawyerly, but yours. You made the arrangements."

"Remember we drove down and you fell asleep in the car—I was driving—and your own snoring woke you up?"

"We had gin in our room."

"You got ice from the lady in charge of the miniature golf course next door."

"There was no phone in the room, and the restaurant sent over a kid telling us dinner was ready. I mean, they really wanted us there."

"They didn't have any other customers.

"The guide had a tongue stud that flashed when he talked."

"A long-hair. His name was Mike. He was from Oregon."

"You always had a good memory."

"He did rock climbing as a sport. Had a girlfriend who piloted one of the other rafts."

"Skinny."

"Skinny but cute."

"Yes."

"And it rained and rained."

"Yes, but that was okay.

"And the fantastic mists and clouds hanging over the gorge."

"And the thunder."

"Echoing."

"And in the calmer water Mike would stop the raft and we could jump in and swim."

"And the water was warm."

"And the lunch—eating grilled burgers standing under plastic sheeting that they had to stretch between the trees because of the rain."

"And we repaired to our motel room."

Smiles of regret. I get this feeling, that the past is beginning to become too much, beginning to stretch out of sight, like a road behind you that disappears when you look back, and runs and runs over the horizon back there, and you've come so far you can't see where you've come *from*.

Liz has gotten a home-alarm system installed with the appropriately threatening paddle-shaped signage in front and back of the house—"This House is Protected by Allied Systems" et cetera—and a cypher-keyed telephone by the front door, ready, Allied Systems says, for all emergencies, medical, fire, break-in, you name it. Liz and the girls are now watched over, 24/7.

Liz said, "Oh, Rick, I feel so bad. I mean the girls. What if?" Her eyes fluttered away from mine, a tremor of guilt in that motion.

You said it, I didn't say.

The girls were not fazed in the least by the event. And both were much smitten by the lead cop who came over, a Sgt. Paquin of the Fairfax County Police, who was young, handsome, polite, businesslike, and sported a silvery laptop, on which he took down details of the crime, such as it was—trespassing, breaking and entering, and not much more, maybe a little vandalism. No violence, nothing stolen. The girls also enjoyed the slightly later arrival of a team of latex-gloved lab techs, who dusted everywhere and turned up exactly nothing, as expected.

Liz waved her bourbon glass, giving me a mock salute. "Like some?" she asked. "Come on, join me. I like to have a little at night. Relaxes me." Made me think of the General: *I like a tot. Sometimes several tots.*

I went to the kitchen for a glass and ice. I noticed she has a new fridge, big thing, looked like it belonged in a restaurant kitchen, the whole left half of it freezer, with an ice-maker on the front, covered with the same old magnetic stickers, digital cooking timers, and little plastic clothespins also attached magnetically holding important notes and reminders.

At the "bar" in the dining room, actually an ugly, dark brown oak side table, a Yoder hand-me-down and keepsake from Liz's childhood in Mifflinburg, I poured myself some Jack Daniels, Liz's drink, from a large bottle, the 1.75 liter size, which I saw was half-empty. Liz doesn't throw parties, doesn't have "boyfriends," as she proclaims and the girls affirm. She's hitting the stuff on her own, her "a little at night." I wonder how fast she gets through a 1.75er, how much "relaxing" she needs. I don't pour myself much. Back in the old days with Liz, Global Reach starting up, ballooning, then bursting, I'd have poured a full tumbler over the

rocks, then—finishing that—maybe poured another, then uncorked a bottle of wine for the dinner Liz would have cooked and which would have
been pretty good and which I could not have remembered for the life of
me the next A.M.

I went back to the living room to sit with Liz.

"If I'd just had an alarm system this wouldn't have happened. They could
have come in when the girls were here. I'm absolutely sick about that."

"Hey, Liz, think: *I'm* the security guy. Why the hell didn't *I* have one
put in? Don't blame yourself so much."

"Oh, Rick," she said, her eyes moist. The bourbon. "Why why why?
You empty out, and nothing but sadness comes in, and it fills you, you
think it's forever." She bit her lower lip, and it struck me that all this evening her eyes had seldom met mine.

Drink to me only.

"The girls," she said again. "I feel so bad."

Quickly, surprisingly, she pressed the palm of her hand to her mouth,
and her shoulder hunched up—just once. Always had great control, Liz,
though the tears came.

When I put my hand to her arm, she didn't pull away. My gesture was
only a gesture, spontaneous and unthought-out, but in the old days that
gesture—a hand on the arm, mine on hers or hers on mine—was one of
our signals: sex time.

"Oh, Rick."

I N BED she was taut, clawing at my back, pushing her face into my neck,
pulling her arms tight around me, sometimes almost crying, "You . . .
you . . . you . . . ," jerking her head back when she came, then coming
again—Jesus, when they do that—then tensed, pausing as if in death, then
silence and soft breathing.

I T DIDN'T mean anything," she says dully.
    "Right," I say, pushing my shirt into my trousers, zipping up, sitting
on the bed to put on socks, shoes, and sweater. Liz watches in silence, her
face, as it's been all this evening, unreadable.

Silent, she follows me to the door in a white terry-cloth bathrobe
(she'd had a blue one in the last days of our marriage), her arm in mine,
her hair unkempt.

At the door she says, "It was crazy, Rick. I don't know what the hell . . ."

"Right. I know." My turn to look away, as from a particularly nasty accident.

I walk out onto the graveled parking apron and start my car, a bright yellow Mustang these days, not an Infiniti. Liz is standing in the doorway—it's freezing—staring at me. When I wave good night she stands immobile. I ease the car up to Dulany, pull past the white brick stanchions, and head home in the frigid night.

HQ: Makes Things Really Problematic

OPCOM/NPTG Session Audiotape, Session 62 (Excerpted).

Attending: J. Gutman (Chair), M. Fiscarelli, C. Lindquist, S. Kremer, R. Eisenberg.

Transcriber: D. Braithewaite.

Mr. Gutman: Okay, let's get moving, next item, contacts between Russian mobsters, crooks et cetera, and Islamists, latest news. Rhoda.

Ms. Eisenberg: Right. We had this contact in Turkey identified as a "well-known and reliable Pakistani businessman"—his crypt is BIKER/5, the cable is ANKARA 20339, it's there in your folders—we had this contact tell of a meeting in Turkey, in Antalya, touristy place on the southern coast, between a Russian national named Ivan Oparin and Amin Tajer, who is an associate, close associate of the nuclear engineer Sajid.

Mr. Gutman: Tajer and Oparin?

Ms. Eisenberg: Right.

Mr. Gutman: [Expletive].

Ms. Eisenberg: The report is a MEMCON from a meeting, clandestine meeting in Istanbul, Agency officer and a Pakistani asset. And no, the meeting between Tajer and Oparin if it occurred was not surveiled. The report is after the fact, simply a source saying that the meeting took place. But if it did, it's very disquieting because of Tajer's connection to Sajid.

Mr. Lindquist: Oparin, I don't recall the . . .

Mr. Gutman: Major jerk.

Mr. Lindquist: I know, but . . .

Ms. Eisenberg: Last OPCOM report on Oparin was probably a year or so back, before your time, but Oparin, as I was saying, we have reports of early contacts between Oparin and the Taliban in Afghanistan when they were ruling that country and maintaining contacts with them after . . .

Mr. Gutman: Oparin ran some kind of cheesy airline, flew matériel, weapons, civilian goods, too, into Afghanistan, into Kabul and Kandahar airports back then, this was before 9/11, before we went into Afghanistan. He's also an arms supplier and shipper to every war on the continent of Africa. Real stinker.

Ms. Eisenberg: And we heard Oparin was continuing to have dealings with Taliban representatives in Pakistan and the UAE, and so we got very concerned about this behavior and felt it had to be monitored. Which we've been trying to do.

Mr. Fiscarelli: Very difficult. He has used his satellite phone openly for deals and we've caught that, but he's gotten more secretive. We're also getting chatter, people mentioning his name here and there. Sometimes they just call him "the Russian," but from surrounding context, other calls et cetera, other facts, we know they mean Oparin.

Ms. Eisenberg: Probably his deals got more suspicious and questionable.

Mr. Gutman: NSA made a small project of Oparin a while back, but they think he knew he was being monitored. He'd move around between calls, throw his cells away, talk in code. We think for long stretches he maintains radio silence.

Mr. Kremer: Radio silence?

Mr. Gutman: Doesn't use the phone—doesn't make calls, doesn't take them. Uses couriers, go-betweens, especially probably when he's working a deal.

Ms. Eisenberg: Oparin's almost impossible. But to get back, Oparin meeting this businessman Tajer—if he did, and this is just hearsay from an agent, there's no evidence—this makes things really problematic, because as we know, Tajer was, is, a close associate of Ahmed Sajid, who has become a major worry. Now if Tajer is out meeting with types like Oparin . . .

"In Her Sleep, They Think"

"MARGE DIED." Sue called from Cleveland this morning to give me the news, her flat metallic voice not quite breaking. "Mrs. Kelso found her."

Virgie Kelso, a neighbor who kept a kind of watch over Marge, checking in on her every day, found her lying in bed, her eyes closed, her face peaceful. Virgie called Sue first, and Sue told her she'd call me.

"Early this morning," Sue said. "In her sleep, they think. They're saying it was a heart attack. Not sure, but that's what they're saying. Maybe a stroke at the same time."

I worked things out with Sue on the phone—when she'd fly in (tomorrow), who'd deal with the funeral home (me), when to decide what to do with the house (indefinite, but soon). The house will be hard to sell in the winter.

I found Marge there in the bed, Virgie sitting quietly at the bedside, her fingers intertwined, as if waiting for something. The police have come and gone. The funeral home hearse has just driven off. Virgie has gone home.

And I remain alone.

I will let Marge's church and her gardening club know, put a thing in the paper. Because she was Walter L. Behringer's widow she may get a notice in the *Post* obits. Maybe with a photo. Marge has been taken to the Loeffler Funeral Home. She'll be buried next to Walt in National Cemetery, out Lee Highway in Falls Church.

And the restless living go on.

Sue and I will divide the heirlooms. Sue might want some of the furniture. I don't. We'll probably dump most of it in an estate sale. I've called Liz, who will break it to the girls. Buttons is with Virgie now, though I don't think Buttons has much of a future.

In the empty house I walk from room to room. Strange to hear only my footsteps, my breathing here. In the back den I sit for a time on the couch, then fish out old photo albums, large things with thick covers, and leaf through the black pages. The photos, stuck in place with little triangular paste-on holders, show Marge and Walt in their early days, Walt's father and mother, Marge's, other family members I barely know, some I don't recognize at all, snow scenes in Minnesota.

I come across a photo of Marge from her time at the U, her thick hair piled high up in front and parted on the side, in the style of the '40s. The way she's posed accentuates the high Conover cheekbones. She's wearing an austere dark dress with a narrow, not too deep V neckline, her arm up on some guy's shoulder—not Walt's, I wonder who—and she has a quizzical, almost puzzled look on her face, as if caught by surprise.

I will come to think of her in some midzone between the fragile old lady she became and the beautiful young woman she was when she caught Walt's eye. And gone now like a dream.

Marge's books. Biography, history. And the old copy of *The Jungle Book*—Kipling—with its worn, dark red cover. Walt and Marge had spent Walt's one and only sabbatical year in India in the fifties, back when Walt was a young professor at Minnesota. For Marge, for Walt, too, the experience had been life-transforming.

Marge, naturally, was anticolonial, but loved Kipling anyway, especially *The Jungle Book,* and among that collection of stories her favorite was the one about Rikki-tikki-tavi, the brave mongoose. The animal's name was Rikki and so, later, was the name of her little boy.

"This is the story," she would read to me, "of the great war that Rikki-tikki-tavi fought single-handed through the bathrooms of the big bungalow in Segowlie cantonment." I almost had it memorized. The battle between the little mongoose, protecting the English family, and the cobra that wanted to kill their baby. The protective mongoose, acting like a good native. I was too young to understand the story, the colonial moral.

I FIND a faded color picture showing me, age about six, in football gear, wearing a silly-looking helmet, acting as center, stooped over the ball, about to snap it, as if I could snap a football at that age, to Walt the quarterback, Walt smiling in his rueful way. It's autumn in our Davidson Street backyard. The skinny sycamore in the background of this picture is now tall and thick-trunked. Around it, new then in the picture, is a circular wooden bench, which has been there to this day, though now much weathered. In the left side of the picture is the de Roodes' dogwood, just at the corner of their lot line. The tree died years ago and was taken out. The de Roodes are gone, too.

IN MARGE's bedroom there is one early picture of Walt, which she kept on a marble top dresser: Walt the young professor. He has long blond hair and a very serious demeanor. The dresser is a Conover family heirloom brought here from Minnesota. Marge had a fight over it once with her sister Pru. Pru's gone now, though her husband, Uncle Eddie is still alive, fading away in a retirement home in the District. Sue will probably want the dresser. It's hers.

Staring into Marge's empty bedroom and its whorled maple double bed and matching highboy, I remember the lullaby of Walt and Marge murmuring to each other in that bed just before sleep. Then I catch a glimpse of our compound in Jakarta, and hear Walt and Marge, who slept in twin beds pulled together, murmuring that same murmur to each other. I see the white walls of my bedroom there, and a small gekko occupying the top left corner of the wall opposite my bed.

The garden in Jakarta that Marge loved: rubber plants growing all around, traces of red under the big green-yellow leaves that spread out above my head. The central pool filled with lily pads that had turned up edges like pie plates and that were big enough—I thought at the time—to walk on.

Beyond the pool and its lily pads, was the big steel gate to our compound, which a skinny, ageless servant named Yusuf would clang shut after Walt drove his Land Rover through. And beyond the gate, the road leading away, lined with impossibly tall palm trees, into a world I couldn't explore.

That's all.

IN THE dining room I turn the heat down to fifty-five, then go up to the attic and stand for a moment in the chill, surveying the cardboard filing boxes, old copies of *The Atlantic* and the *National Geo,* once-used lamps, my red wagon, my Lionel train set, a large playhouse (Sue's), badminton rackets (the badminton net is draped over an ancient end table), wicker baskets, wicker furniture, cartons of clothing, weights (a pair of two and half pounders, one seven pounder—where is its twin?), collapsed aluminum lawn chairs that were deposited here at the end of some summer long ago and never brought back down.

At the far end of the attic, in shadow, beyond the boxes, baskets, and toys, in a corner, lodged between two rafters and two uncovered ceiling joists, is Walt's ancient, beaten-up, dark blue footlocker. I've never had a look in there. I'm curious.

To get to it, I crawl to where it sits, banging my head once on the low rafters, and pull it back to the floored part of the attic. The lock on the front is sprung, and one of the leather handles has been pulled partly off. On the top of the box, in bright, light blue paint, is written, "Walter L. Behringer" and under the name, Marge and Walt's old Trinidad Street address in Arlington, where they lived before moving to McLean.

When I open the locker I see: shoe boxes and manila envelopes full of papers; a jumble of smaller boxes; and, at one end, those two Japanese field telephones Walt and I once talked to each other over. They've been stored away now for over thirty years. They were still connected and operating when Walt died. Marge must have collected them and put them up here.

Rummaging through the rest of the stuff, I find a small box covered in dark blue velvet. It contains a sheet of heavy-grade, ivory-colored paper, folded twice to fit the box, and a round, bronze medal an inch and a half or so in diameter. On the medal is the simple inscription, "For Merit. Central Intelligence Agency." The medal shows an eagle facing right over a shield embossed with compass points in all directions, indicating guard against all enemies. Growing around the shield are oak leaves and some other vegetation I can't identify.

On the paper, in print, is a statement:

> It is recommended that WALTER LOOMIS BEHRINGER be awarded the
> Intelligence Medal of Merit. Dr. Behringer was Senior Intelligence
> Analyst in the Vietnam station's Critical Analysis Division from June 12,
> 1967 until November 25, 1968. He was a true area expert with a depth
> of knowledge of Vietnam seldom encountered in a foreigner to that land.
> During his period of service in Vietnam he demonstrated a keen mind and
> an acute analytical ability as is shown by his promotion to Chief Analyst

*in the Saigon Station, the highest post in-country in the Directorate of
Intelligence, a GS-13 level position. Dr. Behringer showed particular
courage during the Communist Tet Offensive of 1968, assisting one
comrade wounded by enemy fire. It is my whole-hearted recommendation
that Mr. Behringer's talent, dedication, and hard work be recognized by
the award of this medal.*

No signature. Just the text. A jockstrap award is what they call these
things. You collect them, but you do not show them to anyone, you do not
even talk about them, and to wear them you pin them inside, not on, your
jockstrap. Private.

I find a box of letters that Marge and Walt exchanged when he was overseas and she was here, alone with the kids. Some of them are blue light-
weight air-letters, though most are regular letters with APO addresses. In
among these letters for some reason is a photo of Walt and Marge at the Taj
Mahal, from their early, India days. Behind them, the Mogul tomb, the long
pool, and, just visible, a monkey calmly gaping at something not in the
frame.

There's no overt passion in the letters. Walt and Marge didn't do passion
in writing. The letters all begin "Dear Marge," or "Dear Walt," and lay out
the day-to-day stuff of their lives. His deal with embassy matters and his im-
pressions of the cities he was in; Marge's are mostly about me and Sue. Walt
usually signed off with a "Miss you much, dear heart," Marge with, "Want
you home." She'd call him "Sugarplum" now and then. Some of Walt's letters date from the period when he was seeing Donna Blalock. Story of a
marriage.

The manila file folders contain documents stamped CONFIDENTIAL, an old
low-level classification—mostly reports on Vietcong force levels and village
pacification, typed in big clunky lettering. All the official stuff seems to be
from Vietnam. Technically, Walt shouldn't have taken this stuff out of the
building, but no big deal. That was Walt.

In a purple velvet sack I find a heavy gold watch, an ancient Waltham. It's
worn with use. Someone pulled it out of his pocket time and again over the
years, consulted it, wound it, put it back in his pocket. Probably John
Behringer. From what I hear of him it's the kind of thing—a precision
timepiece—he'd have had.

Rolled in a brown cardboard tube is Walt's high school diploma of 1937 and high school graduation photo. Walt, with a thick, slicked-back pompadour of blond hair, is looking affably beyond the photographer's shoulder. In the same tube is Walt's Certificate of Discharge from the Army Air Corps, 1946.

Behind the field telephones, encased in a large, clear plastic envelope, is a yellowed copy of *The New York Times*, dated Wednesday, April 30, 1975. It has a screaming, eight-column headline:

MINH OFFERS UNCONDITIONAL SURRENDER;
1,000 AMERICANS EVACUATED FROM SAIGON IN COPTERS WITH 5,500 SOUTH VIETNAMESE.

FORD UNITY PLEA.
President Says That Departure "Closes a Chapter" for U.S.

REGIME YIELDS
Its Leader Declares He Acts to Avoid More Bloodshed.

The front-page photograph is the iconic image of American defeat in Southeast Asia: a helicopter perched—precariously, it looks—on a metal boxlike structure the size of a small cabin on top of the American embassy in Saigon. On the roof is a crowd of people: most seem to be Vietnamese. Some are filing up a ladder to the copter. A man on the structure who looks American is helping them up. The copter is not large and cannot begin to carry all these people. Hopeless.

I notice one more thing: a heavy manila packet labeled CIRCLE that contains old clips from the *Post*, the *Times*, and the *Wall Street Journal*, most of them dated 1967, 1968, all of them yellowed and crumbling after forty-some years. They seem mostly to be stories about Vietcong force levels. "U.S. Aides Say Foe's Strength and Morale Are Declining Fast," reads the headline of one, dated November 11, 1967. Paperclipped to it—the clip has rusted and has stained the paper—is a copy of a CIA cable dated October 7, the month before. The cable is classified SECRET LIMITED DISTRIBUTION ONLY and was written by a man named Cmdr. James Meacham, USN. It is addressed to Dean Rusk, the secretary of state at the time, and is to be passed on to Walt Rostow, Lyndon Johnson's main Vietnam adviser. Walt is listed as a contributor and "W. Behringer" is on the routing slip.

The cable tells of a fall in VC force levels from 126,000 in August 1966, to 118,000 a year later.

There is another CIA document, a kind of report. On the cover I make out the faint lettering: SECRET SECRET SECRET. The author of the report is WALTER L. BEHRINGER, ASSIGNED MACV J-2 SAIGON (TEMPORARY DUTY). The report is dated October 11, 1967, and was sent from the American embassy in Saigon, addressed to "Helms, DCI, Langley." It, too, speaks of declining Vietcong force levels.

And that's it. Ancient history. Though I wonder about that label, CIRCLE.

MARGE KEPT these things, all the substantial records of Walt's life, unable to throw them away, but unable to keep them in sight, either. I've never seen any of it except for the two field telephones.

I haul Walt's heavy footlocker down the narrow attic stairs, pull it out the door, and hoist it into the trunk of my Mustang. I'll take it home. I'll give Sue a chance to look through it and see if she wants anything. She won't want the phones, and in any case won't get them, but she'll want some of the other stuff.

HQ: Now You See Him, Now You Don't

OPCOM/NPTG Session Audiotape, Session 65 (Excerpted).

Attending: J. Gutman (Chair), M. Fiscarelli, C. Lindquist, S. Kremer, R. Eisenberg.

Transcriber: L. Jamison.

Ms. Eisenberg: Now as to the reported Tajer-Oparin meeting in Antalya, we've scrambled to get this.

Mr. Gutman: And in fact Rhoda tells me only this morning some of it, some of it came in.

Ms. Eisenberg: Correct, and I'm relaying it now. We know from Turkish immigration control and PIA [Pakistan International Airlines] manifests that Amin Tajer, who is a known associate of Sajid, entered Turkey a day before the purported meeting with Ivan Oparin, the Russian arms merchant, and left a day after the meeting. He stayed in the Antalya Sheraton, went back home to Karachi. No other information. I mean, it really does sound like this meeting was the reason for the trip.

Mr. Gutman: Let me jump in. We have no information of Oparin's whereabouts at the time. As I say, he is very hard to track and often maintains radio silence. He has multiple identities and passports issued by the Russian government—he's very close to Russian intelligence and probably has incognito entrée to Turkey and in fact manages to go pretty much wherever he pleases incognito. Now you see him, now you don't.

Mr. Kremer: You say we got no signals traffic? Oparin? Tajer?

Ms. Eisenberg: No.

Mr. Kremer: Sterile cell phones or something.

Mr. Gutman: If he was using anything.

Mr. Kremer: Hey, he lives in the world.

Mr. Gutman: Well, people manage not to use phones when it suits their purposes not to.

EVENING. I'M at home. I've been thinking about those old Japanese field telephones. I wonder what shape they're in, and though I'd never sell them, I wonder what they're worth. They haven't been opened in thirty years. So I go down into my finished basement—den, half-bath, laundry room— where I've stowed Walt's blue footlocker. I haul it into the den, open it with its creaky almost-sprung hinges, and lift out the phones.

The field clunker in its green wooden case seems fine. When I lift the old handset and feel the spring of the talk switch, I'm ten years old again. I will hook them up and test them. I bet they work.

When I open the polished leather carrying case of the other, the elegant phone of blond wood and polished metal, I see rolled and placed under the handset a few—three, when I count them—white, blue-lined pages that look as if they were torn from a notebook. They look as if they're from Walt's Vietnam Diary, and I think they are. The size and shape are exactly the same, the writing is in his hand, and he's used the same system of exact dating. But these notes are not from Walt's Vietnam period; they are from the spring of 1975, a few months before he killed himself. My heart pounds.

One entry reads:

> *Wed. 19 March 75. Too hard. Can't concentrate. Don't want to think. Tired, all too much. Can't write. Must write CIRCLE.*

He was working on something called CIRCLE, the word he used to label that packet of newspaper clippings and two CIA documents.

Another entry reads:

> *Thurs. 27 March 75. Cannot write CIRCLE without documents. Must "borrow."*

The last reads:

> *Tues. 2 Apr 75. Brought docs home, wrapped in saran, then plastic garbage bag, then bag in tupperware bowl (sealed) put under first azalea back row.*

Meaning that Walt, trying to write something he called CIRCLE, stole documents from work, carefully wrapped those documents against moisture in the ground, and buried them in the raised azalea bed behind our house.

Where, three months later, he shot himself.

I rise as if in a trance and drive to Marge's place. I turn on the backyard light, then head for the low metal gardening shed to the side of the azalea bed, where I pull a spade from a cardboard drum where the handled tools—a brace of rakes, the shovels, two mattocks—are kept, and I climb up among the azaleas. They are woodier and thicker now than they were thirty years ago, but they are the same plants.

First azalea, back row.

I suppose that means the one to the far left. I plunge the pointed spade into the earth, stabbing at it. The spade is shiny and its tip is worn concave after much use. It was the spade Walt gardened with. Probably the tool he used to bury . . . what?

I hack into the hard winter ground in front of the azalea, spewing clumps of dirt this way and that, hitting roots that have strayed way over from the Siberian elm, slicing through them. Maddeningly, my spade clunks against rocks—most of the time in this Virginia piedmont soil you have a hard time *finding* rocks—and, digging down a foot or so in front of the shrub, I find nothing but clusters of roots and more rocks, no hint of something buried. I chop crazily at the earth to the left of the shrub, exposing more roots, the earthy smell rising, my heart pounding. I find nothing.

Furious now, I cut into the ground behind the plant, digging a deep circle around the azalea and cursing luck, cursing Walt's directions, when there—my spade exposes something not soil or rock or plant, but a soft but firm presence, pliable and oblong.

Plastic.

IN THE chilly kitchen I place the box—it is rectangular, its sealed lid, a pale, discolored blue, has collapsed into the box itself—on Marge's white formica-topped counter.

Carefully I pull off the lid, still stuck at one corner and see that the leaf-bag has opened—leaking in how many years of rain?—and contains only a black mass of slime. I peel the black plastic away from its contents, which stink, and lay them out on the counter. There: Walt's handiwork. I touch it carefully, testing it. I try to pull it apart, but cannot; the contents have melded together into a solid lump of ancient, rotted paper. Whatever this material once was, whatever information it contained, is lost forever.

Standing at the counter in the cold, empty house, staring at the damp mess, I break down and weep.

NEXT DAY I take the Beltway to College Park and the Archives, where at the CIA declassified document monitor I punch in "CIRCLE + Behringer", but get nothing. "Behringer + Vietcong" gets me a number of documents, including the 1967 cable Walt wrote to Richard Helms that I found in the attic in the packet marked CIRCLE. Nothing else.

At home, I call around to old pals of Walt's whose names and phone numbers I know, or can find and who are still alive, Pappas, of course, others, and tell them of the envelope I found in the attic and of Walt's strange cache out in our azalea bed.

"It was something called 'CIRCLE,' " I say, when I get Pappas. "Some kind of report or project he was working on at home, away from headquarters for some reason. Any ideas?"

"Jeez, wow, caught me off guard. Give me a sec. This was when?"

"Spring 1975. He died in early July that year. He made the notes like in March and April. So he was working on it around then."

Pappas says, "Hun."

"And he called it 'CIRCLE' and it had to do with Vietnam, maybe with Vietcong force levels—that's what the newspaper clips dealt with anyhow and a report, official report he'd done for the Agency. Sent to Helms."

"Hun."

I hear Pappas expelling breath.

"Shit, I'm getting old, and it's been a long goddamn time, like, jeez, thirty years, something like that. I don't think I can tell you what it's about. Be nice to know, Rick, especially for you, I do understand that, but, nah, I don't think I can help."

He tells me he hopes I find out what it's all about and to let him know if I do. We talk a little more and end it. Nobody else I talk with is any help, either. Then I go to bed.

In the early morning—is it three A.M.?—I wake and see a sliver of light from the street lamps cutting across the far wall and reflected in the mirror over the dresser.

I hear occasional traffic out there on Old Dominion: the soft chuff of a truck braking and shifting down, and after a few moments, the far-off wail of a siren—ambulance? fire engine?—that approaches, fades, and is gone.

HQ: FSB Is a (Expletive) Sieve

SCI TOP SECRET GREEN SCI TOP SECRET GREEN SCI TOP SECRET GREEN
SCI TOP SECRET GREEN SCI
OPCOM/NPTG Session Audiotape, Session 67 (Excerpted).

Attending: J. Gutman (Chair), M. Fiscarelli, C. Lindquist, S. Kremer, R. Eisenberg.

Transcription: L. Jamison.

Mr. Gutman: We'll start our rundown in a sec, but I have to flag an enormous problem, just turned up early this morning, and it's a threat to the safety of our agents. Plus viability of ongoing operations and what we may do in the future. Just gotten word. We had a walk-in in Moscow who says Russians have penetrated our most sensitive communications. ODNI is afraid of a real security breach in commo—something out at the Warrenton commo center. Stuff going through there, out there in Virginia, stuff is being read in Moscow. It's making them pretty uncomfortable.

Mr. Lindquist: Everybody's suspicious of walk-ins.

Mr. Kremer: The Warrenton site is as secure as you get.

Mr. Gutman: Sure, as is the encryption. So? The guy, the walk-in has some credibility apparently. Guy said some of the stuff coming out of there, out of Warrenton, was getting read, that the Russian embassy people were collecting it here in Washington. He said he knew of one office in the Defense Ministry that routinely had gotten reports via that route. Routinely. What he saw had to do with nuclear proliferation, stuff we were doing to monitor the trade, people we were using. Which is an enormous concern.

Mr. Fiscarelli: [Expletive] FSB. If they're reading our mail, what they get may not stay confined to FSB and the Russian government.

Mr. Gutman: [Expletive] exactly right. FSB is a [expletive] sieve, and we all know it. They're all . . . all these Russians are on the take. Sources and methods do get out into the private sector. Bad guys, hoodlums find out what you know and how you know it. They get smarter. We can't tell about the breach at Warrenton yet. But it is a dirty business. After our walk-in walked in, NSA redid some of their procedures and encryption methods. Supposedly we're back to being secure. Who [expletive] knows?

Ms. Eisenberg: Jack, this is just terrible. Are we assessing . . .

Mr. Gutman: CI [counterintelligence] people are most definitely currently looking at the time frame on this, what information may have been lost and when it was lost. But whatever it is, it is lost, period, irretrievable. I'm very concerned about this and the threat to operations, and the threat, literal physical threat to our people, who are now in danger, and this is, yes, I agree, terrible. Literally life and death.

"This Isn't a 'Dump'"

"HERON." I point at a tall, gray-blue bird perched on a mud bank, motionless as a statue and looking for prey.

Frannie and I are hiking Roosevelt Island. We are down by the Boundary Channel that separates the island, a small, pleasant "national memorial" to TR, from the mainland of Virginia. (Columbia Island, where Pappas and I have our occasional alfresco rendezvous, is the next island down—you just follow the bike path over a boardwalk and you're there.)

Frannie and I have institutionalized our walks here. We usually meet at one of our places, Frannie's today, on a Saturday afternoon if Frannie can get away from work, and drive down here. We have our walk, sit around, relate a little, then head home for some dinner and a TV evening or not, then, generally, some spirited fooling around.

On our walks here we usually take the looping trail that follows the perimeter of the island down into the low, swampy areas by the river. The trail isn't long, not much more than a mile, I'd say. Once in a while we'll pay a visit to TR's memorial in the middle of the island, a brick-paved plaza surrounded by fountains and reflecting pools at the north end of which stands a dark bronze statue of the old Rough Rider. He's dressed in civvies, not his Rough Rider outfit, delivering a speech somewhere, looking exhortatory, his right hand up, ready to pound home some point he's making. Circling the site are tall slabs of gray marble engraved with TR's thoughts on appropriate subjects—nature, manhood, youth.

Today we're keeping to the path. The weather is clear-skied and sunny-chilly. Frannie's wearing her military khaki parka with brown fake-fur collar and a pair of black jeans she reserves for yard work and hikes. After we pass under Roosevelt Bridge and its rumbling traffic (the Roosevelt is a major artery into and out of the District), we settle on a familiar bench with a view of a quiet inlet that smells nicely of rot and where two late-to-leave mallards, male and mate, are paddling. "They pair up, don't they?" I say. "Like people? Maybe these two'll stay right here. Winter here. Maybe it's warm enough for them. You wonder how they make up their minds."

"Mmmm. I'd head south."

We're quiet for a time. I'm about to tell Frannie about Walt and CIRCLE and the lump of muck I've dug up back in the azaleas, when Frannie, who's been subdued this afternoon, says, "I'm wondering . . ." pauses a sec, then in a nervous-husky way, says, "I think we should step back, Rick. From the relationship. I think we just have to. Where I am—it's just not what I had in mind."

I look at her dumbly, and for all I know my tongue is lolling out of my mouth. "This is kind of out of the blue. I mean way out. I mean, like zero warning. How come?"

"I know, I know, I know. Rick, this isn't a 'dump,' really. I don't want it to be that. It's just a . . . it's a time out. I need to have some time—and some space. And I need to do a little reflection."

I can only stare at her.

Do you love me? Do you? she would ask. And I wonder, Do I?

"It hasn't been a waste of time," I say. "Not for me."

"No no no, of course not, I don't mean that, not for me, either."

"So what's the problem?"

"I think . . . I can't say it exactly. I think maybe I was getting too close to you, that I felt that . . . that I was actually falling in love with someone again, and you're supposed to feel good about that, and I didn't. And that scared me. This has been . . . I've been feeling this for a while." She puts her hand on mine, then withdraws it. "Oh, Rick, am I making sense? I thought I'd gotten through the thing with Jim, that I'd be okay seeing guys. But you can fool yourself that way. I wasn't seeing anybody when we met and I thought maybe it would be okay. I thought, well, let's give it a go. But I'm just not sure now and it's not fair to you. I'm still afraid. Maybe I'm still numb from

Jim. But right now, the way it is . . . It isn't any good. Oh, Rick, Rick, Rick, Rick, Rick."

Tears. She crosses her arms, hugging them tightly to her body. She's staring straight ahead at nothing.

I look away, too. Those mallards are still silently paddling the inlet, clucking—to each other?—and diving occasionally for what it is that ducks dive for.

"You're genuinely kind, Rick," she says, finally, I suppose to buck me up and be positive about all this. "I've seen it and felt it, and you're *not* dishonest. I trust you, I believe you, you don't lie to me"—this is a response to some of Liz's diatribes that I've unloaded on Frannie and is quite true. "You are . . . sympathetic. And I loved it when you played the piano, especially the soft, romantic stuff"—looking my way, small smile through the snuffles— "very seductive. But I'm afraid. Not on the surface. Down deep. Can you see? It isn't you, it's me." She tightens her mouth. "That's what they all say, right? 'It's not you, it's me. It's not fair to you' et cetera et cetera." She lets out a breath. "It's been building over I don't know, weeks, maybe."

"Clueless me."

"And I just have to sort things out."

"Why now?"

She sighs. "Because it's been going on so long."

WE HEAD back in silence over the bridge to mainland America and the parking lot. We board her Chevy, and she pulls out of the lot onto the GW, heading for Spout Run and the crazy Arlington streets that take us to her home, where I've left my Mustang.

When we get out I say, "I don't want to say good-bye."

She nods curtly, her face somber. She ascends the porch stairs, unlocks her door, and with a small wave vanishes into her house.

HEU: "If You Cheat Us, You Will Die."

IN THE parking lot of an abandoned paper mill on a secondary road north of Moscow they exchange the money for the goods. The mill lies next to a canal and across a railroad track from a small gathering of abandoned buildings—a machine shop, a tavern, a few houses. The railroad, which once served the mill, bringing in scrap paper and old rags, taking out new paper, follows the canal. The line hasn't been used for years.

It's late afternoon on a cold, windless day. Snow covers the surrounding fields, which are sodden from a recent drizzle. The day is chilly.

Kolpakov arrived first. He has three men with him, all armed with machine pistols, though Kolpakov himself is carrying no weapon. Their vehicle is a large beige Mercedes-Benz SUV.

Oparin's team, also four men, is led by a tall, redheaded man named Dmitri—"Misha"—Bichurin. They've arrived half an hour after Kolpakov in a white Toyota Highlander. All Bichurin's comrades are armed with Beretta pistols. Bichurin himself carries no gun. Sheathed at his belt is a military knife, his signature weapon. The knife is thirty-five centimeters long and has a grip of black rubber and a silvery cross guard. The blade itself is a gray matte color and has a false edge that slopes down to the true edge forming a sharp point. Bichurin claims he uses the weapon well and likes to show it off.

Bichurin's driver parks the Toyota twenty meters from Kolpakov's SUV. Then Kolpakov and Bichurin get out of their vehicles, approach each other, and stop a few meters apart halfway between their vehicles. They nod hello.

"The material," Bichurin says.

Kolpakov nods again and keeping his eyes on Bichurin signals with his right hand to his man Stegerov, who gets out of the vehicle carrying a black plastic valise, and approaches. He places the valise on the asphalt between Kolpakov and Bichurin. Stegerov's movements show that the valise is heavy.

Keeping his eyes on Bichurin, Kolpakov gestures at the valise with his head. "That's it. The payment?"

Bichurin is staring at the valise, a look almost of wonder on his face. He snaps his eyes back to Kolpakov and says softly, "Yes. Right."

He turns and waves, nodding yes to his comrades in the Toyota. One emerges from the vehicle with a small, gray plastic suitcase and puts it on the ground next to the black valise. Stegerov moves to take the valise. Bichurin says, "Hang on. There are two more of these." His comrade goes back to the Toyota, returns with the other two suitcases, and places them next to the first.

Kolpakov says, "All right?"

Bichurin shrugs. He motions to the man who brought out the suitcases, who then picks up the black valise; making two trips, Stegerov carries the suitcases to the car, puts them on the rear seat, and returns to stand by Kolpakov.

Kolpakov says, "Now we verify."

Kolpakov and Stegerov go to the Mercedes and open the three suitcases. They find forty apparently identical packets of bills, held together by large rubber bands. From among these packets they select four at random and count the bills in each: each contains four hundred apparently genuine 500-euro notes. They take three other samples at random, pull forty or fifty notes from each, and inspect the notes carefully: they examine the holograms and the varicolored inks, they compute the checksums, hold the bills up to the light to view the watermarks and the security threads, they feel the textures. The bills appear genuine. This process takes twenty minutes.

Kolpakov steps out of the Mercedes and orders his other men into the car. Then he approaches Bichurin and says, "All right. Time for you to leave."

Bichurin nods, goes back to the Toyota, and gets in. Bichurin and his men pull away in reverse from Kolpakov's Mercedes, then stop. Bichurin from the passenger seat surveys Kolpakov, his men, the road, the surrounding fields. Then, the Toyota pulls slowly onto the road and disappears in the direction of the setting sun.

A T A second meeting near his Mediterranean-style villa south of Moscow, again outside on the service road, Ivan Oparin had told Kolpakov, "We will take possession of the commodity. We will pay you then and there eight million euros in full and in cash for thirteen kilograms of the commodity. We assume you will be honorable and that you will supply us the commodity as described."

Unsaid: If you cheat us, you will die.

HQ: It's Nukes

SCI TOP SECRET GREEN SCI TOP SECRET GREEN SCI TOP SECRET GREEN SCI TOP SECRET GREEN SCI
OPCOM/NPTG Session Audiotape, Session 68 (Excerpted).

Attending: J. Gutman (Chair), M. Fiscarelli, C. Lindquist, S. Kremer, R. Eisenberg.

Transcription: L. Jamison.

Ms. Eisenberg: To sum, Jack, on the Sajid problem, and we've got these bits of evidence that add up if we look at them to a pretty clear case. We believe Ahmed Sajid, a colleague of A. Q. Khan and a nuclear engineer and a person in deep hiding, is connected to the Pakistani terrorist group Jund al-Haqq, which has known al-Qaeda ties. We think Sajid controls an Islamic charity which is getting Islamist money to finance his work on, nuclear work of some kind. We know Sajid, crazy engineer, is connected with a Pakistani businessman named Amin Tajer, who nominally runs Islamic Relief. This person Tajer, Amin Tajer, who may be a kind of messenger boy, we think has met recently in Turkey with the Russian arms merchant and gangster Ivan Oparin. We don't know why, but . . .

Mr. Gutman: It's nukes.

Ms. Eisenberg: And we do have to do a push on this. Like right away.

"And He's a Killer"

COCKTAIL LOUNGE in the Sheraton Premier, that big glass cylinder on Leesburg Pike, an easy stroll from Global Reach—I've actually walked here. It's late morning and the lounge is almost empty. I'm at a table with Fiscarelli, who looks terrible in the bright, sky-lit atrium, as if he's been needing sleep for days or is nursing a cold. I decide neither is the case: Fiscarelli just looks terrible when the light's on him. He's drinking a martini, stirring it with a little pink straw. I'm doing Sprite.

"Know this guy?" Fiscarelli hands me a color photocopy of a Russian passport. The cover is magenta and is embossed with a golden double eagle. On the first inside page is a portrait of a man in a necktie and suit coat. His face is impassive, flat, Russian. Pale skin, gray eyes. Moles. Mustache. A face you can't read. Could be the face of a dead man.

And, yes, I do know him. He's aged, he's puffed out under his eyes, and his cheeks show flab, but it's Johnny, all right, Johnny Oparin.

Under Oparin's picture are his passport number, birthdate, place of birth, signature in Cyrillic. On the inner pages are visas—UAE, Turkey, Republic of the Congo, Liberia, Sierra Leone. Exit and entry stamps, dates—the official record of some, at least, of Johnny's wanderings. I wonder how Fiscarelli got this.

A memory: Sharjah Airport, eight years back. Blistering heat. In the air, dust, sand, and jet exhaust. I had come to the freight terminal to meet a shipment of equipment—computers, software, and telecoms—for the Bank of Sharjah, a Global Reach customer. Real business, not Black World.

Bored and restless waiting inside the terminal, I walked out onto the warehouse loading dock, and there I saw this tall, thick-armed guy in a billed cap, shirt sleeves rolled up, talking with an Arab. The Arab was wearing a red and white *kaffiyeh,* white *thowb,* and a feather-weight black cloak with gold edging hanging loosely over his shoulders. The Arab had a black spade beard. When he talked he gestured languidly with the ease of a man who was used to having things his way.

The two were overseeing a loading operation, from the warehouse to a waiting Ilyushin 18, a four-engine turboprop, a large plane for large shipments. Forklifts were carrying pallet after pallet of wooden crates marked in Cyrillic characters from the dock to the waiting Ilyushin. On the dock two crates were open. One held AKs, the other ammo—some kind of quality check, I suppose.

You could tell: They were flying this stuff out of Russia or Kazakstan or Ukraine, probably using phony end-user certs, and they had brought it here to Sharjah, where the regulations are light and easy. They were transfering it to another plane, that Ilyushin out there, and sending it to—where? Somalia? Sudan? Central African Republic? Some place like that.

After a time the Arab gathered his cloak about himself and swept from the loading dock, leaving Johnny and some associates. With no one else to talk to and being curious, I walked up to him to say hello. Johnny's men got in my way, but Johnny didn't seem to care. He signaled them to let me by. Eyeing me up and down, he asked, "What are you doing?"

I told him my name, my real one, Rick Behringer, and what I was doing in Sharjah. He nodded approvingly. "Good business." Then I asked him who *he* was and what *he* was doing. At that he just smiled, turned, and walked away, his men closing in behind him.

After Johnny had gone, a Brit working for Sharjah Customs asked me if I'd "seen Oparin, Johnny Oparin—that was him out there on the dock, bloody Satan himself," and in a hushed voice, eyes aglint with excitement, told me a little about the man. But I'd heard of Oparin. Everyone in the FMA trade has.

Fiscarelli smiles at the story. "Still Johnny's main business—weapons. He rounds them up and flies or ships them to customers in Africa, Latin America, and the Caribbean. He owns a fleet of aircraft. His airlines shift names and nominal owners. Believe it or not, some of his cargo planes have flown missions for us in Iraq. Main airline is TAK Air, maybe ten or a dozen old

Russian planes, a kind of mother fleet. Name hasn't changed in ten years. TAK Air leases its planes to temporary little companies that get registered in places like Panama, or Beirut, or"—Fiscarelli gestures with both hands at me—"the Emirate of Sharjah. They fly for a while, then fold."

Fiscarelli leans over the low table, forearms on his knees. "He doesn't travel under his own name in the West, never visits the TAK Air offices, but he is thick with the Russian security services, and they furnish him with multiple identities, multiple passports. He's very discreet. Probably owns or rents places in Western Europe—London, Paris likely—does it through middlemen. Wherever he goes, he keeps his head down.

"We think he was born in Almaty, in 1956. Mom and Pop were Russians. They'd been living in Estonia, but came to Kazakhstan back in the '50s as settlers. The Soviets had this big deal back then, Virgin Lands Plan, Khrushchev's big idea. They were going to develop Central Asia and fill it full of highly productive collective farms, cotton and whatever. Whole scheme blew up in their faces—bad planning, bad weather, bad engineering, bad everything. But Johnny's parents stayed on, and Kazakhstan is where Johnny went to school.

"In 1976, he joined the Soviet internal security forces. They taught him martial arts and how to handle guns. He was stationed around the Soviet Union at a bunch of military bases, last one near Vitebsk in Belarus.

"When he got out of the service he went back to Almaty and made friends with the local drug mafia. After a while he took over a drug smuggling gang—guy's got a way—that was running heroin from Tajikistan and Uzbekistan, even from Afghanistan. They move the product from Central Asia to Russia and Eastern Europe, eventually the EU. Oparin also acts as money launderer and trafficks in 'Natashas'—Russian prostitutes outside Russia. He's involved in legitimate business, too: construction, transportation, oil exports. He owns a transport company, ships goods around Russia by train. When he has to, he pays off local customs services and the transit police. He has allies in Azerbaijan, Georgia, Armenia. He's gotten married, divorced, and married again, divorced again."

Fiscarelli's voice gets confiding. "This is a good one. In the '80s, this was in Kazakhstan, they threw him in prison for rape. When the other inmates found out he'd been in the security service they lit into him, wanted to beat the shit out of him, but he was good at defending himself—he's a genuine tough guy—and they learned it was smarter to leave him alone.

And this tells you something—long before his sentence was up, he walked, free man, absolutely free man. Little help from his friends. Bastard still moves around Kazakhstan. Never been rearrested. Kazakhstan a great country or what?"

Fiscarelli raises his martini in a toast and makes an admiring clicking sound with his tongue.

"And he's a killer. He's eliminated rivals and enemies: a Chechen drug smuggler, the Kazak head of a rival construction company, a journalist—a woman—who had been following Johnny's story as money-launderer. She was shot dead in the street in Moscow outside a restaurant. Nobody ever arrested, of course."

Fiscarelli sucks the last of his martini through the little pink straw, making a small hooshing sound, and signals the waiter for another. "We, ah, we want to learn more about him. His business, his movements, get, ah, get a general fix on the guy. Question is, how do we get in?"

Fiscarelli gets confiding again, lowering his voice, leaning over the cocktail table. "He wanted to come to the States once. Long back. Before any international warrants were out on him. He applied for a visa in Moscow, but the embassy turned him down. They followed the rules, but it was a wrong move. If he'd come here we could have trailed him around. Maybe we'd have gotten lucky and he would have broken U.S. law while he was here and we could have arrested him. Anyhow, he never came. About the same time he applied for the visa we heard that he wanted to buy telecoms equipment here—very sophisticated stuff, stuff's that's very secure and that you weren't allowed to ship overseas back then. He never made it in, but he wanted that commo equipment. Maybe he got it, the export regs are so relaxed these days. But maybe he still worries about security. Maybe a sales guy, security sales guy could get close to him—who knows what the possibilities would be?"

Fiscarelli looks at me steadily.

III: CAPTURE

"Liking Doesn't Come into It Where There's Money"

"WE CALLED him Johnny. Real name's Ivan, of course. Ivan Oparin, but Johnny—in English—was what he liked us to call him. Knew him out there—Africa, off and on, after that, too."

Edward Timperman, General Manager, InterAir Aviation, is telling me the story, lounging back comfortably, his cowboy boots up on his desk. We are up on an open deck in InterAir's warehouse in Dania, Florida, overlooking a clutter of boxes, crates, and shipping modules on the warehouse floor. Nothing is happening down there. In here you can smell diesel exhaust from Route 1 and hear the trucks rumbling by. Jets flying into Fort Lauderdale Hollywood International shake the windows.

"Johnny always preferred his Russians, especially for the African work, but, yeah, he hired me on. A little later"—Timperman's eyes drift— "Afghanistan, yeah, there and the Gulf."

Timperman is large. He has a wide, pink, buttocky face and buggy eyes. He has clipped hair and a mustache. He is wearing jungle fatigues with huge pockets. He has a beer gut. In his accent there's a trace of the Afrikaaner.

"I been in plenty of scrapes flying in Africa," Timperman says. "Real scrapes. You do over there. And I've flown some funny cargoes. Flew the western routes, Fokkers mostly. I never checked out on Russian planes. Johnny's company, TAK Air—don't know what the name meant, some Russian thing, you'd have to ask Johnny—but you'd see their planes, mostly old Antonovs, the odd Ilyushin, see them oh, everywhere out there. Freetown, Monrovia, Brazzaville, Kinshasa—all those towns. Planes weren't very new, of course. But Johnny flew them, out there making a buck."

"TALK TO Eddie Timperman," Ted Pappas told me when I asked him about Oparin. "Down in Florida. South African. Used to be a pilot. He's office manager of a crummy little company in Miami called InterAir. Ought to be called Shit Creek Airlines. They fly execs around the Caribbean—Caymans, Bahamas, wherever. Do freight hauling, too. They're on call, like taxi drivers. Timperman schedules them and bosses the maintenance and cargo crews around.

"Eddie used to fly for Oparin, way back, like in the early '90s, I think. Oparin was flying matériel into Afghanistan for the Taliban, way before 9/11, of course. Got too hot after that, Afghan war and all, right? But back then Timperman flew for him. Timperman says he doesn't know, but everybody thinks Oparin was flying heroin then, too. Either right out of Afghanistan or they'd bring it across the border into Tajikistan, and Johnny'd fly it from there. That's the rumor. Even the Russians disapproved of it, but Johnny never got nabbed for it. Friends in high places.

"Timperman's an asshole, very flamboyant. Once he flew a cow to a friend in Connecticut who owned a 'gentleman's farm'—tax dodge—and Eddie gave him this big milk cow for Christmas, flew it from Wisconsin himself. Whole deal cost him a shitload, but that's Eddie when he's got money. That was back when, of course.

"Then Timperman left Oparin, I don't know why, and he got a job flying for this company, Air Transafricain. Belgian. We used it a lot. Everyone knew the airline had Agency gigs. Shit, that's why they got the *legitimate* business. And that's how I got to know Eddie. After a while the Belgians fired him—for drinking mostly. He'd get violent, get into bar fights, not show up for work, or show up late and hungover. The Belgians, God, they keep anybody on, you can't get people to fly those routes, not Europeans, anyway, which they wanted. But Eddie was too lousy even for them. Lost his license in the wake of all this, couldn't get it back. Screwed. When you're fifty and washed up . . . So Oparin took him back on as a freight manager, the Gulf—Sharjah, I think, then Istanbul."

Timperman has no family. He hates Africans and won't, or can't, go back to his native land. Pappas says the Agency is pretty much done with him, that he doesn't have a handler anymore. "I hear they think he's juiced out. Might have burned him, for all I know—maybe he told them too many lies. Whatever, he's inactive. But guys like Timperman, they're never out of touch with their past, they always want to hear stuff. Sometimes they do. I give him a buzz now and then just to keep the relationship going, see if he has anything to say.

"Anyhow, he knows Oparin. He knows stuff you won't get out of the Agency. You'll have to go down there, though. Won't work over the phone. I'll give him a call ahead of time. He'll be okay."

I can hear Pappas, hear his line: buddy in the phone business I told him about Johnny Oparin ha ha your old pal no hey I heard TAK Air wants phones secure networks that stuff TAK Air's actually in growth mode nah nah this guy's legit very knowledgeable making a business sweep through Europe ten cities five days that kind of thing ha ha I exaggerate but no he's gonna be in Florida more business guy's a maniac thought you could fill him in on the Johnny Oparin account TAK Air all that give him some business pointers maybe some personal insight also might be a good guy to know you might get some work out of him yeah sure InterAir but I mean you you personally good for some bucks maybe a lot no I don't know what kind of work but what the hell use your imagination who knows who knows right?

I'VE RENTED a no-frills Pontiac at Miami International and driven up Biscayne Boulevard through town in sunny, almost warm winter weather, past places called the "Gator Pit" and "Davey Jones's Locker." Fort Liquordale, some call the area.

I found Timperman up Route 1, just inside the Dania line. InterAir rents space here in a block of low, sun-bleached buildings. There are a lot of these blocks along Route 1. They're separated every so often by midrise motels—"Waterbeds, Adult TV"—that also look like warehouses, most of them locally owned, that service the Fort Lauderdale and Miami airports.

The other companies in InterAir's block are service firms for the airports—small aircraft maintenance and parts suppliers ("Dixie Ball

Bearings," "Southern Aircraft Equipment, Inc."), almost-unheard-of courier services and freight haulers—InterAir competitors—and a couple of freight forwarders. Most do business with the other fields in town, too—Miami International, Opa-Locka, Fort Lauderdale Exec.

JOHNNY OPARIN—why do you want to know him?" Timperman asks. "I'd stay away." Pappas has done his job. Timperman is pretending I'm a telecoms guy. Timperman is pretty sure I'm Agency, but he can't figure the arrangement. If he tells me anything, it'll be for the Agency favor bank, not mine. Plus the cash.

"Oparin, Johnny Oparin—he had this way of walking, of holding himself, very jaunty—know what I mean? Self-assured, like a man walking into the wind. The manner of it was, 'Here comes Johnny Oparin and the world better look out.' Always serious face, though. Face, something in it, didn't go with his ease of movement. Funny.

"He liked to talk. Not that he was a sociable guy. Not Johnny. But he liked to know people, talk to them, know what's going on."

I think of Jim McClennan. *He likes talking to people the way other people like to read books,* Frannie said. *He says he learns a lot that way, and I guess he does. That's how you become a good spy.*

"Johnny's very daring, crazy daring—takes chances other men maybe wouldn't take. Part of his game. I'm surprised he's still alive. Some of his work in Africa, you wouldn't believe the places he'd land his planes. Little dirt airstrips, short runways, potholes big as shell craters—goddamn, some of them *were* shell craters. You go in, you bounce like crazy, you think the plane's going to fall apart. These Russian planes, they can take anything, land anywhere. And Johnny always delivered. Point of honor with Johnny. Usually in person. He liked that, showing up, bossing the cargo people, unloading the plane himself. I think he liked the risk. The people he was dealing with—crooked politicians, crazy blacks, superstitious, believe in magic. Dangerous people. Can't trust them. But he went in anyway. And as a result Johnny got known as a man you could trust. Johnny delivered. You could believe in him.

"Had an assistant named Misha, kind of a bodyguard. Misha Bichurin. Big bastard, red hair. Nasty guy. He beat up girlfriends, three or four I know of. I'm not kidding. Did it for the fun of it. The last was a Thai Air hostess. Sharjah. They had to hospitalize her. Nothing happened to

Bichurin, of course. Down there, the Gulf, things are like that. Misha—he carries a knife. Big. Some Russian military thing. Very scary. Shows off with it.

"Well, after a while we started flying for the fucking Afghans. You wouldn't believe those people. Primitives. And their Arab friends—worse! Yeah, in Kandahar you'd see the Arabs, couldn't miss them. They'd be walking around with sat phones all the time talking with their Taliban friends. They'd put these damn carpets down in the maintenance hangar— right down in front of our planes. I mean it wasn't right—stupid!—and have meetings, sitting cross-legged, babbling in Arabic. Sometimes they'd have real feuds right there, tribal you'd think, shouting and hollering and waving their goddamn arms, making gestures at each other. Real comic book.

"Saw Mullah Omar once. Swear to God I did, saw him with my own eyes. Blind man. Not that old, but bent over, walked on a stick. Always led around by kids. Saw him one day when I went into the hangar to check on my plane, it had been days in shop, should have been a fucking four-hour turnaround, but all they were doing with it was—well, not even fuck-all, wanting *bakhsheesh* before doing anything. So anyway I go into the hangar, there he is, the Mullah, sitting on a carpet, talking to *mujahideen* from Tajikistan or Uzbekistan or somewhere, getting salaamed by everybody. Comic book.

"Johnny didn't like these people, neither did I, I can tell you, but liking doesn't come into it where there's money. And Johnny made it in Afghanistan, flying ammo into Kandahar mostly, that and small arms. We flew into Kabul, also.

"Always good on his word as I say. Which is how he succeeded when he succeeded. Harder now. I think he's a little down on his luck. Always lives well—got a taste for it—but that's his problem. He's always a little on the edge financially, know what I mean? Saw him last in Istanbul. Worked for him there. Then came here."

The Agency has debriefed Timperman well. He knows all these stories by heart, he's told them all before. He's gotten his U.S. residence, I'm sure, because he was Agency. Agency probably got him this job.

H E HAD this girl," Timperman says reflectively. "She was Russian. Like him. Tall drink of water, really good looking. Named Marina.

Johnny liked to show her off. Johnny keeps her in Istanbul. Home away from home." Timperman chuckles, but it doesn't sound real. Something in his voice, a harshness when he says "Marina," makes you wonder about Timperman and Marina. His face is empty.

"Hey, can't smoke in here," he says abruptly. "Come on, let's go out. I could use a break." He grabs a pair of sunglasses for the Florida glare.

We go down the metal stairing, and head out a side door to InterAir's private parking lot. The lot is surrounded by a ten-foot-high chain-link fence that has a gate activated by a card-reader. As Timperman leads me across the lot to the fence opposite, he pulls out a pack of Marlboros and lights up with an old-fashioned Zippo lighter that he shuts with a loud click. He makes a kind of gesture of it.

On the other side of the fence is a building site. Two large cement trucks are churning and pouring concrete onto a broad floor area while workers, Hispanics all of them, rake and smooth it. Overhead I-beams jut out beyond the floor.

Timperman puts his thick hands on the fence despite his cigarette, and grips the wires. He looks like a prisoner.

"Another warehouse?"

"Yeah. Lot of traffic at the airport. Keeps growing. Not us though." His voice is disengaged, the voice of a man who is washed up, who will never do better than this, and knows it.

"Oparin." He sighs and turns away from the construction to face me. "You want to fuck him?"

"I want to meet him."

Timperman considers that, looking at me coolly. "Yeah," he says finally. "Right. Johnny. He's in Turkey a lot. Lot of Russians there, you think it's a Russian colony sometimes. Istanbul, Izmir, Antalya—all those places, full of Russians. Playing golf, doing business."

"I've got old some numbers and addresses for him"—thanks to Fiscarelli—"but maybe you've got something more recent?"

"Well, I'll give you numbers—Moscow, Sharjah, Istanbul. E-mails, addresses, PO boxes, whatever you want, whatever I've got. But if you call, you won't get Johnny. You never do. Johnny's always 'out' somewhere or 'away on business.' Johnny *returns* calls, that's how he works. You don't call Johnny, Johnny calls you."

"Anything for where he lives? Addresses, numbers?"

"He lives with his cell phones. 'Course, he's got a place in Istanbul. Couple of places. Don't know them, keeps them secret. Beach place, place in Beyoğlu—you know Istanbul? Beyoğlu's fancy-fancy—the old European quarter. Buildings turn-of-the century. French. Old, but you clean them up, put in good heating systems, you've got a chic product. Prices sky high these days, yes."

"Any addresses?"

"Never been to those places, didn't get invited."

Fiscarelli and the combined forces of CIA and NSA do not know where Johnny Oparin lives in Turkey or Russia. He's used middlemen to buy or rent. For some reason, probably because the place is so small and foreigners get noticed, they know his compound in Sharjah.

I ask, "That girl he had—Marina?"

Timperman looks at me, face still empty, still no emotion. "Yeah, Marina."

"Who is she?"

"Oh, well, she was a 'Natasha.' Russian girl down there in Turkey—you know. She went on her own, though, nobody tricked her, knew what she was getting into as far as you can know that kind of thing, Turkey being Turkey. Had a boyfriend to protect her, went down there together. Well, she got into trouble with him and he treated her badly. Funny thing, she was rescued by Johnny. Johnny—rescuing girls! The idea! So she stays there in Turkey in one of Johnny's places. Got two in Istanbul, got one in the south on the coast. So Marina stays down there. She has friends in the country."

Timperman's voice is flat now. He's leaning back on the chain-link fence, studying the end of his cigaret. "He beat her. Not like Misha with his girls, not that bad, but he beat her. Still there with him. That's loyalty. She's hopeless. She won't leave him. Not ever.

"She had a daughter from a marriage that went kaput. This was back in Russia, before the boyfriend, before Turkey. Husband left her and took the girl. Girl's proper name's Anastasia, but Marina called her Nastoushka. Nastoushka—funny name, don't you think? Nastoushka? Lives in Moscow somewhere with the father. She has to be four or five now. Marina had a picture of her, a baby picture of course. She'd take it out and show it around. 'My Nastoushka,' she'd say. The little girl doesn't know where her mother is. Or who she is really."

"What's Marina's last name?"

He studies my face, his eyelids unmoving. "Oranskaya," he says finally. "Marina Oranskaya."

Timperman's old. He's a drunk, and he's washed up, and he has no money. When he was in Istanbul he dreamed of Marina, who was beyond his reach, and here in Florida he still does. Fiscarelli's never mentioned Marina to me. Timperman wouldn't have told the Agency about her.

"Know how to get in touch with her? Phone number or anything?"

"No, no, I don't have anything like that."

"Where's she live?"

"Beyoğlu somewhere, in that part of town. Don't know the address. You know Istanbul?" He hesitates, his eyes somewhere else. "She has a girl friend, another hooker, Russian, came down with her and her boyfriend. Sonya. Yeah, I know Sonya." He smiles. "I was close to Sonya, if you know what I mean. She's high class. Does the tourist trade, better sort of Turk out-of-towner, Russians. Marina, Sonya, they were thick. I don't know the situation now. She lived with Marina for a while. The two of them, they lived by their wits in the city of Istanbul. Amazing. Sonya acquired a 'boyfriend' down there, too, I think. Didn't work out. Anyway, when Johnny came along, Marina took up with him. Sonya was out on her own. She worked near a hotel called the Küçük Palas. Old place, real hotel. Classy in its day. Maybe a little seedy now. You know Istanbul, you know the Küçük Palas. She had this cheap little apartment around the corner. Hung out nearby, got some of the hotel trade. Never fucked in the hotel. They winked at her, the hotel people. I think they liked her. Didn't bother them. Maybe she paid them a little, who knows? She could be still at it there."

Back up in the office Timperman gives me what he has of Oparin's coordinates and tells me again, "Good luck. You call him, maybe he'll get back to you."

I LEAVE Timperman and have lunch—stone crab claws and potato salad—at a place in Fort Lauderdale called Circe's. Since the temperature is seventy-eight degrees and there's a fine breeze, I ask to eat out on their brick patio. It's sheltered from the sun by thick grapevines, and I like the air coming off the ocean. According to Circe's menu, the patio where I'm sitting is "surrounded by ferns, zinnias, orchids, pencil plants, Scheffleria, and crown of thorns." The menu says that Fort Lauderdale gets 3,000 hours of sunshine every year and that Miami has 165 miles of canals.

"We Find Spies"

I ARRIVE at Ataturk International outside Istanbul in midmorning, clear customs quickly, and check into a glassy hotel at the airport. I haven't slept much on the flight over, but the thin, wintry daylight makes me think I'm awake.

I catch a cab to TAK Air Services, Oparin's Istanbul office, which is in an industrial park to the northwest of the airport. TAK Air's block looks a lot like Timperman's. The company occupies a single large room on the second floor of its building. The back half of the room is glassed in and forms a kind of separate office. Out front are two wooden desks, neither occupied, and a couple of brown plastic chairs. On the walls are faded travel posters in Russian—one of the canals in St. Petersburg, one of Red Square in Moscow. Piled around the edges of the room are cardboard boxes of various sizes labeled in Turkish, English, French, and Russian.

In the back office a short, slight young woman in a business suit is shifting folders of paper on a large table—contracts, maybe, or plans, or correspondence. With her, supervising, is a tall red-haired man. Tieless, dark shirt, hip-length black leather coat, flat Russian face. Bichurin. He notices me, the unexpected intruder, and comes out. "Yes?"

"Hey, Doug Lawson. Good to see you." I put out my right hand, card him with my left, smiling a big Conover smile, all of it in one large, smooth gesture.

Holding the card in two hands—he looks clumsy doing it—Bichurin reads out loud in a thick Russian accent, "Douglas Lawson—Engineering

Associates, Fairfax, Virginia, USA." The information on the card—the landline and cell numbers, the e-mail, the URL, the office address—all run in the end to Langley and will check out nicely.

Bichurin looks at me questioningly.

"Had an appointment in the area, had some time, thought I'd visit some likely customers. You the manager? We do security. Computers, phones, networks. We also help out with secure transmissions—phone-to-phone encryption, e-mail encryption, that kind of thing. We have access to the latest equipment, best stuff they make in the USA." That Conover smile again.

Back in the glassed-in room the computers are hoseable. So are the networking cables. Put an emanation receiver in there, you'll get the signals. Every wire in that room will give them off. Out here the phone looks insecure. Probably hoseable. Everything in this place is. But then, Johnny doesn't do his better deals through this equipment or out of this office. Not a chance he would.

Bichurin stares for a moment. "We are satisfied with our current situation, Mr. . . ."—he looks at the card again—". . . Lawson. Thank you."

"Well, okay, but seriously, I can probably get you a good price, a really good price, on any new equipment or any kind of service you want, probably less than you're paying now. I won't take more of your time. Just let me leave you with some literature," I say, pulling a Virginia Associates brochure out of my jacket pocket. Four-color and glossy. Silvery photo of a secure phone on a black background. In bold, bright green letters below the secure phone is the message, "We stop leaks, we find spies," and below that, the peaks and valleys of a red frequency amplitude wave.

"Okay, good," he says and turns away abruptly, walks back into the glass-walled room.

He tosses the card and the brochure onto his desk.

Something's doable here.

T HE POLICE are not useful. They don't care." Deniz Uzan can barely control his rage. Even now. It's been three months. "They don't like guys like Sasha. They beat. Maybe *they* kill him."

I'm with Uzan in an office off the lobby of his bed-and-breakfast, the Ottoman Saray, in the Sultan Ahmet quarter of the Old City. Uzan was Sasha Geydarov's lover. He is large-chested and muscular. He has a shaved head and wears little cat's-eye spectacles. In addition to the Ottoman Saray,

Uzan owns an expensive seafood restaurant, the Mercan, a couple of blocks away. I've dined there with Sasha, Uzan acting as gracious restaurateur and host, drinks and dinner on the house, nothing too good for a friend of Sasha's. Who, as Uzan knows, is in some kind of black business.

From the restaurant's second-floor windows you can see the Sultan Ahmet Mosque on the Hippodrome. At night, the mosque's six pencil-shaped minarets are illuminated, and white gulls circle them, cruising endlessly into and out of the light.

"He was dealing with Russians. Mafia," I say. "Dangerous people. You haven't heard anything? He never said anything?" Agency people have been through here. But I want to know.

Uzan shakes his head. "That day, afternoon. He walked out. He was all right, okay, happy like a bird. When he doesn't come home I call police. They come here and are difficult people. Shits."

"I know you've told the police what you can . . ."

"I hate the police, they hate me, okay? No, I didn't tell them nothing. What can I tell? I don't know nothing. Sasha came here long time ago. I knew him from first. I tell them that."

Met in a bar probably.

"I tell police he was from Azerbaijan, he spoke Azeri, had a funny accent. My friend . . ." Uzan's voice quavers, and he tears up, his body freezing in place, hands rigid on the top of his desk. He waits out the feeling. After a time he says, "He learned our Turkish. He was okay businessman. He had good enough money. He did a lot of things, knew a lot of people. You can't say who killed him. I say police."

I think there's nothing here to learn. I get a card from Uzan with the address and phone number of the Ottoman Saray and give him my cell number. I tell him I'll be staying in a hotel in the old European part of the city, that he should call me if he thinks of anything to say about Sasha.

As I leave the Ottoman Saray I notice a pretty young woman sitting in a lounge chair in the lobby. Black hair frames her white face. She is doing her nails. She smiles at me as I pass. Her hands are large and strong. She-male.

Friend of a Friend

THE HOTEL Küçük Palas is just off Taksim, in a narrow street. The hotel's name is over its small sheltered entrance in bright red neon. On the hotel's southern side is what looks like an alley, and I think Timperman's memories of Sonya are pretty good. The few shops back in here—a plumber, a picture framer, a mattress store—are closed for the night.

The hotel lobby is brightly lit, full of fat, plush chairs, about eight of them, all occupied, and a sofa flanked by potted palms. Russian tourists who have come in by bus from somewhere are milling around noisily. Could be a Lions convention. Their bags are piling up because bellhops keep pulling them out of the buses and dragging them into the lobby and leaving them there, and the scene looks pretty chintzy because the hotel is basically a good one.

The restaurant is half full, the clientele international, though mostly Russian, and loud. I tell the girl checking reservations that I'm waiting for a friend, and head for the bar.

The lounge here is very dark, American-style, and almost deserted. The bartender is young, balding, mustached. He is leaning on his elbows and seems bored. I sit at the end of the bar, and he comes over.

"*Da?*"

I put twenty dollars on the bar. "I need some help. I'm looking for a friend of a friend. A girl named Sonya."

"Sonya?" He smiles, not deigning to take the money immediately. "Well, if you stay she will come. Maybe. Sometimes she is outside."

"I don't know her to see her. I need some help to find her."

"Stay. Or come back. She is often here. Maybe ten o'clock."

I LEAVE the hotel to take a walk and get some air. It's snowing. I hitch up my collar and walk down İstiklâl, a nineteenth-century street of French-looking buildings and small shops—boutiques, cafés, art galleries, restaurants, lined with small, well-tended trees in protecting iron cages. No auto traffic on İstiklâl, just pedestrians, who this evening hurry past in the falling snow. The old electric tramway, with its two cars, one red, one white, clangs up the street.

In the sidestreets off İstiklâl a few hookers in thick coats stand in door-ways. Beginning of their shift. They look bored. I get some dinner—*yoğurtlu kabap* and a salad—at a place called Kaktus, kill time at the bar, then head back up to the Küçük Palas.

In the lounge I find a single young woman sitting at the bar smoking a cigarette. The bartender I spoke to is still on duty. He recognizes me and gestures at the girl with his head.

She notices this. When she turns to see what's going on she catches my eye and smiles. Her legs are crossed, dress up high. She moves her legs slightly and I can almost hear one thigh rubbing on the other. Her hair is good, simply cut, blonde. She makes a stabbing gesture toward the ash-tray with her cigarette, tapping the end, and lets loose a quarter inch of ash like a soft bomblet, which hits target. She smiles at me again, then stares at me, takes a drag, and stares some more.

I go over and sit beside her. She's not drinking.

"Hey, honey, you speak English?"

She blinks yes.

"My name's Doug. What's your name?"

"Sonya."

"That's a nice name. Sonya. Russian?"

She nods and takes a long drag on her cigarette, looking at me coolly. The look says Russian girls get a premium here.

She says, "You are lonely? You like a date?"

"You have a friend."

"O-o-h." She puts on a little smile, a practiced knowing look, that says, Oh, you naughty boy. Another drag on the cigarette. "Tonight? Maybe.

Yes, why not? Yes, I can do. Four hundred euros for two. You like, very, very nice."

"No no no. Your friend. You have a friend." I slip her twenty dollars. "Your friend Marina. You have a friend named Marina and I want to speak with her. I need some help, and she can help me. Do you have friend named Marina? Russian girl, too?"

She hesitates, her eyes narrow. She looks over at the bartender who is wiping glasses and paying us no attention.

I say softly, "Do you? I'm okay."

She nods once, not looking at me.

"I think I know her. From a long time back. I'd like to say hello. Ah, I think she isn't completely happy."

"Oh."

He beat her, Timperman said. *Not like Misha with his girls, not that bad, but he beat her. Still there with him. That's loyalty. She's hopeless. She won't leave him. Not ever.*

"Just tell her my name's Doug and I want to say hello. Just hello. That's all." Smiling, I say, "I'm safe." Then, "Here's a hundred dollars." I pull the money from my pocket. "You can have it. There's another hundred if you can bring Marina. I *am* a friend. I just want to talk to her. If you can bring her."

"Police."

"No."

I don't mention Johnny. I don't have to. She knows it's about Johnny. She's weighing it. "Give me the one hundred."

I do, and say, "Another one hundred for you tomorrow if I can see Marina." I give her my Doug Lawson card. "Here's my cell number, Sonya. My name's Doug. Give me a call. Tell me when and where. Any place is all right, you say where. I'm safe."

She studies my face, then looking down nods.

"Sonya, give me your cell number." She hesitates for a moment, then pulls a pen out of her purse and writes her number on a napkin. Then, she collects her things, and stubbing out her cigarette, heads for the lobby. Nice demure black dress, black purse, and a nice swaying half moon of an ass as she walks away.

———

I GET no phone call the rest of the night.

Next morning for something to do I walk to the Old City. I cross the Galata Bridge and its hawkers of phony Rolexes and jewelry, its toy-sellers with their boxes of paper cut-out monkeys that jerk their arms and legs when you yank a string, pinwheels that turn in the stiff wind. Down on the lower level are the restaurants and I can smell frying fish. The sun is out, hanging over the Golden Horn and the mosques that rise on the peaks of this old city.

Istanbul: water, hills, minarets.

I catch a streetcar up to the Hippodrome and stare at Aya Sofia and the Sultan Ahmet Mosque and have a coffee in a crowded restaurant called Vi-tamin. Just up the street is Deniz's hotel and I think of Sasha Geydarov.

Around eleven my cell rings. Sonya.

"Hello, are you Doug?"

"Yes."

"We can meet. She will come. This night. In the hotel. In the bar? Okay?"

"What time?"

"Six o'clock? Okay?"

"Good. Six o'clock."

T HEY COME in together, arm in arm, laughing, Sonya and a taller woman wearing a long shiny black dress, silvery bracelets and rings. Cigarette. No purse, thick fleece jacket dyed green.

Sonya points me out and they come over to the table where I'm sitting away from the bar. Marina—*tall drink of water, really good looking, Johnny likes to show her off*—has long flaxen hair that's parted in the center, a large forehead, oval face, high cheekbones. Slender, good figure. She has a curi-ous look on her face. Can't place me. Sonya goes to the bar.

I say, "Hi."

"Hello."

"My name's Doug Lawson."

Pale complexion, hazel eyes. Intelligent-looking.

"Where do we know each other?"

"We haven't met."

Her look doesn't change. She waits.

"I'm in the telephone business. I sell telephones to businesses. I also buy them. Cell phones. Do you have a cell phone?"

"Yes, sure."

"Well, I might want to buy it. Who knows, it could be valuable. Also, I might want to buy other people's cell phones."

She looks steadily at me. She's talked to Sonya and Sonya's filled her in. Marina knows pretty much where I'm from and what I'm up to. And she's shown up. That she's here, just that, means she's open to—something. Now she lights another cigarette, in no hurry to leave. She's thinking, and I wonder if she's thinking of Nastoushka.

I say, "Sometimes people lose their cell phones—know what I mean? Or throw them away. But maybe the phones are valuable. Sometimes they are, old cell phones. Quite valuable."

I put ten one-hundred-dollar bills folded once and held in a silver clip on the table in front of Marina. Just like that. The clip has a replica of a large ancient coin on it, a portrait of some Roman emperor, also silver. "It's yours," I say.

She looks mutely at the emperor, at the hundreds. She makes no move to take the money.

"I can get you away. Someplace safe."

"No."

"I understand. But no one ends well with Oparin. You know that. I can get you away."

"Where?"

"Wherever you want. The United States if you want. I want his cell phone."

"Not possible."

"Tell me about his cell phone. What's it look like? Got more than one? How many does he have?"

She tosses her head. "This is stupid."

"No. And I'm very serious. A lot of money and escape, a way out. People lose their cell phones. It happens. He drinks a lot, goes out a lot. People lose things that way."

"Always the friends. Difficult. Very difficult."

"Hasn't he lost things before?"

"Careful man."

"Does he have a lot of phones?"

She doesn't answer.

"Does he get rid of them? Throw them away? Change them? Maybe he erases them, then throws them away."

"I don't know."

"Maybe when it's time for him to change—know what I mean?—you wouldn't have to do much. Just collect a phone he's thrown away."

"Don't."

"You have a daughter, think of her."

Anger flashes in her eyes. "*Don't* talk about her."

"I can get *her* a life, too. Somewhere safe. The money will be good." I gesture with my eyes at the money clip. "You know I'm serious. And you know that Oparin—nothing ends well with Oparin."

"Oh, stop stop stop. This is crazy. I must go." She starts to gather her things.

"The money is yours. I mean it. I'm giving it to you to show you that I am very serious. Take it. I don't ask for anything in return."

Agency principle: Once they take your money, you own them.

I give her a card. "Marina, here is my cell-phone number. I'm here in Istanbul. Call me. My name is Doug. I can help. It can be a lot of money and a new life. For you, for your daughter. I can get you to a safe place here in Istanbul, then out of the country. We'll talk. I'll tell you how we can work together."

She sits silent for a time.

Subdued, her eyes avoiding mine, she takes the card and the clip of bills and slips them into her coat pocket. Kind of like Frannie taking my business card in that slush-filled Safeway parking lot.

HEU: There, I've Done It

MARINA ORANSKAYA returns to the beach house—Johnny's house, their house—from taking a walk along the shore, looking at the leaden sea. She is wearing her navy-blue pea jacket and a white knitted cap, which she's pulled down because of the wind. She is carrying a brown, coarsely woven hand bag. She's bought *döner kebap* from one of the few open food places up on the Coastal Road and three expensive imported oranges from a stall. Lunch. Later.

With her key she unlocks the door to the house. She enters. Yes: as cold inside as out. They sometimes use kerosene space heaters here, which don't work. They don't spend much time in this house in the winter.

She goes into Johnny's office: papers, files, television. The computer is turned off, the laptop gone. Johnny's gone, too.

She goes into the first-floor bedroom—theirs—and goes to the night table on Johnny's side of the bed. She sits on the bed and opens the upper drawer of the night table. There inside, where he has left it, is a phone, the cell he uses here in this beach house. Johnny has cells in his offices and apartments around the world, cells for Moscow, St. Petersburg, Almaty; for Vienna and Budapest; for Sharjah and Dubai; for those countries in Africa. Different places, different cells. He changes his cells frequently—erases them, destroys them, throws them away and gets new ones. But this cell, the Istanbul but never-in-the office cell, the very private cell, Johnny left. He forgot to throw it away, or thought he had thrown it away, or had just got careless and left it— half a dozen reasons why the cell might be here. But it is here.

She rests her hand on the chilly glass top of the night table and as she does she hears a faint rushing sound, like sea waves crashing on the shore. She thinks what she hears may be the sound of fate.

She thinks of Nastoushka. She thinks of Nastoushka's father, a drunk. Hard face, chin like a stone. He took Nastoushka for spite, not love, and now Nastoushka is with his family, his mother, a good woman, but she has that same hard face. They don't want Nastoushka. Not really. Marina thinks of Nastoushka's small face, her gray-blue eyes so serious as she waves, saying, "Bye-bye, Mama. Bye-bye, Mama," and herself waving back, not even trying to smile through her tears from the rear window of the taxi as it speeds off to Sheremetyevo, where she boards a cheap Aeroflot flight to Istanbul and Johnny. Six months back. Marina thinks: Johnny saved me, Johnny frightens me, Johnny saved me, Johnny frightens me. To leave Johnny is not possible. To leave Johnny . . .

Holding her breath, Marina moves her hand toward the phone, then hesitates, as she hears the rushing sound. She reaches into the drawer and touches the phone lightly as if to see if the touch would hurt her. It does not. She pulls her hand back from the drawer and waits, not just hearing, but feeling the surf entering the beach house, loud now, pounding. Saying, "In God," she snatches the phone from the drawer and thrusts it into her woven bag.

There, I've done it, she thinks. The rushing water has stopped. She can't hear a thing.

Like Magic

EVENING. I AM sitting alone on a bench in a small park by the Bosphorus. A few motor boats moored at a dock here rock gently in the lapping waves. Just to my north is the Dolmabahçe Palace, where the last Sultans lived, who in the end had become prisoners of the army and in the 1920s were at last removed from power. Behind me, floodlights have come on to illuminate the small, gray Dolmabahçe Mosque. Out on the water a freighter is making its slow way down to the Sea of Marmara. Beyond the ship, over in Üsküdar, lights are winking on. A feathery snow has been falling, but the wind picks up and particles of ice prickle my face.

I have talked with Fiscarelli. We will give Marina another $1,000 for whatever phone she brings. If and when the phone checks out, we will pay her more, perhaps a lot more, that depends. We cannot offer her citizenship, but a green card will be doable if—and only if—the phone is genuine.

When Marina called, we arranged to meet near Sonya's pad. Standing with Marina in that sidestreet, around the corner from the Küçük Palas, I relayed Fiscarelli's offer. I also told her, "There's a hotel in the Old City I know. You can stay there. It's safe and you won't be seen. We can get you out of Turkey very quickly." She hunched her shoulders, shivering, and said she would try to bring a cell. She said it was Johnny's, that Johnny hadn't discarded it, just left it behind. She might be telling the truth.

THERE: FROM Necatibey a taxi slowly circles into the park drive and stops close to the entrance. A woman in a dark blue coat and white hat gets out, pays the driver, and comes toward me. Marina.

She sits down, hands in her coat pockets.

"Hello, Doug."

"Got it?"

She takes a cell phone out of her pocket and hands it to me.

"I can't go back there."

"I said I can arrange help. I meant it."

"I want to leave. To disappear. For always."

"You can. Also there's this." I give her the $1,000.

Out on Necatibey we get a cab, and Marina gives the driver directions to Johnny's apartment in Beyoğlu, which turns out to be in a winding street of graceful old buildings west of İstiklâl. Now we—the Agency—know where Johnny lives when he's in town. I wait with the cab as Marina goes up.

The apartment is six stories high. Each floor has a window onto the street, and each window has a small balcony ledge with identical iron balustrades worked in a symmetrical wavy pattern shaped like a peacock's tail. Over the street entrance, so indistinct from age it's just barely visible, is the legend, APPARTEMENTS PANTELIDIS FRÉRES, the building's French-Greek name from a by-gone era. Johnny knows quality. (Timperman: *Beyoğlu's fancy-fancy—the old European quarter. Buildings turn-of-the century. French. Old, but you clean them up, put in good heating systems, you've got a chic product.*)

Marina brings down a single suitcase. I give the driver directions to the Ottoman Saray, where Uzan has a room waiting. Before Marina registers she has to think for a second to make up a name. At the Ottoman Saray they're not always fussy about identification.

In her room I sit on one of the twin beds. "Your daughter?"

"She has gone to different place. She's okay. But only for now." Marina's face is haggard.

"I'll call in the morning."

JOHNNY'S PHONE, once a sterile instrument and never before connected to the man, now is. And we have it. It's a prepaid wireless—has to be— that Johnny most certainly got under a false name. With these phones you have no contract, no credit check, no security deposit, no activation fee. If you end the service—say, by throwing the thing away—there's no discontinuation fee. And you have no phone bills; instead you buy prepaid cards. The phone itself tells you how much airtime you've used, how much you've got left. Great little service. A bunch of companies make these phones, a bunch of other companies furnish the service.

Fiscarelli and I wanted to clone this cell—we could have done it overnight—and have Marina return it to its place, Johnny none the wiser. We'd then have a copy of the phone, and any future calling done on this instrument, in or out, the Agency or NSA would listen in on. But Marina refused to return to the beach house and we didn't push her.

In my hotel room, I try to turn the cell on, but it's dead. When I snap open its back panel I see the batteries are still there—a good sign of carelessness—as is the gleaming little SIM card and the gray and red SD memory card. Very good.

These cards are the keys to Johnny. The SIM card you can lock with a PIN, but most people don't know that. Did Johnny? And you cannot encrypt data on either of them. To hide your data, your only recourse is to wipe your cards. Has Johnny ever done that? Most people don't. Even if he has, there are ways to retrieve material, some of it anyway, that a user thinks he's gotten rid of forever.

So, at Fort Meade what might the resident techies find? For starters, maybe Johnny's address book, the names and numbers of his clandestine businesses, of his friends and lovers. Maybe also, the text messages he's sent and received, maybe spreadsheets, other documents, photos even. The log will tell the Fort the phone numbers of people Johnny has talked to on this cell and when he's talked to them. Computers at the Fort will listen in on the numbers they find on the log, to all the calls made to and received by those numbers. They will know the locations from which those calls are made, in many cases down to a few meters, and the times they were made. They will learn who many of the callers are. Monitoring Johnny's contacts, they may even catch Johnny himself calling one of them from another of his cells.

On the particularly interesting phones their computers turn up NSA cyberspies will try to install password sniffers, little programs, maybe only a few K in size, that detect a target owner typing in his secret passwords to the programs he runs and to the Web sites he logs on to. The program will acquire these passwords along with the target's usernames and send them to the Fort. With this knowledge, Fort personnel will rummage through their targets' program data to see what they can see. If they want, they will manipulate that data. They will also log on to the Web sites their targets have visited and see what the targets have done at those sites.

Other programs will capture text as it is being typed, before it is encrypted, and, if so instructed, will send that text elsewhere—to the servers at Fort Meade, maybe, or at Langley, where it will be perfectly readable. Like magic.

FRIENDS IN the business tell me NSA and CIA persuade or force antivirus companies to design their programs to recognize lists of these government-created viruses—password sniffers and keyloggers—and not flag their presence to the user. Or, my friends say, our spook agencies persuade anti-virus companies to design their programs so that they will not flag specially-marked NSA- or CIA-created viruses. Either way, with whitelisting or white-tagging, NSA and CIA viruses can enter target cells and computers unnoticed and operate on those devices undetected. My friends think NSA and CIA go through secret courts to compel the software companies to cooperate, if they go through courts at all.

I WALK from my hotel to Taksim Square. The pavement is wet with melted snow. I enter a sidestreet of shuttered shops south of the square where two or three bars are still open and I hand Johnny's phone to a young American woman who's been waiting for me with a male companion in a parked car. She has a lovely smile.

HEU: The Money Trail

ISLAMIC RELIEF electronically transfers 55.5 million euros into three accounts controlled by a Saudi trader named Ismail Hamawi, suggested by Johnny Oparin and agreed to by Amin Tajer, in three different banks in Geneva and Basel, Switzerland. By courier—the process takes twenty-four hours—Hamawi notifies Oparin in Sharjah and Tajer in Islamabad that the funding for their transaction, whatever it may be, is in place.

Hamawi will now wait for Tajer to confirm that the goods, whatever they are, have been delivered and approved. When Hamawi receives Tajer's confirmation, he will then transfer from his Swiss account 55 million euros, in three unequal amounts, into three accounts, two in the Cayman Islands, one in Switzerland, controlled by Oparin under three different pseudonyms.

Where the trail will end.

HQ: Code Red, Blinking

OPCOM/NPTG Session Audiotape, Session 70 (Excerpted).

Attending: J. Gutman (Chair), M. Fiscarelli, C. Lindquist, S. Kremer, R. Eisenberg.

Transcription: L. Jamison.

Mr. Gutman: Okay, emergency. Heads up, everybody. Mike, the business with Sajid and the transfers?

Mr. Fiscarelli: Right. Just in. The bank transfers, you can see in your materials today, this is page one, just last week, a bunch of bank transfers out of Islamic Relief, that account they have in Bahrain, Gulf Commercial. These transfers were indeed at Ahmed Sajid's direction, and went to five Swiss accounts, in three separate banks, that Sajid controls. They total up to 55.5 million euros. From these same accounts on separate days, you can see this, three separate days over the course of last week, the sum total of 55.5 million euros were transferred to one bank account, also in Switzerland. We do not know the owner of that account or who might control it. It's very opaque, and we have no way in there, but thanks to the electronic take on the bank in Bahrain, the account there, we do have these transfers.

Ms. Eisenberg: But no assets at the Swiss bank, so to speak.

Mr. Gutman: No, not at the Swiss bank, no. Now what is troubling me right now is the size of these transfers. 55.5 million euros is a considerable sum of money, and I think this may mean a sizeable quantity of merchandise, maybe contraband, is involved here, which if it is HEU, is very, very disquieting, and we must act and must focus full resources here. Code Red, blinking.

"WE GOT the merchandise," Fiscarelli says, "and we're looking at it closely. It's a great thing you've done. I mean that."

It's a Friday afternoon in early February. We're watching skaters at an open air rink in Reston, Virginia. Among all those out on the ice this day, one lovely girl with beautiful thighs and calves—a teenager—in a short red outfit trimmed with white, looking like a living valentine, stands out, skating like a pro, cutting the ice with a swish sound as she glides past us. Then moving fast away on one leg, bending forward, the other leg and her lovely young ass elevated, to the far end of the rink, then back again— swish, and the slushy ice sprays up toward us.

When I got back from Istanbul—this was three weeks ago—Fiscarelli told me the young woman from the embassy, the woman I gave the phone to, "took the case over." He tells me the cell "has worked out very well," and that Marina and her daughter are in "a European location," happy as clams apparently, and maybe headed for the States. I hope. I liked her.

After staring at the skater doing her loops for a time Fiscarelli sighs, and it sounds genuine. "Look, Rick, ah, we want more. I know you may have problems with this, but is there anyway you can head over again?"

"Mike, for God's sake."

"What you've done is really good work. I mean it. But we still may need your, ah, access. It's your call, obviously, I can't order you, but it could be enormously helpful. I don't want to get heavy about this, but it *is* your country and this is extremely important. And I mean that, too."

Nukes.

"For how long?"

Another sigh, then in a low voice he says, "That could be indeterminate. There's a major push here on all this. We're going to need more . . . more technical help. It's got to be done, and it's got to be done soon. TAK Air. You know the layout there, you've got an excuse to go back. Sales call, right?"

I mull this.

He asks, "How's the risk element?"

"The what?"

"The risk. Any risk to you, I mean."

"I don't know. It's there. I can't quantify it. I've been low profile. They'll miss the phone at some point. When they think about that, they'll think Marina. Sonya could connect me and Marina, but Sonya's loyal to Marina and probably won't blab. I don't know. You figure it out." I think some more, watching that lovely skater in red and white, and finally say, "I want a Glock 26 and some ammo."

"That's nuts."

"No. The gun. I want the gun. Fucking Station's got them lying around. If they're all out on loan, get one brought in. No gun, no go, all right?"

Fiscarelli looks at me closely. "I'll try."

After Fiscarelli leaves, I call my secretary Argaysha who's holding the fort this late Friday afternoon and give her the news. Heading on another trip, no, leaving this weekend, I won't be in, lot of prospects, staying maybe a week, Vienna first, then maybe head for Paris, I'll be checking in. I call Pappas and ask him to pay a visit or two to the office to see things are okay, and he agrees.

HEU: "The Engineer Will Be There"

IVAN OPARIN punches Amin Tajer's number stored in his phone and writes the text:

> John here. I see the fonds have been deposted. Are you available in one week, ten days for delivery? do you agree? is that possible?

Half an hour later Tajer replies:

> *Right. yes. It is okay.*

Oparin replies immediately: We will meet then. good. we'll meet where we agreed

> Yes, sure
>
> And the enginer will be there?
>
> Yes. the engineer will be there. He is in Dubai and will meet
>
> Okay. we make arrangements here. i will be in touch. very soon
>
> yes. Okay. Very good
>
> okay, then. good bye
>
> good bye

HQ: We Simply Must Ramp Up for This Right Now

SCI TOP SECRET GREEN SCI TOP SECRET GREEN SCI TOP SECRET GREEN SCI TOP SECRET GREEN SCI

OPCOM/NPTG Session Audiotape, Session 71 (Excerpted).

Attending: J. Gutman (Chair), M. Fiscarelli, S. Kremer, C. Lindquist, R. Eisenberg.

Transcription: L. Jamison.

Mr. Gutman: Because of the emergency nature of the case, we've put Alpha Priority on the known calls from Oparin and the numbers we've been acquiring of his contacts and we've been doing this on an ongoing basis for some time using, using various approaches and with some real success. The document you all have, it's the transcript of an intercept of a call, actually texting via cell phone, four days back from Ivan Oparin in Moscow to Tajer in Dubai. They were writing in English, no translator problem. And as I said when calling this special session, calling you, this intercept is very, very troublesome. It looks like a meeting with Sajid is imminent, and it may involve transfer of contraband HEU and will take place in Dubai. We have almost no time and we simply must ramp up for this right now.

Ms. Eisenberg: No time or place—it's maddening.

Mr. Fiscarelli: We are putting an eavesdropping device in Oparin's Istanbul office, which might, we hope might be helpful in tracking him, determining the venue of meeting, time et cetera.

Mr. Lindquist: But we have no information on Oparin's whereabouts?

Mr. Gutman: He is almost impossible to surveil. He made this cell call from central Moscow, we do know that, but have not been able to surveil him in Russia. Period.

Mr. Fiscarelli: We have people on the ground in Dubai and Sharjah alerted as is Abu Dhabi Station, and should be able to detect his entry into the UAE, probably at one of those airports.

Mr. Gutman: If that's the intended country of meeting.

Mr. Fiscarelli: Sure, sure. I should say too that DNCS is aware of this operation and is taking a special interest in this matter, and may drop in on this meeting this morning, by the way, and it's the Agency approach that Ahmed Sajid is a big focus of this exercise. Now, our people in Dubai and Sharjah of course will be prepared to seize Oparin and seize any contraband he may be carrying, but we will try to seize Sajid as well, which would be the optimum result, and that means we will try to sur-veil and track Oparin visually and also with any electronic means we may have and at the appropriate time seize both Oparin and Sajid.

Ms. Eisenberg: And the HEU.

Mr. Gutman: And the HEU. Okay, right, that said, we start now on an operational, very emergency operational plan. Mike has been surveying the possible re-sources and will coordinate the effort, which will not be easy in this short a time frame, but we don't get to set the parameters in these things.

The Fit Feels Very Secure

WHEN I walk into the Tak Air premises, the same young woman is there. No one else. I smile when she comes out. She doesn't recognize me.

"Hi, Doug Lawson. Remember me? Security man? I was here a month ago, ha ha."

She says she remembers. "No one is here now."

"The gentleman I met, tall guy"—I gesture with my hand—"red hair? Is he the manager? Is he going to come back?"

"Maybe one hour, maybe half an hour, I don't know."

"Great! Super! I'd really like to see him again. He may want to talk. I've got some time, okay if I wait for him? Hey, no problem, I'm used to it. Brought a book." I smile again and sit at a desk, put my briefcase down on the floor, and pull out a paperback which I wave at her.

I don't take off my coat. In the right pocket is my Glock 26. Base Chief Istanbul was not happy to supply me the weapon, but Fiscarelli—not happy himself—persuaded him. I feel pretty good with it.

She shrugs reluctantly and says, "Yes, okay." She goes back to the glassed-in office, and busies herself at the large table back there. The phone rings, she answers, speaks in Russian, seems to forget me. The phone conversation over, she sits idly at the table and lights up a cigarette.

I'm carrying a "block," the old name for a sneaky. The block, which is the size of a deck of cards, can catch emanations from computers, phones, and copying machines, and broadcast what it picks up to a receiver—a radio, a laptop with WiFi, a cell phone. It has a large passive memory that fires off only in bursts. If you're not continuously monitoring for radio transmissions, you'll miss the output of this little buckaroo.

I can drop the block out here, and it might do some good. This desk where I'm sitting would do. The wooden cabinet over on the far wall would not be bad either. But better back there where she is, in the glassed-in room. The big table back there—stuck under it somewhere. Good place. No—great place.

The young woman is still sitting, smoking, gazing off into nowhere, bored.

I reach into my briefcase and fish out a small, secure phone, a business sample, a cute little silvery thing, like the phone on our brochure—nice functional key pad, big display. It has an encryption chip and can communicate securely with another phone, cell or landline, fitted out with a similar chip. Smiling, I walk back and invite myself into the glassed-in room.

"Hi. Tired of reading. Been reading this whole trip. Airport literature, ha ha. Hope you're not too busy. Don't want to bother you." I sit down, smiling, at the table across from her. Her face—she's about to tell me to get the hell out. Still smiling I wave the phone. "This is the thing I provide to companies. Great, great phone. Absolute security. And it's just like a cell phone—feels like one, acts like one." I punch the green On button, then punch in YouTube and get a rock group. The sound comes out in small, squeaky pulses, and I hold up the phone, show it to her. "Here, take a look. No no no, go on, take it, hold it in your hand, it's so light you won't believe it." The phone grabs her, its screen full of little rockers and their tiny voices, pumping their little hips. She smiles.

The block is attached to the underside of the wooden table.

The adhesive has already dried.

The fit feels very secure.

I look at my watch. "Well, I'll tell you, maybe I won't wait around," I say. I fish into my briefcase and pull out a little white manual for our phone and chip. "Look, here's a little book describing the phone. Tell you what, I'll leave the phone and the little book with you. The manager can take a look at the book if he likes, play with the phone. Might be interested." I put up my hands. "No obligation. I'll come back in a couple of days and pick the thing up. If he wants to talk some more, great. If not, no problem. Okay?"

HEU: "You Can Receive It?"

FROM MOSCOW, Ivan Oparin texts Amin Tajer and gets him immediately:

Hello, hello. john here
How are you?
Two days? Is that okay?
yes, and we are okay
You can receive it?
yes
Very good. I am coming in Thursday. Sharjah. Can we schedule for
Friday?
Yes, no problem, friday
Then Friday morning, that good, yes?
Yes, good
Is ten o'clock okay with your side?
no problem
Then, we meet at agreed location?
Yes
Very good
Good bye

NIGHT. HASSAN Zaheer, a night guard of Pakistani nationality employed by Ivan Oparin, visits the three vehicles Oparin keeps for himself in his Sharjah villa, parked side by side in the blue moonlight—the Highlander, the BMW, the Mercedes.

Zaheer is the guardian of the villa. But who will guard the guardian?

Zaheer is carrying three transceivers, each no larger than a cigarette pack, supplied to him by his American handler, who in cables to Langley refers to Zaheer as TOGGLE. Each transceiver has a unique, coded identifier. Each is a tiny radio, but will signal only when signaled. Each broadcasts its GPS position, the coordinates accurate down to five meters.

You don't call Johnny, Johnny calls you.

But with these you *can* call Johnny, only Johnny won't know it.

Zaheer attaches one transceiver, concealed in a synthetic substance much like tar, in the cavity of the rear bumper of each vehicle.

Work done, trembling and perspiring in the cool night air, Zaheer returns to his modest quarters, the gatehouse of the villa.

HQ: The White House Is Involved for Obvious Reasons

SCI TOP SECRET GREEN SCI TOP SECRET GREEN SCI TOP SECRET GREEN SCI TOP SECRET GREEN SCI
OPCOM/NPTG Session Audiotape, Session 72 (Excerpted).

Attending: J. Gutman (Chair), M. Fiscarelli, S. Kremer, C. Lindquist, R. Eisenberg.

Transcription: L. Jamison.

Mr. Gutman: Command of the operation is out of our hands now since the White House is involved for obvious reasons and they've taken over, NSC has taken over the general command and control on this, though of course we'll be the hands-on. I want to congratulate Mike, by the way, on a really first-rate fast job of planning. You catch up on your sleep? You were up nights for a time there.

Mr. Fiscarelli: I'm fine.

Mr. Gutman: Right. Good. Okay, on the operation, they, NSC concurs that Sajid and the stray HEU are the real targets of this operation, and because we do not know what his location will be with any . . .

Mr. Fiscarelli: It's pretty certainly the hunting lodge.

Mr. Gutman: We do not know that. NSC concurs that the need to get Sajid impels us to follow Oparin rather than arrest him outright and on the spot and seize the contraband. I've have been given assurances by Abu Dhabi Station that we have the ability to track Oparin's local vehicles, that's vehicles he has in Dubai and Sharjah, track them electronically. I'm not privy to the details, but we know his vehicles and we have the capacity to do that. The operational plan is, this is a White House decision, highest levels, and this is still sketchy, but the notion is for DOD personnel to follow Oparin at a distance in a number of helicopters, carrier-based choppers. I forget the make and type, but military, Blackhawk probably, and well-armed, two choppers as I understand it, then close in for . . .

Mr. Fiscarelli: For the snatch.

Mr. Gutman: For the snatch. When the parties, Sajid and Oparin have rendezvoused. We will also have an armed drone, a Predator, also carrier-launched, in the air as backup and for tracking, particularly as the helicopters will stay out of the line of sight of the targets and the Predator at 15,000 feet is as good as invisible.

Mr. Fiscarelli: We moved heaven and earth to get that Predator. It was a White House decision. Went through the SECDEF.

Ms. Eisenberg: Absolutely essential we capture these people, Jack. Loss of either one them would be a tragedy.

Mr. Gutman: That is universally agreed. We will recover the contraband and make arrests of the targets. As to the choppers and personnel operating in UAE airspace, we have a modified go from the UAE Defense Ministry. Under an MOU signed with the Ministry in 1981 and updated since then, last time updated was— Stu, help me out, when was . . .

Mr. Kremer: Last updated 2005.

Mr. Gutman: Okay, right, last updated with the Ministry in 2005. We can operate U.S. military aircraft in UAE air space provided we get prior general permission, meaning we can specify general dates, times, locations, aircraft et cetera and work within those parameters pretty much ad lib, which we do on a routine basis. This will cover the Predator as well.

Mr. Fiscarelli: Let me add, these drones are hard to track by radar and they, the UAE military, are known not to put great effort into radar surveilling the south of the country, so this will be as low profile as possible.

Mr. Gutman: Also, the location of the probable meeting site is close to a live ammunition target range, which they have several in the southern desert, and it's my guess why the house, the sheikh's house, is not used much these days. Not the danger, the noise. The site being there is not crucial for our planning, but it's a fairly useful fact and if necessary might be helpful in giving us cover in case God forbid there's a [expletive]. Mike, on the Istanbul offices . . .

Mr. Fiscarelli: We did get a device into Oparin's premises at Istanbul airport, but the take has been negative, negative as far as this operation.

Mr. Lindquist: Null? Useless?

Mr. Fiscarelli: About the size of it.

Who Are They? What Do They Want? What Will They Do?

LAST DAY in town, I see Deniz Uzan at the Ottoman Saray. I want to know if anyone's been around asking about Marina.

"No problem. No police, nobody." Deniz's face registers a grim kind of happiness. Putting up the woman incognito, whoever she was, was a good way to get back at the police and the system. We talk a little more, but that's all I get from him. So far I think we're in the clear.

From the Ottoman Saray I wander down the steep backstreets of Sultan Ahmet toward the Sea of Marmara, through a neighborhood of decrepit wooden houses. They are paintless and browned in the sea air. From the side windows of some, clothing hangs out on lines to dry. Over the roofs of buildings below me I catch a glimpse of blue-black water and ships lying at anchor in the rosy dusk with their lamps on, waiting to put into harbor.

I enter a small square. At the far end is a single newspaper kiosk, and standing at it a man in a dark green parka, facing my way but reading intently something he's picked up at the kiosk—a magazine or a newspaper. His breath hangs in the cold air. The man does not look at me directly, but as I move across the square he reacts. He is aware of me—I can sense it in the his movements—and he doesn't want me to know he is aware. My hands are in my coat pockets. I ease off the safety on my Glock.

Who are they? What do they want? What will they do?

And then from behind: a hard tug on my right arm, someone spinning me around. Two of them, big. Punched fast in the gut and I cannot breathe—it hurts so bad—black gloved fist right hand coming at my face, glancing off under my right eye, left punching at my mouth, connecting, right punching at my ribs, punching, punching, my arms held from behind, gloved fist in my eye again, then ribs face gut gut gut. Down. Kicks.

They pull me lungs airless into the backseat of a car—it must have been waiting or following—and the car jerks into motion. I am between two men. Someone jams cloth into my mouth, I gag, puke, breathe my puke in, choke, think I'm dying. They pull the cloth. Something goes over my head and face, a knitted woolen cap I think. Someone cuffs my wrists. Plasticuffs. They cut. A hard piece of metal—I feel it through the knitted cap, I know it's a pistol—at my right temple. Someone says, "Shut up. You are coming with us." The accent is Russian. I am then shoved face down toward the floor, where it's cold. I ache from the beating. They shove the cloth back in my mouth.

The car moves quickly, makes a stop, then a couple of slow turns, another stop, then after a turn, speeds up again, heading down a ramp, I think, and starts going very fast.

We travel in silence for a time that I cannot estimate. Just a time. I think of my useless Glock. And I ache.

The car slows, pulls to the right, then stops for a moment. A red light, I think. Then it moves forward again, slows, turns right, and stops again. This time the passenger in the front seat gets out, slams the door. He doesn't return, but the car starts again, pulling forward slowly, briefly, stops. I hear the engine cut. Keys rattling. Emergency brake engaged.

I am pulled from the car. Two men walk me over a tiled courtyard. We come to a step. I am pulled up, then shoved through a door into the interior of a house. They walk me forward, I cannot count the paces. My coat is stripped off. I am pushed into a chair. I feel them using tape to fasten my arms to the arms of the chair, my legs to the legs. They pull off the knitted cap, and I see I am seated in a single wooden chair, like an office chair, in the center of a large room. There are men in the room. They are speaking Russian. When I turn my head to look around they don't object.

There is a wide, square plastic sheet under the chair.

Someone comes into my view from behind. Tall, red-haired. Bichurin.

For a moment he looks intently into my eyes, then nods and says to the others, *"Da, tak."* Then to me, "You are a spy. Yes. Who are you, Mr. Lawson? Who sent you?"

Pain back of my neck, hurting so badly dizzy in the chair, pain left shoulder, wad of cloth in my mouth suffocating. I.

HQ: Now Let's Get Over to the Center

OPCOM/NPTG Session Audiotape, Session 73 (Excerpted).

Attending: J. Gutman (Chair), M. Fiscarelli, R. Eisenberg.

Transcription: L. Jamison.

Mr. Gutman: I'm hoping Carl and Stu can make it in, they've both phoned and said they're on the way. Recap, Oparin arrived in Sharjah at 10 P.M. their time, which is eleven o'clock this morning D.C. time. News: We have absolute confirmation of that now, his arrival, from our surveillance team, and further strong indication that a meeting will take place with Ahmed Sajid. The meeting will occur sometime in the A.M. their time, meaning possibly in a few hours, the whereabouts from our surveillance unclear, but . . .

Ms. Eisenberg: And the operational elements?

Mr. Gutman: Three armed Blackhawk helicopters and an armed Predator. Now let's get over to the Center.

"TARGET ONE latitude twenty-five oh two nine seven, longitude fifty-five two five oh two, closing. No visual yet."

"Roger that."

The Director of Central Intelligence, three of his deputies including the Director of the National Clandestine Service and five other NCS officers are in the OPCOM/NPTG Operations Center, fifth floor, CIA headquarters, Langley, Virginia. With them are Jack Gutman, Michael Fiscarelli, and Rhoda Eisenberg of OPCOM/NPTG. It is 11:33 P.M.

They are watching three large flat-panel displays showing the identical image of pale, rose-pink land, the desert south of Dubai, slipping beneath the belly-mounted camera of an MQ-9 Predator. The Predator is armed with six Hellfire AGM-114 air-to-ground, laser-guided missiles. The voices belong to the pilot of the craft, who is flying it remotely from an underground control room at Nellis AFB, Las Vegas, Nevada, and to the Special Operation Commander, who is in direct charge of the operation, and who is based at Central Command HQ, in Doha, Qatar in the Persian Gulf. Both the Pilot and the Operation Commander are Clandestine Service officers.

It is early morning. The sun is just coming up, casting long shadows from the east over desiccated hill country of rippling sand and pale green brush.

The Predator is in a holding pattern over a long, almost empty six-lane highway called the Al Ain Road, which leads to a wildlife reserve. As the vehicle circles, the pilot will occasionally zoom the camera in to view the sparse traffic on the highway, the isolated settlements, and the highway turnoffs that turn off to nowhere.

The Predator banks, the soundless picture tilts.

JOHNNY OPARIN and three of his men are heading south on the Al Ain Road in a red Toyota Highlander. They've come from Oparin's villa in Sharjah and have been driving for an hour. Oparin's men are armed with AK-47s and Beretta pistols. Oparin himself carries no weapon. They have just crossed the east-west Sweihan Road, a landmark. Five kilometers farther south on this desolate highway, they are to meet The Engineer, Ahmed Sajid, who will be in a white Range Rover accompanied by three armed men. Oparin is bringing 12.7 kilograms of HEU in an aluminum container, which, as his men cover him, he will turn over to The Engineer. The two parties will then separate, Oparin returning to Sharjah, Sajid to the desert.

"Target One latitude twenty-four five nine five eight, longitude fifty-five two eight oh four, closing," says the pilot at Nellis AFB. His voice is soft, a young man's voice. He has no accent. "No visual yet," he says. "Lead helicopter, Beta Blue. We have you at 10,000 feet, and your coordinates are seven point four miles from Target One."

"Copy that."

"Maintain standoff," the commander says.

"Roger that, Command."

Three support helicopters, Beta Blue, Beta Red, and Beta Green, are maintaining a distance of at least five miles from Target One. One hour before, they were launched from an aircraft carrier in international waters in the Persian Gulf.

A FEW moments go by. No one in Virginia speaks. On the Al Ain Highway sparse traffic passes soundlessly.

Then: "Beta Blue, we have a visual. Visual Target One, visual Target One. We have Target One in sight. Altitude of the aircraft is fourteen six five oh. In range, in range."

"Zoom it down, Pilot" says the Operation Commander, "take a look, better look."

"There," Rhoda whispers. "My God, there, it's them—Oparin."

The view on the screens shows three vehicles on the highway, all approaching from the north. The vehicles are so small, smaller than toys, and barely visible. The mid vehicle of the three slows, pulls to the side, stops on the shoulder. The two others traveling from the north move slowly to the bottom of the screens, then disappear.

The Director is tapping the table with his spread fingers. "Beautiful," he says softly. "Beautiful."

The Pilot says, "Target One latitude twenty-four five four four one, longitude fifty-five three oh five eight. Halted, no motion."

"Maintain altitude at fourteen thousand," says the commander. "Maintain visual."

"Ah, check that. Going for a turn."

The horizon rolls, the vehicle is lost from the screens. The sky is blindingly blue and cloudless. In the angled distance loom mountains, naked gray rock. Below now, as the aircraft rights itself, the camera catches a large compound broken into plots of green, regularly spaced plants.

O PARIN EXITS the rear seat of his halted red Highlander, comes around to the front, and orders his driver out. He gets in and takes the wheel himself. He will drive south, cross the median, and, as agreed, return up the highway to an unfinished turnoff. There, Sajid will meet him.

O N THE flat-screens again a view of the rosy, rippling landscape. The camera searches up the highway and locks onto a red vehicle. Target One is back in sight.

"Command Central, we have visual," says the pilot. "Target One. We have visual. Target One is moving. Moving south."

Silence.

"Zoom out for a larger visual. Target One is proceeding south. Beta Blue, do you read?"

"This is Beta Blue."

"Maintain standoff."

"Roger that."

"Target One has crossed the median. Target One is moving north slowly. Beta Blue maintain standoff."

"Roger that, Command."

Two other vehicles, both large trucks, come into view quickly from the south, passing the red Highlander.

"Target One has stopped. He's stopped on the shoulder. Zoom in."

The top of the red Highlander fills the picture.

"This is Beta Blue. Standing off."

"Maintain that, Beta Blue. We are waiting for Target Two. We do not have a definitive Target Two. Aircraft showing other vehicles."

"Where is he," Gutman whispers. "Where's Sajid?"

The Director says, "This could go on all morning. At some point—I'm concerned about fueling—at some point we may have to bring down the choppers. Anne, give me the Sit Room." An aide hands the Director a secure phone. "Mac? Hi, Mac. Lindsay here. Uh, look, if this keeps up and the choppers start getting low on fuel we may have to engage targets and get what we get. Right . . . Right . . . Concur." Speaking to Gutman, the Director says, "Decision at the White House is, and they're passing this on to Central Command, we'll stand off if we have to until the last minute before we have to bring the choppers down, then we'll go for an arrest of Oparin, Target Two or no Target Two."

"Could be pretty soon," Gutman says.

"Well, that's right."

The Predator is flying a lazy circle now, locked on Johnny's Highlander.

OPARIN SITS at the wheel, scanning the road ahead, scanning his rearview mirror. "The handoff is here. Where is the son of a bitch? The GPS coordinates are exactly right, the exit here."

A gray water tanker rumbles past. On its side a sign painted in black letters on a white eliptical background reads, HAITHAM FIELD SERVICES LTD.

"Maybe he's not coming."

Oparin shakes his head. That can't be.

A WHITE vehicle approaching from the south passes the parked red Highlander, drives for a time, then slows, loops over the median of the highway, turns back, then slowly comes to a stop on the shoulder. The two vehicles are a kilometer apart. The Predator banks slowly, keeping both vehicles in view.

OPARIN SAYS, "That was him," and brings his Highlander back onto the highway, driving slowly north toward the white vehicle, a Range Rover.

THE CAMERA sweeps, pauses: a white vehicle, stopped.

"Visual. Visual. Possible Target Two in sight. Target One is closing on a stationary white vehicle."

"Copy that, Command."

"Zoom in, zoom in on Target Two."

"Bring in the choppers."

"Beta Blue, move to arrest."

"Roger that, Command." A few moments pass. "Ah, Beta Blue here, Command, we have target in sight. Proceeding to engage and detain."

"Beta Green, arrest Target Two. White vehicle approximately five hundred yards north of Target One."

"Command, Beta Green. Roger that. Moving to engage."

In the bottom of the screens, a helicopter moves into view, then two more.

OPARIN HEARS the rhythmic slapping of rotor blades over his head, the sound becoming louder, becoming a roar, and he sees a helicopter one hundred meters in front of his vehicle.

And he understands.

He jerks the wheel to the right and stamps on the gas pedal, taking his Highlander fast off the highway onto the desert.

"For God's sake, Vanya!"

COMMAND, BETA Blue. Beta Blue, Beta Red are on Target One. Target One attempting evasion. Permission to fire a warning."

"Beta Blue, fire a warning."

"Roger that, Command."

A SPRAY of sand erupts diagonally in front of Oparin's Highlander, but Oparin keeps driving fiercely, twisting the wheel right and left in evasive maneuver.

"Vanya, you must stop!"

COMMAND, TARGET One is continuing evasion."

"Beta Blue, disable Target One."

"Roger that, Command."

———

Wᴵᵀᴴ ᴀ deafening crack the Highlander's tail door and roof fly into the air, orange flames fill the interior, and greasy, black smoke pours from the vehicle and rises into the air. Hands on the wheel, Oparin stares ahead mutely. Then, his body begins to thrash and his mouth opens in a scream no one can hear. He beats his head on the steering wheel, beating, beating, until he stiffens like a scarecrow set on fire and consumed as flames engulf the vehicle. In the air, there is a sweet smell of oil and the odor of fuel and burning rubber.

Cᴼᴹᴹᴬᴺᴰ, ʙᴇᴛᴀ Green. Target Two halted and in sight. Proceeding to detain."

"Copy that, Beta Green."

EPILOGUE

The Inquiry of Mike Fiscarelli

IN THE silence of his office, Michael P. Fiscarelli, Special Assistant for Nuclear Nonproliferation to the Director of Central Intelligence and Co-Coordinator, Operations Committee/Nonproliferation Task Group, has compiled a small database of files of the twenty-two session transcriptions of OPCOM/NPTG that pertain to the work of CASTLE-MARLIN (the original audiotapes of the sessions, in accordance with Agency policy on the preservation of tapes of routine meetings, have been destroyed). Thus far, he notes, no session transcription has been accessed or copied to another site. Good.

In working with CASTLE-MARLIN, Fiscarelli disobeyed direct orders from the Director of Central Intelligence and the Director of the National Clandestine Service not to employ such contractors in certain clearly defined geographic areas. A problem. In doing so he fabricated a cryptonym—MARLIN—for the contractor he misused and, in effect, ran an operation against his own agency. Furthermore, in the CASTLE-MARLIN operation Fiscarelli was responsible for numerous large unauthorized and unjustifiable expenditures. All this and what he had wrought with SLIDER and CASTLE put him in danger of severe administrative, if not legal, sanctions.

As Special Assistant to the Director, Fiscarelli has the unilateral power to classify documents in his area of operation, and his actions are not subject to routine review. On this late Friday evening, Fiscarelli first tags each file in his database with the classification level TOP SECRET GOLD. He then tags each file TOP SECRET DRAGON.

Because the two classification keys, GOLD and DRAGON, are compartmentalized and are of an extraordinarily high level, it is unlikely that any of the OPCOM/NPTG CASTLE-MARLIN files will ever be accessed or seen by anyone. The documents have in effect disappeared. Barring investigation by the Inspector General, they will never be retrieved.

Fuck 'em, he thinks, logs off his computer, and heads home.

The Draft Final Report on Operation Green Fire (OPCOM/NPTG OPREP 3203/229), which Fiscarelli himself wrote and circulated among relevant Intelligence Community officers, draws the following conclusions:

> •Four occupants of the Target One vehicle, a red Toyota Highlander, including the Russian arms trader Ivan Oparin, indentified by DNA analysis, were killed in the operation.

> •11.1 kilograms of contraband HEU were recovered in and around the Target One vehicle, some as far away as one hundred meters.

> •No individuals were detained at the Target Two vehicle, a white Ranger Rover, which had been left deserted by the side of the Al Ain Highway. It is presumed the occupants escaped and are alive and at large.

Fiscarelli sits late this Friday night, lonely, at home, sipping a martini and watching the History Channel. He's muted the sound. They're showing something on World War II. British. Tanks strain over hedgerows. Troops walk along tree-lined roads past signs pointing to towns with French names. It's snowing.

Oblivious to the scenes of an old war, Fiscarelli is thinking of a man named Sasha Geydarov. The in-house damage assessment on Geydarov is in. Fact one: A cable naming Aleksandr "Sasha" Geydarov—HIGHBEAM—as an American agent and describing him as an "informant for the Turkish police" went out of the Warrenton, Virginia, communications center addressed to the CIA station in Ankara, Turkey. The cable was sent when the Russian FSB was thought to be successfully monitoring CIA transmissions from

Warrenton. It is assessed, therefore, that the FSB had access to HIGH-BEAM's real name and function. The cable also mentioned Geydarov's role in the sale of Russian military equipment to U.S. Government purchasers, including the sale to CIA via agent CASTLE of the internal electronics of an S-300 anti-missile system. Geydarov facilitated the sale by arranging a meeting between CASTLE and corrupt elements of the Russian military in a Moscow park. This sale represented a major intelligence loss to the Russian military, and a revenge motive is therefore not ruled out. It is assessed probable that personnel within the FSB leaked Geydarov's name and other role—informant to the Turkish police—to the Russian underworld.

Fact two: The Georgian in the Turkish jail, the man whom Geydarov identified as a nuclear materials smuggler and who was apprehended and convicted for trying to sell nuclear slag on the black market, has begun to give information to the authorities. He has named as his supplier a man named Dmitri—"Misha"—Bichurin. Bichurin was associated with a Russian air services company headquartered in Moscow called TAK Air. TAK Air was owned by Ivan Oparin.

Johnny. Who is dead.

FISCARELLI, NOW in a soft, even agreeable state of melancholy, thinks of Dawn Braithewaite. She is long gone to Sci Tech in the north wing of the building, a transfer Fiscarelli helped arrange. He seldom sees her. Once in a while, she calls over for advice, which he gives. As far as he can tell she never caught a carnal vibe from him. Fine.

Her replacement Lynne is a pretty woman. Lovely blue eyes. Blond. In her fifties, can't be a real blond. Wears sneakers to work, then changes to sensible shoes. Married, kids raised. Very nice person.

Fiscarelli's thoughts drift to Rhoda Eisenberg. Another pretty thing—slender, with freckles and long, frizzy auburn hair. Wears pants and boots. Intense, self-contained. Brainy. Rhoda . . . Not so much of an age difference as with Dawn. She's what—forty? That would be in the ballpark. Religious differences? That stuff can be worked out. But a long while back, at an office birthday thing, he'd met Rhoda's partner, Joyce, a large, personable, outspoken woman, also an officer in Analysis. Rhoda is taken.

They're so open about it these days. At the Agency, it's no big deal anymore. Thinking on the seventh floor is, if you're out of the closet you're out, and you can't be blackmailed over it. If you can't be blackmailed, you're not a problem. We need good people. Competence counts. Period.

About such relationships Fiscarelli once felt, two pretty women off the market, what a waste. But now not so much. Someone loving someone else. Why not?

On Fiscarelli's TV screen: a destroyer is dropping depth charges into the gray ocean. Probably a British vessel, probably the North Atlantic. Now a shot of a submarine crew, close-ups of their faces—silent, perspiring, their eyes tense and staring: Germans.

Largest theft of HEU on record, 11.1 kilograms, big part of a bomb. Any more of it out there? The rest of the bomb? Where? Who has it?

And Ahmed Sajid. Where's Sajid? Is there a Sajid?

The ocean behind the destroyer erupts with spray.

"I Think They Were Serious"

"YOU GOT banged up pretty bad," Ted Pappas is saying.

"No shit."

"What happened?"

"I'll tell you sometime."

"Line of duty?"

"I'll tell you sometime."

He nods his head jerkily, a gesture of acknowledgment, and smiles a little. "Well, that's okay," he says.

Pappas called. He said he wanted to talk, that something had been bothering him, that it was "about Walt and all that," and could he come over?

I said sure.

It's late in the evening. We are on the couch in my den, Miles Davis on the stereo doing "Funny Valentine." I've poured Pappas a scotch. As he takes a first sip, his eyes raise and play over my face, lock briefly on the purple sack of blood that's collected under my left eye—"Jesus Christ, you look like an eggplant," he said when he first came in the door and saw me—then move to the lump, now diminished, on my left temple, then to the "multiple contusions," as the Turkish doctor put it, around my jaw, right cheek, and forehead.

As Davis plays, his muted trumpet's phrasing of the Rodgers so nuanced, so right, I think of Hart's lyrics: "Your looks are laughable . . . unphotographable . . ." and wonder if Pappas would get the joke. I let it go.

A TURKISH SWAT team took down the beach house. I am told they wore black ninja uniforms and masks, and that things went very fast with much yelling in Russian and Turkish. There were four Russians. They all resisted. Two were shot dead, two wounded and arrested. No Turkish casualties.

Before I woke in the ambulance I heard someone moaning in the darkness, then realized it was me. I saw first the face of a young EMT nurse peering down into mine, moving his hand back and forth in front of my eyes. Someone behind him said in English, "What's your name?"

I said, "Doug Lawson," then, "No. No no no. Behringer. Rick Behringer."

"What day is this?"

"Thursday."

"What month is this?"

"February."

I noticed I couldn't move my head and got good and scared about that, then realized they had put heavy blocks on each side of it. Like chocking a tire.

The EMT worker asked again, "What's your name?"

"Rick Behringer."

"What day is this?"

"Thursday."

I felt the ambulance move.

"What month is this?"

"February."

In the hospital the nurses didn't speak English, but hummed around efficiently enough and seemed to know what they were doing. An English-speaking doctor, a stout, bushy-haired little guy with a kind face, stood by my bed and and said, "You have two cracked ribs. You cannot see them easily on the X-ray. Very small. No teeth damaged, which is good. Internal organs seem okay. I see from your chart you were concussed. The CAT scan shows a small subdural hematoma—blood clot on the brain. Don't worry, it's stabilized. It will dissolve, go away. Nothing to do. Just wait. Maybe three weeks. For the ribs you wear a corset bandage. Try to breathe deeply, otherwise you get pneumonia." He leaned in toward me. "The men who did this, I think they were serious."

"Yes," I said.

I told the Turkish police some of what I knew of my attackers, not much. The embassy—Fiscarelli—managed to get the police inquiry cut short and got me out of the country. The Russians who survived the SWAT team raid—Bichurin was not one of them—are now in a Turkish jail, probably headed for a Turkish prison.

Fiscarelli told me on my arrival home—we were trudging in snow on a bike path in Reston—"You've had backup for a lot of your stuff. Not easy. You did in Turkey, most of the time. Well, a lot of the time." That man in the green parka at the kiosk, working hard at reading a newpaper, following my movement through the square. Probably him.

Fiscarelli said, "Police were on standby."

"Could have gotten there sooner."

"Don't complain."

Fiscarelli also said the investigation of Ray's murder is stalled. "Pak police say they got no leads. But if Pak security had anything at all to do with it— I mean, you know, solving it might be . . . inconvenient." Change of subject: "By the way, dropping the sneaky at TAK Air was a great help, a very great help. I can't say more than this, but it was very useful, and what happened, what occurred, was not, ah . . . in vain."

I wonder.

When they took down the beach house, the police seized the Glock 26, and it is now part of the evidence in the case. Istanbul Base isn't happy about this, but the police, whatever their private thoughts on the matter may be, are not connecting the gun to the embassy or the Agency.

AND NOW I am with Ted Pappas in my den/piano room. He's nursing his scotch, looking subdued. On the stereo Davis has moved into "Blues by Five."

"Well, CIRCLE," Pappas says. "Uh . . . I liked Walt." His eyes flicker to mine. "A lot. Felt really sorry about what happened with him. Never wanted to talk too much about it." He breaks off, sloshes his drink in a moody, meditative way.

Pappas, like a lot of Agency people, like a lot of ordinary people for that matter, has the knack of telling the truth deceptively. As he did when I called him about the lump of muck I'd found in the azalea bed and asked him if he knew anything about a document called CIRCLE. *I'm getting old,* he said, *and it's been a long goddamn time . . . I don't think I can tell you what it it's about. Be nice to know . . . Don't think I can help.*

None of this was untrue. All of it was misleading. Pappas did remember CIRCLE. He's been thinking about it, and now has come over and wants to talk. I think he wants to get it off his chest.

"Started out as a report Walt was doing," Pappas says. "This was like in late '74 going into '75. Walt and me, we were both in Washington, though I was shuttling back and forth between here and Saigon. End was in sight over there. We all knew what was coming, and Walt was distraught over it. Just killed him. 'Our friends are in danger,' he'd yell at meetings, actually yell, which wasn't like him, 'people who trusted us, they're going to die for it. Because they *believed* in us.' Then that spring the commies took Saigon. Goddamn shambles. Walt was crushed. Wasn't too long after that that he started going . . . showing symptoms. Mostly not talking much, keeping to himself, drinking more.

"Now, about this time Walt gets tasked to put together a thing on the intel we'd produced, CIA'd produced, over the course of the war. Not to be any big deal, just a kind of summary. We do these reports all the time— learn from your mistakes, right? Contribution to institutional memory and so on. But it was nothing we really needed right then. In fact, it would have been premature. Colby, I know, gave it to Walt as a kind of make-work thing 'cause by now everybody knew Walt was . . . was having emotional troubles, and Colby wanted to give him some simple thing to do, probably as a way to ease him out and into retirement, probably thought it would be just kind of routine, something Walt could handle. Big mistake. The assignment, hell, it was just the thing to set Walt off. And Walt, God, he took it and ran with it. Report grew into some kinda . . . it got crazy"—Pappas blows through his lips—"a monster, just a monster. I remember it was so obvious with this thing that your dad was becoming, you know, really, really unstable.

"He'd gotten obsessed with lying. Sort of a fixation with him. Partly 'cause of all the lying he had to do in his job over the years and all that. But other lying, too, lying he shouldn't have done. He told me once, 'Ted, I've done terrible things, terrible.' I said, 'I can't believe that.' And he said, 'I've been wracked with guilt for years over things I did in the '60s, false reports. Back then,' he said, 'back then the White House didn't like some of the intel they were getting, especially on VC force levels. We knew damn well the force levels were big and growing. White House didn't want to hear that. So they misrepresented it. And they wanted us to gin up reports downplaying how popular the VC were, write up stuff full of good news and happy talk. When the White House is hell-bent on believing something, they'll just believe it.' "

Pappas grimaces at me. "Sounds like Iraq, doesn't it? Some things don't change. Same goddamn deal. Well, hell, they all knew better about the VC, but in the end Walt and the others gave them what they wanted. Now, Walt was chief officer in charge of producing the intelligence. 'I signed off on reports I knew weren't true,' he said. 'We made it look like VC cadres were shrinking, that main-force North Vietnamese soldiers were dying and not getting replaced.'

"Of course, this stuff got cleared at the top of the Agency—Helms signed off on it, sent it over to the White House. White House loved it. And Johnson, LBJ, he'd run around with this little summary in his pocket and pull it out whenever he'd talk to a congressman.

"So, Walt thought back on that, on the false reporting and on a lot of other stuff he did in the course of the war, mostly giving in to 'misrepresentation' now and then, or at least not standing up for the truth. I don't know if it drove him crazy or not—Jeez, Rick, maybe he'd just had his breakdown by that time and just seized on the lying. But he thought that he personally prolonged the war. Blamed himself. I'd tell him, 'Walt, that just isn't so,' but he'd say, 'I swore to be an honorable officer and I helped mislead people' and so on.

"Then one day—I remember this so clearly—he takes me aside and says, and he's serious about this, he says, 'Know what I'm going to do? I'm going to expose all the lying.' He was going to name names, he said, 'nail the sons of bitches.' Everybody was culpable, he said, and he'd blow them, shit, everybody, I guess, blow them out of the water, and on and on and on.

"So he changes course on this report, this dumb, make-work thing Colby dreamed up for him, and he turns it into an exposé which he called Project 'CIRCLE.' Title came from 'squaring the circle,' the idea being numbers that didn't compute—those VC force levels. And everything else about that war that wasn't honest, either.

"He'd come in every day, put all his time in on it, pull documents from here and there, sit in his office alone, reading, typing. He was going through all the old stuff out of Saigon, from the early '60s on—reams of it, piles and piles of paper, talking out loud to the paper, saying stuff like 'What the hell does this mean?' 'What the hell does that mean?' 'You son of a bitch, how could you *say* that?'

"Sometimes he'd pace in his office, up and down, up and down, muttering to himself. Or he'd be sitting at his desk, stone dead silent, staring, just staring. I'd go in, his eyes'd be glazed over. About now was when he stopped worrying too much about the way he dressed. One time he came in in sneakers, his shirt half out. Marge, I don't know how she dealt with it. I'm sure it was a terrible burden. In all this, by the way, he never yelled at me or got angry. Don't know why. I was a kid basically, wet behind the ears, so maybe I was somebody, somebody 'uncorrupted' he could talk to, some kind of confidant, maybe, 'cause he'd show me drafts of what he was doing. Jesus, they just got more and more bizarre. It was a history of all the lying in the Vietnam War. Well, that could get pretty long.

"Anyhow, after he'd been working on CIRCLE for a while, detailing all the lying about the war, he decided he was being 'watched,' that 'they' were watching him, spying on him. And maybe they were, who knows? So, he got secretive. He decided he'd work on CIRCLE at home and he took to walking out with documents, classified stuff. He'd fold them in his newspaper and just walk out—you could do that, get away with that back then. Told me about doing it—me!—and had this funny smile on his face when he did. He also told me he was afraid of what they'd do to him if they found out. 'Ted, if they see this, they'll crucify me.' Thought they'd take away his pension or throw him in jail or something. They wouldn't have. I'd been telling my superiors that Walt was in trouble, pushing at them to do something. They knew by that time that he was ill, and way I heard it, they were going to put him on leave, let him rest, get him some help. But they just didn't get there fast enough.

"On CIRCLE, from what I saw of it and from the way he talked, I could tell CIRCLE was turning into an indictment not of the Agency so much but of Walt himself, Walt and his career. Began as a simple project, this dopey report, but Walt made it first a judgment on all the crimes and stupidities of CIA, then turned it into a judgment on his own life. Which he found hollow. That's the word he used, 'hollow,' said we were 'hollow men.' I remember he burst into tears when he said that.

"Now, he was afraid they'd find out about his report, what he'd done.

But he didn't want to destroy it, either. It was some kind of major statement he was making to himself and he couldn't let it go. So, he didn't
burn it or shred it, he took it out—I didn't know this till you told me—
took it out and buried it in his backyard."

"And then killed himself," I say.

Pappas sighs. "Great sadness everywhere when that happened. He was
liked and respected, Rick. Really was. He was a good intelligence officer.
Everybody at Langley was like, we knew so why didn't we do something
sooner? But we didn't. Not enough, anyhow. And so what happened happened."

I think of the Behringer family—gloomy Germans out on the Minnesota prairie—and their predisposition to madness. I think of Walt's father's suicide back in the Depression, of my uncle Hen on the streets,
dying crazed in that mental institution in Bethesda. And of Walt.

You can go mad with secrets—secrets about secrets, lies about lies. Walt
had a strict code of truth-telling, which he tried to teach me and Sue. But
he couldn't reconcile that code with the rest of his life. I think of Walt
standing silently in the backyard in the twilight, arms crossed, staring at the
azalea bed—where now I know he had buried CIRCLE. I think of the rotted Tupperware bowl I dug up and the lump of black muck it contained—
a kind of metaphor for Walt's madness, perhaps for his life.

Walt had a finely wrought, too-finely wrought, moral sense, part of the
Behringer craziness, and it eventually drove him to insanity and suicide.
That, or something like that, is his story. It's as close as I'll ever get.

"Well, that's what CIRCLE was," Pappas says.

LATER, I drive into Arlington to see Jack Gutman, mostly for my own
comfort. In the foyer, when he gets a look at my wounds, he asks in
astonishment, "What the *hell*? Jesus Christ, Rick, what *happened*? You look
like . . ."

"Barroom fight. Nasty place. Bikers."

"Jesus." He stares at me for a time in wonder, then swiftly a look comes
over his face. His eyes get shrewd and steely, he's calculating something, no
longer astonished—then he nods a couple of times, throws his head back,
and barks out a laugh. "Oh, my," he says. "Oh, my my my." Grinning, he
pats me affectionately on the back and puts his arm around my shoulder.
"Well, come on in. Jesus Christ."

He knows.

We smile at each other in mutual understanding and say no more on the subject. He puts on some Mozart. I don't talk of Walt, or Project CIRCLE, but I tell him of Liz and Frannie. He listens sympathetically.

I HAVEN'T "seen" Frannie again, though I bumped into her not long back at a Starbucks on Fairfax Drive in Arlington. I was just arriving, she just leaving, carrying a tall latté and a little brown bag, probably a chocolate chip cookie in there—she loves the things. She was wearing a lavender beret, her blond hair tucked in.

She smiled and said, "Oh, hi," that simple greeting so freighted.

I smiled and said "Hi" back. We did the usual how's-it-goings? and chit-chatted a little. Then she said, "Good to see you," bobbed her head in a positive way to show she meant it—the saleswoman—and walked out onto Fairfax, where she'd parked her maroon Chevy, and, not looking back, got in, pulled away from the curb into light traffic, and was gone.

I T'S TEN or so at night, and I'm sitting in my den, back home after seeing Gutman. I think of the women in—or out of—my life. Marge gone. Frannie gone. Pennie and Sam, well, they're still in my life, still love "silly daddy." But they're not in my life that much, not really. And Liz. What was that—TV off, girls at their slumber party—what was that *all about?*

I go to the piano and sit, thinking now of Walt and his lonely torment. I think of those pages he tore from his Vietnam diary telling how he buried Project CIRCLE in our backyard. Those pages—he didn't destroy them, he tucked them away. Why? And why he did he tuck them away in the Japanese field telephone that *I* used when we spoke to each other, basement-to-den? Did Walt, in some deranged attempt to communicate, leave those pages for *me*—in a telephone, no less—hoping they would lead me to Project CIRCLE, that in time I would learn of his anguish over what he considered his wasted life? I'm guessing yes, but I'll never know. In any case, it was madness, all of it.

Softly I start a blues line, just a couple of measures, a quiet, melancholy little tune in a minor key. I plug it into a blues progression and find the results not bad. Seems to work. I take it where it can go, which isn't far, then leave it, and get into some Handy:

I hate to see . . . that evening sun go down,
Hate to see-ee . . . that evening sun go down . . .

Here I pause and let the last chord, unresolved, die out in the silence of my house. I sit for a time, then—hell, why not?—do a couple of runs in a major key, have some fun at that, getting a little boppy. I once could imitate Monk doing "Well You Needn't" as a solo piece. I give it a try and—land o' Goshen, as Marge used to say—what comes out is, well, not that great, frankly, but not all that bad either. Briefly I bounce along at Monk's piece (dah *dah* dah dah DAH . . . dah DEE dah . . . dah *dah* dah dah DAH . . . dah DEE dah), lose my way—had to—but get into my own improv, which is very jivey, with spikey off-beats, intended wrong notes, not Monk but Monkish, feeling very good. Slowing down, but still jivey, I shift into some Kern—"Lovely to Look At," "A Fine Romance"—then into Arlen's "Paper Moon." I take the signature line, "But it wouldn't be make believe if you believed in me," play it a couple of times with some Monk-like fillips and jerky, jagged-edge rhythms till the thing gets unrecognizable, then come back and play the whole song straight, the way Arlen wrote it, and end in a full, two-handed g-major chord.

I stop here and let the music go. I am in a region where everything is cool, right, true, beautiful: boplicity.

It's late, but I think I'll give Liz a call.